Praise for *Silen*

MW01074600

Silent Horizons is more than just a military thriller; it's an unflinching look at the clandestine warriors who operate in the most dangerous environments, setting the stage for the battles that follow. Robichaux and Stewart deliver a raw, intense, and authentic experience that pulls back the curtain on a world most will never see. A read you will not forget!

Jack Carr, #1 *New York Times* bestselling author of *Red Sky Mourning*

Silent Horizons gives readers a behind-the-scenes look at the dark side of special operations and the toll it takes on those who navigate the battlefields of spiritual and mortal warfare. A riveting thriller you won't want to put down!

Shawn Ryan, former US Navy SEAL, CIA contractor, and host of *The Shawn Ryan Show*

Chad Robichaux's latest book, *Silent Horizons*, eloquently depicts a warrior's journey on and off the battlefield. It's the human side of the operator that hits hardest and resonates with my own experience. This book doesn't glorify war—it shows what it really means to those who live it. I'm proud to call Chad a friend and fellow warrior that's sharing his journey to help others—maybe even you.

Mike Glover, US Army Special Forces (Retired), founder of FieldCraft Survival and national bestselling author of *Prepared*

Propulsive and inspiring! Robichaux and Stewart clearly know firsthand the world of special operations and the toll it can take on those who serve. They also know how to keep you turning the pages! Absolutely fantastic storytelling.

Marc Cameron, *New York Times* bestselling author of *Bad River* and *Tom Clancy Red Winter*

Balancing commitment to family and commitment to the mission is a duty made harder by the secrecy surrounding clandestine operations and the work that feeds it. In *Silent Horizons*, Robichaux and Stewart show what reaches deep into the soul of every operator and reveal what many never get to say about the missions of elite operators.

> **Marcus Luttrell**, US Navy SEAL (Retired) and author of the *New York Times* bestseller *Lone Survivor*

Real experience, valuable lessons, and exhilarating moments are captured in the pages of *Silent Horizons*. It's uniquely told through the lens of fiction by Robichaux and Stewart, men who have survived the pinnacle of military operations. But this is more than just a good story; it's an opportunity to see into the lives of those who chose sacrifice over peace and comfort.

> **Chadd Wright**, former US Navy SEAL, ultrarunner, and founder of the Three of Seven Project

If you're looking for a military thriller that strips away the gloss and glamour, *Silent Horizons* will feel like an intense debriefing from a covert mission. There are few men, and fewer authors, who have walked in those shoes, and the authenticity is undeniable. This is what it's really like when you're operating behind enemy lines and carrying the weight of family and unspoken duty on your shoulders.

> **Andy Stumpf**, US Navy SEAL (Retired) and host of the *Cleared Hot* podcast

The tension, the terminology, the thrills, the tradecraft—this is as real as secret intel ops get. Chad and Jack have opened a door to a world only a select few get to see. You won't be able to stop turning pages.

> **Andrew Bustamante**, former CIA intelligence officer and founder of EverydaySpy

Silent Horizons is an amazing, heart-pounding thriller, but it's so much more. It's a deep dive into the personal battles we fight when the mission ends and the reality of life as a husband, father, son, brother, and teammate kicks in. I still often miss the relentless focus and comradery of a career in special operations, and this novel really tells the whole story.

Jason Redman, US Navy SEAL (Retired), *New York Times* bestselling author of *The Trident* and *Overcome*

Silent Horizons is a high-octane thriller that plunges readers into the gritty, dangerous world of special operations with breathtaking authenticity. Foster Quinn isn't just another action hero—he's a man grappling with loss, loyalty, and the weight of responsibility, making him as emotionally compelling as he is tactical. If you're looking for a gripping military thriller that offers both emotional depth and tactical brilliance, this is it. Fans of Brad Thor and Mark Greaney will love this book!

Ryan Steck, *The Real Book Spy* and author of *Gone Dark*

This story is brimming with authenticity and a jet-fueled pace. Robichaux and Stewart crushed it with *Silent Horizons*. I can't wait to see what these two write next.

Connor Sullivan, acclaimed author of *Wolf Trap*

Silent Horizons is a gut-punch of a thriller. Yes, it's an adrenaline rush of authentic action and suspense that takes us inside the secret world of special operations, but Robichaux and Stewart have also managed something much deeper (and more difficult): an exploration of the warrior spirit, the meaning of honor, and the costs borne by those who serve. Force Recon Marine Foster Quinn is the real deal.

David McCloskey, former CIA analyst and author of *The Seventh Floor*

Silent Horizons captures the unrelenting intensity of covert operations while honoring the quiet struggles that follow. Robichaux and Stewart have crafted a story that resonates deeply with anyone who's operated in the shadows. This is fiction, but it hits close to home for those of us who have lived it.

Sarah Adams, Former CIA targeting officer and author of *Benghazi: Know Thy Enemy*

Silent Horizons is an inspiring, fearless look at the unsung heroes of covert warfare. It takes you inside the missions but also into the hearts of the men who have to leave it all behind both when they deploy and again when they come home.

Mark Smith, CEO of Smith & Wesson

SILENT HORIZONS

A THRILLER

SILENT HORIZONS

CHAD ROBICHAUX

WITH JACK STEWART

Tyndale House Publishers
Carol Stream, Illinois

Visit Tyndale online at tyndale.com.

Visit the authors online at chadrobichaux.com and jackstewartbooks.com.

Tyndale and Tyndale's quill logo are registered trademarks of Tyndale House Ministries.

Silent Horizons

Cover designed by Ron C. Kaufmann

Edited by Sarah Mason Rische

Published in association with The Howard Literary Agency, 102 Yellowood Drive, West Monroe, LA 71291, represented by John Howard

Scripture quotations are taken from the Holy Bible, *New International Version,*® *NIV.*® Copyright © 1973, 1978, 1984, 2011 by Biblica, Inc.® Used by permission. All rights reserved worldwide.

For information about special discounts for bulk purchases, please contact Tyndale House Publishers at csresponse@tyndale.com, or call 1-855-277-9400.

Library of Congress Cataloging-in-Publication Data

A catalog record for this book is available from the Library of Congress.

ISBN 978-1-4964-8869-5 (HC)
ISBN 978-1-4964-8870-1 (SC)

Printed in the United States of America

31	30	29	28	27	26	25
7	6	5	4	3	2	1

Every man and woman who has put on the uniform and served honorably deserves special recognition for the roles they played in the defense of our nation. While it would be impossible for us to name every person who has done so within the pages of this book, we chose to honor the legacies of four individuals who impacted our lives:

Sergeant Foster L. Harrington

United States Marine Corps

Force Recon Marine

3rd Force Reconnaissance Company, 4th Marine Division

September 5, 1973–September 20, 2004

Sergeant Major Robert J. Cottle

United States Marine Corps

Force Recon Marine

4th Force Reconnaissance Battalion, 4th Marine Division

February 18, 1965–March 24, 2010

Chief Special Warfare Operator William "Ryan" Owens

United States Navy

Navy SEAL

East Coast–based Special Warfare unit

March 5, 1980–January 29, 2017

Commander Seth A. Stone

United States Navy

Navy SEAL

Special Operations Command Pacific

September 17, 1976–September 30, 2017

From time to time, God causes men to be born—and thou
art one of them—who have a lust to go abroad at the
risk of their lives and discover news—to-day it may be
of far-off things, to-morrow of some hidden mountain,
and the next day of some near-by men who have done a
foolishness against the State. These souls are very few;
and of these few, not more than ten are of the best.

RUDYARD KIPLING

Then one of the Twelve—the one called Judas Iscariot—
went to the chief priests and asked, "What are you
willing to give me if I deliver him over to you?" So they
counted out for him thirty pieces of silver. From then on
Judas watched for an opportunity to hand him over.

MATTHEW 26:14-16

Prologue

FOSTER QUINN STOOD AT THE EDGE of the fifty-meter pool with his toes wrapped around the bullnose tile coping. He wore only goggles and a pair of sand-colored UDT swim shorts with the front pull strap cinched tight around his trim waist, and he shivered as the wind whipped down the hills from the north and crossed the exposed pool deck. He carried one hundred and ninety pounds of lean muscle on his six-foot frame, and the just-completed twelve-week course had erased any remaining fat, as if God Himself had sculpted a model Marine from stone.

"Enter the water!" The instructor's voice boomed from over his shoulder.

Foster took one last breath and filled his lungs with the crisp morning air, then stepped off the deck into the deep end. Despite the water's bitter temperature, he felt instant relief at being insulated from the wind. The ten-pound brick he held in both hands carried him quickly to the bottom. There, he set it on the solid line of miniature black tiles and started swimming while pushing it in front of him.

Nice and slow, he reminded himself.

He knew it was counterintuitive to move slowly when the objective of the exercise was to reach the other side without surfacing for a breath. Slower meant he had to hold his breath longer, but if he moved faster, his body would burn through his oxygen quicker. The only way he could complete the test was by remaining calm, and he forced himself to look down at the black tiles and ignore the wall that seemed impossibly far away. He tamped back the fear that was certain to cause his heart rate to spike.

Left . . . right . . . pull . . . relax.

Pushing the brick out like a spear, he scissored his legs and pulled with his free hand in a modified sidestroke. It moved him the greatest distance while exerting the least amount of energy. Nothing could be easier. And yet, it was so hard.

Left . . . right . . . pull . . . relax.

The pool's bottom sloped upward, and despite his best effort to ignore the enormity of the task, his mind registered the first of several landmarks that keyed him in on his progress.

Fifteen meters, he thought, then he exhaled a thin stream of air to relieve some pressure on his lungs. His feet continued churning at the same slow cadence he had set out on, and his free arm continued pulling him onward.

The brick slid across a black line perpendicular to his path, and again his mind announced its significance.

Twenty-five meters.

He exhaled a second stream of air, more forcefully than the last, and the bubbles shot to the surface as the fear he had kept at bay beat against his resolve.

You're almost there.

His heart thundered in his chest, its sound drowning out everything else around him in his liquid cocoon.

It's too far!

Left . . . right . . . pull . . . relax.

Each stroke was a battle of wills, pitting the hardened and competent Marine against the terrified boy held hostage in his mind. While one fought with each pull to reach the objective, the other fought to give up. All he had to do was let go of the weight, push off the bottom, and he could taste the fresh air once more. He could be free from his watery prison before it became his watery grave. All he needed to do was give up.

The end was now in view, but before he could rejoice in being nearly two-thirds of the way across the pool, his vision narrowed until only the black-tile line remained.

Nice and slow, the Marine pressed.

But the frightened boy countered, *You won't make it!*

Left . . . right . . . pull . . . relax.

Foster's body screamed at him to give up. His chest spasmed and expanded, trying to draw breath into his lungs, but he kept his mouth clamped shut. His heart raced faster, fueled by the trickle of adrenaline that had become a torrent. He moaned and let another burst of air escape to the surface, but still he kept moving forward. One kick. Then the next. One pull. Then another.

Forty meters.

He was almost there, but his vision continued closing in on him, leaving him with only a soda straw to look through. He no longer sensed the other Marines around him or felt the sting of the frigid water and the rough plaster beneath the brick. He felt only a warm, comforting embrace as his thrumming heart consumed every other sensation. Even the fear that had gripped him seemed to have vanished.

Forty-five meters.

Suddenly, his vision returned. It was as if somebody had flipped a switch and turned on the lights, unveiling the wall just in front of his face. His shoulders sagged with relief, and the tension he carried in his muscled upper back dissolved into the water around him as his classmates on either side surfaced. He reached out with both hands, inching the brick closer to the pool's edge, then stopped.

Fifty meters.

The frightened boy was gone.

Foster twisted his body and placed both feet on the wall, then pushed off with the brick stretched out in front of him. Even starved for oxygen, his powerful legs propelled him another five meters before the weight carried him back to the bottom. One leg. Then the other. Slowly, he scissored his legs together and resumed his swim.

Left . . . right . . . pull . . . relax.

He had completed the task, but something compelled him to go farther. It wasn't vanity or boastful arrogance, but the discovery of an untapped reservoir of determination. Unbidden, the words of the Recon Creed echoed in his mind and drowned out even the deafening cacophony of his heart's beating.

Exceeding beyond the limitations set down by others shall be my goal . . .

One kick. Then the next. One stroke. Then another. Foster pulled and pushed his body farther along the black line, beckoning him back to the deep from where he'd come.

Sixty-five meters.

To quit, to surrender, to give up is to fail. To be a Recon Marine is to surpass failure . . .

BOOM!

The sound resonated through the water and seemed out of place as the bottom again flattened out, but Foster just tilted his head forward and sighted in on the black line that was his goal. It had never been his ambition to break the record. He hadn't dropped into the deep end intending to go more than fifty meters. It was as if he felt a direct connection to those who came before him—to James Roosevelt and Merritt Edson, to Samuel Blair Griffith and Alan Shapley.

Foster Quinn was a Recon Marine.

I shall be the example . . .

He opened his mouth to shout in triumph as he reached the seventy-five-meter mark, but . . .

BOOM! BOOM!

He squinted with confusion, and his world went dark.

Foster bolted upright in his bed and gasped at the booming sound still echoing in his ears. It took him a moment to realize where he was—in his one-bedroom flat in Isfahan, Iran—and he clamped his hand down over his racing heart and clawed at the matted hair on his chest.

The nightmares had become more frequent, but he didn't have the luxury of slowing his frenetic pace to figure out why. Maybe it was just stress. Or maybe it was because he was alone, deep behind enemy lines, and subconsciously longed to be a member of a team again—just one of many.

But now, it didn't really matter. Now, it was just him.

Just one man.

Alone.

BOOM!

Foster looked left and right at the shadows in his room, identifying and dismissing them. His heart rate slowed, but his lungs burned as if he had just surfaced from the weighted underwater swim, not from the dream of its distant memory.

He swung his legs out from under the thin bedsheet and set his bare feet on the dusty floor. Even in the dead of night, the ornate ceramic tile still retained a modest amount of heat from the previous day. He wiggled his toes, almost surprised to discover the tile's smooth touch and not the pool's rough plaster.

Groaning, he leaned forward and rested his forearms on his thighs, a thin stream of light falling on the bracelet Haili had made for him. He steepled his fingers and stared at the solid ground underfoot as if expecting to see the same black line that had beckoned him to test his limits. There was no line, but he knew he was still on its path.

Foster Quinn might not be a Force Reconnaissance Marine any longer, but he still embodied the same principles.

Honor. Perseverance. Spirit. Heart.

Those were the things that had guided him during his twelve years in the Marine Corps. Just like that day in the pool, Foster set the standard in everything he did. And he demanded the same measure of excellence from his teammates.

Yet here you are. All alone.

BOOM! BOOM!

The loud banging on the front door downstairs returned his focus wholly to the present, and he rose silently from the twin mattress and crossed quickly to the window. Pulling aside the rug he had hung in front to insulate his room from the sun's brutal rays, he peered through the dirty glass onto the street below. Two red Toyota Hilux Vigo trucks were parked directly beneath his window, and a quick scan in either direction revealed similar trucks with armed men in the back at both ends of the block.

He considered going for the hunting rifle he had locked away in a case across the room. But there were too many of them, and he was just one man.

The racing heart and crippling fear returned, plunging him once more into the deep end. But, like he had done in the Camp Pendleton pool, he confronted his fear head-on.

Nice and slow, he thought.

Foster's heart rate dipped as he drew a long slow breath in through his nose and held it for a beat before exhaling. Like any good Marine, he wanted to fight. Just over thirty years old, he was no longer the chiseled specimen he had been after completing the Basic Reconnaissance Course, though he was still in remarkable shape. But he knew it was a fight he wouldn't win. He had made his way into Iran under a nonofficial cover, and he would use it to get himself out.

The pounding on the door resumed, and Foster resigned himself to his fate and turned to the chair in the corner where he had draped his clothes. He stepped into a pair of faded jeans and pinched the coin pocket's left rivet to activate a distress beacon. It would be active for an hour before self-destructing and becoming nothing more than an inert fleck of metal and silicone. He pulled a partially buttoned solid blue shirt over his head, then slipped his feet into a pair of leather boots.

The door crashed open, and Foster slowly turned for the stairs as his heart pounded in time with the beating of feet running up the worn treads. When the first man appeared, he feigned shock and held up his hands.

"Don't shoot," he said, letting a quiver of fear break through his otherwise calm baritone voice.

The first man reached the top of the stairs and swung the butt of his rifle up into Foster's chin. His head snapped back, and stars ringed his vision, but he had expected the strike and had already begun moving backward to soften the blow. It still hurt like the dickens, but it hadn't knocked him out cold.

A second man reached the landing and darted around the first to grab Foster's arms and wrench them behind his back. The man was strong, but his technique was flawed. Had there not been more men scrambling up the steps in reinforcement, Foster could have broken the hold and turned the tables on his assailant.

"Why are you doing this?" Foster pleaded, letting a hint of fear and confusion intermix with genuine pain. But he knew why, and he had expected somebody to come for him eventually.

They yelled at him in Farsi, but his mastery of the language was marginal at best, and he only caught bits and pieces of what had them worked into a frenzy. Unfortunately, he caught enough to know his fears were warranted. Somebody had ratted him out.

He'd thought that somebody was a friend.

"You are an American spy," a third man said in surprisingly good English. He stepped forward and placed a thick hood over Foster's head.

"What? A spy?" He shook his head against the rough burlap. "N-n-no," he stammered. "I'm just a hunter!"

"No! You are a spy!"

An invisible fist slammed into Foster's stomach, and he doubled over at the blow, despite half expecting it. The punch wasn't very well placed, and he suspected the offending wrist had probably taken the worst of it. But it still took the breath out of him.

He opened his mouth under the hood, trying in vain to inhale, but the punch had seized his diaphragm. His heart rate ticked up with another injection of adrenaline, but so far, he had kept the frightened boy banished from his mind. The Recon Marine was still in charge, and after only a few seconds, his heartbeat slowed again.

Unseen hands gripped his upper arms and the back of his belt, lifting him slightly off the ground as they carried him to the stairs leading down into the warehouse. He shook his head and continued asserting his innocence, slowly twisting and jerking his body to resist his captors' efforts to abscond with him. He knew enough about how this usually went to abandon hope of surviving through the night.

They would beat him and question him, then torture him and interrogate him until he gave them whatever answers they sought. Whether at the behest of MOIS or worse, in the end, they would kill him and dump his corpse somewhere public as a gruesome warning.

Unless Seth got the message.

"Please," he moaned. "I'm just a hunter. I'm not here to hurt you. Please, let me go."

"Just a hunter!" the third man scoffed.

Foster protested, "Call Director General Ghorbani! He'll confirm I'm only a guide—"

The man struck him in the side of the head, ending the conversation as they reached the warehouse floor. Foster felt the cool night air wash over him as they carried him through the front door and out onto the street, where he heard only the soft puttering of a truck's idling engine through the thick burlap over his head. He knew what was about to happen.

"You're no guide . . . *Foster Quinn*," the menacing voice said in his ear. He had the presence of mind to recognize that the man had used his true name, confirming his fears that somebody had discovered who he really was. There would be no chance of talking his way out of this.

He just needed to survive. At least long enough for Seth to send help from Abu Dhabi.

A rifle struck the back of his head, and that hope disappeared along with the world around him.

SEVEN MONTHS EARLIER

ONE

Foster sat in the back seat on the right side, peering through a sliver of a window in the shape of a Dorito. He lamented the poor visibility compared to the older Humvees he had grown up with in the Marine Corps but admitted the Oshkosh Joint Light Tactical Vehicle had several advantages.

Ting!

The improved armor was one, but he still flinched with each round that impacted the side of the four-seat Combat Tactical Vehicle.

"How much longer, Foster?" Seth asked from the seat directly in front of him.

Using his plaid shirtsleeve, Foster wiped the sweat from his brow and cursed the air-conditioning system. Despite promises that it could withstand extreme temperatures, it seemed overwhelmed by

13

Somalia's sweltering spring. It spat water and lukewarm air, when it worked at all.

Ting! Ting!

Foster pressed the push-to-talk on his plate carrier and shouted into the microphone perched on a boom in front of his mouth. "We need air support!"

The voice transmitted back from the joint operations center was maddeningly calm. "Angel One Zero, ETA on your ISR is five mikes, over."

Foster groaned. As their JTAC, or Joint Terminal Attack Controller, he was responsible for providing air support, and five minutes was a long time to be stuck in a tin can—even one with comfortable seats—waiting for an intelligence, surveillance, and reconnaissance drone to arrive overhead. But at least it would bring a bigger gun to the fight. And right now, they needed it.

"Foster! How much longer?" Seth asked again, his gaze fixed through the forward windshield on the tracers streaking into their convoy from both sides. Technically, they weren't supposed to be in harm's way. At least, that's what their task force headquarters had told them. The nine Americans—seven SEALs, one Marine, and one Agency operations officer—were there to *advise, accompany, and assist* their partner forces but remain at the last line of cover and concealment.

Too bad the enemy got a vote.

"Five minutes."

"Too long," Justin Salters said. The lone Agency man sat next to Foster and nervously tugged on his chest plate. "Is it armed?"

"Two Hellfires and a GBU," he replied.

The MQ-9 Reaper was primarily used to locate and track high-value targets, but it never flew in theater without the ability to deliver hate if needed. Armed with two AGM-114 Hellfire air-to-ground missiles and a single five-hundred-pound laser-guided bomb, the Reaper had the potential to turn the tide on this ambush. The Kenyans and their American advisors just needed to hold out long enough for the remote-controlled cavalry to arrive.

"Do you think he's here?" Ryan asked from the driver's seat.

When Justin didn't answer, Foster elbowed him. "That's a question for you, Hoss. It's the CIA's intelligence."

"He should be."

"Should be," Ryan echoed in dismay.

Foster wasn't so sure. All the intelligence their JSOC, or Joint Special Operations Command, task force had collected pointed to the man known as SANFORD returning to the al-Shabaab stronghold in southern Somalia. But something about it didn't feel right to him. From the moment their convoy came under attack, Foster had begun having second thoughts about the intelligence they'd received. It seemed SANFORD had been one step ahead of them their entire deployment.

Ting!

Foster flinched again as the small screen in his lap flickered to life, and the Reaper began broadcasting images of the ambush. "Holy . . ."

"Angel One Zero, what's your status?"

Yeah, now you're concerned.

"Stand by," Foster said, ignoring the question as he began planning how the Reaper could deliver its ordnance to have the greatest impact. After seeing their small convoy surrounded by large groups of insurgents closing in from all directions, there was no longer a question of authority. This was cut-and-dried self-defense.

"How bad is it?" Seth asked.

"Bad."

"Angel One Zero, Bravo Six . . ."

"We're the last two trucks at the rear of the convoy, marked with IR beacons," Foster replied, his strained voice laced with frustration. The lights blinking on the two JLTVs were visible on the Reaper's feed, and their status should have been evident. The African Union Mission to Somalia vehicles at the front of the convoy were engaged in pitched combat and had dismounted their Kenyan soldiers to repel the attack while their American "advisors" sat comfortably behind two inches of armor at the rear.

"Copy, we're diverting everything we have to you."

Good call.

"What are we doing, boss?" Hunter asked from the second vehicle.

Seth keyed the microphone to reply. "Sit tight. Foster's drumming up air support."

"We need to do something!"

Foster understood the SEAL's frustration. They were on the tail end of the United Nations Security Council mandate and were sticking to the tired playbook of hanging back and letting others do the fighting for them. At least with a Reaper overhead, he had the chance to do something meaningful. But he only had three shots, and he needed to make them count.

"Angel One Zero, this is Envy Six Two, over." Another calm voice.

"'Bout time," Ryan muttered.

Foster ignored him. "Envy Six Two, this will be type two control . . ."

Despite the intensifying gunfire, he relayed the first set of target coordinates to the MQ-9 Reaper crew who sat thousands of miles away in an air-conditioned trailer at Creech Air Force Base in Nevada. He waited patiently with his eyes glued to the small monitor while the crew slewed their sensor to the right spot and positioned their aircraft.

"Envy Six Two in," the voice said, indicating that the Reaper was on its attack run.

"Cleared hot," Foster replied.

"Ten seconds."

Foster echoed the Reaper pilot's call on the intrateam net and continued watching the drone feed, his eyes darting from one heat source to the next as he added up the number of terrorists under the crosshairs. When the missile impacted, he saw the glow through the windshield, but his eyes remained fixed on the screen as the Reaper crew widened the sensor's field of view to gain a better perspective of the damage the Hellfire had caused. Foster figured they had taken out six or seven with that shot. But it wasn't enough. The insurgents still crawled like ants across the screen.

"Good effects," he said over the radio. But he didn't have time to savor the minor victory and wanted to hit them again hard and fast to break their will. He shifted the Reaper's sensor to another sizable group of insurgents on their left flank.

"Envy Six Two in."

"Cleared hot."

The second Hellfire missile detonated fifteen feet above the ground and dispersed shrapnel in a cloud over twenty al-Shabaab fighters. But, even with the two back-to-back missile attacks, the insurgents demonstrated a resolve he found unnerving.

He's got to be here, Foster thought hopefully. *Why else would they fight like this?*

It would be a nice feather in his cap to end his task force deployment by nabbing the number one bad guy in East Africa, but he was more concerned with just making it through the night. Foster directed Envy Six Two to target the center of what looked to be the principal element near the front of the AMISOM convoy with its five-hundred-pound laser-guided bomb. Even at the opposite end, they were well within the bomb's blast radius. But it was a risk Foster was willing to accept.

"Tell the Kenyans to button up," Foster shouted to Seth, who quickly relayed the message to the African commander.

"Angel One Zero, confirm target . . ." The Reaper crew was understandably hesitant to drop so close to friendlies.

"Danger close. My initials: Foxtrot Quebec, over."

"Envy Six Two copies." The calm voice had developed a slight tremor. "Envy Six Two in."

"Cleared hot."

Foster noticed Justin reach for something in his cargo pocket but was fully engrossed in watching the Reaper approach weapons release. The Agency man removed his cell phone, silenced it, then looked up long enough to see the Kenyans retreat to the relative protection of their vehicles. There was nothing left for them to do but sit and pray.

"Ten seconds," the Reaper pilot said.

Instinctively, Foster crouched lower in his seat and stared at the flashing cursor on the screen as the Reaper sent laser energy into the target to guide the weapon in flight. The phone in Justin's hand lit up again, and Foster glanced over as the spook unlocked it to read the text message. Through the dim glow reflecting off his face, Foster saw a panicked look that made him forget about the bomb hurtling through the night sky toward them.

"What is it?" he asked.

"SANFORD's not here," Justin replied, just as a deafening concussion rocked their vehicle.

Two days later, the team arrived at the objective exhausted, filthy, and completely unsurprised to find a dry hole. Foster cradled his SOPMOD M4 as he leaned against their truck and sat in a sliver of late-afternoon shade, looking out across the swath of dirt Seth had hoped would pass the Air Force sniff test. Their last gunfight had ended less than an hour before, and he felt his weary body sagging into the dirt as he enjoyed a brief respite from the truck's confines.

The door above his head opened, and Foster looked up into Seth's scowling face.

"Uh-oh. Not good?"

"Some bird colonel hoping for a star denied our request for a C-130," the SEAL replied.

Foster sat up and stared at the towheaded officer in open-mouthed bewilderment. "You're kidding me."

"Wish I was."

Foster removed his ball cap and ran his fingers through his long hair, then shook his head and glanced over at what remained of their battered convoy. The Kenyan and Ugandan forces had comported themselves well in the heat of battle, but five days of near-constant firefights had all but depleted their rations and ammunition supplies. There was no way they would survive a return trip through the gauntlet.

"What about an Osprey? We can give the Kenyans our trucks," he suggested.

Seth squatted down and pinched his stubbled chin in thought. Had they not been deep in the heart of al-Shabaab territory and hundreds of miles from the ocean, Foster might have expected to see the SEAL cradling a longboard and headed into the surf. Instead, the Texan held a carbine across his knees like it was a Gibson acoustic. "Too far, bro. The JSOAD looked into air-dropping a fuel bladder to set up an ad hoc FARP, but the risks were too high."

"So, what's their plan?"

"Sit tight," Seth said, finally giving in and shifting his weight to collapse onto the ground next to Foster. "They said the Air Force already has an approved LZ survey, so at least that hurdle has been crossed. If we need more food or ammo, they'll emergency air-drop a resupply bundle for us."

"Can always use more five-five-six and Rip Its."

Seth chuckled. "I'll put in the order."

Foster pulled the ball cap back onto his head, then climbed to his feet and kicked a stone, watching it skitter across the dirt onto the makeshift runway. "All we need is a freaking cargo plane. How hard is that?"

As if sitting on the ground had taken the fight from him, Seth leaned back against the JLTV and closed his eyes. But he nodded anyway.

"When's the next update?"

"Top of the hour," Seth mumbled. Foster could tell the frogman would be asleep well before then. Though they had all endured training that required them to go inordinate lengths of time without sleep, the last five days had sapped them of their strength. And whether Navy SEAL or Force Recon Marine, the adage *Sleep when you can* was tried-and-true.

Seth's breathing slowed, and Foster walked away, letting their team leader catch up on some much-needed rest. He nodded at a few of the Kenyan soldiers, standing sentry at their end of the landing zone, then made his way to the second truck, where Hunter and Hayden had cornered Justin and were grilling him on what they considered faulty intelligence. They looked like Viking pillagers preparing to claim their spoils of war.

Foster only caught the tail end of the spook's reply: ". . . was corroborated by SIGINT."

"So what the heck happened?" Hunter asked.

"Beats me," Justin replied. "But I can promise you we've got a lot of people working to figure that out."

Foster sidled up next to him while scratching at his thick beard. "You said signals intelligence corroborated your assessment that SANFORD was here?"

Justin nodded.

"Like *here* here? Baardheere?"

"As late as twenty-four hours ago, a cell phone we assessed as belonging to him was active in the camp. And . . ." He paused for dramatic effect. "Two others associated with his entourage were active up until the moment of the raid."

"So where are they?" Hunter asked.

Justin's head whipped from Foster to the SEAL, and he shrugged. "Had to be a ruse of some kind, right?"

"Yeah, but why?"

As much as Foster held a healthy dose of skepticism for the mystical arts of the Central Intelligence Agency, he knew the men and women of the intelligence service were exceptionally good at their jobs. Both Justin and his predecessor, a man by the name of Luke Chapman, had been exceptionally gifted case officers with keen eyes for the intricacies of building target packages in the Wild West of Somalia. He didn't think it was fair to place the blame squarely on their shoulders.

"Does it really matter?" Foster asked, trying to divert the conversation to a more productive topic. "A dry hole is a dry hole. Now we just need to get our butts home in one piece."

Hunter held his gaze on the Agency man a while longer, then finally turned to Foster. "Yeah, so what's the status of that? We got a bird coming or what?"

"The Air Force denied our request for a C-130—"

"You're kidding me!"

"—but the JSOAD is figuring something out."

"Right," Hayden said. "I'm sure they're going to be in a real big hurry from their air-conditioned tent six hundred miles from the fight."

Hunter swatted at the other SEAL. "Stop being so cynical."

Hayden responded by opening a can of Rip It and bringing it to his mouth. He drained it in one long pull, then crushed the squat can in his bearlike grip. "You're right. I should count my blessings."

"A good measure, pressed down, shaken together and running over, will be poured into your lap," Foster said.

"Confucius say what?"

He gave Hayden a crooked smile. "Just something my mom used to say."

A long burst from a nearby Kenyan HK21 machine gun halted their banter, and they swung into action.

TWO

TING! TING! TING!

The Duramax V8 roared, and Ryan drove the truck up and over a berm on the west side of the landing zone as rounds impacted their forward armor plating. Foster gripped the seat in front of him and stared through the windshield at the line of Kenyan Hizir vehicles that had set up a blocking position to keep the insurgents from swarming the landing zone. Their Katmerciler armored personnel carriers were equipped with remote weapon platforms on their roofs, and the nearby trucks glowed with the staccato of 7.62mm machine-gun fire.

"So much for *last line of cover and concealment*," Justin muttered next to him.

Seth leaned over and slapped Ryan on the shoulder, pointing to a gap in the line on the right side. The SEAL yanked the wheel hard over and guided the JLTV into place before slamming on the brakes. Without waiting, Foster and Justin opened their heavy doors and jumped to the ground to join the Kenyan dismounts, firing American-made M4 carbines at the advancing al-Shabaab fighters from behind cover.

Foster sprinted from the safety of their armored truck into a ditch in front of and parallel to their line of vehicles, then flopped down against the earthen embankment between two Kenyan soldiers. Flames leapt from the ends of their barrels as they raced each other to be the first to empty their magazines.

"Slow it down!" Foster yelled.

The soldier to his right gave him a sideways glance but seemed to heed his American advisor. The deafening reports slowed, but the soldier on his left continued his breakneck pace until the bolt locked to the rear. He ejected the spent magazine and fumbled for a full one, but Foster placed a heavy hand on his arm to calm him.

"Take your time," he said. "Pick your targets."

The soldier stared at him bug-eyed but nodded in assent. "Yes, Mistuh Quinn."

Foster lifted his head to peer over the embankment, but the growing darkness had made it difficult to see anything other than a dozen AK-47 muzzle flashes scattered across a front stretching over one hundred yards. The enemy's advance seemed to have stalled, but he knew from past experience that looks could be deceiving.

I need to get eyes on.

He rolled onto his back to look up into the deep purple sky and reached for the push-to-talk on his plate carrier. "Advocate, Angel One Zero, what's the status on our ISR?"

The reply was immediate, and the voice predictably calm. "Vader Two Six is overhead your position."

Seth's voice interrupted. "How about our ride out of here?"

Over his shoulder, Foster heard a metallic *tang* as the second Kenyan soldier sent his bolt home and chambered a round to get back into the fight. Despite his assurances to the contrary, he resumed his fevered pace and fired indiscriminately on phantom shadows downrange.

Any disappointment in the young soldier's verve was over-shadowed by the JOC's reply. "Wombat Three Three is en route. ETA ten mikes."

Foster glanced over at Justin, who shouted, "What the hell's a Wombat?"

But Seth beat him to the punch. "Copy all, Advocate. Say type of platform."

"Wombat is a Combat Spear."

Again, Justin shouted from across the ditch. "What the hell's a Combat Spear?"

Foster had never been on one, but he knew the MC-130W was a replacement for the older MC-130E/H/P Combat Talon and Combat Shadow platforms. "A spec ops Herc," he replied, then keyed the switch. "How'd we get the Air Force to pony up a Hercules?"

"The JSOAD managed to cajole a transient crew to fly you out."

"Tell 'em beers are on us," he said, then pushed himself off the ground and raced through the dusk for the JLTV, already thinking about the drone orbiting overhead. "Break, break. Vader Two Six, Angel One Zero, over."

"Angel One Zero, Vader Two Six is visual two IR strobes. Go ahead."

Foster rotated the handle to unlock the back door, then climbed up into his nest and shut himself inside. He picked up the tablet computer resting on the center console between the two back seats just as the Reaper began streaming video. "Copy Vader Two Six, you are visual the friendlies. Can you see the landing zone to our east oriented north-south?"

The sensor's field of view zoomed out to show the entirety of the five-thousand-foot-long dirt strip. "Contact the landing zone."

"Copy. Using that as your centroid, I need you to scan the area in all directions."

Immediately, the imagery shifted as the sensor operator slewed the Multi-Spectral Targeting System in a box pattern around the improvised airstrip.

"How's it look?" Seth asked.

Foster squinted as he studied the infrared imagery but waited until the Reaper had completed its circuitous scan of the area. "Just this one element on the west side," he replied. "Looks like they've stalled their advance and are possibly falling back on the north flank."

"Aardwolf Six, this is Angel Six," Seth said, trying to raise the Kenyan commander over the intrateam net.

"Aardwolf Six," the raspy voice of Colonel Njeri replied.

"The enemy is weak on their north flank. I would advise you to advance your forces there."

A warm static replaced Seth's soothing voice as Foster and the SEALs waited to see if the Kenyan commander regarded his suggestion. They stared at the armored trucks on either side, silently willing them to move forward and press the advantage. Suddenly, the driver-side rear door opened, and Justin climbed up into the truck.

"They're getting ready to go on the offense," the spook said.

As if on cue, the surrounding deep bass of Cummins turbocharged and intercooled diesel engines whistled as the Kenyan Hizirs sprang into action, surging forward into the ditch and across to the flat earth beyond.

"This is our chance," Seth said. "Foster, bring in Wombat."

Ryan put the JLTV in reverse, and they backed away from their blocking position. As long as the Kenyans continued driving the insurgents back, they would have a narrow window to bring the MC-130W Combat Spear into the LZ, load up, and get the heck out of Dodge.

"Angel One Zero, Wombat Three Three," the Herc pilot said. *Speak of the devil.*

After leaving their blocking position, Ryan drove their Oshkosh JLTV north to the far end of the landing zone with Hunter and the other SEALs hot on their heels in the second truck. The Combat Spear pilot had elected to make his approach and landing from the south, where Foster had placed bundles of ChemLights in the shape of a box to give the pilots a visible cue to the entry point. The Herc would roll out to the north end, load up, and take off back the way they had come. It was going to be a quick turn, and they had all hands on deck to get the four-engine cargo plane back in the air as soon as possible.

Foster glanced up from the tablet at the shadow racing toward them. A giant cloud of dust blossomed around it, and he could just begin to make out the sound of the turboprop engines roaring over the distant sound of machine-gun fire as the Kenyans kept the insurgents at bay on the western side of the landing zone. He glanced back down at the Reaper imagery and frowned when he saw a second cluster of hot spots growing on the southeastern side of the airstrip.

"Angel One Zero, Vader Two Six, are you seeing this?"

Seth heard the hesitation in the drone pilot's voice and walked over for a closer look.

"Vader Two Six, can you zoom in?"

"What's going on, Foster?" Seth asked.

The MC-130W came to a stop in front of them, then spun one hundred and eighty degrees to point its nose back down the dirt strip. With its engines still running, the cargo ramp lowered, and a crew chief jumped out and ran at them. But Foster was focused on the infrared images of a dozen insurgents creeping toward their position.

"Possible hostiles advancing from the southeast," Foster said.

The crew chief skidded to a halt in front of them. "Sir! Let's get you loaded up!"

Seth looked from the tablet in Foster's hands to the crew chief, then to Hunter and the other SEALs who were all waiting for him to make a call. After a few seconds of consideration, he sprang into action.

"Hunter! Load up your truck and men. We're taking ours to intercept—"

The crew chief cut him off. "Sir, we don't have time for that!"

"We'll be back before you're done loading that first one," Seth said, then turned and sprinted for the idling JLTV. Foster raced after him, scrambling up into his seat just as Ryan put the truck in gear and surged forward.

"Vader Two Six, can you see what kind of weapons they're carrying?"

Foster gripped the tablet with both hands as their truck bounced and jostled across the uneven ground to where the second group of insurgents had amassed. He couldn't make out their armament, but he had a sinking feeling that if they managed to get close enough with a rocket-propelled grenade, or worse, a man-portable air-defense surface-to-air missile, they could take out the Combat Spear. On a blacked-out dirt strip in the middle of Somalia, the cargo plane was a sitting duck.

"Negative, Angel."

Foster looked up. "I don't like this, Seth. Can't you get Njeri to send some men?"

Seth apparently agreed. "Aardwolf Six, Angel Six."

"Aardwolf Six," Colonel Njeri replied.

"We have a second group of insurgents closing in on the LZ from the southeast, over." Seth paused as he considered how to phrase his request. "We are moving to intercept but request your assistance."

Well, that was open-ended, Foster thought. But he couldn't blame him. How could you spend a week fighting alongside somebody then ask him to wade into the fray and provide cover for you to make your escape? It almost felt like they were leaving a teammate on the field of battle. And that didn't sit well with any of them.

"Aardwolf Six," the raspy voice said.

"Was that a yes?" Ryan asked.

Seth shrugged, then pointed at the shadowed outline of an acacia tree that might provide suitable concealment from the advancing al-Shabaab fighters. "Park there and we'll dismount," he said. "Foster, you ready?"

Ryan slammed on the brakes, and before they came to a stop, Seth had his door open and leapt for the ground with his carbine in hand. Foster followed quickly behind and hit the ground running as they bounded away from the truck toward the western flank. They were outgunned and outmanned, but they still had the Reaper overhead providing cover.

Hunter's voice broke through over the radio. "Seth, we've almost got our truck tied down and these airdales are getting nervous."

Click. Click.

"Angel One Zero, Vader Two Six, you are one hundred yards from the closest hostile," the drone pilot said. "Doesn't look like they know you're there."

"Copy," Foster replied, looking over his shoulder at the cargo plane's shadow at the far end of the landing zone. He'd never felt the need to be in two places at once more poignantly than at that moment. But there was nothing he could do other than trust Seth's judgment.

Foster followed the SEAL around the far side of the acacia, sighting down his carbine at the approaching al-Shabaab fighters. His thumb reached up and flicked the selector switch off safe, and his finger stroked the soft curve of the Geissele trigger, but he waited to press it. He was still hoping the Kenyans came through to relieve them of the burden.

And he felt guilty about that.

"Angel One Zero, you have two vehicles approaching your position . . ."

"From where?" Foster asked.

"The west," the drone operator responded.

Hunter's voice broke through again. "Seth! You need to get back here!"

Foster's finger came off the trigger, and he rotated the safety selector back to safe. Seth relaxed his posture and spun back for the waiting JLTV. Without another word, Foster turned to follow the SEAL just as the Kenyans' remote-mounted machine guns opened up on the terrorist position, ripping through the deepening night like a scalpel.

THREE

FOSTER KNEW HE WAS TIRED, but he didn't realize just how tired until the Combat Spear took off from the landing zone and climbed away from the firefight. Despite being forced to wedge himself into an uncomfortable webbed seat between two filthy men who resembled prison inmates more than SEALs, he was asleep before the landing gear retracted. A little more than two hours later, he awoke with a start when the special operations Hercules touched down on the ten-thousand-foot runway at Djibouti-Ambouli International Airport.

"Morning, sunshine," Seth shouted over the din.

Foster blinked, then wiped away his drool and rubbed at the kink in the back of his neck. But he ignored the SEAL officer. After almost a week of being stuck inside a cramped vehicle or engaged in pitched battle, his fatigue had become overwhelming, and he wasn't in the mood to be messed with.

The cargo plane jostled from side to side as the Allison turboprops droned a deep harmonic and lulled him back to sleep. He railed against it and forced himself to stay awake by yawning compulsively. When the Herc came to a stop with its open ramp facing the fenced perimeter of the Navy base south of the airport, Foster shook his head and slapped his cheeks.

Let's go, Marine.

"Alright," Seth shouted. "Let's not waste any time. Off-load the trucks and get them to the motor pool, then meet back at the team room in thirty for the hot wash."

A chorus of groans echoed off the Herc's thinly insulated walls, but Tre's seemed the loudest. "Can't it wait?"

Seth held up his hands to placate them. "This will go a lot faster if you quit your moanin' and pitch in."

"Yeah, yeah, I'm just sayin' . . ."

Will cut him off. "We know what you're sayin'. But we're *all* tired."

A few others chimed in, and Foster listened to the banter as it faded into background noise. It was almost as if the entire scene wasn't real. Their voices became muted, his eyelids sagged, and he knew that if he didn't start moving—and stay moving—he would slip into a deep sleep and stay there for two days straight. Even the cold steel floor of the transport plane beckoned to him as if it were a Westin Heavenly Bed with a supportive pillow-top mattress wrapped in three-hundred-thread-count Egyptian cotton sheets . . .

The noise was gone.

"Foster?"

He shook his head and blinked to focus on the SEAL. "Yeah?"

"You with us, buddy?"

He stood from the webbed seat and stretched. "Good to go, boss."

"Come on," Seth said. "Let's get to the team room."

"But the . . ." Foster gestured at the JLTVs they were to off-load, but they were already gone. The rest of the team too. He and Seth were the only ones still on the plane. No trucks. No team. Only an Air Force loadmaster tidying up the mess their motley bunch had left behind. "What . . . what happened?"

"You knocked out," Seth said, placing a sympathetic hand on his shoulder.

Foster flushed with embarrassment but knew Seth hadn't meant to call him out. Every member of the team had played an important role during the operation, but as their only JTAC, Foster was the one who had kept the jihadists at bay with persistent air strikes. While the others managed catnaps here and there, he had skipped out on his sleep to keep the armed drones busy twenty-four hours a day.

He shook his head. "Sorry 'bout that."

"Don't be. If it wasn't for you, we probably wouldn't be here right now. You did good work out there."

"Yeah, but the other guys . . ."

"The other guys know what you did. Nobody even batted an eye at you catching a few more winks." Seth paused, then quickly added, "Besides, you just helped prove what we already knew."

"What's that?"

"SEALs are tougher."

Foster looked up at the mischievous grin on his team leader's face and laughed. With the gauntlet thrown, he bent down and scooped up the Mystery Ranch backpack that held everything he had needed for a week away from base. He was back in the fight.

"Thanks, boss."

Seth picked his pack up off the floor and slung it over his shoulder. "I don't know about you, but I could go for some hot chow."

Other than sleep, nothing had a greater impact on their morale. The food that had sustained them in the field was adequate, but it was nothing compared to what they could get once their chores were complete. Camp Lemonnier had once been a garrison for the French Foreign Legion before the Djiboutians leased it to the United

States to become their only permanent military presence on the African continent. Not trusting the Army with it, the Department of Defense had handed control over to the Navy, who promptly built the Dorie Miller Galley—a five-star dining facility that rivaled even the best back home.

"Hot chow always sounds good." Foster tossed his bag over his shoulder and turned for the exit.

Together, the two men stepped off the ramp onto the tarmac in front of the JSOC task force compound. While the others had to hoof it back from the motor pool at the other end of the flight line, he and their team leader walked straight to the gate in the fence leading to their team room. With his momentary fatigue forgotten, Foster focused on putting one foot in front of the other. One step at a time. One task at a time.

Seth reached the gate first and was about to enter his access code when it swung open from the other side with a muted curse. Both men stopped and stared at the lieutenant commander, whose face was redder than normal.

"What gives?" Seth asked.

"You ain't gonna believe this." The task force intelligence officer looked close to bursting with anger and let out another string of curse words Foster suspected were unique to his corner of Alabama.

"What?"

"I'll show you *what*," the J2 replied, then he spun away from the gate and stormed for the TOC.

"Guess chow can wait," Foster lamented.

A few minutes later, Foster and Seth stood next to the J2 on the worn plywood floors at the rear of the TOC, looking up at what the men and women who worked there wryly referred to as their "Twitter porn." As hard as it was for Foster to believe, much of the intelligence the task force analysts evaluated was gathered from open sources—primarily social media channels, with Twitter as the primary purveyor.

"You can't be serious," Seth said.

"As a heart attack," the J2 replied.

The large flat-screen monitor mounted on the wall displayed a constant stream of tweets with hashtags or locations that bore some relevance to their operations in East Africa. While most were largely meaningless—like most social media posts—a few contained information that impacted their work. It was why they streamed the tweets in the TOC twenty-four seven for all to see. And it was why one particular tweet was front and center.

President authorizes elite Navy SEAL Team 6 to capture Mahmud Abu Hassan in daring headhunting mission. #Somalia #SASC #Oversight

"When did this go out?" Foster asked.

"Before your convoy left Kenya."

"What are we doing about it?"

"Well, the Beach is fit to be tied," the J2 said, referring to their leadership located in Virginia Beach, Virginia. "Pretty sure a few of our boys will be making their rounds inside the Beltway. But who knows what good it'll do."

Seth let out a disgusted grunt, then bent over and retrieved his pack from the dusty floor. "I'll save you the suspense. None."

Foster shook his head as he read the tweet for the seventeenth time. Each iteration, he tried reading it from a different perspective, hoping to unearth what possible reason the staffer could have had for what amounted to a gross breach of operational security.

"You said she's on Senator Ord's staff?" Foster asked.

"Yeah, pretty new too," the lieutenant commander said, then

turned away from the Twitter porn and returned to his desk set on a dais at the rear of the room. "She graduated last spring from the University of Chicago with a master's in public policy where she completed two internships on Capitol Hill—one with Congressman McKenzie."

"The Democrat from Illinois?"

He nodded. "District ten. She grew up in Mundelein, a suburb north of Chicago. Her second internship was with the Council on Foreign Relations, which is where I suspect she met Senator Ord."

"A Republican from Texas," Seth said.

"And ranking member on the Senate Armed Services Committee," the J2 added, flopping down in his slightly less-than-ergonomic chair from Office Depot.

Foster squinted at the monitor before finally looking away. "Wait a second. Isn't she that redhead who was out here on some sort of staffer field trip a month or two ago?"

"Yeah, I knew something was fishy about her."

Foster saw the stern look on Seth's face. "How so?"

"She looked at me like I had two heads when I said she needed to try Truth Barbecue in Houston."

Foster already knew Texans took their barbecue seriously. He turned back to the J2. "We were pretty tight-lipped around those staffers. You think she picked up on this when she was here?"

"There's no telling where she got it. She could have overheard something said in committee and decided to score points with her liberal followers by letting it leak that the administration had approved . . . what did she call it?"

"A *headhunting mission*," Foster said.

"A *daring headhunting mission*," Seth corrected. "But does it really even matter? Republicans? Democrats? They're all the same. They'll say whatever they have to say and do whatever they have to do to retain power. This . . . *woman*"—he thrust a finger at the scrolling

Twitter feed—"doesn't care about us. She doesn't give two hoots that we were in a weeklong firefight for nothing. She doesn't care that we came up empty because the man we were—"

"Headhunting," Foster offered.

"—targeting is the same man she tipped off for political points!" Seth clamped his mouth shut as if embarrassed he had let his emotions get the better of him. But Foster understood. He knew the SEAL still felt responsible for the mission's failure, even if all evidence now pointed to an errant tweet that had given SANFORD all the heads-up he needed to set up an ambush and beat feet for greener pastures.

"Power and money," Seth whispered. His outburst seemed to have sapped his remaining strength.

Foster cocked his head. "What?"

"That's all they want, man. Power and money."

Before either could rebut his argument, the blond SEAL spun for the door and left the TOC in shambles. Weeks had gone into preparing for the operation, but one hundred and thirty characters had ruined it.

FOUR

A little over a week later, Foster finally set foot on American soil. Even after eight deployments downrange, it was an event that never lost its luster. He might have expected it to lose some of its meaning after the first, or its novelty after the fifth, but it was still a moment that gave him pause. He stepped from the back of the Air Force C-17 Globemaster, inhaled a deep breath of cool ocean air, and closed his eyes to let the sun wash over his face.

I'm home.

"Sir, do you need a ride?"

Foster exhaled and opened his eyes. The wind caught his long hair and tossed it in his face. "Thanks, but I've got somebody coming."

I hope.

The senior airman nodded, then returned to his duties off-loading the cargo they had flown halfway around the world. Foster watched him climb back up into the massive transport aircraft, then picked up his backpack and strode for the air operations building—the same walk he had made a half dozen times before, and one he wasn't sure he would ever make again.

Halfway across the tarmac, he reached inside his pocket and pulled out his phone. He powered it on and waited for it to connect to the nearest cellular tower before opening Signal to read his last message.

LOADING UP NOW. WILL BE HOME SOON.

The message had two little circled check marks next to it to show it had been delivered. And they were filled in, which meant Rebecca had read it.

But she hadn't written back.

Disappointed, he inhaled another deep breath and slipped the phone back into his pocket. As a young Devil Dog, he had joked that the only way he would ever take a wife was if the Marine Corps issued him one. But, in the end, it was God who had done that, and Rebecca had turned his world upside down.

Foster took several deep breaths to calm his budding anxiety and ignored the jet noise surrounding him as he climbed the steps and walked through the automatic sliding doors into the air operations building. For close to ten years, Rebecca had been the one person he could always count on to be there for him, even when his thoughts became too dark to bear alone.

And now she had gone silent.

Where are you, Beccs?

"Can I help you, sir?"

Foster turned to the sailor who stood behind the counter in open-mouthed amazement at the long-haired bearded warrior who had just walked in like he owned the place. He shook his head. "Just waiting for my ride."

"You're welcome to wait right over there," the petty officer said, gesturing to a sitting area next to the main entrance. "Do you need to use the phone to call them?"

Foster caught a glimpse of himself in the mirror behind the petty officer and understood why the sailor seemed so eager to be rid of him. He looked more like a caveman than a Marine staff sergeant. He pulled out his phone again and held it up. "Got one. Thanks."

Foster was unaccustomed to being alone. As a Force Reconnaissance Marine, he could always count on having one of his brothers at his side. From the first day of training and through every deployment in a platoon of four six-man teams, he'd never been alone. That continued after joining the JSOC task force. He might have been the only Force Recon Marine in the squadron, but the SEALs, combat controllers, and pararescuemen were brothers all the same. They left together and came home together. Except for those who never came home at all.

And now here he was. Alone.

He opened Signal again, and his fingers hovered over the keyboard as he debated sending Rebecca another message. Maybe she had been distracted taking care of Haili and forgot to write back. Or maybe she was waiting to hear from him once he had landed. Things had undoubtedly been tense between them over the last several months, but that was to be expected with the operational tempo the command had forced on them.

Racked with uncertainty, he tapped out a quick message.

I'M HOME.

He watched the single check mark become two, then held his breath and waited for them to fill in. One minute became two, and two minutes became ten. When it finally showed she had read the message and still hadn't responded, he knew things were more than just tense. At least for Rebecca, his time in the military had come to an end.

Foster waited another ten minutes before he gave up and scrolled through his contacts for a backup. The first name he came to was Robert James, his best friend, and another Force Recon Marine who had made the move to JSOC from the vanilla side of special operations. Foster was almost closer to Robert than he was to his own wife. But like most in their community, they hadn't spoken in months. He tried Robert's number, but it went straight to voicemail. He was disappointed but not surprised.

He continued scrolling, past family who had sacrificed for his sense of duty, and past friends whose sense of duty was unparalleled and whose sacrifice had been absolute. When he came to Jeff Wilson, he paused. They had served together in another squadron, but he couldn't remember if Jeff was home or not. For those in the command, even time at home was defined by time away. He rolled the dice and dialed.

His call was answered after one ring. "Brother! It's been a minute."

Even hearing a friendly voice helped settle the storm within. "Just got back into town."

"Haven't seen your car in the driveway," Jeff said, confirming he hadn't moved on or left for yet another school they frequented to keep their skills sharp.

"No, I mean I *just* got back into town."

"Then why you calling me? Where's Rebecca?"

Foster felt the lump in his throat choke off his answer. He wanted to say she was on her way to get him and would soon welcome him into her loving embrace.

But she hadn't written back.

Thirty minutes later, Jeff pulled in front of the air operations building in the same beat-up Ford F-150 pickup truck he had driven for as long as Foster had known him. It wasn't for lack of money either, since he was single and had spent enough time downrange that most of his income was tax-free. He just enjoyed the classic look, the shot muffler, and the way it burned more oil than gas.

Jeff pulled Foster into a bear hug. "Welcome home, brother."

It wasn't quite the embrace he had hoped for, but it felt good all the same. "Thanks for coming to get me."

"Man, don't even sweat it." The SEAL released him, then bent over to retrieve one of Foster's duffels. He hefted it over the side and tossed it into the truck bed, then walked around and climbed into the driver's seat. "I was just puttering around in the garage."

"Obviously not working on this old beater." Even for as close as the men were, it was an unspoken rule that you could bad-mouth a teammate's mom, but his old lady and his ride were off-limits.

Even if it *was* a hunk of junk.

But Jeff just laughed it off. "Actually, yeah. Just finished changing the oil when you called."

Foster looked in the side-view mirror as they pulled away from the curb and saw a trail of blue smoke. "I think you're burning it all up."

"That's the old stuff. Now, where we going? Am I taking you home, or do you need some time?"

That's just how it was. They hadn't seen or spoken to each other in months, but they shared a bond that others couldn't understand. Some guys were able to come home and slip back into their family's routine with ease. But others needed to unpack more than the gear they had brought with them. Jeff knew things weren't kosher in Denmark by the simple fact that Foster had called him and not Rebecca.

"Can you take me to the command?" It almost felt like admitting defeat, so he quickly added, "My car's there."

Jeff didn't press the issue. He just nodded and drove.

It was a short jaunt from the naval air station to their compound at Dam Neck Annex, and they passed the time catching each other up on the goings-on in their respective worlds. For Jeff, it was the political pitfalls of being in the rear with leadership breathing down their necks while they waited for their turn downrange. For Foster, it was the political malfeasance that let bad men go free on the field of battle.

"A freaking *tweet?*" Jeff was incredulous when Foster told him about their last operation.

He shook his head at the memory. "A week of living in the suck with nothing to show for it."

"What happened to her?" Jeff turned off Atlantic Shores Drive onto Dam Neck Road and drove toward the naval base.

"Who knows. Probably nothing," Foster said, shrugging it off as just another example of how the political elite viewed the military. He remembered the redheaded staffer complimenting Seth on his grasp of geopolitics, then nullifying it by asking why he had chosen to go into the military when he could have gone to college. He had patiently responded that he graduated from the Naval Academy, and she repeated her question—oblivious that he had gone to a school with a single-digit acceptance rate where he graduated with honors.

"And they wonder why we avoid Washington like the plague."

Foster nodded in agreement. Each election cycle, it seemed more and more veterans were stepping up and wading into the political arena, and he had hope that things would change in DC. But his thoughts had returned to what concerned him even more than what he saw as a constant failure of leadership—the more pressing matter was how he was going to bridge the gap that had grown between him and Rebecca.

Jeff's phone rang, and Foster let him answer it while he stared into the trees whipping by outside his window, lost in his own thoughts.

"Yeah, I'm on my way there," the SEAL said. Then his tone changed. "What? When?"

Foster shot a glance across the cab and saw Jeff's downcast face.

"I've got him with me." Jeff shifted the phone to his other ear and started cranking his window down as they neared the main gate. "Sit tight. We'll be there in five minutes."

When he ended the call, Foster didn't bother asking him questions. The look on his face and tone in his voice were all the evidence he needed to know Jeff had received some bad news. He handed his military ID across to the frogman as they neared the gate.

After the guard scanned their ID cards and handed them back, Jeff rolled his window back up and pulled away. At the traffic circle, he turned down Terrier Avenue for their compound, where they would undergo even more screening before being permitted access. It wasn't until they were through that Foster finally ended the silence.

"Okay, what gives?"

"We lost another one."

Foster nodded. The loss of a teammate wasn't as common in the years following the end of full-scale operations in Afghanistan or Iraq. But it still happened. They both had brothers in harm's way in almost every corner of the world, and it was only a matter of time before one of them paid the ultimate price.

"Who?"

Jeff ran a hand across his bearded face, then reached over and rested it on Foster's shoulder. "Robert James."

Foster felt like he had been punched in the gut.

FIVE

Foster spent the week before the funeral in a fog. Even the cooling of his relationship with Rebecca had taken a back seat to his grief. Robert wasn't just a teammate or a fellow Force Recon Marine. He wasn't just another young man taken far too soon. He was Foster's best friend—the best man at his wedding, and Haili's godfather. He might not have been blood, but Robert was his brother in the truest sense of the word.

And now he's gone.

Foster sat in the driver's seat of his Land Rover Defender and stared out at the gray clouds rolling across the sky, mindlessly caressing a set of worn gold Master Parachutist wings and ignoring the empty seat next to him. Rebecca had already gotten out to join the family. He took a deep breath and let the cool spring air fill his lungs.

It was a bitter morning, and he could already feel the cold seeping through his midnight-blue suit coat.

Foster had been to enough funerals in the last decade to know what awaited him up the hill. The slow march to the graveside, the somber faces of the mourners, the sound of the guns firing in salute. But it was what the others wouldn't see that kept him from stepping out into the cloud-filtered daylight. It was Robert's smile and infectious laugh. It was his irreverent humor, doled out when it was needed most. It wasn't Robert the Marine or Robert the warrior, but Robert the friend—the man who would give you the shirt off his back and show up for you ten times out of ten.

And now he's gone.

A black Mercedes S500 pulled up to the curb and parked behind Foster's Land Rover. He watched the driver climb out, then reach back inside for a dark blue suit jacket that he slipped on over a white dress shirt. Foster squinted at him through the mirror and watched as he straightened his cuffs and used his reflection in the tinted window to adjust his red tie. But when he turned to walk toward the waiting crowd, Foster saw the man's face and recognized him instantly.

All hesitation gone, he slipped the wings into his pocket, opened his door, and climbed out to face his old teammate. "Luke?"

The slender man paused and appraised Foster almost as if conducting a uniform inspection. He started at his feet, looking for scuffs in his brown leather oxfords, then up to the gold Master Parachutist and Marine Combat Diver badges pinned to his lapel.

"Foster? I thought you were deployed."

Foster ran a hand through his hair and walked back to greet freshman congressman Luke Chapman. "I got home the day we found out."

The two men embraced as brothers, beginning with a handshake they used to pull each other in for a hug. It was a scene that had played itself out far too many times at countless cemeteries all over the country over the last two decades. But one that far too few were ever forced to endure, laden with the burden that had fallen onto only those who had stepped up to answer their country's call. Two men who had once been strangers became family, forged in the furnace of combat and their shared experiences. When they released each other, both men had tears in their eyes and stared at each other without shame.

"I'm sorry for your loss, brother," Luke said. "I know how close you two were."

Foster nodded and swallowed back the lump in his throat. He quickly cleared it. "It's good of you to make the time to be here."

Luke gave a wry chuckle and gestured over his shoulder, where Foster could just make out the domed roof of the US Capitol Building. "You came a lot farther than I did." He paused. "You're still with . . ."

Foster nodded. "For now."

Luke cocked his head as if to catch the hidden meaning, then nodded. It wasn't uncommon for the life they had chosen to take its toll on the ones who survived. Their physical and mental health took a hit, and many turned to drugs and alcohol to numb the pain of invisible wounds. Relationships of all kinds suffered, and marriages ended in divorce. As a former case officer with the Central Intelligence Agency, Luke understood.

The congressman handed Foster his business card. "We should talk."

"I'll give you a call," Foster said, taking the card and rubbing his thumb across the gold embossed logo for the US House of Representatives. The former spook representing North Carolina's ninth congressional district would be as good a place as any for Foster to start looking at what he wanted to do with his life beyond the Marine Corps.

"I'm sorry for your loss," Luke said again, then turned to join the others.

Foster watched him walking away and felt the gloom settle onto him once more. Without the distraction of a friendly face, the realization of why he had come to the final duty station for far too many of his friends hit him like a sledgehammer. He exhaled loudly to suppress his anguish and inhaled another lungful of cold air to calm him.

Turning to follow Luke to where the others waited, he couldn't see the faces of strangers or mourners gathered for the procession. He saw only the faces of his family, clad in Marine dress blues or Navy service dress blues, adorned with parachutist and diver badges, Marine Special Operator badges, and Navy SEAL Tridents. Like Foster, some had long hair and beards and wore suits to disguise what they were—elite warriors, agents of wrath to bring punishment on the wrongdoer.

And they were waiting for him to join them.

When Foster reached his brothers, they welcomed him into their circle. They stood off to the side and provided a protective ring for Robert's family, standing behind the black Cadillac hearse with Eagle, Globe, and Anchor displayed in prominence on the rear doors that sealed their loved one inside.

Up the road, members of The President's Own—the United States Marine Band—stood at attention in their red dress uniforms, their scarlet blouses trimmed in blue, contrasting both the somber mood and dark uniforms of others in attendance. Behind them, Marines from Barracks Washington also stood at attention and waited for the procession to begin.

When it did, the hearse started rolling forward at a slow pace, its yellow emergency flashers signaling to the cemetery's visitors that a son of the Republic was inside. Members of Robert's family who were physically able set out on foot and followed the Cadillac as it made its way up the hill.

"What's *he* doing here?" Jeff whispered as he and Foster set out to bring up the rear.

Foster followed his gaze and saw it settle on Congressman Luke Chapman. "He was with us a few times downrange. He came to pay his respects."

"Don't you mean score points with his constituents?"

Foster shot an incredulous look at the long-haired SEAL. "He wouldn't do that."

"They *all* would," Jeff said. "He's not one of us."

Foster heard Seth's words echoing a similar sentiment as the Cadillac stopped near the band. Over the blustery wind Foster heard the soft rolling of drums followed by the slow triumphant proclamation of trumpets announcing Robert's presence. The band marched off the field in front of the hearse, followed in steady cadence by the 8th and I Marines. As the song's notes reached a crescendo, Foster recognized the hymn "God of Our Fathers."

With The President's Own leading them again, the Cadillac resumed its steady crawl onward. In his mind, Foster heard the hymn's words punching through the thin wall he had built around his heart, buttressing it against the crushing agony of Robert's loss.

From war's alarms, from deadly pestilence,
Be Thy strong arm our ever-sure defense;
Thy true religion in our hearts increase,
Thy bounteous goodness nourish us in peace.

When the song ended, the drummer continued beating an even cadence to guide the Marines on their march. Few, if any, of the Marines who had shown up to render honors to Robert had known him. But he was one of them, and they felt his loss all the same. It was that deep connection, that bond, that held Foster in its grip and tormented him with his decision to leave the military behind.

"Robert wasn't even from his district," Jeff whispered.

"Can you give it a rest?"

The SEAL harrumphed but thankfully fell silent. Foster didn't blame him. They had all seen politicians snatch defeat from the jaws of victory, but this wasn't the time or place. With each step, Foster felt his chest getting tighter, and he prayed for the procession to stop. If they could just keep from lowering Robert into the ground, then maybe he wouldn't have to accept the reality that his brother was gone.

But when it did stop, it was too late. The hearse came to rest only a few paces from where his best friend's body would be buried. The band resumed its mournful dirge, and the 8th and I Marines stood at attention as the honor guard removed the flag-draped casket from the hearse, hoisted it to shoulder height, and carried it to a spot in the grass that had been swept clean.

Robert's family took their seats in chairs draped in dark green cloth as the Marines lifted their fallen brother in a final triumphant salute to heaven, then lowered him slowly to the ground accompanied by a fading drum roll. A Navy chaplain saluted and began speaking, but his words were muted by Foster's thundering heart.

I can't believe he's gone.

By the time the seven rifles fired and shattered the silence around the grave site, Foster knew his life would never be the same. He felt each of the three volleys of gunfire hitting him in the chest. But when the Command Master Chief began the roll call, he felt Robert's loss like a fist to the gut. He heard the names being called but barely registered their responses as he focused on the simple task of breathing.

"Special Operations Chief Wilson!"

Jeff didn't hesitate. "Present!"

"Staff Sergeant Quinn!"

Foster blinked the tears away and cleared his throat. "Present."

"Master Sergeant James!"

The silence was deafening as only the wind responded to the master chief's call for muster.

"Master Sergeant Robert James!"

The President's Own bugler began playing taps, and Foster gritted his teeth as tears flowed freely down his cheeks.

"Master Sergeant Robert M. James!"

A commercial jet on approach to Washington's Reagan National Airport drowned out the bugler's final notes, as if to remind Foster that his time of service had no end. For those who accepted the calling to serve their nation, even death wasn't an end. The Marine Band played "Eternal Father, Strong to Save" while the honor guard folded the flag and prepared it for presentation.

Foster saw Rebecca lean forward and place a comforting hand on Robert's wife as the Command Master Chief knelt in front of her and uttered the words no spouse ever wanted to hear. "On behalf of the president of the United States, the United States Marine Corps, and a grateful nation, please accept this flag as a symbol of our appreciation for your loved one's honorable and faithful service."

Foster stared into the distant horizon and knew he could never turn his back on his brothers.

I can't quit.

SIX

A week later, Foster woke early and squeezed into his wet suit before slinking away from their cottage on Vanderbilt Avenue like a thief in the night. He crept past the playset he had built—when Haili had been too little to fully enjoy it—and around the side of their house to his shed in the backyard. He knew exactly what he was looking for and didn't bother turning on the light. Within minutes, he retreated to the front yard and left through the gate in their white picket fence with his longboard tucked under his arm.

He cut over to Aqua Lane in his bare feet, then turned toward the sound of waves crashing against the shore only a block away. The proximity to the ocean had been the deciding factor when buying their house. For Rebecca, it had been the ease of access to a world-class beach where she could lounge under the sun. For Foster, it was the daily opportunity to sit astride a surfboard and harness the power of nature to calm the storm within.

Crossing Atlantic Avenue, Foster stepped off the cracked asphalt onto the cold sand of the path cutting across the dunes. It was still hours before the sun was expected to rise, but Foster didn't mind. He was comfortable in the dark and welcomed the anonymity it afforded him. Not that anyone would be awake to see, but he would be long gone before dawn officially fell on their little beach in Croatan.

Today's the day, he thought.

Descending on the beach, Foster broke into a run and raced for the frigid water. Without hesitation, he sprinted into the ocean and took three paces before a wave caught him square in the midsection. He powered through it and, holding his longboard in front of him, dove on top and began paddling down the back side of the wave.

His board had a deep, long blended concave in the nose that helped him glide farther into the ocean. While Croatan wasn't known as one of the premier surfing spots—even in Virginia Beach—just north of him, the 1st Street Jetty and its mushy right peeler often played host to surfing competitions throughout the year. From the Eastern Surfing Association to the East Coast Surfing Championships, 1st Street was where surfers went to surf and everyone else went to heckle. But Foster wasn't a surfer, so Croatan was just fine by him.

He felt another wave approaching and grabbed the rails at his chest, took a deep breath, and rolled underwater to let the wave crash on top of him. After the white water had passed, he pushed on one rail and pulled on the other, then kicked his legs to propel him back up onto the board. He shook the cold water from his hair and resumed his paddling.

After several more turtle rolls, Foster had paddled through the breaking zone and coasted to a stop in the pitch black. He sat upright and let his legs dangle on either side of the board, bobbing with the gentle swells while staring up at the stars above and across at the faint glow on the horizon.

"What should I do?"

He didn't hear an answer. He never did. But it still felt good to believe.

"She hasn't said it, but I know Rebecca wants me to get out. And if I'm being honest, she deserves to have me around more. Haili's getting older, and she needs her dad more than ever." Foster kicked his legs in an eggbeater and turned the board to look back toward shore. "I should want to be around more, shouldn't I? For both of them?"

After almost an hour of sitting in silence and listening for an answer on the wind, he watched a few lights flicker on as his neighbors who were early risers woke to greet the day. But Foster wasn't eager to return to the real world just yet. Sitting on his surfboard, surrounded by nothing but darkness and water, he felt completely at ease. He didn't feel the tension in his marriage or the weight of his responsibilities bearing down on him. And he didn't feel the pressure to give his command an answer either.

He wished he could stay there forever.

"I just can't walk away. They're my brothers, and they need me." He felt his throat tighten up with the one thing that had been gnawing at him for weeks. "Robert needed me, and I wasn't there for him."

Foster felt the water retreat underneath him with the telltale sign of a coming wave, and he didn't hesitate. He never did. He flopped his chest down onto his board with his knees bent and the bottoms of his feet facing the stars, then started paddling. With long powerful strokes, Foster drove the longboard toward shore while waiting to feel the wave swelling. When it did, he popped up onto the board and planted his feet along its waxy surface.

The wave was less than two feet high, but it propelled him to shore with ease and carried him into the breaking zone, where he dropped to his knees and paddled the rest of the way through the surf. When he reached the shallows, Foster slid off his board and planted his toes in the sand with the hint of a smile cracking his face. Most mornings he paddled back without even catching a wave.

But it wasn't the ride that kept him coming out each day. It was the opportunity to cleanse himself and believe that there was actually a purpose to his existence.

With salt water in his hair and his longboard tucked under his arm, the heaviness had lifted from his heart, and he set out for the dunes and the short walk home. It was time to face his fears and confront what he knew was waiting for him.

Today's the day.

When he reached their cottage, he didn't bother putting the longboard away, just left it leaning against the brick exterior next to the front door. He stripped out of his wet suit and draped it over a chair on their front stoop, then silently opened the door and slipped inside.

"We need to talk."

Rebecca's voice startled him, but it still had that soothing, melodic quality that first captivated him. He pushed the door closed and turned to face his wife of almost ten years while his heart hammered with fear. "Okay," he said. "Can I shower first?"

She shook her head and gestured to their kitchen table. She had already poured him a cup of coffee and made him a plate of bacon and scrambled eggs with two slices of buttered sourdough toast, and Foster suddenly felt his stomach twist into knots. She hadn't made him breakfast once since he'd returned home, but he knew she cooked for the same reasons he surfed. He hesitated for only a moment, then sat in front of the meal she had prepared for him.

Rebecca took several breaths before sitting down in the chair to his right and folding her delicate fingers around the steaming cup of coffee in front of her. She stared through the table at some invisible scene and worked her mouth as if trying to recall the words she had rehearsed. Tears filled her eyes, and Foster reached out to place an encouraging hand on her arm. "It's okay," he said.

She made eye contact with him, took a deep breath, and slowly exhaled before speaking. "I want you to stay."

He swallowed. "I don't want to leave."

As if the sudden agreement had unlocked the door holding back her emotions, Rebecca visibly deflated with relief and started talking. "I knew what I was getting into when I married you. I knew how you felt about serving your country, and I loved that about you."

Foster relaxed his grip on her arm.

But she let go of the coffee cup and placed her hand on top of his. "I *love* that about you," she said. "You are a man of honor who always steps up to carry the burden for others. You sacrifice for your country. You sacrifice for the Marine Corps and your teammates. You sacrifice for Haili and . . ."

Foster's heart slowed as if her words had the power to let him live or die.

"And you sacrifice for me," she said, squeezing his hand with a sad smile. "As hard as it can be sometimes, every day I wake up and thank God that He made you that way."

"I love you both so much," he said, dismissing the idea that what he did to provide for his family was a burden. "I would do anything for you."

Silence hung in the air between them, and neither wanted to be the one to break it. In his two weeks at home, there had been a tension between them that was more palpable than after any of his previous deployments. But he knew the stress of military service was cumulative and eroded even the strongest relationships over time. He knew it was a choice they each had to make, and he wanted to let her know he had made his.

"Even get out of the Marine Corps."

Her lips parted as she inhaled softly with surprise, then she quickly shook her head. "But I don't want you to get out."

He cocked his head, unsure he had heard her correctly. "I thought . . ."

"Foster, this is a hard life—Lord knows it's pushed me to my limits—but I signed on for better or worse. If I let you get out before you're ready, you wouldn't be the man I married. And there's no future for us in that."

"But Haili . . ."

"She loves you, Foster. You're her hero and can do no wrong."

Foster looked from his wife's brown eyes to the plate of food she had prepared for him. He wasn't sure how he could have misread things so poorly, but he had never been more conflicted. Standing next to other Marines and SEALs at Robert's funeral, he'd known with certainty he could never turn his back on them. Sitting next to the woman God had blessed him with, he knew with certainty he could never fail her the way his own father had failed his mother.

"I can't keep doing this to you," he whispered.

"You're not doing anything *to* me," she said softly. "We're doing this together."

He kept his eyes turned down. "I have to give them my answer today."

"I know. And I'm sorry I waited so long to let you know I've still got your back. Haili and I will be fine."

Foster looked up at her and saw the smile return to her eyes. "I've missed you," he said.

"I'm right here."

He pushed back from the table and stood, then pulled Rebecca to her feet and wrapped her in his arms for a hug that was two weeks overdue. She buried her face in his chest and cried, and he couldn't have been happier.

I'm home.

SEVEN

Foster parked his two-door Land Rover Defender 90 over the oil spot it had made after sitting there for the last several months. He climbed out and walked across the parking lot, pulling his hair back and tucking it underneath a faded baseball cap. A huge weight had been lifted from his shoulders, but his only regret was that they had waited so long to clear the air between them. Rebecca's support had been the one thing missing, and now that he had it, he was confident in the decision he was about to make.

The sun had just risen, but already the compound was abuzz with activity. Unlike other military bases in the Hampton Roads area, Dam Neck Annex was home to the Naval Special Warfare JSOC task force, and it was a near certainty that Foster would run into someone he knew. Even at that early hour. So he wasn't that surprised when the first person he saw on his way into the team room was one of the few who never grew his hair out—his squadron commanding officer, Commander Doug Belloni.

"Welcome back, Foster," the SEAL officer said, stopping to greet him just outside the door.

"Thanks, sir."

Doug eyed Foster carefully as if assessing his mental state. "Sorry I missed Robert's funeral. We all loved him."

Foster nodded in thanks. He knew the words weren't mere platitudes—Doug actually meant it. Most of the officers Foster had served alongside during his time in Force Recon and JSOC were leaders in the truest sense of the word. And they proved it by enduring the exact same grueling training shoulder to shoulder with their enlisted teammates. But guys like Doug and Seth went above and beyond and modeled the standard Foster had always aspired to—which was why he'd put off making his decision for as long as he had. "He was a special man."

Doug was dressed in his type III Navy working uniform in the green AOR2 camouflage pattern with a black embroidered oak leaf cluster on a tab centered on his chest and subdued SEAL Trident above the US Navy name tape on his left breast. It was unusual to see the SEAL in uniform, and it made Foster uncomfortable.

"You got a minute? I think we've got some things to discuss."

Foster nodded. He knew Doug would be eager to get an answer from him and put him back in the rotation. If he didn't reenlist, the command would cut orders for him to return to the Marine Corps for out-processing and fill his vacant billet with another qualified person fresh from selection. "Yeah, I was actually coming to find you so we could talk about that."

Doug nodded, then gestured for Foster to turn back toward the headquarters building. "Well, hold that thought. There's something you need to know before you make your decision."

He eyed the commander suspiciously. "Do I need a clean shave and uniform for this?"

Doug shook his head. "It's probably better you don't."

Before Foster could ask any more questions, the SEAL commander started walking across the parking lot at a brisk pace. Foster easily kept up, but they made their journey to the headquarters building in silence. Though he had never been inside before, he wasn't nervous. Doug had probably sensed his hesitation in reenlisting and called in a leadership quick reaction force to persuade him to stay. Propelled onward by his curiosity, Foster wondered what bit of intelligence awaited him when they arrived.

"You know I'm going to re-up," Foster said, hoping to avoid wasting anybody's time.

"Just hold that thought," Doug replied without breaking stride.

They entered the headquarters building and breezed through the layers of security preventing those already cleared to work on the compound from reaching the inner sanctum. When they arrived at the commander's conference room, Doug held the door open for Foster and gestured for him to take a seat.

"Just wait right here," Doug said, then closed the door behind him.

Alone with his thoughts, Foster started to second-guess his decision to reenlist in the Marine Corps. Despite Rebecca's assurances that she had his back and would support his continued service to the country, he wondered if she fully understood what that meant. Sure, she had endured countless deployments, but as he looked around a room he had never seen before, he wondered how much deeper the secrecy went. And he couldn't help but wonder if it might be a bridge too far.

The door swung open, and Foster instinctively jumped to his feet as Captain Timothy Cross swept into the room and closed the door behind him. He walked around the table, took a seat across from

Foster, and placed a manila folder containing a thin stack of papers on the table.

"It's good to see you, Foster," the captain said as he leaned back into his chair.

Foster looked at the door over his shoulder, then back to Captain Cross. "Are we waiting for Commander Belloni, sir?"

The senior SEAL shook his head. "This conversation will be just between us."

Despite having found himself in stressful situations numerous times before, Foster felt his heart rate tick upward at sitting across from the task force commander wearing only flip-flops, cutoff shorts, and a faded Iron Maiden T-shirt. "I already told him I was planning to reenlist. This isn't necessary."

Captain Cross nodded. "He told me."

Foster let the comment hang in the air for several moments more while wringing his hands beneath the table. He inhaled slowly and held the lungful of air for a four count before exhaling and expelling his anxiety and worry. Rebecca's words echoed in his head, drowning out the deafening silence.

I've still got your back.

"Sir, why am I here?"

"Because I don't want you to reenlist, Foster. I want you to get out."

The words hit him like a hammer, and he sat back in his chair, wondering what he could have done wrong. He had spent the last two weeks agonizing over a decision he had never wanted to make—turning his back on his teammates or turning his back on his family—and now it seemed that decision was being taken from him. As the seconds ticked by, Foster's confusion turned to hurt, then to anger.

"Excuse me?" he hissed through gritted teeth.

"I don't want you to reenlist," Captain Cross said again, his voice deliberately calm. "You're a model Marine and one of the finest assaulters we've had at this command, and I'm going to hate losing you."

Foster blinked several times and shook his head. "Then why?"

"Eventually, the Marine Corps is going to want you back. And, as much as we would like, we can't keep you forever . . ."

Foster cut him off. "So if you can't have me, they can't have me? Is that it?"

Captain Cross sniffed and squinted at him, then leaned forward and steepled his fingers in an overt display of confidence. "Maybe I should explain."

"Maybe you should," Foster said, a bit too acerbic for a staff sergeant addressing a Navy captain.

But the task force commander didn't seem to mind his brusqueness. "As you well know, our ability to succeed on the field of battle is predicated on our ability to acquire and analyze quality intelligence. We study networks to identify key nodes, name the target, establish a pattern of life, and build a target package to execute. We have access to every source we could possibly need—imagery, measurement and signature, signals, human—and we could still miss out on our target."

Foster thought back to the errant tweet that had tipped off SANFORD he was being targeted by the JSOC task force.

"You know how frustrating that is," the captain added.

His curiosity overshadowed his anger, and he nodded. "Yes, sir. I do."

"Which is why you are the perfect person to make sure things like that don't happen again."

Foster took a deep breath and tried collecting his thoughts to follow the captain's logic. There was no question it was a team effort to eradicate the terrorists they hunted around the globe, which was why for every Navy SEAL assaulter in the task force, there were ten enablers who managed everything from communications and logistics to intelligence and administration. But he still didn't see what this had to do with him getting out of the Marine Corps. Did Captain Cross want him to hang up his rifle and become an intelligence analyst?

As if reading his mind, the captain opened the folder in front of him and slid it across the table to Foster. At the top of the stack of papers were several photographs showing what looked like a large bomb or missile with a wide delta wing and a propeller at the rear. The images were grainy and appeared to have been taken clandestinely.

"What's this?"

"That is the Shahed-136," Captain Cross answered. "The Shahed Aviation Industries Research Center developed it at the behest of the Islamic Revolutionary Guard Corps Aerospace Force."

"Iran?" Foster thumbed through the remaining photographs. "For what purpose?"

"That is what we need to find out. All available sources of intelligence are pointing to this being what we are calling a *suicide drone*."

"A suicide drone?"

The captain nodded. "We believe the drones are employed in batches of five from a vehicle-borne launcher and can fly autonomously to their targets over six hundred miles away."

"What kind of payload?"

The SEAL shrugged. "Best guess? An eighty-pound warhead."

Foster whistled. "What is Iran doing with them?"

"Selling them."

"To who?"

Captain Cross gestured for Foster to turn the page. When he did, he saw several more photographs that were equally grainy and showed a large bearded man, who obviously wasn't Persian, wearing an expensive tailored suit. "That man is Oleg Volkov."

"A Russian."

The captain nodded. "We believe he is a facilitator for the Wagner

Group, the private military company Putin uses to conduct his proxy wars around the world. We have had our eyes on him since he first popped up on our radar in Syria and were preparing to shift a squadron to focus on his network."

Foster noticed the subtle change in the SEAL's demeanor. "*Were* preparing? What happened?"

"After we received those pictures, our asset went silent."

Foster focused on the picture of the dark-haired Russian with a neatly trimmed beard and military-style haircut. The quality of the photographs wasn't nearly good enough to give him the kinds of details he would need to be able to positively identify Volkov through a rifle scope, but it was a start. Maybe with a few more photos and a better idea of his pattern of life, Foster could develop an adequate target package for a snatch-and-grab operation. "How long has it been since you've been in contact with your asset?"

"Two weeks," Captain Cross said.

Foster set the photos back into the folder and looked across the table at the senior leader. "I'm not sure what you're asking of me, but if this is a bad guy who needs to be taken out, you can count me in."

The captain pursed his lips and nodded.

"How soon do you think we can reestablish contact with our asset?"

Captain Cross exhaled. "We can't. He's dead."

A chill ran down Foster's spine as he stared across the table at the SEAL. His stomach twisted into knots as he worked his mouth to form the question he needed to ask, though he wasn't sure he wanted to know the answer. "Who . . . who was our asset?"

"Robert James."

EIGHT

FOSTER JUST STARED AT THE CAPTAIN as if still waiting for an answer. He couldn't have heard him correctly. There was no way Robert would have kept this a secret from him. There were no secrets between them, and there hadn't been for as long as Foster had known him. Robert certainly would have said something if he had gone over to the intelligence, reconnaissance, and surveillance squadron or been involved in an SAP, or Special Access Program.

"What did you just say?"

"Turn to the next page," Captain Cross said.

Foster sat immobile for a few seconds before finally trusting himself to move. Still shell-shocked, he reached for the folder and moved the photograph of Oleg Volkov to see the sheet of paper underneath. He had signed enough nondisclosure agreements during his time with JSOC that he recognized it immediately.

"I need you to sign that for me," the SEAL said.

Foster shook his head. "What did you say? I thought you—"

Captain Cross held up his hands to calm Foster. "I will answer each and every one of your questions once you sign that NDA. Then, after you've heard what I have to say, if you want to go back to being just another assaulter, I'll reenlist you right here and now. Master Chief already has the paperwork ready to go."

After his conversation with Rebecca, Foster had felt like he finally had a grip on his life and knew the direction he wanted to go. For the first time since coming home from Africa, he had felt at ease with his conflicting obligations and believed he had finally struck a balance. But, in a blink and with a short stack of photographs, the captain had torn that precarious peace asunder.

Foster swallowed. "Do you have a pen?"

The captain offered him a simple black Skilcraft pen, then leaned back and waited. Foster didn't even read the agreement. He hastily scrawled his signature along the bottom of the form before pushing it across the table and leaning back to wait for the task force commander to enlighten him.

Captain Cross pushed his chair back from the table and appraised Foster with what seemed like tired eyes. The senior frogman had seen things in his day and had been with the command long enough that Foster knew this wasn't the first time he had lost someone. Why this required him to sign an NDA was still something of a mystery to him, and had it been anybody other than Robert, he might have just left.

But Robert was more than just his brother.

"I'm all ears."

The captain took a long, slow breath before speaking. "As I said, we were preparing to shift a squadron to focus on Volkov's network. As part of that, we recruited Robert to conduct Advanced Force Operations."

Their Army brethren from "the unit" at Fort Bragg had been

conducting AFO far longer than they had and were the recognized experts within JSOC. After jihadists from the Sunni pan-Islamist militant organization Al-Qaeda attacked the United States on September 11, the organizational structure of JSOC and their task forces had changed to meet the demands of the new global war on terrorism. As part of that, Naval Special Warfare recognized the need for its own in-house capability to send a single man ahead of its squadrons to prepare the battlefield.

Just one man to develop plausible access and placement. One man to build out a clandestine infrastructure to put assaulters on target. And one man to account for every contingency to ensure the success and safety of the mission.

Robert had been that one man.

"Which squadron?" Foster asked.

"He wasn't in a squadron," the captain replied. "He reported directly to me."

Foster glanced at the NDA he had just signed and noticed that it was for a Special Access Program under the code name SILENT HORIZONS. "And he was targeting the Volkov network?"

Captain Cross nodded.

"Where?"

"Iran. Outside Tehran."

"What was his cover?"

"We started an adventure travel company that he ran. It catered to recreational climbers and offered several multiday trips to places like Alam Kuh, Bisotun, and Lajvar. Most were simple climbing expeditions of the big walls, but some included trekking along German Ridge. Most importantly, it offered credible access and placement for the command."

Foster shook his head while trying to process everything at once. The cover made sense. Before joining the Marine Corps, Robert had been a self-proclaimed dirtbag who had lived out of a van in

Yosemite while climbing its iconic routes. But Foster didn't think his background was enough of a reason for such an elaborate cover. "Robert was a gifted climber, but what was the rationale for using mountaineering?"

The captain's eyes sparkled as if he was pleased that Foster had picked up on a nuanced aspect of the operation. "The Agency believed Volkov spent his free time in one of the coastal cities on the Caspian Sea—maybe Chalus, or someplace less populous like Nashtarud. As the second-highest peak in Iran, Alam Kuh afforded us an opportunity to establish a signals collection outpost that could cover the most likely coastal locations and much of northern Tehran."

"And?"

Captain Cross folded his arms across his chest. "We were wrong."

Foster couldn't help himself—he leaned forward to hang on every word.

"Robert learned that Volkov fancies himself a big-game hunter and has traveled the world in search of the biggest prize. When the Wagner Group sent him to Syria—where we first picked up on his network—he used his connections with the Assad regime to receive written permission to hunt endangered wild cats known as Euphrates River tigers."

Foster was losing his patience. "I could care less about Volkov's hobbies! What's this have to do with Robert? And why did you make me sign that NDA?"

The captain pursed his lips as if to bite off a scathing reply. "When Robert discovered Volkov was traveling to Isfahan to hunt mouflon, he went off script and ventured outside the Alborz mountain range. Because his business had no legitimate reason for being south of Tehran, we think his trips to Isfahan put him on Volkov's radar."

"Or MOIS," Foster said, referring to Iran's Ministry of Intelligence.

Captain Cross shook his head. "We don't know that."

"And they had him killed," Foster concluded.

"His death was an accident."

Foster recoiled as if slapped. After everything the SEAL captain had just told him, there was no way Robert's death could be chalked up to an accident. But he needed to know more. "How did he die?"

"In a climbing accident on the Alam Kuh Big Wall."

Foster laughed at what had to have been a joke. It was preposterous to think that Robert could have died doing what was almost second nature to him. Sure, climbers died all the time, pushing the limits of their capabilities. But for Robert, those limits probably far exceeded the difficulty of the Iranian climb, and he was unlikely to try something as dangerous as a free solo when he was only using climbing as a cover. "I don't believe it. What's your evidence? Were there witnesses?"

Captain Cross shook his head. "All the details we have are from the State Department, who got them from the Iranian government."

"I'd trust Casey Anthony as a babysitter over them as a source," he said with overt sarcasm. "Do the Iranians know he was one of ours?"

The Ministry of Intelligence had a reputation for being ruthless in uncovering threats to the Islamic Republic and had expanded their reach into Europe and North America. If they had discovered that Robert was part of a JSOC task force, they wouldn't have hesitated to eliminate him.

But the captain's response was less than satisfying. "State said they received notification of his death through the same channels as for any other citizen. We don't have reason to believe they discovered his true identity."

"Then why would they kill him?"

The captain sighed. "It was an accident, Foster."

Maybe it was his patronizing tone, or his clear dismissal of what Foster saw as the obvious truth, but the task force commander's comment struck a nerve. "There was no accident! Robert was a world-class climber. He's climbed some of the hardest routes in the country."

"Foster . . ."

But he couldn't let it go. There was no way his best friend had made a mistake like that. "He's climbed Screaming Yellow Zonkers in Oregon, Cocaine Rodeo in Wyoming, and Colossus in Idaho. Do you know what those are?"

Captain Cross just stared at Foster like he had grown a second head.

And that head was full of steam. "Only some of the most technically challenging routes in the US! Robert would not have made a mistake on a climb—especially when he was there on task force business. He wouldn't have put himself in a position to screw up. He just wouldn't. They killed him, sir."

"Okay," the SEAL said, conceding the point. "Let's say they did kill him. Why?"

"Because he was onto something. Because Volkov knew he was being watched. Because the Iranians knew he was one of ours and would jeopardize their sale of drones to Russia. Because he was just another good guy trying to stop a bad guy, and . . ."

And I wasn't there when he needed me.

The captain waited until Foster's frustration fizzled out. Even as he fell silent, his mind continued dropping pieces of the puzzle into place. It was really quite simple. Oleg Volkov was a rabid dog that needed to be put down. Even if the Russian had only been the triggerman, and the Iranians were behind the murder of his best friend. He wasn't going to let either get away with it.

At last, Foster asked, "What can I do?"

"You can get out of the Marine Corps and sign on as a contractor to pick up where Robert left off. Your contract will be with the command, and you will report directly to me or my deputy. None of your other teammates will know where you are going or who you are targeting. We will develop a complete backstopped identity, and you will travel to Iran under a nonofficial cover and continue to build out the access and placement needed to execute a capture-or-kill operation when the time is right and the president authorizes it."

Foster sat mute as the captain made his pitch.

"You will make connections, establish safe houses, find and track the target. You will build out a means of ingress and egress for the assault force, and you will meet the team and provide anything they need at H hour. Think of anything and everything you needed when you were a shooter, and you will have the full backing of this command to acquire it."

"Anything?"

He felt a twinge of excitement at the prospect of being given that much latitude to take down the person responsible for Robert's death. But what the captain was proposing was insane. If he had thought he was failing as a husband and a father before, this new life would make it next to impossible to sustain what was already hanging on by a thin thread. There was no way he could leave Rebecca behind and run off to Iran on his own.

"Anything."

Foster didn't hesitate. He never did. "Where do I sign?"

NINE

IT HAD ALL HAPPENED SO FAST. He had arrived at the annex that morning with the intent of reenlisting in the Marine Corps to continue serving the command as a shooter in one of its assault squadrons. But now, as he stepped from the headquarters building into the crisp morning air, Foster realized he had just decided against the future he and Rebecca had mutually agreed upon. And he wasn't sure how she was going to take it.

What did I just do?

As if on autopilot, Foster walked past his Land Rover Defender and navigated his way across the parking lot and into the warehouse-like building that was home to his squadron. He knew he probably should go home and face the music with Rebecca, but he wasn't in the right frame of mind for that just yet. He still wasn't sure how it had happened, and he was certain Captain Cross had orchestrated the whole thing to cajole him into it. But the decision just felt right.

Is it though? Did I make a mistake?

"Hey, Foster," a friendly voice called out from across the open bay, interrupting his brooding.

He turned and saw a dreadlocked SEAL carrying an M91 sniper rifle—a favorite among the Teams. Foster's eyes traced the sleek lines of the bolt-action weapon system manufactured by Redick Arms Development. It was based on the Remington 700 long action, chambered in 7.62 x 51mm, and could reach out and touch enemies of freedom—at incredibly long distances in the hands of the right person.

And Desobry was definitely the right person.

"Hey, Des, where you going with that thing?"

He smirked but stalked over to Foster's cage. "Just staying lethal, my man."

"Mind if I tag along? I need to throw some lead downrange."

"Always welcome." The SEAL ran a hand through his shoulder-length dreadlocks and studied Foster for a moment. "Everything good?"

"Just need to clear my head," Foster said, walking into the ten-foot-by-twelve-foot cage to gather his gear. Though most SEALs in the command opted to shoot the M91 sniper weapon system, Foster had come up in the Marine Corps and still preferred the short-action version of the Remington 700 with a twenty-five-inch Schneider Match Grade stainless steel barrel.

"With that old thing?"

Foster picked up the M40A5 and cycled the bolt to verify it was clear, then cradled it in his arms like a newborn baby. He had modified the rifle to suit his specific needs and replaced the Schmidt and Bender Scout Sniper Day Scope with a Razor HD Gen III from Vortex Optics. "Pretty sure this old thing can give you a run for your money."

"My money, huh? Alright then, Devil Dog."

Uh-oh.

"Let's do snaps and movers. Ten bucks a target?"

Foster scowled.

Desobry had grown up in Compton, California, where he had been a star running back and five-star recruit before a stray bullet had ended his football career. But his competitive nature and athletic ability carried over into the military, where he accomplished what too few Black men did and became a Navy SEAL. Not only was he the honor man of his BUD/S class, but he and his partner had finished as the top pair in the SEAL sniper course too. Foster would be a fool to take the bet.

But Foster wasn't known to back down from a fight. And he was no slouch on the gun either.

"Let's make it twenty."

Desobry flashed him a mouthful of brilliant white teeth as if he knew he had just won the lottery, then offered his hand to make the wager official. "You're on."

Snaps and movers was a test that involved two different types of targets—ones that snapped upright in a variety of locations at irregular and unpredictable intervals and others that moved left and right at random. There were six human-sized E-silhouette targets—three head snaps and three movers—at two hundred yards, four hundred yards, six hundred yards, and eight hundred yards each. Foster swallowed when he did the math.

Twenty-four targets at twenty bucks a pop?

Desobry must have seen Foster blanch. "It's not too late to back down."

But Foster saw the sparkle in the SEAL's eyes and knew there was no way his pride would allow him to crawfish his way out of the challenge. Rebecca would be upset if he lost almost five hundred dollars, but maybe that wouldn't be such a bad thing. Maybe it was just what he needed to keep her from focusing on the life-altering decision he had made without talking to her first.

"Not a chance."

Desobry nodded with something akin to respect, then hefted his range bag onto his shoulder and headed for the door. "I'll meet you there."

After the SEAL walked out, Foster was again left alone with his thoughts. Only this time, they weren't on the fragile state of his marriage or the loss of his best friend. His thoughts weren't on Iranian suicide drones or a Russian arms facilitator. They weren't even on the politicians who sent warriors like him and Robert into harm's way only to yank the rug out from underneath them with an errant tweet.

No, Foster was in the zone. He felt the familiar calm that came with focus, and all he could think about was the satisfying *ping* of targets dropping under his crosshairs. He felt a subtle shift in his body as he mentally prepared to become one with his rifle. He thought about his spot weld, bone support, muscular relaxation, and natural point of aim. He thought about holds and leads and a host of complex calculations he would need to make on the fly in order to find his mark.

And he was ready.

The knot of anxiety in the pit of his stomach had loosened, and he felt completely at ease in his environment. It had been months since he took up position behind his beloved long gun, but if the SEAL thought the competition was going to be a walk in the park, he had another thing coming.

I am a hunter of gunmen.

But Desobry wasn't just a professionally instructed gunman. He was one of the Teams' best snipers, and he quickly put on a clinic that left Foster feeling silly for accepting the match.

Ping!

"Hit," Foster said for the tenth consecutive time.

He leaned back from the Leupold spotting scope and glanced over at Desobry. The SEAL sat at the bench next to him with his cheek welded to the stock and his eye two inches behind the scope. He looked relaxed in what Foster knew was the practice of follow-through—the continued mental and physical application of the fundamentals after each round had been fired. He wasn't sure, but he thought Desobry was smiling.

Ten for ten . . . he'd better be smiling.

Desobry reached up and cycled the bolt to extract the spent cartridge and load a fresh one from the four-round internal magazine. The action was smooth and silent, and the SEAL was ready to engage another target within seconds.

Foster shook his head, then dropped his eye back to the scope and scanned the range for the next target. Movement caught his eye, and he focused on a black silhouette that had snapped up at six hundred yards. "Shooter, by eye, go to the six-hundred-yard marker."

Desobry's deep voice sounded like rolling thunder. "Contact."

"From the six-hundred-yard marker, go to the three o'clock, approximately ten mils."

"Contact."

"Go to glass."

Desobry shifted the rifle slightly as he sighted in on what he thought was the target. He began describing the scene to Foster. "The target has dried grass around the head and shoulder area and is leaning slightly right. There's a sand berm at the six o'clock—"

Foster cut him off. "That's your target. Check parallax and mil."

Desobry removed his firing hand and adjusted the scope's parallax knob to crisp up the target, then canted the rifle to align its reticle vertically. Then he called out the mils: "Three point one."

Foster agreed. "Check level." While Desobry readjusted the cant of his rifle to ensure it was level, Foster calculated the drop and reported it to his shooter. "Holdover five point four."

"Ready."

He checked the wind and announced the correction as his command to engage the target. "Left point four."

Less than a second later, Desobry had made the correct adjustments to his point of aim and the rifle bucked. Before Foster heard its report, he saw the bullet's vapor trail in the spotting scope and followed it through its arc as it descended onto the target.

Ping!

"Hit," he said.

Eleven of eleven.

Again, Desobry's voice rolled across the stillness between them. "What is that? Two hundred and twenty? We can call this off anytime you want." He cycled the bolt to let Foster know he was more than ready to keep going.

But Foster wasn't thinking about the money anymore. He wasn't even thinking about how Rebecca would respond to him leaving the Marine Corps to become a singleton operator for the command. He was thinking about how natural it felt for him to sit behind the spotting scope and call shots for his partner. He had done it during the nine-week reconnaissance sniper course at Camp Pendleton, and he marveled at how easily he had slipped back into that role for Desobry.

"Foster?"

The voice startled him, and he looked over to see that the SEAL had backed away from the gun.

"Yeah?"

"You okay, brother?"

He nodded, but his eyes were playing out a distant scene. He saw himself perched behind a spotting scope for a very different reason—sighting in on a mouflon navigating the treacherous terrain of the Zagros Mountains west of Isfahan. He saw himself calculating the holdover for a shooter who had paid him a lot of money to hunt the prized species with its full-length black neck ruff extending to the brisket. He saw the white saddle patch, muzzle, chin, throat, and lower part of its legs. And he saw the supracervical and perverted horns curving above and behind the neck.

"You want a turn on the gun?"

Foster blinked and the image was gone, but he still felt its presence in the same way he might if he had awakened in the middle of a dream and wondered if it was real. He shook his head and leaned forward to sight in through the spotting scope again. "Shooter, by eye, go to the four-hundred-yard marker."

The SEAL hesitated for only a moment then quickly fell back into the practiced cadence of communication between spotter and shooter. "Contact."

"From the four-hundred-yard marker, go to the nine o'clock, approximately four mils."

"Contact."

"Go to glass."

TEN

The sun was directly overhead when Foster parked his Land Rover on the crushed gravel in front of their cottage. He turned the key to silence the 2.5-liter turbo diesel engine and stared through the windshield at his longboard leaning against the house. Part of him was tempted to try and catch a couple sets before going inside, but he knew that would only delay the inevitable.

He got out and walked through the white picket fence while avoiding thinking about what waited for him inside. Before his last deployment, coming home with a sense of dread or unease would have been completely out of place. No matter their arguments or differences—and there had been plenty—Rebecca had always made him feel welcomed and celebrated. Their home had always been a sanctuary to him, but he wondered if his decision to accept the contract role would strain her tenuous support of his service.

He glanced at the surfboard once more—*It's not too late*—then turned the handle and walked inside.

"Rebecca?"

The cottage was an older home with small rooms compared to the modern monstrosities that dotted the Virginia Beach oceanfront. It was barely over one thousand square feet with two bedrooms and a bathroom they shared with their only daughter. And with Haili at school, it was silent.

Swallowing back his worry, he walked from the front room into the galley-style kitchen where Rebecca had prepared his breakfast that morning. He could still smell the bacon grease hanging in the air, though she had already washed and put away the dishes.

"Rebecca?" he called again.

"I'm out here," she replied.

His eyes went to the window over the sink, and he saw her sitting in a chair with a book in her lap and her face tilted up toward the sun. For all their troubles and struggles since he had come home, she still took his breath away, and he felt his heart thundering in his chest.

But like he did with everything, Foster threw himself into the fray. He opened the back door and stepped out onto the weather-worn deck that was in desperate need of another coat of stain. Just one of the many things he had planned on doing after returning from deployment that would have to be put off. Again.

Rebecca turned and saw the worried look on his face. "Everything okay?"

Foster nodded, but he didn't feel like it. He had felt such relief after their talk that morning that he was hesitant to risk ruining it. Even if she had promised to have his back and vowed to support his continued service, he couldn't help but think that this new challenge might be a bit too much for her. But he also knew he couldn't do it without her.

"How did it go at work?"

Just tell her.

"Fine."

She closed her book and turned her body to face him. She knew him well enough to know that *fine* didn't really mean *fine*, and she braced herself for whatever bit of bad news he had come to deliver.

With a sigh, Foster pulled up a chair and sat down next to her, then reached across and took her hand in his. They interlaced their fingers while he avoided making eye contact with her. It would have been easier just to tell her he had made a bet with one of the best snipers at the command and lost a ridiculous amount of money, but that wasn't what happened.

After Foster brushed aside his worry over his new role in the command, Desobry had finished the round by dropping only one shot of the twenty-four targets. He set the bar, but Foster made up for it when it was his turn as the shooter. He felt rusty and had rushed his first two shots—missing them both—but then quickly settled into the same rhythm he remembered sharing with Robert during their hours together at the range. Foster went on to score twenty-two consecutive hits and only had to pay the SEAL twenty bucks.

Not quite enough to distract Rebecca from the bigger issue.

"What?" she asked, clearly losing patience with his silence.

"I'm not going to reenlist," he said, opting to start with the least controversial decision he had made that day.

"Okay . . ." She placed her other hand on top of his, a clear sign that she was still firmly in his corner and believed in him. But that subtle act of kindness made him feel even more guilty that he hadn't spoken to her first. "So what are we going to do?"

He looked from the faded wood planks under his feet up into her big brown eyes, holding her gaze as he worked his mouth to try to find the words he wanted to say. But he wasn't quite ready to answer her question. "The skipper told me how Robert died."

The look in her eyes softened, and she squeezed his hand gently.

"He was alone," Foster said.

"Why?"

"He was part of a covered program targeting a Russian arms dealer." Foster swallowed. "And they asked me to take his place."

Rebecca scrunched up her face in confusion. "Take his place? What does that even mean?"

He knew he couldn't tell her everything. He couldn't tell her where he would be going or what exactly he would be doing, but she deserved to know something. She deserved to know enough to understand why he felt compelled to step in where his brother had left off. "It's called Advanced Force Operations," he said.

She removed her hand from his, and he felt a twinge of guilt. After everything she had been through during their time in the Marine Corps and years at JSOC, it almost felt criminal to ask her to endure even more hardships.

"Before an assault squadron deploys to an area of operations, the command sends in a singleton operator to prepare the battlefield," he said, opting to give her the textbook definition.

But she wasn't falling for it. "Singleton. You mean alone."

He nodded. "I can't tell you where Robert was or who he was targeting, but he was undercover when he was . . ." He almost slipped up and quickly corrected himself. "When he died."

Again, Rebecca was too smart for him. "When he was killed, you mean."

He gave her a weak smile to acknowledge his gaffe, then waited for her to say more. But when she remained silent, he continued. "All I can tell you is that the person he was targeting needs to be taken out."

"And the person to do it needs to be you?"

Yes, he thought. But instead, he said, "No. Shooters from one of the assault squadrons will do that."

"That used to be you," she said, reminding him that if he had only reenlisted like they had agreed on that morning, then he might have been the one to sight in on the person responsible for his best friend's death and pull the trigger. "Now what will you do?"

This was it. This was the moment he had been fearing since he signed his name to formally accept the command's offer of employment as a contractor. In one fell swoop with a Skilcraft pen, he had left a life of running and gunning behind for one he wasn't sure he was prepared for. And now he needed his wife to understand why.

"I'm going undercover to pick up where Robert left off."

She recoiled as if he had slapped her, and he saw the hurt look on her face. He reached out for her hand, and she quickly pulled away, then stood, knocking her paperback to the ground. "What are you saying, Foster?"

He felt his heart rate tick up, triggered by his biological fight or flight response, and he poured all his energy into remaining still and keeping his voice calm. He didn't want to lash out at her or abandon her, leaving her to cope with her grief and confusion on her own. She didn't deserve this, but he needed to convince her it was his only choice.

"I was going to reenlist like we talked about . . ."

"Then why didn't you?" Her voice had risen in pitch.

He knew she was hanging on by a thread, desperately hoping and praying her husband hadn't just thrown away their marriage on a whim. With as much love and compassion as he could muster, he fixed her with his eyes and began explaining it to her. "Because my best friend died doing something he believed in—something so important that the president of the United States personally authorized the mission. And because that mission still isn't complete. I need to be the one to finish it."

His earnestness had calmed her somewhat, but still she hovered over him as if trying to decide whether to hug him, slap him, or run to her parents' house in North Carolina. "How can you do this if you're not in the Marine Corps?"

He felt a bubble of anxiety deep in his gut burst with the relief that came from sharing his secret. "I accepted a contractor position with the command. The pay is far more than what I received as a staff sergeant—"

"It's not about the pay, Foster."

"—and I'll report directly to the task force commander. I won't be in an assault squadron, but I will contour the landscape for them—building out safe houses, establishing logistics to get them to and from the target, and developing the intelligence we will need to go after this guy."

"By yourself," she said. "Like Jason Bourne or something?"

He gave her a little smile but shook his head. "My job won't be to kick in doors and take out the bad guy. If I do it right, they won't even notice I'm there."

Rebecca lowered herself back into the chair. Her initial reaction had been fueled by fear, but he knew his wife had turned a corner and was no longer approaching their conversation with an adversarial bent. She didn't want to fight him. She wanted to fight *with* him.

"Is it dangerous?"

"Not if I'm smart."

"But you've never done this kind of thing before," she said, vocalizing the same worry that gnawed at the back of his mind.

"They'll teach me."

Then, as if accepting their new life and the challenges that awaited them, she asked what every military spouse wanted to know. "When do you have to leave again?"

This time when he reached for her hand, she didn't pull away. "I have a lot of training I need to do between now and then."

"When?"

"Not until the fall."

He saw tears filling her eyes, and his heart broke.

ELEVEN

Five months later, Foster sat in a faded La-Z-Boy recliner with a set of gold jump wings in one hand and a tumbler holding only an oversized ice cube in the other. His eyes were glued to the talking heads on TV offering their expert opinions on the Russian invasion of Ukraine, but he wasn't really listening. Most of the analysis they put in front of their viewers as fact was fundamentally flawed and only drove ratings. And that's all that seemed to matter.

Foster watched it, but his mind was on a distant scene he hadn't thought about in years. Since Robert's funeral, a vision of the dank First Reconnaissance Battalion paraloft filled with testosterone-fueled young men had played on a loop in his mind. The room was divided into two camps—one of seasoned and senior Recon Marines who already wore their gold jump wings, the other of newbies who looked up to them.

He could still remember Gunnery Sergeant Robert James—one of his instructors at the Basic Reconnaissance Course—removing his gold Master Parachutist wings before walking up and putting Foster in a headlock. With Foster bent over at the waist, Gunny James led him to the far wall while whispering in his ear.

"You ready to become one of us, Quinn?"

"Yes, Gunny!" he shouted.

Gunny James stood Foster up and pushed him against the wall, placed his gold wings on Foster's chest, and looked him in the eyes. "Make me proud," he said, then rammed the wings into Foster's chest through the thin white T-shirt he wore, grinding the sharp points against his ribs.

Foster winced but refused to let Robert down, even after the next Marine performed the "Rigger's Bite" by biting down on the wings to crimp the pins and lifting. One by one, the seasoned Recon Marines each took their turn pounding the wings Robert James had given Foster into his chest. By the end of the night, his shirt was bloody and his chest was bruised, but his heart was full.

I'll make you proud, Robert.

He tipped the tumbler back, trying to eke out any remaining bourbon, as the video cut from a general who had retired when the Soviet bear was still the biggest bully on the block to images taken from correspondents on the ground outside Kyiv. Foster's eyes were drawn to the sunken faces of the men, women, and children who were forced to live in a nightmare. He had spent his entire adult life learning to be comfortable with violence, but as he transposed Rebecca's and Haili's faces onto those of the Ukrainian women and children who had been robbed of their innocence, he felt sick to his stomach.

It wasn't until he felt Rebecca's hand on his shoulder that he realized she had been talking to him. He looked up and met her emotionless gaze, then offered her a sheepish grin. "I'm sorry. What did you say?"

"I asked if you were ready to go."

"Yeah. Sorry."

The last thing he wanted to do was leave his family again—especially sooner than he had expected—but events in Ukraine had necessitated the change. Of course, Rebecca didn't understand that, and her simmering resentment toward him and the command had caused their relationship to cool over the last few days.

"You might want to talk to your daughter before you leave," Rebecca said, then wheeled away from him for the kitchen.

Their pastor had reassured them that an increase in emotional distance was a normal part of deploying, but that didn't make it any easier to bear. After his separation from the Marine Corps became official, things had almost returned to normal, and they fell into a familiar routine of Foster being home for a few days in between weeks away for training. They made their time together count, and it seemed like their relationship was on an upward trend.

But then Captain Cross had summoned him. Foster had met the task force commander outside one of their compounds in West Virginia, where he had been undergoing lone survivor, evasive driving, and trauma medical training. Without preamble, the captain had shown Foster footage from Ukraine that looked like any other video the networks aired to drive their ratings up. But then the video paused on the remains of what looked like a weapon.

"Is that . . . ?"

Captain Cross had nodded as the image of a Shahed-136 drone was superimposed over the frozen video. There was no question that the smoking apartment building and the crying faces of the suddenly homeless women and children had been caused by an Iranian suicide drone. In that moment, he knew that his looming mission to hunt down Oleg Volkov took on an urgency that hadn't been there before.

Foster shook away the memory and reached for the lever on the side of his recliner to bring the footrest in. He pointed the remote control at the TV and turned it off, then slipped into the kitchen to set his empty glass on the counter. Rebecca leaned against the far wall with a dazed look on her face, and he knew he should say something to her. But as hard as he tried, he couldn't find the words to assuage her suffering. So he let her be.

He returned to the main room and set Robert's gold wings on their place of honor next to the certificate commemorating the day he received them, then walked down the hall to the smaller of the cottage's two bedrooms. He knocked softly on the door and paused before letting himself in to his daughter's room. Haili sat on the floor with a large case of ceramic beads in various colors, shapes, and sizes opened in front of her.

She looked up, the spitting image of her mother. "Hi, Daddy."

"Hey, monkey," he said as he sat on the edge of her bed. "Whatcha workin' on?"

She held up a thin strand of red and yellow beads with the word *DADDY* spelled out in the middle. "Making you a bracelet to wear while you're gone."

He leaned forward to get a closer look at her handiwork and noticed the obvious love and care she had put into making the custom piece of jewelry. "I love it. Did you pick out those colors yourself?"

She grinned. "Mama said that even though you're not in the Marine Corps anymore, you're still a Marine."

"That's right. Once a Marine, always a Marine." He held his arm out for her to drape the bracelet across his wrist, then waited patiently while she proudly affixed the clasp to keep it in place.

With the presentation of the bracelet complete, her smile faded, and she stood to face him, wearing a forlorn look. "Is it time for you to go?"

He felt a lump in his throat and quickly cleared it. "'Fraid so."

Without hesitation, she flung her arms around his neck and

squeezed with all the might her eight-year-old body could muster. His heart broke as he wrapped her in his arms and lifted her off the ground. He rocked her gently from side to side and savored the moment with the second most important person in his life.

"I don't want you to go, Daddy," she said, her voice muffled against his neck.

He lowered her gently to the ground. "I know, monkey. But you know why I have to go."

She nodded earnestly. "Because you have to stop the bad guys."

He grinned at her through his gut-wrenching sadness. "I'm going to miss you."

"I'm going to miss you too, Daddy." She gave him a sad smile, then stepped in close and squeezed him one more time. Then, like the tough little trooper she was, she stepped back and put on a brave face for him. "Don't take that off," she said, pointing to the bracelet on his wrist. "It will keep you safe."

"I won't, baby girl."

"I love you, Daddy."

"I love you too."

They hugged and kissed one more time, then Foster slipped out of her bedroom and quickly closed the door on half of his entire world. Like her mother, Haili knew how to tug on his heartstrings without even trying, and he didn't want his daughter to see him cry.

~

NORFOLK, VIRGINIA

A short while later, Foster's stomach dropped when he exited Interstate 64 onto Norview Avenue and drove toward the international airport. He looked at the clock on the dash and felt the burden of his upcoming task weighing on him. A glance in the rearview mirror at the empty back seat reminded him that Haili was staying with friends while Rebecca sat next to him but felt farther away than just three feet. He felt his heart pounding like a metronome, beating an incessant cadence as he marched onward into the unknown.

And all he wanted to do was stop. He could have reached out and touched her or said something to close the distance between them, but he was hesitant to do anything that might make things worse. Swallowing back his fear, he steered her Ford Explorer in silence and looked across the water covered in lilies at the runway in the distance.

"What time is your flight?"

He knew she already knew the answer to that question but had asked it to break the silence. Neither one wanted him to leave with things as they were. "Five oh seven," he said.

Rebecca turned away from the view outside her window and looked at the clock. Almost as if seeing the time confirmed her fear about him leaving again, she broke down and sobbed into her hands.

Foster steered the SUV onto a tree-lined street to the right toward departures. He reached over and placed his hand on Rebecca's leg to comfort her while searching for the words to say. He opened and closed his mouth several times, unsure what he could possibly tell his wife that would make her understand why he felt the need to leave his family behind. The core values that had always guided him— honor, courage, and commitment—sounded trite at a time like this.

So he settled for speaking what was on his heart. "I love you."

The words only seemed to make her sob harder, and he fought the temptation to remove his hand from her thigh. Love was the one thing he knew would see them through the trials they were both going to face. *It always protects, always trusts, always hopes, always perseveres. Love never fails.* He had to believe they would make it through this, because without her, he wasn't sure it was worth it.

As he rounded a bend in the road toward short-term parking, Rebecca stopped crying and wiped the tears from her eyes. She placed her hand on top of his and squeezed. "You know how much I love you, don't you?"

He looked over at her and nodded. "I do."

"Then you know how hard this will be for me," she said.

Again, he nodded.

He pulled into the short-term lot and found a parking space close to the terminal. They hadn't discussed how this was supposed to go, other than that she would see him off at the airport, then return home to Haili. But they were treading new ground. Unlike previous deployments when he had been surrounded by his teammates and Rebecca had the support of other spouses in the command, they were on their own.

That he was still going to be in the US made it even worse.

He put the Explorer in park and turned it off, then shifted in his seat to face her. She looked up at him with red-rimmed eyes and a pleading look on her face that battered against his resolve. Despite his reasons for taking on the role the command had offered him and all the training they had given him, that one look from his wife caused him to question everything he had done since returning home from Africa.

"Am I doing the right thing?" he asked.

He saw her shoulders relax as she turned her body toward his. "Only you can answer that."

Foster knew she wasn't putting the burden on him to make all the decisions for their family. They had always been a team. But she was asking him to listen to his head and not his heart. She was challenging him to put aside his fears and decide if he was sacrificing for the right reasons.

He took a deep breath.

"Do you feel called to do this?" she asked.

Foster nodded.

"Then it's the right thing."

And just like that, he knew he had his wife back.

They got out of the car and embraced in the short-term parking lot at Norfolk International Airport as if they were the only two people in the world. Foster and Rebecca were the only ones who mattered in that moment. For all the tension and stress brought on by his new position and the uncertainty of his deployment, that hug was the only thing he needed in order to know they would make it through to the other side.

When she let go, he opened the rear hatch and removed a brand-new Eberlestock Hercules rolling duffel he had packed for his trip. With a hard-sided bottom and rip-stop nylon material, it had a comforting familiar feel to it, though there was nothing inside that would ever connect him to the military. He closed the hatch and looked at his reflection in the Explorer's rear window. A stranger with a neatly trimmed goatee stared back at him.

"Are you ready?" Rebecca asked.

Foster swallowed and took her in his arms again. "I'm going to miss you, babe."

"I'm going to miss you too," she said, looking up at him. "Foster Cottle."

A switch had been flipped. Foster Quinn, former Marine staff sergeant and devoted husband and father, was no more. In his place was Foster Cottle, world-class hunting guide and owner of Shinar Outfitters.

TWELVE

Foster turned off the asphalt county road onto the gravel drive, slowing just enough so the cattle guard didn't rattle his molars. He drove a lightly used 2015 GMC Sierra 1500 Denali with all the bells and whistles, but part of him still wished he was driving his Defender, which was twenty years older. After two weeks in his cover life, he was still unaccustomed to having such nice things. But someone of Foster Cottle's stature was expected to drive in luxury. Even if it was just a pickup truck.

He parked it in the freestanding carport, then opened the door and stepped out onto the running board that automatically dropped into place. After two weeks of living another man's life, he was finally beginning to settle into a routine, but he couldn't help but think about Rebecca and Haili living their real life without him in Virginia Beach. Despite his commitment to the mission, that was where he really wanted to be.

The waiting was the worst part.

Closing the door behind him, he walked across the lawn—more weeds than grass—to the fifteen-hundred-square-foot house of the same vintage as his Defender. It had been remodeled within the last two years and was the perfect place for a newly divorced Army veteran to call home. If anybody took the time to look, they would see that the house was owned by Shinar Outfitters, LLC, the same company that owned almost two thousand acres between Lake Tawakoni and Lake Fork.

Foster let himself in through the back door and kicked off his boots in the mudroom. He had spent the day at the ranch mixing up a batch of soured corn, then riding around in the Polaris to add it to his feeders. A group of four hunters from Fort Worth had been the first to book a feral hog hunt during the ranch's opening weekend, and he wanted to make sure the lodge was squared away and that he had enough bait to make their stay worthwhile. Shinar Ranch would only succeed if its reviews were glowing.

He walked through the galley kitchen, pausing long enough to remove a tumbler from the cupboard and fill it half full of Buffalo Trace. Normally he'd prepare it with a sugar cube saturated with bitters before filling it with the bronze liquid and garnishing with an orange peel and cocktail cherry. But today was a straight bourbon kind of day.

Today was Haili's ninth birthday, and he was missing it.

Foster carried the tumbler into the living room and flopped down in his recliner before reaching for the remote. For the two weeks he had been living in his bachelor pad, he'd ended his days the same way—a predinner cocktail, followed by a shower, then a simple home-cooked meal of venison steak, grilled javelina backstrap, or chile verde. Particularly stressful days saw him in an Adirondack chair on his back porch after supper with another cocktail in hand while studying Iran's history, culture, politics, and laws.

He already saw himself pouring that second drink tonight.

The TV came on—already tuned to FOX News—and he took a sip while catching up on the latest headlines making waves. The crawler at the bottom of the screen showed an assortment of headlines from Ukraine—including the shelling of a hospital in Velyka Pysarivka and the counteroffensive in Kharkiv—as well as an announcement that the Department of Treasury had sanctioned the Iranian Ministry of Intelligence in response to a cyberattack against Albania.

"Swell," Foster said.

The last thing he needed as he prepared to infiltrate the Islamic Republic of Iran was an increase in sanctions by the US government. If he had any hopes of establishing his cover for status without added scrutiny, the Treasury Department had just dashed them.

His cell phone rang, and he muted the TV before answering. The caller ID showed a 418 area code, but he didn't recognize the number. "Shinar Outfitters, Foster Cottle speaking," he said, trying to sound like the owner of a premier hunting outfitter instead of a former Marine pretending to be one.

"*Bonjour*, Foster," the voice said. "*Comment ça va?*"

He recognized the voice immediately and leaned forward in his chair. "Simon! How are you, my friend?"

Simon Gervais switched to English. "I am well. How have you been?"

"Busy. The ranch is hosting its first guests this weekend."

"Bravo!" Foster could hear the genuine excitement in Simon's voice. "I hope my suggestions were of help."

"Very much so," he replied.

He had met Simon in June at the Game Fair en Loir-et-Cher—a region in France named for the two rivers that crossed it. His command had arranged for the Browning arms company to invite Foster Cottle as their guest to the premier event, which catered to hunters and outdoor enthusiasts in France and Europe and saw more than eighty thousand visitors and six hundred exhibitors. Simon's company, Dion Outfitters, offered a luxury experience in the northern region of the Lac Saint-Jean, four hours from Quebec City, and had been an exhibitor in the Game Fair's Premium Village.

"*Bien,*" Simon said. "I call with good news."

Foster set his bourbon on the end table. "You're coming to Texas to hunt pigs with me?"

Simon laughed as if the idea of staying in a Texas hunting lodge was humorous. But given the luxurious accommodations he offered his guests in lakefront chalets set in the middle of twenty-eight thousand acres of raw wilderness, Foster couldn't blame him. "No, my friend. But I think you might not be in Texas much longer."

This is it.

Over dinner one evening, Simon had introduced Foster to the man he had traveled across the Atlantic to Lamotte-Beuvron to meet. When JSOC had learned from multiple agencies within the intelligence community that the Republic of Iran's Department of Environment intended to send Bijan Ghorbani, the director general of Wildlife Protection and Management, to the Game Fair, Foster knew it was his in. He needed someone from Iran's government to sponsor an entry visa, and Director General Ghorbani was the perfect person to do so.

"Are you saying what I think you're saying?" Foster asked, trying to rein in his nerves.

"Our mutual friend has extended an invitation for you to visit."

"When?"

"Next week."

Foster whistled. "That's not much time."

"He asked me to convey to you that your letter of invitation and entry visa will be waiting for you at the Pakistani embassy in Washington, DC." Simon paused before voicing his reservations. "Are you sure you want to do this?"

He appreciated Simon's concern. Dion Outfitters had the prestige and clout to attract hunters from around the world and charge exorbitant fees for trophy hunts in Canada. They didn't need to travel halfway around the world to a country that was openly hostile to the West. But Shinar Outfitters was new and unknown to wealthy clientele. Sure, it was an up-and-coming operation—with a wealthy uncle for a benefactor—but it needed something to set itself apart from the others.

Guided hunts for ibex, urial, or mouflon in Persia would be a great place to start.

"I'm sure," Foster said. "I can't grow by offering only whitetail and wild pig hunts."

Simon sighed. "In that case, I will wish you safe travels and recommend you to our clients. *Bonne chance, mon ami.*"

After Foster had hung up, he unmuted the TV to provide background noise while he scurried around the house to gather what he needed for his trip. With the trip still days away, he only needed to make the necessary arrangements to travel to Tehran. But he still set about to pack his things in order to lose himself in the mundane and forget the enormity of the looming task. He pulled out his large Eberlestock rolling duffel, set it on the floor at the foot of his bed, and began filling it with enough clothing to last him a week. If his initial meetings with the director general panned out, he would arrange to have the rest of his things sent over.

Once he had packed his clothes, Foster returned to his recliner and took another sip of bourbon to calm his nerves. Then he picked up his phone and dialed the number to his travel agency. Like everything in his house, the agency was real enough, but it served more than one purpose. The three-digit extension he dialed took him directly to a travel agent whose job it was to forward his itinerary to an innocuous email address. Captain Cross monitored that email account, knowing it was the only way he would learn of Foster's travel plans.

"Four Ten Travel," the woman's voice said.

"Yes, my name is Foster Cottle with Shinar Outfitters . . ."

"Mr. Cottle, of course. How may I help you?"

Foster spent the next several minutes selecting a flight from DFW to Ronald Reagan Washington National Airport with a two-night stay at the St. Regis. Though Simon had told him that his letter of invitation and visa would be waiting for him with the Interests Section of the Islamic Republic of Iran at the Pakistani embassy, he wanted to ensure he had enough time before leaving the country.

"Would you like coach or business class from Frankfurt to Tehran?" she asked.

"Business class," Foster replied without hesitation.

"And the Parsian Azadi Hotel?"

"Correct."

She placed him on hold for several minutes while she ticketed the flights and secured his hotel reservations, but he barely heard the music playing in the background. His mind raced with budding anxiety, now that all his months of training were about to be put to the test. From evasive driving to tradecraft, surveillance detection to high-risk SERE—survival, evasion, resistance, and escape—and corporate cover, he felt overwhelmed with the amount of knowledge he had shoved into his brain.

Just breathe, Foster. If Robert did it, so can you, the commanding Recon Marine inside of him said.

But Robert was killed, the frightened boy countered.

He took a long, slow breath and held it.

One . . . two . . . three . . . four.

Foster exhaled through pursed lips when the music stopped.

"Mr. Cottle?"

"I'm here."

"You're confirmed on American Airlines flight twenty-eight seventeen, departing DFW on Tuesday, September thirteenth, at ten twenty-five a.m., and arriving at Reagan National at two twenty-nine p.m." She continued reading him his travel plans, including his hotels and confirmation numbers, then asked, "Is there anything else I can do for you?"

"That's all I needed. Thank you."

After hanging up, he picked up his tumbler and drained the rest of his bourbon. He considered skipping the shower and dinner for another online Farsi cram session but opted to stick to his routine. After all, once he arrived in the Islamic Republic of Iran, his routine would be the only thing that kept him alive. He couldn't pretend to be Foster Cottle. He needed to *be* Foster Cottle.

"Giddy up," he said, then climbed out of the recliner and headed for the shower.

THIRTEEN

The Lufthansa Airbus A330-300 touched down in the Islamic Republic of Iran just before 9:00 p.m., five hours after leaving Frankfurt, Germany. But because he had arrived in one of only eight countries with a thirty-minute offset from Coordinated Universal Time, Foster had to spin the minute hand on his Tudor Submariner one and a half times.

After screwing down the crown on his watch, he leaned forward in his business class seat and looked through the window at the darkened parking apron, his thoughts turning to Robert. He wondered if his best friend had seen what he saw—a handful of large commercial aircraft with livery from Mahan Air, Iran Air, and others, parked under orange halos cast from a row of sodium lamps on the otherwise vacant tarmac. For an airport that serviced a city of nine and a half million people, Imam Khomeini International seemed almost sleepy. But he had expected that.

The passenger jet slowed and then came to a stop at one of the few gates that used jet bridges for deplaning. During training, Foster learned that the airport had begun as a joint venture between an American engineering and architectural consulting partnership and a local firm overseeing design. But construction halted when a rebel faction led by the religious cleric Ayatollah Khomeini ousted the Shah during the 1979 Iranian revolution. What was supposed to have been a modern Western-style facility based on the Dallas Fort Worth Airport slipped into irrelevance. Now, Tehran's international airport serviced only fifty flights a day, compared to a volume twenty times that in Frankfurt.

Foster leaned back in his seat and tried to calm his nerves. Had Robert felt like this?

The war in Ukraine and Russia's use of the Geran-2—their name for the Shahed-136 suicide drone—had necessitated his deployment sooner than the command would have liked. When he should have spent over a year learning everything he needed to know to conduct Advanced Force Operations, the command had crammed what they could into a third of the time.

But there was nothing he could do to change that now that he was in Iran. He had a job to do.

Ding.

The *Fasten Seat Belt* sign extinguished, and Foster stood and stretched his legs. Though this flight had been far shorter than his trip across the pond from Dulles International Airport to Frankfurt, it was the culmination of fifteen hours of flying. And he was ready to be off the plane.

Foster opened the overhead bin and removed his cobalt-blue Eberlestock Switchblade backpack. Unlike the handful of other passengers in business class who carried designer briefcases from fashion houses like Valentino, Gucci, or Fendi, Foster's simple style fit both his personality and his cover identity. He wore a pair of stretch woven twill pants and plaid flannel—both from California hunting apparel company KUIU—and a pair of leather Scarpa hiking boots to travel in. But he had packed a modest suit for the business meetings he hoped to set up in the coming days.

"Danke," the petite flight attendant said as he walked past. "Thank you for flying with us."

"Bitte," Foster replied with a relaxed smile, all but exhausting his mastery of the German language.

He followed his fellow business class passengers off the plane into the jet bridge, unable to help second-guessing his decision to leave the Marine Corps behind and slide headfirst down a rabbit hole of espionage and intrigue. As a Force Recon Marine, Foster had been behind enemy lines many times before. But this was his first time doing it alone. No teammates, no air support, no quick reaction force. He was completely alone and couldn't help but wonder if Robert had also struggled with his self-imposed isolation.

His stomach rumbled—probably more from nerves than the cod wrapped in smoked salmon with stewed leek and Venus black rice they had served on the flight—but he put aside his misgivings about the mission and focused on his next task. He knew that was the only way to get through it. One task at a time. One day at a time.

The queue wended its way through a narrow corridor that ended in an area reserved for customs and immigration. Foster noted the separate counters for foreigners and Iranian citizens and waited his turn to approach an officer of the Immigration and Passport Police, sitting inside a booth behind a glass window. He watched other foreigners in front of him take their turn at the window, confer quietly with the officer, then continue on their way.

When it was his turn, Foster stepped up to the window and smiled at the officer. *"Salaam alaykum."*

He was met with suspicion. "Passport."

Foster ignored the man's brusqueness and handed over the falsified passport his command had provided him. Because Iran participated in the International Civil Aviation Organization Public Key Directory, it made entering the Islamic Republic with a fake almost impossible. But technically, his passport wasn't a fake. The State Department had issued Foster Cottle the biometric passport with descriptive data and a digitized passport photo on its sixty-four-kilobyte contactless chip.

The immigration officer scanned the passport, then turned to the page containing his entrance visa. "You have an invitation?"

"Yes, I do." His passport had entry and exit stamps for a half dozen countries going back two years—each of which could be verified—and a Category A visa he had secured through the director general's invitation. As a guest of Iran's Department of Environment, he wasn't required to show proof of a return flight ticket or travel insurance like those with tourist visas. But that didn't mean he was immune to added scrutiny.

"May I please see it?"

He generally thought he had fifty-fifty odds of making it through this first layer of security without having to resort to the connections he had made over the last several months, so it wasn't entirely unexpected. He opened his backpack and removed an envelope containing the letter of invitation that was required to secure his entry visa. Foster handed the officer the letter while surreptitiously studying the room and looking for signs that he would be under continued surveillance once he cleared passport control.

The officer read through the letter and held it up to the light, looking for the absence of a watermark or another indicator that it was a forgery. But like his passport, it was genuine. Apparently satisfied, the officer folded the letter, slipped it back into Foster's passport, and added an entry stamp to one of the many blank pages.

"Enjoy your hunt, Mr. Cottle," he said, before dismissing Foster and waving over the next passenger.

I plan on it.

~

After clearing customs and retrieving his rolling duffel, Foster exited baggage claim and made his way to the curb where dozens of young men clamored to attract his attention. This late in the evening, the temperature had dipped into the low eighties but felt colder thanks to a stiff westerly breeze. He paused and reached into his backpack for a charcoal-gray sweater vest, then took his time pulling it on while scanning the throng of drivers for an ideal candidate.

Like in most countries he'd visited, groups of young men gathered at the airport for a chance to claim fares into the city. While some were registered shuttles or private taxis, a few—known as *shakhsi*—were nontaxi drivers who earned money by giving people rides in their personal vehicles. Their cars were of various makes and models but weren't yellow and green like the others, and they were easy to spot.

"Darbast?" a taxi driver called out to Foster, asking if he was interested in a private ride.

Foster shook him off. He zipped up his sweater vest and started walking along the curb as he scanned the faces of the Persian men vying for his attention. Most were in their late twenties or early thirties and competed for the potential payday. But the one who would win would be the type who stood apart from the others and toed the line between eager and aloof.

Foster saw him standing near a white Peugeot Pars ELX, a facelifted version of the Peugeot 405, and they made eye contact.

That's the one.

Foster made a beeline for the Peugeot, and the driver took a few steps to greet him, holding out his hand in an apparent offer to take the Eberlestock rolling duffel. *"Salaam alaykum."*

"*Wa-alaykum-salaam,*" Foster replied.

"Need a ride?"

"Do you speak English?"

"Yes."

"How much to the Parsian Azadi Hotel?"

The young man paused and scrunched up his face as if performing complex algebraic calculations in his head, then replied, "Two hundred toman."

Foster had done his research and knew that the standard fare into the city from the international airport wasn't quite half that amount. He shook his head and waved the young man away. "Too much," he said. "Far too much."

He started to walk off, but the young man stepped in front of him. "One hundred fifty toman."

"Seventy-five," Foster countered.

"One hundred and twenty-five. Best offer."

Foster appreciated the time-honored tradition of negotiating for goods and services. Even in a theocratic republic with laws and regulations based on Ja'fari Shia Islam, Iran retained a capitalist view of its economy. With the second-largest population in the region, Iran had seen its number of high-net-worth individuals increase by more than three times the global average. Forbes had reported that there were more than two hundred and fifty thousand millionaires in Iran— more than its regional rival, Saudi Arabia—with a significant number known as *Shaazdeh,* or *noble born,* who flaunted their extravagant lifestyles on Instagram.

Negotiating with the young driver left little doubt that hustling was alive and well in Iran.

"What is your name?"

The first test.

"Reza Rajavi," he replied.

Foster held out his hand. "Foster Cottle. One hundred toman," he said, already knowing it was a fair rate for traveling the forty-odd miles.

But that didn't mean Reza wasn't going to try to squeeze the American for more. He shook Foster's hand, then with exaggerated disappointment said, "I can't do it for less than one hundred and ten, Agha Foster. I'm sorry."

Foster let the final offer hang in the air for a moment as if considering turning it down. "One hundred toman to deliver me to my hotel," he said. "And another one hundred toman if you pick me up in the morning and give me a tour of your city."

The second test.

The man's face lit up at the offer, and he quickly nodded. "Okay."

Foster handed over his rolling duffel and followed the driver to his car. He knew he still had a long way to go before he could consider Reza an asset, but it was a start. It would take an hour or more to reach his hotel on the north side of the city—more than enough time to begin vetting his suitability.

Reza tossed the duffel into the trunk, then opened the rear door for Foster to climb in. The interior was simple but well-appointed, and he could tell the young Iranian took pride in the car. He buckled in and looked out the window as Reza pulled away from the curb and began their drive north.

FOURTEEN

EARLY THE NEXT MORNING, Foster busied himself with the multitude of mundane tasks that came with being just another visitor in a foreign country, including converting almost eleven thousand in cash from dollars to rials, buying a new burner cell phone from a local carrier, activating a VPN with 256-bit AES encryption to access the internet, and downloading the apps he would need to communicate with his command.

Of course, Foster was anything but just another visitor. Even with all the added layers of security, his communications were at risk of being compromised by MOIS or other hostile actors, so he had to ensure each message he sent was absolutely critical.

He dressed in a pair of denim jeans, a simple and conservative collared button-down shirt, and the same boots he had worn on the flight from Frankfurt, then sat on the edge of his bed and mentally reviewed the surveillance detection routes he had established while still in Texas. Though he didn't plan to remain in Tehran very long, he needed routes he could use if his location at the Parsian Azadi became compromised.

Unlike most foreign countries he had visited, Iran didn't have formal diplomatic relations with the US, and there hadn't been an embassy guarded by Marines since 1979. Without a place of sovereign US soil to fall back on, he was left with only the Foreign Interests Section at the embassy of Switzerland. So he had plotted out primary, secondary, and tertiary routes to the embassy from his hotel in the Evin neighborhood—each with multiple stops and cut-throughs he could use to spot a tail.

His primary route was the quickest. It was a direct shot that followed the busy Chamran Highway almost the entire three miles there. The secondary route cut north toward Shahid Beheshti University and avoided the busier highway in favor of tree-lined residential streets, before rejoining the primary route on Fereshteh Street. His third option was the longest and cut south around the Enghelab Sport Complex—home to Iran's National Olympic Committee—and through Mellat Park before turning north and ending at the nondescript building across from the Russian Embassy Gardens.

When Foster left his hotel on foot, he still had over three hours before Reza returned in his Peugeot to give him a more comprehensive tour of the city—the next in a series of tests after driving in from the airport with no red flags. It was just over seventy degrees, but Foster knew it would quickly warm and reach the midnineties by the early afternoon, so he left his sweater vest and light jacket behind in his room.

Still, Foster walked at a brisk pace to keep warm as he surveyed his surroundings. The Parsian Azadi was one of the largest and tallest hotels in the city, and Foster walked in its shadow—away from the Alborz Mountains—and followed the route he had memorized. Less than a block from the 475-room hotel, he climbed an exposed staircase to a pedestrian bridge that had been planned as his first opportunity to detect surveillance. He was halfway across the highway when he noticed him.

Game on.

He knew he had probably picked up his first shadow even before concluding his business with the officer from the Passport and Immigration Police, but he was still somewhat surprised to spot a tail so soon. In Iran, MOIS, or the Ministry of Intelligence, was both adept at surveillance and exceedingly skeptical of outsiders. Americans even more so. That he had spotted a man following him so soon after leaving his hotel brought into question whether it was sanctioned surveillance or a potential criminal element.

Either way, Foster continued walking as if he didn't have a care in the world and used his preplanned stops and cut-throughs to observe the team surveilling him. If there was one shadow, there would be others; it was just a matter of how many and how easy they would be to spot. Regardless, he didn't want to give them reason to think he was on to them or up to no good. His only goal at this stage of the operation was to establish his legitimacy. And the best way of doing that was by being legitimate.

Other than the man who had shadowed him for several blocks before disappearing—only to be replaced by another—the walk to the embassy was uneventful. By the time Foster reached the diplomatic neighborhood, he had identified at least three men on foot, and two cars—both Saipa Pride sedans—that didn't fit with the normal flow of traffic in the city. On one hand, he was honored that whoever was following him had devoted so much manpower to a person ostensibly there to gain approval as a hunting outfitter catering to wealthy foreigners. But on the other, he was almost offended they hadn't been more discreet and had allowed themselves to be spotted.

"You caught yourself a tail," a British voice said from a café's recessed entrance on his right.

Foster had reached the end of his surveillance detection route and was only a block from the embassy. He debated ignoring the voice to keep walking, but between the accent and astute observation, he figured it was worth the risk. With no outward sign he had heard the man, Foster ducked into the café and took a seat at a table near the entrance. The gray-haired gentleman who had caught his attention remained in his seat at an adjacent table and waited several minutes while Foster ordered a cup of chai and fussed over the menu.

"I recommend the *nān-e barbari*," the man said, as if sensing Foster's hesitation.

Foster placed an order for the thick flatbread with an airy and doughy texture, then turned to look at the older man. "Thanks for the tip."

"I take it you're new in town," he replied.

Foster nodded.

"The name's Duncan Riley," the man said, standing from his chair and moving to join Foster at his table. "Shell Global."

Foster studied Duncan as if he had never seen a Westerner before. He was similarly dressed, in casual pants and a loose-fitting button-down shirt, but he had a more dignified appearance. Maybe it was his full head of gray hair, or the fact that Iran referred to Great Britain as the "old fox," but Foster instantly dubbed him the Silver Fox.

"Foster Cottle," he replied. "Shinar Outfitters."

Duncan cocked his head to the side. "Shinar Outfitters, is it?"

Foster nodded.

"Sounds about right for a Yank in Persia." Duncan snickered as if he had made a joke, then took a sip of his tea. "How long have you been in town?"

But Foster had seen a twinkle in the man's eye—much like the kind he'd seen in the likes of Justin Salters or Luke Chapman—and he suspected Duncan Riley was more than an executive for Shell Global. "I just arrived. How long have you been here?"

Duncan sat up taller as if to exert his dominance over the new arrival. "Two years next May."

Foster thought that was an odd turn of phrase, since it was closer to *this* May than *next*, but he brushed it off. "And what do you do for Shell Global?"

"Oh, this and that," the Brit replied.

It was exactly the kind of thing Justin or Luke might have said if Foster pressed them on what their day-to-day looked like working for the Central Intelligence Agency. Between that and Duncan's observation of Foster's tails, it was beginning to look more and more like what seemed to be a chance encounter was anything but.

"Come here often?"

"Only when I have reason to," Duncan replied, his smirk betraying the genuine pleasure he was taking from their banter.

The waiter arrived and set a steaming cup of chai in front of Foster, and he inhaled deeply to take in the full-bodied aroma of the warm spices. He turned away from Duncan and looked through the café's open door onto the street, catching just a glimpse of a Pride rolling by a little slower than it should. When he looked back, he saw the Brit studying him.

"How many of you are there?" Foster asked.

Duncan paused. "How many . . . ex-pats?"

Foster nodded.

"More than you might think." He took a sip of his tea as if to draw out his answer. "Would you care to meet a few?"

"Should I?" *Did Robert?*

"Never hurts to have friends," Duncan replied.

Foster wasn't sure exactly when it had happened, but he noticed the conversation had taken on new meaning. Instead of idle chitchat between two strangers a block from the Swiss embassy, it became almost ritualistic foreplay filled with doublespeak and hidden meanings that both understood clearly. He still didn't know exactly who

Duncan Riley was, but he had the feeling it was in his best interests to accept the man's offer.

"I'm still getting my bearings," Foster said. "How can I reach you?"

Duncan reached into his pants pocket and removed a business card adorned with the Shell logo. On one side, his contact information was written in Farsi and on the other was an address on Khakzad Street written in English. "My office," he said.

"How far is this?"

Duncan nodded toward the open door. "Only a few blocks from here. You're welcome to stop by any time if you need any . . ."

"Advice?"

The Brit smiled and nodded, satisfied he had conveyed his message. "But seriously, if you need to reach me, you can usually find me here." He scooted his chair back and stood, then dropped two blue-colored bills on the table. Foster noticed the face of Ruhollah Khomeini on one side and the Mausoleum of Poets on the other. "Try the *khagineh*. You won't be disappointed."

Foster stood and shook Duncan's hand, then watched the Silver Fox slip back out into the Persian morning before taking his seat to finish his tea. But before he had taken a sip, the waiter returned and placed a dish on the table in front of him—a dish Foster was quite sure neither he nor Duncan had ordered.

"What is this?"

"*Khagineh*. It's a sugar omelet."

Foster turned to look for the Brit again, but he had already disappeared around the corner.

"It is stuffed with cinnamon-and-cardamom-spiced crumble from ground walnuts and Medjool dates."

With the dish delivered, the waiter gave a slight nod and retreated to the kitchen. Foster waited until he was alone again, then poked at the dish while searching for a hidden message of some kind. He was almost certain Duncan was an agent of Britain's Secret Intelligence Service and had suggested the sugar omelet for a reason.

But after just one bite, he gave up and settled on satisfying his hunger with the tasty treat.

Foster finished his breakfast and tried to pay, but the waiter told him that Duncan had left more than enough to pay for both their meals.

After noticing the time, Foster reluctantly stood and headed for the door. He made note of the café's location, knowing he would most likely return. The Swiss embassy was only one block away, but he planned on taking the reverse of his longest route back to his hotel. He still had enough time before Reza arrived to take him on a guided tour of Tehran, but he couldn't afford to get waylaid again.

Foster walked outside and turned right toward the embassy. He took only two steps before stopping.

"Would you please come with us, Mr. Cottle."

Foster noticed that the uniformed police officer had phrased it more as a statement than a request. Between that and two other officers—both wearing patches bearing the green logo of the Security Police—blocking his path to the Swiss embassy, any foolish notion he might have had of trying to make a run for it disappeared as quickly as Duncan had.

"Of course," Foster replied behind a feigned smile.

FIFTEEN

FOSTER WASN'T SURPRISED when the police officer ushered him into the back of an unmarked Saipa Pride sedan. He followed one of the uniformed men into the back seat and was quickly followed by the other, finding himself squished between two men who smelled of equal parts body odor, aftershave, and tobacco. The one who had spoken was obviously in charge and climbed into the front passenger seat.

"Foster Cottle, I apologize if I have alarmed you," he said.

"What's this about?"

The man turned and spoke to the driver in Farsi. But even after several months of one-on-one instruction with a tutor from Berlitz, Foster found he couldn't keep up with the rapid-fire instructions.

The officer turned back to Foster and met his gaze with a wide smile. "Director General Ghorbani sent us to collect you."

He tried keeping his face passive, but he slowly exhaled with relief.

Bijan Ghorbani was the director general of Wildlife Protection and Management in the Department of Environment. It was his invitation that had secured Foster's entry visa. He had planned on scheduling an appointment with the director general in the coming days, but now he needed to adapt to the changing situation.

Just go with it, he thought.

"Are we going to his office now?"

"Yes, Mr. Cottle," the officer replied, seeming pleased that he wouldn't have to explain more.

"Can we stop by my hotel first? I'm not dressed for a meeting with the director general."

The man shook his head, as if the notion of being afforded an opportunity to be in appropriate attire was ludicrous. "I'm sorry, but no."

After all, Foster was there at the director general's pleasure. If Ghorbani wanted to see Foster in his office, then he had every right to send officers to retrieve him. That's just how things worked in Iran. But Foster couldn't help wondering if it was Ghorbani's men who had shadowed him on his walk from the hotel or someone else's. He pondered the thought while staring straight ahead through the dirty windshield and trying to ignore the tightness in his chest.

The driver merged onto the Sadr Expressway without looking for a gap in traffic, then weaved between slower moving cars into a lane for the Niayesh Tunnel. From his route study, Foster knew the tunnel went underneath Mellat Park and headed south into the government sector of Tehran. After exiting the tunnel, they merged onto the Kordestan Expressway and passed the Ministry of Energy and the Islamic Republic of Iran Police headquarters.

"What is that?" Foster asked, pointing to a tower that stood out on the cluttered Tehran skyline.

The officer followed his gaze and beamed with pride. "That is the Milad Tower," he said, though Foster already knew. "It is the sixth tallest tower in the world and is located at the International Trade and Convention Center."

"Is the director general's office there?"

The officer smirked. "No. The director general's office is at the Department of Environment headquarters in Pardisan Park."

Of course, Foster already knew this as well. But the more questions he asked and the more the officer felt inclined to answer, the more he gave the impression he was just a clueless Westerner, enjoying a private tour of the city. Anything to keep their suspicion away from him being an American operator building out a covert logistics network and infrastructure for special operations forces. Anything to keep them from learning his true reason for being in Iran.

"And Pardisan Park is nearby?" Foster leaned forward and craned his neck to look beyond his minder through the side window as the tower retreated into the distance.

As if in answer to his question, the driver exited Hakim Expressway and followed a narrow road up the hill into the park. Foster had studied satellite imagery of the area and knew that the Department of Environment headquarters sat in a cluster of buildings that had chosen utility over aesthetics.

The driver parked the car in front of the tallest building in the compound but left the engine running. The officer who had done all the talking climbed out of the front seat and opened the rear door. Foster followed his minder out of the sedan and stood in the driveway, looking up at the government building. No matter the country, all government buildings seemed the same, lacking even a modest effort to look appealing to visitors.

"This way, please," the officer said, gesturing for Foster to walk up the steps and through the double doors into the gray building.

Foster's heart pounded in his chest, but he clung to the hope that Ghorbani was only eager to help him. He knew business was conducted differently in Iran, but it still made him uneasy.

One step at a time. One task at a time.

He took a calming breath, then walked up the steps and through the double doors as if he owned the place. Despite his uncertainty, he knew that the only way he could convince doubters was if he convinced himself he belonged there and his hosts wanted him there. He was a skilled hunter and astute businessman with investors who had deep pockets.

Very deep pockets.

"Salaam alaykum," Bijan Ghorbani said from just inside the double doors, his arms stretched wide in greeting.

The smile on the director general's face was disarming, and Foster felt himself relax. *"Wa-alaykum-salaam,"* he replied.

"It's so good to see you again, my friend."

Director General Bijan Ghorbani shooed away the police officers who had plucked Foster from the streets and dropped him at the headquarters building. Foster's elevated anxiety eased somewhat when he noticed that the officers had nodded reverently to Ghorbani and retreated to the Saipa sedan.

"I'm sorry if my men startled you," Ghorbani said, leading Foster to the only elevator in the cramped lobby. "I knew you had just arrived and were eager to discuss business. But unfortunately, duty is calling me away for some time, and I didn't want you to miss out on this opportunity."

You mean you didn't want to miss out, Foster thought.

He knew the only reason he had been given an invitation in the first place was because he had promised to bring investors who wanted to shower Ghorbani's department with money. What had started as the Hunting Club of Iran in 1956 had evolved into an organization that oversaw hunting and fishing activities in the country, with the aim of safeguarding the environment and preserving Iran's natural treasures. For a country with twenty-six cultural sites inscribed on the World Heritage List, Iran's Department of Environment oversaw twenty-three national parks, thirty-two national natural monuments, thirty-seven wildlife refuges, and one hundred and seventeen protected areas.

Hunting was imprinted on their culture. And Shinar Outfitters offered a solution to their financial woes.

"I apologize for my appearance," Foster said when the elevator doors opened, drawing attention to the fact that he was entirely unprepared for this meeting. "If I had known you had other pressing matters, I would have arrived sooner and made myself available to fit into your schedule."

But Ghorbani waved away the remark, then stabbed at the button for the top floor. "Nonsense. Men like you and I needn't worry ourselves with the traditional stuffiness of bureaucrats and businessmen. We are hunters!"

It was true. Ghorbani wasn't dressed in a suit—tailored or otherwise—and wore clothing much like Foster's. He stood a head taller than Foster but was easily twenty pounds lighter and had a full head of jet-black hair that was parted and neatly combed. But despite his manicured appearance, he had a rugged look that betrayed him for who he really was—a hunter, just like he had said.

"Thank you for your understanding," Foster said.

The elevator sounded a soft, metallic *ding* when it reached their floor, and the doors opened onto an open space filled with cubicles that could have been in any office building in any city in America. Despite the early hour, several of the cubicles were occupied, and heads turned and eyes followed the director general as he led Foster to his office in the far corner of the room.

"Please, have a seat," Ghorbani said, gesturing to an avocado-green leather armchair that seemed to have been plucked from a 1970s Palm Springs resort.

Foster took a seat and looked beyond his host at the expansive view of Pardisan Park while waiting for Ghorbani to open discussions. It was in that moment that Foster allowed his firm grip on the reality he had crafted to weaken. For just a second or two, he allowed himself to remember that he wasn't just a businessman seeking the Iranian government's approval to guide hunts in their national parks and wildlife refuges. It was only a second or two, but it was long enough to recognize that he was an American operator who had successfully infiltrated an office of the government that regularly chanted "Death to America" at political rallies.

But, in a blink, Foster Cottle banished his old identity.

You must believe it, he reminded himself. *Like Robert believed it.*

"So, Mr. Cottle, I believe the prudent first step in this endeavor would be to establish if such an undertaking is even feasible. Wouldn't you agree?"

He almost smiled at the suggestion because it was what he had intended to propose. He needed to slowly gain Ghorbani's trust, and the last thing he wanted to do was rush the director general into making a decision. His entire purpose for being there would be in jeopardy if he spooked the bureaucrat and forced him to decide too soon.

"I think that's a fantastic idea, Director General."

Ghorbani smiled as if pleased with himself, then nodded as he studied his guest. "I understand you are staying at the Parsian Azadi Hotel?"

Foster nodded. "For now."

"Are the accommodations to your satisfaction?"

Again, Foster nodded. "It rivals even the best hotels in America."

"Very good. Very good." Instead of taking offense at the insinuation that, by default, hotels in America were nicer, Ghorbani beamed with nationalist pride. "I should return from my business dealings by early next week. In the meantime, I might suggest you find a more permanent place to stay."

A glimmer of hope. "Does that mean you believe our venture to be feasible?"

Ghorbani smiled and stood, indicating that the meeting was nearing its conclusion. "One step at a time, Mr. Cottle. But I have faith the next week will give us the answers we need to move forward."

Foster stood and met his gaze, smiling with genuine satisfaction. It was even better than he had hoped. The director general was about to endorse his presence in Iran, giving him the freedom to scout locations and begin to build out a more permanent footprint. "I look forward to our next conversation, Director General."

"Please. Call me Bijan," he said, holding out his hand for Foster to take.

He shook it. "And I am Foster."

Ghorbani ushered Foster to the door. "My secretary will have the documents you require to gain access to our protected areas. Might I suggest you always keep them on your person? Sometimes, my country's law enforcement can be overzealous in their protection of our lands."

"Of course, Bijan. I am honored to have the opportunity."

Ghorbani led Foster to a desk outside his office where a young man—most likely a recent university graduate—stood and waited for his instructions. "Please provide Mr. Cottle here with the letters we have prepared for him."

"Yes, sir."

Then, almost as an afterthought, he added, "And call Dom Theriot. He can give Mr. Cottle a ride back to his hotel."

Foster furrowed his brow in confusion.

Who the hell is Dom Theriot?

SIXTEEN

THE DIRECTOR GENERAL MUST HAVE seen the confusion on Foster's face, because he smiled sheepishly as if suddenly remembering he had previously failed to mention the involvement of another individual.

"You needn't worry about Mr. Theriot," Ghorbani said.

Foster wasn't worried, but he suddenly doubted that Ghorbani's efforts to see him safely to his hotel were entirely altruistic. Still, he played the part of confident businessman without hesitation, even though every fiber of his body hummed with nervous energy. "I figured you would tell me what I needed to know. But he shouldn't need to be put out on my behalf. I can take a taxi back to my hotel."

Ghorbani led Foster to the elevators, and again Foster felt eyes on him as they walked past the cubicles. "Nonsense. I have already taken up too much of your time when you have only just arrived. It's the least I can do."

Foster knew better than to argue, so he thanked the director general for his thoughtfulness and followed him into the elevator. They descended to the ground floor in silence, and when the doors opened, Ghorbani led him outside before speaking.

"I hope you understand that you are not the only Westerner who has shown an interest in doing what you have proposed. I have a fiduciary responsibility to consider all potential partnerships."

Foster knew for a fact he wasn't the only Westerner, but he also knew he was the only one with a benefactor of unlimited resources. His command would stop at nothing to ensure he had every advantage in beating out his competition and securing the Iranian government's support of Shinar Outfitters. It wouldn't matter what Dom Theriot brought to the table. Foster brought more.

"Of course," Foster said. "I understand perfectly. And I am certain I can win your confidence over the coming weeks." He paused, then added, "Is Dom Theriot my competition?"

The director general laughed but shook his head. "No, no. Of course not. He is a hunter—like us—and I thought you might benefit from meeting him and sharing your collective experiences with one another."

So, he is my competition, Foster thought. "I appreciate your thoughtfulness, Bijan."

Ghorbani nodded with apparent satisfaction that his guest understood the conditions of his support. Without saying as much, he had just told Foster that he and Dom were the only two competing for his department's endorsement. The one who most freely greased the wheels of bureaucracy with *facilitation fees*—what the US government called bribes—would earn the director general's support and secure the desired license.

Dom was in for a rude awakening when he realized he wouldn't be able to keep up.

Ghorbani turned at the sound of a pickup truck making its way toward them. "Here he is."

A brand-new red Toyota Hilux came to a stop in front of them, and the driver's door opened. A man with an unruly mop of blond hair jumped out and scampered around the front of the truck. His eyes flicked toward Foster for the briefest of moments, but he practically beamed with exuberance at the director general. "Mr. Ghorbani! It's so good to see you again!"

"*Salaam alaykum,*" Ghorbani said.

"And to you, my friend!" The newcomer turned and looked at Foster as if he was almost surprised to see another person standing there. "And you must be Foster," he said, holding out his hand. "Dom Theriot."

Foster shook it, careful not to squeeze as hard as he might had the two men met under different circumstances. It was good to show strength, but too much might make him appear hostile. "Foster Cottle," he said. "Shinar Outfitters."

"Shinar, huh? Well, it's good to meet ya!"

Bijan Ghorbani brought his hands together as if he had just closed a major deal. "Dom, I trust you will see Foster back to his hotel for me."

"Of course!"

"It's really not necessary," Foster said.

Dom gestured to the Hilux Vigo pickup truck. "Well, I'm already here and have the room. Would be a shame to come all this way and leave with an empty seat. Especially if we're going to the same place."

"Oh, you're at the Parsian Azadi too?"

Ghorbani interrupted them to excuse himself, then slipped back inside the headquarters building. When they were alone again in the driveway in front of the government building, the smile on Dom's face and his accompanying enthusiasm vanished. "I could really go for a drink," he said.

Despite himself, Foster laughed. "Know where we can get some whiskey around here?"

Dom apparently thought the comment was worthy of a chuckle,

then slapped Foster on the back and walked around the truck to climb into the driver's seat. Foster climbed in on the passenger side and had barely buckled himself in before his new American friend shifted the Hilux into gear and lurched forward.

"Seriously, are we staying at the same hotel?"

Dom shook his head. "I've got a house nearby, but it's really not a big deal."

"It's not necessary, but I do appreciate it."

"No biggie," Dom replied, before turning onto the highway and accelerating away from Pardisan Park.

Foster studied his competition to get a read on him. Dom was in his late forties with tanned and weathered skin, and he looked every bit the part of a hunting guide. "Where you from?"

Dom downshifted to pass a slower-moving Peugeot, then said, "Louisiana. You?"

Foster didn't answer the question. "Get back much?"

"Every September. Just to dip my toes in the swamp and get the most out of alligator season. Never miss it."

Foster wondered why Dom was missing it now.

Foster's initial hesitation at being in the car with Dom Theriot slowly diminished as the two made their way north to the Parsian Azadi Hotel. But even though the other American seemed congenial, Foster had to remind himself he was his competition. Worse, he seemed to have already gained some favor with Ghorbani, which in itself was troubling.

"Where do you plan on hunting?" Dom asked.

It was almost so nonchalant, Foster had to force himself to pause before answering. He had been trained to avoid giving away too many details, but he quickly turned the question on its head and used it as an opportunity to gain more information for himself. "Around

Isfahan," he said. "I understand the mouflons in the Tangé-Sey-yed and Kolah-Ghazi wildlife refuges are prized trophies."

"I was thinking the same thing. At first. Now, I might stay near Tehran and hunt red sheep in the Alborz."

Foster looked through the windshield at the mountain range stretching across the horizon north of the city. He knew his best friend had been killed in those mountains, and it did little to comfort him to know that the person who had been foisted onto him by a representative of the Iranian government intended to hunt there. It was too much of a coincidence for his liking.

"Have you been to Isfahan?" Foster asked, trying to get a feel for the freedom afforded to Dom.

"Oh, yes. It's a beautiful city—covered bridges, grand boulevards, tiled mosques—about the size of Houston, I guess. It was once the capital of Persia. I think you'll enjoy it there."

Every few minutes, Foster glanced in the sideview mirror at the flow of traffic behind them, but he didn't see anything that raised his suspicion. After leaving his room that morning and spotting the first tail outside the hotel, he had assumed that he would be under constant surveillance. But he had seen nothing since leaving the Department of Environment headquarters. Not even a hint of something. And that bothered him.

"How long have you been here?" Foster asked.

Dom downshifted and passed a green and white taxi—reminding Foster that Reza was supposed to be waiting at his hotel—then weaved back into the far-right lane before answering. "Only about a week. But Bijan gave me temporary permission to scout locations in the Alborz, near Isfahan, and to the east near Birjand."

Foster wasn't sure why, but he felt like the last location Dom mentioned had been thrown in to test him. "Afghan urial," he said knowingly. "I did a spot-and-stalk hunt for them in Texas a few years back. Northwest of San Antonio."

"Probably nicer than Birjand," Dom said. "Too close to Afghanistan for my liking."

Foster laughed. "Must be a veteran."

Dom turned and studied him. "You too?"

He nodded. "Army. Six years active duty."

"All the way!"

"Airborne!" Foster wasn't sure if Dom had studied up on him, but he replied exactly how a former paratrooper—like Foster Cottle—might.

If it had been a test, the Louisiana native quickly moved past it. "I got out when they wanted me to go to Fort Polk."

"What? You didn't want to go home?" Foster knew the sprawling post of almost two hundred thousand acres, home to the Army's Joint Readiness Training Center, was in Vernon Parish, Louisiana.

"Fort Polk ain't home, brother!" He turned and locked eyes with Foster. "I'm from South Louisiana. I mean *way* south. You ever been there?"

"South Louisiana?"

Dom laughed. "Polk."

"Once. Jumped with some Brits from Second Battalion, Parachute Regiment during Exercise Rattlesnake. More than enough time in the swamp for me."

"You need to come see my people when you get home. Give you a better taste of Louisiana." Dom steered the Hilux Vigo toward an exit—well short of the one Foster knew led to his hotel. But he didn't let on that he knew it was the wrong turn and forced himself to relax in his seat.

"I might take you up on that. I hear y'all know how to cook."

Dom whistled as they came to a stop at a traffic light. "Shoot. You ain't eaten until you had jambalaya and étouffée on the bayou!"

Foster grinned at how easily the Louisiana native slipped into his Cajun accent. But he was still on guard and kept his cover story at the forefront of his mind. Same age, same first name, but Foster Cottle grew up in East Texas and spent six years in the Army as a paratrooper before settling in North Carolina. Not Fayetteville—where he had spent the bulk of his time with the Eighty-Second Airborne—but near Elizabeth City on the Albemarle Sound. While there, he fell in with some fellow veterans who were guiding hunts in the States—mostly mule deer, elk, and black bear, with the occasional feral hog thrown in for good measure. But he had grander ambitions.

Dom turned left and pulled into a spot in front of an unmarked building. "Quick detour," he said. "You don't mind, do you?"

"I just appreciate the ride," Foster said.

Dom opened the door and started to climb out but stopped short. "Want to come? It'll be just a second."

"No. You go on ahead. I'll wait."

Dom shrugged then hopped out and slammed the door behind him. Foster watched him walk around the hood of the truck and disappear inside the building without an apparent care in the world. He envied the former paratrooper's confidence and studied it as a way of building on his own cover.

Foster Quinn might be unaccustomed to being alone and uncomfortable being in Iran on his own. But Foster Cottle had swagger and would give Dom Theriot more than he bargained for.

Then he saw Dom's phone sitting in the cup holder.

And it looked like it was on.

SEVENTEEN

AS HARD AS HE TRIED, Foster couldn't keep his eyes from zeroing in on Dom's cell phone. He couldn't be certain that the other hunter had left it there intentionally, but it seemed far too coincidental to ignore. Of course, even if the phone had been left there with the purpose of eavesdropping on his conversations, Foster didn't have anyone to call. That was as much a reminder of how alone he was as anything else.

After about ten minutes of waiting, Dom emerged from the building carrying a package wrapped in butcher paper. He shot Foster a friendly smile, then walked around the front of the truck and deposited the package in the back seat before climbing in behind the wheel.

"Sorry 'bout that," Dom said.

Foster looked at the package over his shoulder. "Not a problem. I'm still getting the lay of the land."

The truth was, he had studied this part of the city in detail before leaving Texas and knew exactly where he was. But he couldn't help but wonder if Dom had added the stop as part of a surveillance detection route. It was the kind of thing he might have done in order to see if the person he was giving a ride to had a team following him. But Foster was alone. So even if that had been Dom's objective, it only confirmed that Foster was exactly who he said he was.

Dom put the truck in drive and pulled away from the curb. "Mind some friendly advice?"

Foster shot him a skeptical glance. "Would love some."

"If you're anything like me, I assume you brought in quite a bit of cash."

Dom paused for confirmation, but Foster remained silent. Even if Dom *was* another American and a fellow veteran, Foster wasn't about to tell someone he had just met how much cash he was carrying or had stashed in the safe in his room at the Parsian Azadi.

Dom seemed to take the hint and moved on. "Yeah, well, you should get prepaid debit cards. They are accepted everywhere. I would use those instead of cash for most things."

"Thanks for the tip. I've been thinking of asking the concierge at the hotel what I should do."

But he hadn't. He had done his research and already knew which bank Shinar Outfitters intended to open an account with. Bank Pasargad had a branch just down the street from his hotel and was generally well respected—making the list of top five hundred global banking brands the year before. Best of all, it was part of the Shé-Taab banking system—officially the Interbank Information Transfer Network—that did business with countries like Bahrain, Qatar, and Kuwait.

But, most importantly, they were linked to banks in the United Arab Emirates.

"Yeah, well, no reason you need to make the same mistakes I made."

Foster thought there were plenty of reasons a competitor might want him to fall flat on his face—fellow vet or not. "Appreciate it."

Dom exited the Yadegar-é-Emam Expressway and turned onto the hotel's driveway. Foster looked through the windshield, hoping to spot Reza's Peugeot sitting out front but not really expecting it. He didn't believe one hundred toman would be enough to secure the man's patience beyond twenty or thirty minutes, and a glance at his watch showed he had far exceeded that.

The Hilux came to a stop in front of the hotel's grand entrance, and Dom thrust his hand out to Foster. "Well, it was great meeting you!"

Foster shook his hand, just a little more firmly than before. "You too. Thanks again for the lift."

"Don't mention it." Dom handed Foster his business card. "Call me so I have your number."

Foster pulled out his burner phone and dialed. He waited until Dom's phone lit up with an incoming call, then opened the door and climbed out. He scanned the parking lot for Reza's Peugeot but didn't see it.

Back to square one.

He rapped on the top of the truck and turned to walk up the steps as Dom pulled away. His day hadn't gone as he had expected or planned, but that didn't mean he hadn't accomplished anything. He had met with Director General Ghorbani far sooner than anticipated and confirmed that his wasn't the only outfit competing for the government's approval to operate in their country. That he had actually met his competition and spent some time in the car with him was a real coup for his mission, but he needed to figure out how to capitalize on it.

He was already thinking through the myriad of things he needed to do before leaving Tehran. First on his list was to open a bank account and contact the shell company the command had established in UAE for a much-needed infusion of capital.

"Agha Foster?"

Even as aware as he was of his surroundings, the voice caught him off guard, and he turned and saw a sheepish-looking Reza standing off to the side of the entrance.

"You waited?"

The young Iranian nodded, apparently content that Foster hadn't completely forgotten him. Either he was in desperate need of the money or thought his fare had untapped potential.

"Where's your car?"

Reza gestured toward the corner of the building. "I parked it over there."

It was a good sign that Reza had even shown up but a better one that he had waited beyond the agreed-upon time. Foster couldn't afford to miss this opportunity to further vet Reza and develop him as an asset. If his unexpected meeting with Dom had shown him anything, it was that things were moving far quicker than he had planned. It was in his best interest to strike while the iron was hot.

"Go ahead and pull around. I have a few stops I need to make if you don't mind."

"Yes, Agha Foster!" Reza beamed.

Before the young Iranian scampered off to retrieve his car, Foster stopped him. "Hold on just a second." He waved the concierge over and gave him the burner phone with the camera app already open. "Let's take a quick picture to commemorate the occasion."

Foster draped his right arm around Reza's shoulders and threw a Hawaiian shaka at the concierge with his left. The young Iranian looked uncomfortable but put a hesitant smile on his face. The concierge snapped the photo, then returned the burner phone to Foster, who looked at the picture and showed it to Reza.

"It's a good picture, Agha Foster."

He grinned. "Sure is. Now, let's go for that tour."

Reza relaxed, and Foster watched him leave. He wondered how the young man would respond to going to Isfahan.

Only one way of finding out.

As soon as Reza was out of sight, Foster opened the Onion browser on his burner iPhone. Unlike mainstream internet browsers, Onion was specifically designed to access Tor—a network banned by the Iranian government. But by using a VPN and a pluggable transport that made Tor traffic look random, he could access the dark web while avoiding government censors. There was only one site he needed to visit—one that wasn't indexed or visible to search engines—and he quickly entered the address into the browser.

Once the website had loaded, Foster uploaded the picture he had just taken and slipped the phone back into his pocket.

They drove aimlessly around the city while Reza took the opportunity to point out landmarks he thought Foster might be interested in. He showed him the Tehran Grand Bazaar, the Tabiat Bridge, and the Azadi Tower. But Foster was only interested in using the first part of the guided tour to discover if he was being followed.

"Turn right," Foster said.

Reza shot a questioning glance at him in the rearview mirror but followed the instruction. He steered the Peugeot down the narrow side street while Foster looked over his shoulder to see if anybody had followed. It was barely more than an alley connecting to a parallel street, but it was a perfect cut-through to spot a tail if they had one.

At the end of the street, Foster repeated, "Turn right."

Again, the young Iranian did as instructed, but Foster could tell he was more than a little confused why his passenger had apparently wanted him to turn back in the direction they had come from.

"Pull over here."

Reza did so, and Foster climbed out of the back seat and walked into the shop they had stopped in front of. There was nothing he needed inside, but it gave him an opportunity to do a few things.

First, he could observe the street in both directions from the store's front window, giving him a chance to spot surveillance. Second, he could test Reza's willingness to go along with whatever Foster had in mind. Of the two, that was probably the most important.

He studied the street for several minutes but didn't see anything that set off alarm bells in his head. Even that made him uneasy. What if Reza had been a plant and had been waiting for him at the airport? He wouldn't need to have been his driver to be effective—he would have only needed to follow whoever Foster had selected. Before Foster could move on to the next test, he needed to make sure he could trust Reza. But how?

Foster focused on the young Iranian through the shop's window as he contemplated his latest dilemma and wondered how Robert had found someone he could trust.

Did he? Or did someone betray him?

Reza looked relaxed in his seat with his elbow propped on the windowsill while he waited for Foster to conclude whatever business he had in the shop. He looked unconcerned and gave no outward sign that he was anxious to be on his way. Foster felt trapped between healthy skepticism and a constant state of paranoia, but so far, his Iranian driver had given him no reason to think he couldn't be trusted.

Foster returned to the cooler at the back of the store and retrieved two bottles of water, then walked to the counter and paid for both with cash. He hesitated for only a second before leaving through the front door and climbing into the Peugeot's back seat.

"Where to now, Agha Foster?"

Foster handed Reza a bottle of water. "How much time do you have?"

His driver accepted the water graciously and turned to appraise his American passenger. "For the right price, I can be free the rest of the day. Where would you like to go?"

"How much to Isfahan?"

Reza squinted his eyes as he mentally calculated what a private taxi to the former capital of Persia might be worth. Then he added a premium surcharge to that value and probably doubled it. "Fifteen hundred toman."

Foster wasn't sure if the Iranian had given him a high price because he was hoping it would be too much and dissuade him from going forward with the almost five-hour drive or if he was a hustler who knew his value. Foster didn't know which of the two he preferred but figured he would call his bluff either way.

"Deal."

Reza grinned. "Thank you for the water."

"You're welcome."

As Foster leaned back in his seat, Reza put the car into gear and pulled away from the curb. He expertly weaved the sedan through the narrow streets and onto the tangle of freeways that crisscrossed the capital city. By the time they had reached the edge of the sprawling metropolis, Foster was certain they weren't being followed.

"Do you mind if we stop at the Mouteh Wildlife Refuge? I want to get a closer look at it before we reach Isfahan."

Reza looked at him in the rearview mirror. "It is off-limits, Agha Foster."

He already knew the wildlife refuge was off-limits to those who lacked permission from the government—which Director General Ghorbani had given him—but he wanted to see how Reza responded to the request. "Just for a few minutes. I only want to see it with my own eyes."

Reza looked in each sideview mirror as if expecting to see a police car following them and preparing to arrest them before they even reached the international airport south of the city. "I don't think we should. We could get in a lot of trouble."

Foster feigned frustration. "Well, how do we get permission?"

"You have to apply with the Department of Environment for a permit."

"How long does that take?"

Reza shrugged. "One to two weeks? I don't know."

The correct answer was two weeks. "I don't have that long," he said, hoping to convince his driver it was worth the risk. "I'll pay extra."

Again, Reza paused as he undoubtedly considered what rate he was comfortable charging to break the law and risk jail time. "Another five hundred toman," he said.

Foster grinned. Unlike the first rate he'd been quoted, this added cost seemed reasonable. Most importantly, Reza had shown his willingness to break the law and implicate himself in a crime, thereby binding himself to the American's fate. It didn't matter that Foster already had the required permission. Reza didn't know that.

I think I might have found my guy, Foster thought.

Surprisingly, it made him feel less alone. "Deal."

EIGHTEEN

As promised, their visit to the Mouteh Wildlife Refuge had been brief. But it was long enough for the photo to make its way back to the command, where it was run through facial recognition to compare Reza against a list of known individuals. When Foster received an innocuous text message informing him he had won a contest, he had his answer.

Reza is clean.

Once they had left the restricted area and were back on the road to Isfahan, Reza visibly relaxed and became surprisingly chatty. "What brings you to Iran? What is your business here, Agha Foster?"

"I'm here to *shikar*," he replied.

Reza turned and looked over his shoulder, giving him a surprised look. "What do you know of *shikar*?"

Foster knew that while it was often translated from Persian into

English by oversimplifying it to mean *to hunt*, no word in the English language properly captured its true meaning. To *shikar* was to go out into nature and to toil over the hunt. It wasn't about killing as many animals with as little effort as possible, but about being respectful of the land and its inhabitants.

"I know that to be successful here in Iran, I have to bring clients who will honor your customs and traditions. I don't want to simply kill animals—I can do that anywhere. I want to show my customers the joy of the struggle."

"You don't speak like an American," Reza said.

"How many Americans do you know?"

"Just the ones I've met in my travels and seen in the movies."

Foster filed that morsel of information away for later and focused on the topic at hand. In truth, he had known nothing about *shikar* until his research for this mission had brought him to the book *Large Game Shooting in Thibet, the Himalayas, and Northern India*. In the book's introduction, Alexander Angus Airlie Kinloch mentioned the word as a way of comparing the tendency to "debase sport in England by rendering it too artificial and making everything subservient to the one object of obtaining the heaviest possible bag in the shortest time and with the least possible trouble." Colonel Kinloch had written that in the East, "game cannot be killed in any quantities without considerable personal exertion."

"Most of my countrymen are weak and lazy," Foster said, truthfully. "I want to bring clients here who are not. I want them to experience all that Iran has to offer and leave with a new respect for your land."

Reza fell silent as they continued their drive south into Isfahan. It was as if he was ruminating over Foster's words and deciding whether they were worthy of his time. Foster already knew his driver had ambition and the work ethic he would need to be successful if they continued their relationship. He knew Reza was willing to blur the lines of legality but still retained a moral compass and respected tradition. But what Foster really wanted to know was whether the young man would be willing to subvert the ayatollah's regime and help him hunt down a Russian arms dealer named Oleg Volkov.

It would be the ultimate *shikar*.

He considered his next question carefully. "What do you think of my country?"

Reza glanced in the rearview mirror, and they made eye contact. "What do you mean, Agha Foster?"

He understood Reza's reluctance to answer the question. Not being careful with one's words was a surefire way of ending up in prison or beaten to death. The Guidance Patrol, a vice squad in FARAJA, the Law Enforcement Command of the Islamic Republic of Iran, was charged with enforcing Sharia law and reported directly to the Supreme Leader. While they mainly harassed women who did not adhere to an oppressive dress code, they were also known to violently enforce the values decreed by the ayatollah.

Gotta roll the dice, Foster thought.

"Do you chant, 'Death to America'?"

Reza did not break eye contact and answered simply, "No."

When he seemed reluctant to go further, Foster pressed him. "You don't hate me?"

That simple question seemed to break through Reza's hesitation and open the floodgates. "No, I don't hate you. Know who I hate? The men who arrested my cousin for *improperly* wearing her hijab. The men who detained her because they could see some of her hair. The men who said she had suffered a heart attack—a perfectly healthy twenty-two-year-old—and died after being comatose for two days. The men who said they didn't know how she had sustained bruising to her face or legs. I hate the men who tortured her to death just because she was a young woman in Iran!"

As much as Foster had suspected Reza would be a suitable asset, his impassioned outburst almost stunned him. Reza had been reserved during most of their drive, and Foster had accepted that he would need more time to develop him. But there was no question now.

He's the one.

"I want you to work for me," Foster said.

Reza's hesitation was gone. "Doing what?"

"I need to find a place to live here in Isfahan, and it would be useful to have someone I can trust drive me around."

"I would just drive for you, Agha Foster?"

He smiled. "Not just. I would like you to be my interpreter and help me navigate the vast cultural pitfalls of your country. You can offer me counsel and help me secure your government's blessing to *shikar*."

Reza hesitated, and Foster took that as a good sign. He wasn't interested in hiring someone who was reckless.

"How much would I be paid?"

"Fifty-three million toman each month."

Reza's mouth fell open slightly, and Foster knew he had hit the right number. The average Iranian made the equivalent of between three hundred and six hundred dollars each month. The salary he had offered Reza was just over one thousand dollars. It was more than enough to entice him, but not so much that he might think it was too good to be true.

"Each month?"

Foster nodded.

"I accept."

And, just like that, he no longer felt alone.

With Reza's help over the next week, Foster made a list of several properties on the outskirts of town that might be suitable to rent or buy and establish residence in Isfahan. He was taking the director general at his word and looking for more permanent accommodations, though his house hunting served more than one purpose.

"I don't understand, Agha Foster," Reza said.

"What don't you understand?"

They were parked along the curb across from Moshtagh Park, and Foster's eyes were glued to a sculpture of a hand with its palm facing skyward and a delicate blowball pinched between its thumb and forefinger. He stared at the fluffy seedball as if expecting to see a gust of wind carry its spores away into the trees or across the Zayandeh Rud.

"This one is too small," Reza said, pointing to one of the properties Foster had insisted on seeing. "This one is too far from the city." He turned the page. "And this one is a simple one-bedroom flat over a warehouse."

Foster had moved into the front seat so they could both look at a map and the list of properties. "I'm a simple man."

Reza shook his head. "If you are going to win the government's approval to do your business here, you must project power. These properties"—he stabbed angrily at the list—"will not do that."

Reza had gone from being aloof and reserved to becoming Foster's biggest fan. After Foster had told him of Shinar Outfitters and the unexpected competition with Dom Theriot, the young Iranian had taken it almost as a challenge to win the government's favor. It was ironic that a man who had such a deep passion for opposing the regime wanted to gain its approval.

But as much as Foster appreciated his support, he couldn't tell him the real reason for wanting to check on those properties. He couldn't tell him that the one he called too small was an ideal safe house for SEALs from a Special Missions Unit to remain out of sight if things didn't go as planned. He couldn't tell him that the one he thought was too far from the city would be the perfect staging location for an assault team that had infiltrated Iran for a capture-or-kill operation. But he had a plausible explanation for the third.

"Let's go see the flat over the warehouse," Foster said.

"Agha Foster . . ."

He held up his hand to silence Reza's objections. "I need a place to store the off-road vehicles we will use on our hunts." He paused. "And the flat is for you."

Reza looked surprised. "For me?"

"I can't do this without your help. And you can't help me from Tehran. I need you here, Reza."

The young man opened his mouth as if to speak, then quickly snapped it shut. Foster could see his wheels spinning and knew Reza was considering the offer. He knew little about the younger man's life other than that he had a cousin who had been murdered at the hands of the ayatollah's thugs. Reza was a proud Persian, but Foster knew he was embarrassed by the actions of the zealots in control.

"Will you do it?"

Reza turned his head away from Foster and looked across the park at the Khaju Bridge. "Did you know that bridge was built under the reign of Abbas II?"

"I did not," Foster said, though he had read some on the city's history.

"He was the seventh Safavid Shah of Iran."

Foster looked at the stone-and-brick arch bridge with sluice gates underneath that regulated the river's flowing water. It was a masterful piece of craftsmanship, made only more remarkable by the fact that it had been built almost four hundred years earlier.

"He built it on the foundations of an older bridge to connect the two districts of Khajoo and the Hassan-Aabad Gate with Takht-e Foolad and Shiraz Road." Reza pointed to a pavilion at the bridge's center. "He would sit there and admire the view."

"How do you know all this?"

Reza looked back at Foster. "I studied history at the university."

Foster wasn't sure what any of this had to do with Reza moving from Tehran to Isfahan and living in a flat Shinar Outfitters had procured for its operation. But he had the feeling Reza was working up to something, so he sat in silence and waited.

"Those in charge of my country do not build upon the foundations of our ancestors. They tear down and destroy." Reza set his jaw. "I would be honored to move to Isfahan to help you, Agha Foster."

When Foster smiled, Reza followed suit. For the first time since Foster had arrived in Iran, he not only didn't feel alone, but he felt like he had an ally who would ensure his success. Not just with the Department of Environment, who would approve his legitimate business operation, but with his true purpose for being there.

Finding Oleg Volkov.

And figuring out what really happened to Robert James.

Foster held out his hand, and when Reza took it, he said, "Let's go see your new flat."

NINETEEN

FOSTER STOOD BACK AND WATCHED REZA speaking with the older man, who had a weathered, suspicious face and wore long pants and a tunic. He admired the way the younger Iranian showed respect to the landlord without cowering under his scathing outbursts and listened as the men spoke in rapid-fire Farsi while gesturing angrily around the room. Every few seconds, their gaze fell and lingered on Foster.

Finally, after almost half an hour of heated negotiation, the older man threw up his arms and stormed out of the room in a gust of frustration. Reza dropped his chin to his chest in a clear sign of defeat, then joined Foster near the narrow window looking down over the courtyard at the rear of the property.

"I'm sorry," he said. "I failed you. I was not able to talk him down lower."

"How much?"

"Two-point-one billion toman," Reza said, then clucked in disgust.

The number seemed staggering, but Foster did the quick math and calculated the sum out to roughly forty thousand US dollars. Too much. "Just for the flat?"

The young Iranian shook his head. "The flat and the warehouse. That's what you wanted, is it not?"

Foster nodded, almost giddy with excitement that a property of this size could be purchased for that amount. It was more than he had been allowed to bring with him into Iran, but once he opened a bank account, he would have access to unlimited funds. The warehouse was large enough to store three off-road SUVs that he could use on hunts and, most importantly, to move the assault force into position when they were given the green light. "That's exactly what I wanted."

But Reza was still disappointed in himself. "I know I could have talked him down even more, but he said he has another interested buyer—a wealthy Russian who—"

"Wait. What did you just say?" Foster's blood ran cold, and his skin prickled.

"I could have talked him down . . ."

"No. The other thing."

"He has another interested buyer?"

Foster's heartbeat quickened. "You said it was a wealthy Russian."

Reza cocked his head and confusion etched his face, but he nodded at his American employer. "He said the man was coming back today to put down a deposit. I don't know if I believe him. He was probably just trying to drive the price even higher and make you pay far more than it's worth."

If the Russian is who I hope it is, this place is worth ten times that amount, Foster thought.

His mind raced through a dozen plausible scenarios, all centered around the Russian. He was certain Volkov wasn't the only Russian in Iran—or even in Isfahan—but he couldn't afford to ignore an obvious opportunity to gain additional intelligence on his target. Even if the potential buyer wasn't Volkov, he might have some of the same acquaintances and know something of his fellow countryman's whereabouts. Even just a whiff of a rumor would give Foster a place to begin his hunt.

He turned and looked to where the landlord had disappeared to give them some privacy while they discussed the terms, then back to Reza. "I need you to do something for me."

"Anything."

"Go tell the man we will pay double his asking price if he waits twenty-four hours."

"Agha Foster . . ."

"Twenty-four hours," Foster repeated. "But tell him not to say anything to the Russian until he shows to put down the deposit."

Reza clearly thought Foster had lost his mind. He had just spent the better part of twenty minutes negotiating the price down to what he already thought was too high for a basic eighty-five-square-meter flat above a small warehouse in an industrial district on the outskirts of town. But now Foster wanted to undo all his hard work just to beat out a Russian. "I don't think this is a good idea."

"I know it doesn't make any sense, but I have my reasons."

They stared at each other for a moment before Reza finally nodded. With a resigned sigh, he turned to speak with the landlord in the next room and make him the happiest man on the Iranian Plateau.

"And one more thing," Foster said.

The young Iranian paused and looked back.

"Find out when the Russian is coming."

A little while later, Foster and Reza sat in the Peugeot's front seats two blocks from the warehouse they had just agreed to purchase for four billion toman. Despite Foster's insistence that they double the landlord's asking price, Reza couldn't bring himself to waste his hard-earned gains and had only doubled the negotiated price.

"What are we looking for?" Foster asked for the third time.

"He said the Russian drives a Mercedes G-Wagen," Reza said. Again.

As a Force Recon Marine, Foster was accustomed to being still and remaining in one place to observe a target location. But that didn't mean he wasn't bristling with nervous energy as he waited to catch a glimpse of who he hoped was the man his command had sent him to find.

Part of him wanted it to be true. Then he could take out Volkov the moment he saw him and avoid the months of work he would have to put in building out the infrastructure needed to support a task force operation. He knew it would be suicide, but mission accomplished. One more bad guy taken off the battlefield, and he wouldn't have to risk losing any more friends to do it.

But Rebecca . . . Haili . . .

He glanced down at the bracelet his daughter had made for him, the red and yellow clay beads framing the name *DADDY* and reminding him why he couldn't go out in a blaze of glory. As much as he wanted to, he needed to refrain from giving in to his baser instincts and do it the right way.

"Agha Foster?"

He looked over at Reza and saw a concerned look on his face. "Yeah?"

"Are you okay?"

Foster's heart was racing, and his skin felt flushed and damp as if he had just finished a twelve-mile run on a beach. He had been through some of the toughest training on the planet, first to become a Force Recon Marine, then to become a shooter in a JSOC assault squadron—not to mention the last five months spent preparing for his current mission. But he was surprised at how his body reacted to the stress of waiting to see if the man who showed was the man he believed was responsible for his best friend's death.

He took a deep breath and held it for a four count before slowly releasing it in a thin stream of air. "Yes. I'm fine."

Reza handed him his half-empty bottle of water. "Here. Finish mine."

Foster tried waving away the gesture, but the young Iranian was insistent. At last, he gave in and upended the bottle, draining its contents in one long pull. As if the water contained magical cleansing properties that had washed away all his stress and worry, Foster set the empty bottle down and felt remarkably at peace.

"Is that . . . ?" Through the haze in the distance, Foster saw a boxy matte-gray SUV round the corner and pull up to the warehouse he had just agreed to buy for almost twice the market value.

"That is a Mercedes G-Wagen," Reza said with a hint of admiration.

Foster didn't know how much those went for in Iran, but he knew it was well beyond his budget in the United States. "So that's him."

"Looks like it."

Foster watched a large man with a neatly trimmed beard exit the luxury SUV and walk into the warehouse. He had only caught a glimpse, but the Russian seemed to be an exact match with the man Captain Cross had shown him in the grainy photos.

The photos Robert had taken before he was killed.

It's him.

"What do we do now?" Reza asked.

"Now, we wait." Foster clenched his teeth together to keep from saying more. He wanted to climb out of the Peugeot, race into the warehouse, and wrap his fingers around the Russian's neck. He wanted to squeeze the life out of him for being a merchant of death who brought nothing but misfortune and misery to the innocent people of Ukraine. He wanted to slowly choke the man who had murdered his best friend.

"What are we waiting for?"

Before Foster had a chance to respond, the Russian stormed out of the warehouse and scanned the street as if looking for someone. He had a feeling Volkov hadn't taken kindly to an American outbidding him on a property he had wanted for himself, and he was out for blood. They both sagged low in their seats as the Russian's gaze swept across the Peugeot.

"He looks angry," Reza said.

Foster didn't reply. He was zeroed in on the Russian arms dealer and watched as the large man opened the door and climbed into the Mercedes. When it pulled away from the curb and executed an abrupt U-turn in the middle of the street, Foster knew it was his chance.

"Follow him."

Reza's head whipped toward him. "What?"

"Follow the Russian." When the young Iranian failed to react fast enough, Foster snapped at him. "Now, Reza!"

To his credit, Reza put the Peugeot into gear and pulled out from behind the truck that had obscured Volkov's view of them. He drove quickly to catch up with the G-Wagen, but not so fast as to draw attention or so close as to give the Russian a chance to ID them. The closer they got to the city center, the heavier the traffic and the more difficult it became to keep sight of the SUV.

"I'm going to lose him," Reza said.

"You're doing fine. Don't get any closer." Foster's eyes were glued to the boxy roofline of the Mercedes while he mentally plotted its route away from the warehouse.

Where are you going, Volkov?

TWENTY

FOSTER WASN'T BEHIND THE WHEEL, but he still applied his skills in countersurveillance and evasive driving by guiding Reza through the streets of Isfahan. They remained several car lengths back as Volkov drove the G-Wagen aggressively through the heart of the city before slowing and turning onto Aatash-Gaah Boulevard, headed west.

"Why are we following him?" Reza finally asked.

"I just want to see where he goes," Foster said. The young Iranian had calmed somewhat since kicking off their pursuit, but Foster could tell he still felt uneasy following the wealthy Russian from the city. "He might be able to give me leads on clientele."

Reza gave him a sideways glance but remained silent, and Foster knew he was pushing the young man to his limits. Though Reza had willingly elected to uproot from Tehran and move south to work for Shinar Outfitters, Foster had to remind himself they had only just met. Neither man fully trusted the other, though he was certain they wanted the same thing.

"It looks like he's slowing," Reza said.

"Where does this road lead?"

"Najaf-Aabad."

Maybe it was the tone of his voice, but Foster got the distinct impression his new sidekick didn't like where the Russian was leading them. He glanced at the map in his hands and saw nothing to stoke his worry. "What am I missing?"

"What do you mean, Agha Foster?"

"You seem concerned."

Reza chuckled to himself. "Following a wealthy Russian for no reason isn't concerning enough?"

Touché.

They reached a traffic circle at the end of the road and followed the Mercedes SUV around the fountain at its center, exiting south. Foster noticed Reza falling farther behind the G-Wagen, and he glanced across at his companion. "Are you okay?"

Reza nodded, but he still looked nervous. "I don't know if this is a good idea."

Up ahead, the Mercedes pulled off the road and came to a stop in front of a gated compound. Foster felt Reza's foot come off the gas pedal. "Keep going," he said.

The young Iranian complied, and they rolled past a walled compound just off the main highway at the eastern entrance to the city. Reza kept his eyes focused on the road ahead, but Foster turned and studied the Mercedes and the compound, noticing what looked like uniformed men who were opening the gate for the Russian.

"What is this place?" Foster asked.

Reza shook his head. "Najaf-Aabad has a large military presence. The Saheb-é-Zaaman of the Islamic Revolutionary Guard Corps have an outpost here, but they aren't the only ones."

"Who else?" Foster asked, watching through his side-view mirror as Volkov pulled into the compound and the uniformed men closed the gate behind him.

"The Eighth Najaf Ashraf Brigade. Quds. Ashura." Foster felt the younger man's foot press harder on the gas pedal.

"Easy, Reza."

His foot relaxed and they maintained a comfortable speed. "We shouldn't be here, Agha Foster. We should return to Isfahan."

But Foster wasn't so sure. The picture was becoming clear in his mind. He didn't know if the compound belonged to the Saheb-é-Zaaman, Quds, Ashura, or any of the other military units that called Najaf-Aabad home, but he knew why Volkov was there. "Better yet. Take us back to Tehran. I think the Russian has given us a business opportunity."

Reza shot him a sideways glance but didn't reply. He continued driving south until they reached the next traffic circle, then followed it around and exited to the northeast—avoiding the compound where the Russian had led them.

Foster had set the bait, and he was content riding in silence while he waited for the young Iranian to ask the question he desperately wanted to ask. After receiving clearance from the task force to continue with his recruitment, his next step in the process was to let his new employee believe they were engaged in illicit activities. Guns. Drugs. Girls. It was the same in almost any country around the world, and Foster wanted to see how far the young Iranian was willing to go.

But Reza didn't ask. He seemed less nervous as they continued back toward Isfahan and the main highway leading north to Tehran. Foster had nothing but time, and he was more than happy leaning back against the headrest and thinking of all the tasks he still needed to accomplish to build out his network.

First, he needed to open an account at Bank Pasargad and receive a wire transfer from his benefactor so he could purchase the apartment for Reza. Second, he needed to set up a feasibility study by arranging for a hunt on protected lands. But, most importantly, he needed to figure out how to get Reza to Abu Dhabi in the United Arab Emirates, so the command could give him a polygraph. Only after that could Foster unveil his purpose for being in Iran.

And he wouldn't even broach the subject until Reza demonstrated a willingness to go along with something that would end in his arrest if the Iranian government ever discovered what they were doing.

Foster closed his eyes and listened to the sound of the road underneath the Peugeot as Reza guided them north. His outward demeanor was calm and relaxed, but his mind raced with anxiety over the seemingly insurmountable task ahead of him. The only thing he could do was rely on his training and have faith that he had picked someone worthy of his trust.

After almost thirty minutes, Reza broke the silence. "What business opportunity?"

Foster smiled.

On the road between Isfahan and Tehran, Foster painted a picture for Reza that was only partially true. He still couldn't reveal his full purpose for being in Iran, but he gave his young driver enough information to know that it wasn't for something as benign as gaining government approval as a hunting outfitter.

"Guns?" Reza asked.

It had seemed the most logical choice. He knew Volkov was an arms dealer and had negotiated purchases by the Russian private military company, the Wagner Group, from the Iranian government—or at least elements from within the Islamic Revolutionary Guard Corps. Volkov's presence in Najaf-Aabad all but confirmed that he was still engaged in arms trafficking, and Foster wasn't willing to miss out on an opportunity to disrupt the Russian's business dealings.

He nodded. "But I have morals. Do you understand?"

Reza shook his head. "How are you any better than the Russian?"

Foster had to give him credit. He didn't think he would have had the guts to challenge his new employer in this situation had the roles been reversed. He only hoped he could convince the young Iranian that while they would be engaging in illegal activity, it would not be unethical or inimical to do so. "Because I don't sell weapons to murderous thugs who use them on women and children," Foster said, recalling the videos he had seen of innocent Ukrainians slain by invading Russians. "Think of me as an angel of mercy that stands up to the angel of death."

"Who do you sell them to?"

Foster knew this was a critical time during the recruitment process. It would be easy for Reza to decide he wanted no part of this and turn Foster in to the authorities in exchange for leniency. So far, all he had done was escort the American to the Mouteh Wildlife Refuge without express permission—an offense that merited little more than a slap on the wrist. But, if Foster's instincts proved correct, the young Iranian wouldn't turn him in.

"To freedom fighters," Foster said. "To people who only want to defend their families and their homes from oppressive governments. Uyghurs in China. Kurds in Turkey, Syria, and Iraq."

"And Persians in Iran?" Reza asked.

Foster considered the question for a moment, studying the younger man for signs that his sentiment was anything but genuine. He knew there were many young people in Iran who stood in opposition to the ayatollah, and he suspected the murder of his younger cousin had swayed Reza's view of the regime. But still he was hesitant to claim he was there to provide weapons of war to the freedom-loving people of Iran.

At last, he nodded. "There are anywhere from twenty to forty million Muslims in China, but only the Uyghur people—a population of around eight and a half million—of the far western part of the country have been targeted by the government. The Kurds have established a self-governing territory in northern Iraq that is relatively prosperous and peaceful, but they lack the international support for gaining their own homeland. And, yes, there are people in your own country who are persecuted by their government and even murdered for not wearing a hijab properly."

Reza turned and made eye contact with his American employer. "And these are the people you help?"

Even though he wasn't there to buy weapons from rogue elements within the IRGC and sell them on the black market to oppressed peoples, he felt comfortable in nodding his assent. It struck the right balance between illegality and morality to guide Reza into making a decision. "These are the people I help."

When Reza looked away and studied the road ahead of them, Foster fell silent and allowed his driver to come to his own conclusion. He knew he had placed an enormous amount of trust in the younger man—a man he had only met by chance at a cab stand outside the Imam Khomeini International Airport—but he was beginning to realize just how much faith was required for a mission like this.

"Okay," Reza said at last. "I will help you."

Foster hadn't been holding his breath, but he felt himself deflate with relief anyway. "Thank you."

Reza nodded. "Where to?"

"Take me to my hotel," Foster said. "I'll call you in a few days."

"Yes, Agha Foster," the younger man replied.

Foster felt the phone in his pocket vibrate, and he scrunched up his face in worry. There was only one person he had given the number to, and he fished the phone from his pocket to answer. "Hello?"

"Foster! It's Dom Theriot. Have I got a good deal for you."

TWENTY-ONE

Opening a bank account and having funds wired from Abu Dhabi was surprisingly difficult. Though it would've only taken a few hours back home, it took days for Shinar Outfitters to become the signatory on a business account in the Islamic Republic. Finally, with an endless supply of capital—courtesy of Uncle Sam—Foster wasted no time cutting his first check to take ownership of the warehouse property in Isfahan.

As he walked back to his room at the Parsian Azadi Hotel, he was still puzzling over Dom's phone call and his unexpected invitation. If he really was his competitor, it seemed like an odd thing to do. Why would someone—even a fellow veteran—give up an advantage in securing the director general's approval by inviting him along on a hunt? Unless, of course, he was merely a plant by MOIS to root out Foster's true purpose for being in Iran. Then it made perfect sense.

Regardless, he needed to gather more information on the Louisiana native and intended to live by the old saying *Keep your friends close, but your enemies closer.*

Despite the excitement of the day, Foster had no difficulty going to sleep that night. It was hard to believe he had been in the Islamic Republic for a little more than a week and had already checked off several critical items on his list—and a few he hadn't even known would be on there. He had found a driver—who, so far, looked to be an ideal candidate for longer-term employment as his interpreter and cultural specialist—opened a bank account, and purchased a property he intended to set up as a safe house. And he already had a good lead on the Russian.

But there were some unknown variables that vexed him. Dom Theriot. Duncan Riley. Either could be good for the mission or spell serious trouble, and he wasn't sure which camp they fell into. He had a feeling the next twenty-four hours would provide the answers he needed.

Foster woke up the next morning, momentarily forgetting where he was. He rolled out of bed, thinking he was back in his fifteen-hundred-square-foot house in Emory, and almost ran into the wall on his way to the bathroom. But within seconds he remembered he was nowhere near the Lone Star State—and even farther from Virginia Beach. He swallowed back an initial feeling of trepidation and focused on the opportunities of the coming day.

One step at a time. One task at a time.

If all went according to plan, he would have gained another ally and taken one more giant step in establishing a legitimate cover in Iran. From there, it would be only a matter of time before the command authorized an operation to capture Volkov and take the dangerous Russian arms dealer off the board for good. The thought made Foster smile.

Reorienting himself to his hotel room's floor plan, Foster crossed quickly to the bathroom and started the shower. It would be another long day, but he was ready for the challenges ahead. After his shower, he dressed in another casual KUIU hunting outfit, laced up his hiking boots, and packed up the rest of his belongings in his Eberlestock rolling duffel. Then he opened the Onion browser on his burner phone and accessed the website he used to communicate directly with the command.

CUSTOMER REQUESTS A MEETING IN ABU DHABI AT EARLIEST CONVENIENCE.

"Well, that was quick," he muttered.

He exited the app and switched over to the phone to dial Reza's number. The young Iranian answered after only one ring—another positive sign that he had picked the right person for the job. "Good morning, Agha Foster."

"*Salaam alaykum.*"

"*Wa-alaykum-salaam,*" Reza replied. "Are you ready for me to pick you up?"

They had entered the final phase of his recruitment, and Foster hesitated for only a beat. "Actually, I have another job for you."

"Anything," Reza replied.

I wonder if you really mean that, Foster thought. "I have a customer in Abu Dhabi who has requested a face-to-face meeting."

"But you have the hunt with Mr. Theriot today."

He was glad Reza remembered he had agreed to join Dom on a guided hunt for red sheep in the Alborz Mountains. It made it that much easier to pitch him on what he really wanted him to do. "I know, and I can't afford to miss that."

"What can I do?"

He sounded genuine, and Foster wondered if he would feel the same after returning from Abu Dhabi. "I need you to fly there and represent Shinar Outfitters in my absence."

Reza paused, and Foster worried that he'd overplayed his hand. "When?"

He exhaled with relief, but he wasn't out of the woods quite yet. "Today."

"But what about your errands? You needed me to drive you today."

Foster wasn't sure how he would have responded if their roles were reversed, but he got the distinct feeling that Reza was more concerned with logistics than the potential danger of traveling abroad while engaged in illicit activity. Did he even consider for a moment that he would be asked to bring something back into the country that would get him in trouble? Or did he just accept the risks that came with being in business with a criminal?

"This is more important," Foster said. "Will you do it?"

"For you, Agha Foster, I will."

Foster uttered a silent prayer for a successful polygraph and that Reza would respond well to learning that he was actually working for the American government.

After making Reza's travel arrangements to Abu Dhabi, Foster left the Parsian Azadi on foot and followed the same surveillance detection route he had used the week before. Only this time, nobody followed him from the hotel or over the pedestrian bridge crossing the highway. He made several more stops and utilized cut-throughs to add unpredictability to his route, and by the time he reached the café, he was relatively certain he hadn't been followed.

A small brass bell attached to the door tinkled to announce his presence, and Foster stepped across the threshold and paused to survey the room. The elder Brit was nowhere to be seen, but he also hadn't expected him to be. A waiter approached and gestured for Foster to take a seat at the same table where he had sat before.

"What can I bring you?" the waiter asked in surprisingly good English.

Foster waved away the offered menu. "I'll have the *khagineh*, please."

The waiter nodded, then turned and ducked back behind the curtain that separated the dining room from the kitchen. He returned a few minutes later with a cup of chai, which he set on the table.

Foster leaned back in his chair and casually sipped the chai while studying the street through the front window. Like the last time he had been there he'd seen limited foot traffic and only a handful of cars drove past, but none appeared to behave strangely or even turn to look into the café as he might have expected if somebody had been following him or keeping tabs on his activities.

He was halfway through the cup of chai when the bell above the door chimed and Duncan Riley walked inside, dressed in a pair of summer-weight trousers and a long-sleeve linen shirt with the sleeves rolled halfway up his forearms. He made eye contact with Foster and smiled, then walked over and joined him at the table.

"How was the *khagineh*?" Duncan asked.

"Sweet," Foster replied.

"I wasn't sure you had picked up on my meaning."

He almost hadn't. When Duncan had suggested he try it, he knew it was more than a sugar omelet, but it didn't dawn on him until later that the Brit was offering it as a signal of sorts to request a meeting. Foster looked over his shoulder at the conspicuous absence of the waitstaff or other patrons.

"You can speak freely here," Duncan said.

"Who do you work for?"

Duncan threw his head back and laughed. "Well, aren't we direct this morning? That's a bit like asking a woman her age, don't you think?"

"No offense intended," Foster said.

"None taken. But I should think you'd understand my reluctance to share more intimate details about my employment. After all, we have only just met."

Foster nodded. He agreed that their relationship hadn't quite progressed beyond casual acquaintances, but he had hopes to accelerate it quicker than he suspected Duncan was comfortable with. "Maybe a mutual sharing of information, then?"

"You've only just arrived," Duncan replied. "What information could you possibly have?"

"Probably not the kind your employer would be interested in," he admitted.

"You mean Shell Global?"

The question was little more than flirtatious banter, because both men knew that Duncan's position in the oil company was about as legitimate as Foster's fledgling outfitter. "I can tell you that I have no interest in stepping on your toes here in Tehran."

Duncan raised a bushy eyebrow. "Leaving so soon?"

"I've purchased a warehouse in Isfahan."

"Well, aren't you an enterprising chap," he said, sounding almost impressed that Foster had moved so quickly for only having just arrived in-country.

"I don't mess around, Duncan."

"I can see that." The older man narrowed his gaze and appraised Foster in silence as the waiter emerged with a second cup of chai and set it on the table in front of Duncan. The Brit gave him a subtle nod, then waited until he had retreated to the kitchen before speaking. "Then without lifting my kilt—so to speak—is it safe to say that you understand I don't mess around either?"

Foster nodded.

"Then what can I help you with?"

He had thought carefully about how he would ask for Duncan's help. "Will I be stepping on your toes in Isfahan?" *Do you have assets or interests in Isfahan?*

The Brit pursed his lips as he considered the question. "No. Shell Global has no interests in Isfahan."

He hadn't thought so, but he was happy to confirm it, even if it meant he wouldn't be able to leverage an existing network to build out his target package on Volkov. "Do you know an American by the name of Dom Theriot?"

Duncan nodded. "I don't know him personally, but I know of him."

"Has Shell Global done business with him?" *Is he an asset for the British government?*

"No, we never have." Duncan paused for a moment. "And I would be hesitant in doing business with him, if I were you."

Foster received the message loud and clear. *The British government has looked into him and can't be certain of his motives. The American government should be leery of engaging with him too.*

"He invited me on a guided hunt," Foster admitted.

Duncan took a sip of his tea and nodded. "You don't intend on going, do you?"

Foster remained silent but held the older man's gaze.

"Well, isn't that interesting."

TWENTY-TWO

FOSTER AND DUNCAN CONTINUED dancing around the pachyderm in the room until both were satisfied that they shared mutual interests. Maybe their targets were different, but the end goal of weakening the Iranian regime was the same, and Foster made it clear that Duncan could count on him as an ally in that fight. It went beyond his mandate, but he was the man on the ground and could use a friend in his back pocket should the need arise.

"You already know how to reach me here," Duncan said. "I don't know who or what you're after, but I promise you can count on me to assist where I am able."

Foster nodded in thanks, satisfied that he had read the older man correctly. "Thank you, Duncan."

The two sat in silence for a long moment before the Brit cleared his throat and spoke again. "But what *can* you tell me about your purpose here?"

It was surprisingly candid after the lengthy conversation filled with doublespeak, but he was more concerned about talking openly about the topic in the middle of a café.

Duncan saw his hesitation and grinned. "We sweep it for bugs three times a day, and every employee submits to routine polygraphs. This isn't quite a SCIF, but it serves its purpose."

Foster was impressed at the level of sophistication, though he was still hesitant to talk about his mission with anyone other than his commander. Sensitive Compartmented Information Facility or not, the list of people who knew Foster's true purpose for being in Iran was exceedingly short. And Duncan wasn't on it.

But he was fixing to change that.

"Do you know a Russian by the name of Oleg Volkov?"

Duncan leaned back in his chair but made no outward sign that he recognized the name. At last, he spoke. "Wagner Group facilitator and arms dealer. I have heard rumors that he has been spotted here in Iran, but I don't have firsthand knowledge of that."

"I do," Foster said.

Duncan whistled. "Where?"

"Isfahan."

The older man rubbed his chin. "So that explains why you are leaving our fair metropolis for half the world."

Foster nodded, recalling that Reza had described the once capital of Persia with the proverb *Esfahān nesf-e-jahān,* which translated to *Isfahan is half the world.* "And why I wanted to make sure I wouldn't be stepping on the toes of His Majesty's Section Six."

Duncan's mouth curled up at a corner, all but confirming that Foster had guessed correctly. What had been called Military Intelligence, Section 6—or MI6—during World War II was officially known as the Secret Intelligence Service and had been popularized by the novels and movies starring a secret agent under the code name 007. And while Duncan Riley was a far cry from James Bond, his mission of protecting the United Kingdom's interests abroad was the same.

Fortunately, those interests tended to align with the United States'.

"I don't specifically have reason to target Volkov, but my employer would not be opposed if he were removed."

"You mean Shell Global?" Foster said with a smirk.

"Precisely," the older man replied.

"All I can say is that my employer has reason to believe the world would be a better place without Oleg Volkov walking free," Foster said, purposely being vague about who had ordered him to Iran. Though it mattered little since the order—when it came—to remove Volkov would have to come from the president of the United States.

"No objection," Duncan said. "I do most of my work in Tehran, but we have offices throughout the country that might be of interest to you—namely in coastal cities like Imam Hassan, Bushehr, and Bandar Abbas."

He wasn't sure if Duncan had given him those locations because they were MI6 safe houses he could use if needed or because they were port cities that might be used for smuggling people into—or out of—Iran, but he filed the information away in the back of his head for later. He still had a lot of work ahead of him if he wanted to establish his own logistics infrastructure for a future operation, but it felt good knowing there was an ally in the country he could rely on.

"Should I call you directly to set up appointments with those offices if needed?"

More doublespeak.

Foster's phone rang and interrupted Duncan's reply. The older man pushed away from the table and stood. "You do have my number."

Foster nodded. "Thank you for the tea and your time."

The Brit glanced down at the phone in Foster's hands. "If you're going to go through with this silly idea of a hunt with Dom Theriot,

I suggest you take extra care. I don't know what to make of him, but I don't trust his motives."

The phone continued to ring as Foster thought about that statement. "You've looked into him?"

Duncan nodded.

"Did you look into me?"

"I trust your motives," Duncan said with a smile. "Good day, Mr. Cottle."

With that, the British intelligence officer turned and walked through the front door, leaving Foster alone with the phone ringing in his hand. He glanced down at the caller ID and saw the same number that had called the day before. He swiped his thumb across the bottom of the screen to answer.

"Mr. Theriot."

Two hours later, Foster sat in the back seat of a Land Rover Defender 110 as they followed an identical off-white SUV into the foothills northeast of Tehran toward the village of Kond-Olya. The lead vehicle was driven by Farhad—a local hunting guide—and carried two clients, Viraj and Arun, both of whom Foster learned had traveled from India to hunt the Alborz red sheep, a hybrid between the Armenian mouflon and the Transcaspian urial.

Dom rode shotgun in the rear truck, driven by Ahmad, a man Foster learned had spent his entire life hunting in the Alborz Mountains.

"The village is very excited to meet you," Ahmad said. "The government has not issued quotas for red sheep in some time, and your fee will go far in helping us."

"Well, for what I'm paying, I just hope I come away with a trophy," Dom said.

Foster stared at the back of the other hunter's head in disbelief. The more he encountered other Americans abroad, the more he came to understand why so many around the world viewed them as uncouth. Almost as if Ahmad could sense his unease, he turned and looked back at Foster. "Don't worry, Mr. Foster. I am certain you will return with a trophy."

"I'm not worried about trophies, Ahmad."

The comment seemed to stun the Iranian, but Dom was even more floored and spun to face his American counterpart. "You're not?"

"No, I'm not. I'm here to *shikar*. The experience of being here is my trophy."

"Shi-what?"

But Ahmad smiled at the response and gave Foster a subtle nod of acknowledgment.

"*Shikar*," Foster said again. "It's about being respectful of the land and its people. It's not about collecting trophies in the shortest time with the least trouble, but about the process and act of approaching the hunt with humility."

Dom stared at him with open-mouthed bewilderment, then turned back to look at the mountains rising in front of them. "Well, you can *shikar* all you want to, but I'm coming back with a skull mount."

Ahmad glanced back at Foster again and gave him a sheepish smile. "I think you will have good luck, Mr. Foster."

"I think so too, Ahmad."

Though Foster was still unsure what that meant for him. From all outward appearances, Dom behaved just like a stereotypical entitled American, but that didn't make him evil. He might have bribed his way into favor with Director General Ghorbani, but that didn't mean he was working with him to ferret out Foster's true purpose for being there. Maybe he really was who he said he was, and Foster's paranoia had turned him into an antagonist ripped from the pages of a thriller novel.

Don't forget Duncan's paranoia, he reminded himself.

They were quiet for the remainder of the drive, occupying themselves with taking in the sights as they crossed the Jaajrood River and drove through the hamlet of Lavaasan and deeper into the mountains. Foster saw stands of scrub oak, walnut, pear, and sour cherry trees, but most of the surrounding hills were sparsely covered with shrubs and cheatgrass. It didn't look like the vegetation would impede their views during the hunt.

"How much longer?" Dom asked when they broke away from the main road in Lavaasan and started up a one-and-a-half-lane road in a narrow ravine.

"We're almost there," Ahmad replied.

Foster bit his tongue, reminding himself that he was Dom's guest and that his purpose for coming was to decide if the American was more than simply a business threat to Shinar Outfitters. Until he had secured the director general's blessing for establishing his business in Iran, he needed to know who stood in his way. But, more importantly, he needed to know if Dom intended to do something that might spook Volkov before he could even get close.

The convoy turned off the paved road onto a crushed gravel road leading into another ravine, and Foster leaned over to watch the lead Defender navigating the undulating terrain as they neared another village. "Is this your village, Ahmad?"

The driver nodded and smiled. "This is Kond-Olya. My home."

"It's beautiful," Foster said, surveying the modest village.

"It's small," Dom added.

Foster clenched his jaw to keep his frustration from boiling over into anger, but it quickly evaporated when he saw a crowd of two dozen smiling men and a handful of women and children lining the sides of the road. As the Land Rovers drew closer, they pushed up against the vehicles and looked inside at the foreigners who had paid them handsomely for several nights in their guesthouse and the opportunity to hunt on their land.

"Is it like this every day?" Foster asked.

"No, Mr. Foster. They are here for the welcome party."

The lead Defender stopped in front of a small house set off to the side of a gravel clearing, and Foster could see that several villagers were already there preparing for the celebration. He reached into his backpack and removed a carton of Winston cigarettes, then handed them across the front seat to Ahmad. "This is just a small token of my gratitude for you and your village's hospitality. Thank you, Ahmad."

Ahmad accepted the gift with a toothy smile, then opened the door and motioned for his American clients to join him in celebration.

TWENTY-THREE

The next morning, Foster opened his eyes and listened to the sounds echoing off the thick walls. To his left, the deep wheezing of Dom's breathing more than hinted that the Louisiana native was still sleeping, though he wasn't sure how much longer that would last. The rest of the guesthouse seemed to have already come alive, based on the noises coming from outside their cramped bedroom.

It was about what he'd expected as far as accommodations went. The walls were sparse and made of wood and clay, but the ornate rugs covering the floor and the décor dangling from the wooden beams made it feel warm and cozy. Their beds were little more than mattresses set atop the rugs, but Foster had found it to be quite peaceful. Aside from the occasional loud stretch of snoring from his roommate, he had slept harder than he had in weeks.

And he hadn't needed the gentle nudge of Kentucky's magical elixir to do it.

"Mr. Foster?" a soft voice called out from just beyond his door. "Are you awake?"

He glanced over at Dom, saw that he had no intention of rousing soon, then tossed back his blanket and crossed quickly to the door. Though he was still dressed in a pair of loden-green midweight hunting pants and a long-sleeve merino wool hoodie, he had removed his boots before coming inside the night before. That short distance across the rugs felt almost luxurious to his bare feet.

He cracked the door. "Yes?"

"One of the other hunters is going to sight in his rifle and asked if you would accompany him," Ahmad said.

The request caught him off guard. As far as he knew, Dom was the only one who even knew who Foster was, and he had intended on remaining in the shadows during the hunt and letting the others claim kills. "He asked for me?"

"Yes, Mr. Foster."

"Who?"

"Mr. Oleg," Ahmad said, though he looked almost embarrassed.

The name sent a chill down Foster's spine, and his skin flushed. He had met the other two hunters before leaving Tehran and had spent several hours with them at the welcome party the night before. Neither of the Indians' names could be mistaken for Oleg, and the addition of a third hunter to their party at the last minute only reminded him how isolated he was. But even that wouldn't have worried him.

"I don't know a Mr. Oleg," Foster said, hoping to draw out more information before being forced to leave his bedroom enclave and face his fears head-on.

The door opened wider, revealing a man over Ahmad's shoulder who was easily a head taller with a barrel chest and trimmed beard. "I am Oleg Volkov," the Russian said. "I arrived late and was unable to make the welcome party. I apologize for my tardiness."

Foster's heart hammered in his chest as he stared into Volkov's soulless eyes. Less than three feet away stood the man who was responsible for murdering thousands of people in Syria and Ukraine at the behest of the Russian government. But he had killed Robert, and that made it personal. His blood burned hot with a sudden and intense hatred for the merchant of death, but he forced a smile on his face.

"No apologies needed. Let me get dressed, and I'll meet you outside."

Volkov narrowed his eyes as if to divine a hidden meaning in Foster's response, then he nodded.

Foster closed the door quietly but stood there for several seconds while focusing on his breathing to quell the tempest of emotions swirling inside of him. He inhaled slowly through his nose, held the lungful of air for four seconds, then exhaled through his mouth. A necessary calmness came over him, allowing him to compartmentalize the simmering hatred for the Russian waiting for him outside, while he tucked away the feelings of fear and isolation inside a cranny hidden deep in his mind.

"Morning," Dom said.

The fear broke free again at hearing Dom's voice, but Foster controlled it and turned slowly to see the Louisiana native propped up on his elbows, looking up at him. "Morning," he replied, then walked to his duffel to retrieve his insulated hooded jacket and pull it on over the clothes he had slept in.

"Who was that?"

Foster sifted through his bag and removed a wool beanie and a pair of gloves, stuffing both in his coat pockets while trying to rein in his fear and banish the man he used to be from his mind. "New hunter. Russian by the name of Oleg?"

Dom yawned and flopped back onto the mattress. "What'd he want?"

Aside from his boots, which remained near the guesthouse front door, Foster was dressed and ready for whatever awaited him outside.

Beyond his initial misgivings about joining Dom on the hunt, it seemed as if their foray into the Alborz Mountains had been orchestrated for some greater purpose.

Is this what happened to Robert?

"Foster?"

He shook away his suspicion and looked down at Dom. "He wants to sight in his rifle."

Dom groaned and closed his eyes. "Have one of the guides go with him. It's going to be a long day."

But he knew that wasn't an option. Regardless of whether Volkov knew Foster's purpose for being in Iran, he couldn't jeopardize the mission by behaving as anything other than a hunting outfitter. "No, it's fine. I could use the opportunity to check out the area anyway."

"Better you than me."

With that, Foster left the bedroom and joined the others in the guesthouse's main room. Ahmad and Farhad sat on the floor next to Hamed—the game warden assigned to their hunt—and ate from a simple spread of flatbread, feta cheese, jam, and honey. The scent of black tea infused with rose petals wafted through the air, and Ahmad gestured for Foster to join them. "Would you like to eat, Mr. Foster?"

His stomach grumbled, but he knew Volkov was waiting for him. "No, thank you," he said with a shake of his head, then repeated it in his best attempt at Farsi. *"Naa mam-noonam."*

He walked to the rifle stand next to the front door and reached for his Ruger Hawkeye bolt-action rifle with American walnut stock and alloy steel blued finish chambered in the venerable 270 Winchester caliber. Though he knew he had already sighted in his Vortex Optics Razor HD Gen III scope, he wasn't about to head off into the morning alone with the Russian without a weapon slung across his back.

"You won't need that, Mr. Foster," Hamed said.

His hand paused, and he looked over his shoulder at the game warden, who gave him a crooked smile.

Not wanting to raise suspicions, Foster left the rifle in the stand and shrugged before slipping on his boots and stepping outside into the crisp morning air. The village of Kond-Olya sat in a valley in the heart of the Varjeen Protected Area, about twenty-five miles northeast of Tehran and almost four thousand feet higher in elevation. The stark contrast between where they were and the crowded and polluted city below couldn't have been more evident.

"Have you ever hunted here before?" Volkov asked when he saw Foster emerge.

Foster shook his head and walked up to join the Russian at one of the hunting party's Land Rover Defenders. "This is my first time in Iran," he said, then held out his hand. "Foster Cottle, Shinar Outfitters."

"Oleg Volkov," he replied, squeezing Foster's hand in a viselike grip. Foster noted that the Russian hadn't named his employer and held his hand for several seconds before releasing it and pushing off from the Defender's bumper. "Let's go, Mr. Cottle."

Their designated hunting area was less than two miles away, but the Russian slipped behind the wheel of the SUV and cranked the diesel motor. Reluctantly, Foster climbed into the passenger seat while scanning the Land Rover's interior for anything he might use as a weapon. He spotted Volkov's rifle resting in a cradle behind the front seats.

"Have you ever fired a Mosin?" Volkov asked.

Foster shook his head. "A Mosin-Nagant?"

Volkov laughed. "Of course, an American would call it that."

Foster glanced over at the Russian, unsure what to make of the comment, but he remained silent. Volkov put the Defender into gear and pulled away from the guesthouse onto the crushed-gravel road leading north from the village.

"What do you know of its history?"

Foster knew that the rifle had a long history in conflicts around the world. It had been fielded as a sniper rifle in the urban battles of the Eastern Front in World War II and widely exported by the Soviets during the Cold War to global hot spots like Korea, Vietnam, and Afghanistan. It had even been found in the hands of conscripts during Russia's recent invasion of Ukraine. "Some."

"Then you know it began as the Model 1891 Infantry Rifle." It seemed Volkov was eager to share his knowledge of Russian weaponry.

Foster nodded.

"Imperial army captain Sergei Ivanovich Mosin submitted his 'three-line' caliber rifle for consideration to replace the Berdan single-shot rifles that were used in the Russo-Ottoman War."

Foster couldn't help himself. "So did Belgian designer Nagant."

The Russian arms dealer laughed. "And so did Captain Zinoviev. But who cares? Mosin's design won."

They drove to the end of the gravel road and parked in a clearing adjacent to a stream flowing down from the mountains. Foster waited until Volkov turned the engine off, then both men climbed out. Foster shivered as much from the cold air sweeping down the hills as from sharing the peaceful morning with Robert's murderer. He reached into his coat and removed his beanie, pulling it down on his head low enough to cover his ears.

Volkov retrieved the Mosin-Nagant from its cradle and joined Foster at the edge of the clearing, where he shoved a spotting scope into his hands. "Have you ever spotted before, Mr. Cottle?"

"I wouldn't be much of a guide if I hadn't," he replied, taking the scope and tripod and slinging them across his back. He still felt naked without a traditional weapon, but the tripod could be used to do the job if it came to that. Though he didn't have any reason to think his cover was already blown, he suspected Volkov was either intrigued by the American or doing his due diligence to vet Foster's presence in a place he felt he owned.

Volkov slung the Russian bolt-action rifle across his back and started down a trail in the scree toward the creek. Foster followed two paces behind, studying the Russian's body language while scanning the surrounding terrain for signs that he was being led into a trap. Not that there was anything he could do about it. Even if he managed to survive an initial skirmish, it would be next to impossible for him to escape Iran if he ended up on the run.

Unless Duncan can hide you and smuggle you out, he thought, reminding himself that he wasn't entirely alone.

Suddenly, Volkov stopped and spun toward Foster. "There are assassins in these mountains."

Foster froze. His eyes swept the ridgelines on either side of him, looking for whatever had alerted the Russian to the danger. In that moment, he was no longer Foster Cottle—owner of Shinar Outfitters and big-game hunting guide. The sudden fear had snapped the thread of restraint holding back Foster Quinn—Force Recon Marine and JSOC assaulter.

Volkov saw the look on his face and tilted his head back and laughed again. "Not *real* assassins, Mr. Cottle."

Foster winced when he realized how close he had come to shedding his cover in front of the very man he had come to hunt. "What do you mean?"

"The Order of Assassins," Volkov said. "A Nizari Ismaili order founded by Hassan-i Sabbah that committed covert murder of Muslim and Christian leaders. Their fortresses—Alamut and Lambsar—were in these mountains and were the backbone of the Assassins' power."

Another history lesson?

Foster's patience for Volkov's effusion had worn thin. "Do you want to dial in your rifle or not?"

The Russian's smile faded, but he nodded. "Just up here."

They walked another hundred yards before Volkov gestured for Foster to set up the spotting scope next to a large boulder at the stream's edge. Using a laser range finder, he then found what he was looking for and walked another twenty-five yards, where he affixed a paper target to a tree. Foster sighted through the scope at the target, confused by the close range.

"Most hunters zero at two hundred yards," he said when Volkov returned.

"Most hunters don't have my skill." He unslung the Mosin-Nagant and cradled it in his arms as he lowered himself to the ground, dropping his right leg flat, bent, and set under the supporting side knee. With his left arm resting—muscle on bone—atop the knee that nestled into the underside of the elbow, he rested the Russian rifle in the crook on the top side. Foster recognized the seated sniper cradle immediately.

"How far is that? Twenty-five yards?"

"Twenty-six," Volkov replied.

"What's the benefit?"

"Our game has a kill zone of six inches. Anything more than three inches high or three inches low will only wound the animal and end the hunt." Volkov flipped up the lens covers on his scope and set his relief, looking more relaxed than Foster had felt behind the M40A5 on the range with Desobry back in Virginia Beach. "By using a twenty-six-yard zero, if I hold dead center, my bullet will hit two-point-eight inches high at two hundred yards, dead center at two hundred and seventy-five, and three inches low at three hundred and ten."

Volkov took in a breath, held it for a beat, then let half of it out while melting into his final position.

Crack!

Foster peered through the spotting scope as Volkov worked the bolt to extract the spent casing and chamber a fresh round. He saw a hole dead center in the bullseye. "Hit."

"Now, tell me why you bought that warehouse in Isfahan."

Crack!

TWENTY-FOUR

Foster's brief conversation with Volkov had left him anxious. Though he had sufficiently deflected the Russian's question about the warehouse, Foster worried that he had drawn unwanted attention to himself, and for the remainder of the hunt, he spent more time observing Dom and the Russian out of the corner of his eye than red sheep through his spotting scope. He awoke each day on edge and collapsed each night exhausted from the stress of pretending to be somebody he was not. It was all part of the mission he was eager to do, but he hadn't anticipated having to interact so closely with the man he thought of as Robert's killer.

At the end of the three days, each of the hunters had bagged a trophy, and the village celebrated with a feast that surpassed even the exuberance of the welcome party. Though his nerves were shot, Foster felt certain Volkov wasn't on to him, and he let his guard down just enough to relax and enjoy the evening's festivities. But the Russian still made him nervous, and he'd limited their interactions and kept a safe distance.

At least until the party prepared to depart camp and return to Tehran. As Volkov climbed into his own SUV, he had hailed Foster and promised to call on him in Isfahan, apparently having already forgotten his irritation that Foster had outbid him on the warehouse property. Though Volkov had never admitted his intent for the property, Foster already had his suspicions. Over the previous three days—especially during the concluding celebration—the Russian had all but bragged about his business dealings with the IRGC. His arrogance was astonishing, but it gave Foster all the information he needed.

After the two Defenders made their way back to the city and dropped Foster at the Parsian Azadi, he gathered his rolling duffel from the rear of the truck and turned to walk into the hotel. He felt an overwhelming sense of relief as the vehicles pulled away, but it was short-lived. From the corner of his eye, he spotted a young man studying him from the shadows.

"Hello, Reza," he said.

"Agha Foster," the Iranian replied, stepping out into the sunlight.

"Shall we go for a drive?"

Reza nodded and gestured for Foster to follow him to his car.

With a glance up at the hotel and the soft bed that waited for him in his room, Foster pulled his duffel behind him and followed the young man across the parking lot. He knew Reza would have questions for him, and his presence there only meant that the polygraph had been successful and that he was now a fully vetted member of the team. Their relationship would never be the same, but Foster wasn't yet sure whether that was a good or bad thing.

They reached the Peugeot, and Reza opened the trunk for Foster to deposit his duffel inside. Without saying a thing, the two men climbed into the car and waited until they were far away from the hotel before speaking.

"Reza—"

But the young Iranian cut him off. "I understand why you lied to me."

Foster could tell Reza wanted to get something off his chest, so he remained quiet and waited patiently for the young man to continue.

"But I am embarrassed I agreed to work for you—especially after you led me to believe you were buying and selling guns."

"Reza—"

"Please. I'm sure you knew that if I didn't agree to your *customer's* terms, I wouldn't have been allowed to return. You sent me to Abu Dhabi knowing that I might disappear and never return home."

Foster wanted to explain. He wanted to apologize for foisting that decision onto Reza. But he couldn't bring himself to only offer platitudes. The truth was, Foster believed in free will, and he believed that each of Reza's decisions had led to that pivotal moment inside a windowless room in Abu Dhabi. Foster had given him ample opportunity to walk away.

The deed is all.

"But I understand, Agha Foster."

The Iranian turned, and Foster met his gaze. There was a fierceness behind his eyes that Foster recognized. He had seen it in the other Force Recon Marines and Navy SEALs he had deployed downrange with. It was a look that said, *I've got your back, brother.*

"I'm not sorry, Reza. This is very important, and I need you."

He nodded. "What do we do next?"

For the next hour, Reza drove around the city while they plotted their next moves. They both agreed they needed to leave Tehran behind and return to Isfahan to begin setting up shop in the new Shinar

Outfitters warehouse. Foster still needed to find a place to live, but he planned to share the one-bedroom flat with Reza until the right opportunity came along.

"How will we get the team to the target?" Reza asked.

Foster had been thinking of nothing else since leaving Kond-Olya, and the simplest solution was to drive them there. "Probably by car," he replied.

"From the coast?"

Foster almost chuckled at Reza's panicked expression, but he understood why the Iranian would balk at the thought. Isfahan was almost two hundred miles from the Persian Gulf, and the notion of transporting a team of JSOC operators by car over that distance was absurd.

"No, Reza. They will jump into Iran and make their way to the warehouse."

"Jump?"

Foster had to remember that he wasn't dealing with a combat-seasoned operator like he had grown accustomed to during his time in the Marine Corps. Reza had guts and had shown a determination that could rival any of the bearded and brawny warriors he had served alongside, but he was in uncharted territory.

"They will have to HAHO," he said. "It stands for *high altitude, high opening* and is used for the clandestine insertion of operators. They will jump from and open their parachutes at a high altitude."

"Why?"

"Because they can use their parachutes to navigate and fly to the target area at night without being seen."

Reza seemed shocked by the idea. "And they can go two hundred miles?"

Foster shook his head. "Not quite that far. The plane that drops them will either have to fly through Iranian airspace or the drop zone will have to be somewhere south of Isfahan."

"How far south?"

Foster looked at his fully vetted companion. "I have some ideas, but we need to go check them out."

Reza's mouth curled up at the corner in just a hint of a smile. "I really like this idea, Agha Foster. And then we meet them at the drop zone and drive them to the target location in Isfahan?"

Foster shrugged. "That depends on where we establish the drop zone."

"What else do we need to do?"

Foster was surprised at how eager Reza seemed to be to get involved in the operational planning. In truth, he hadn't even had time to consider all the variables that went into a capture-or-kill operation. Much of it depended on what the national command authority decided to do. If the president wanted to capture Volkov—a distinct possibility, given the breadth of intelligence he could provide on the Wagner Group's involvement in Putin's wars—the logistics became much more complex.

"We'll need vehicles one way or another—to get the assault team on and off the target—and a concrete plan for getting them out of Iran."

"With the Russian?"

Because that would be the more complex option, Foster nodded. "We have to assume so."

"How?"

This was why Foster had invested his time and energy into developing Reza as an asset. He needed someone who understood his country's infrastructure and could guide him through the cultural pitfalls of being a foreigner in Persia. "What do you suggest?"

"Flying out from a major airport is out of the question," Reza said, talking his way through the problem. "But maybe a smaller plane from a remote airport?"

The botched 1980 hostage rescue mission known as Operation

Eagle Claw immediately came to mind. Foster knew there were a host of reasons why the mission had failed and that most of those reasons were mitigated seven years later with the establishment of the United States Special Operations Command. But still, the risk of conducting an egress by airplane seemed too great to even consider.

Even so, he appreciated Reza making suggestions and didn't want to stifle his initiative. "It's an option. What else?"

"Driving across the border into Iraq?"

"We would need to know where all the military outposts are and what kind of patrolling they do close to the border. My guess is it will probably be too dangerous—especially without any kind of air support providing us top cover on the move."

Reza nodded. "What about by sea?"

As a Force Recon Marine, Foster was comfortable in the water. He knew the SEALs who would conduct the raid would agree with him, but there was still the issue of getting almost two hundred miles from the target location in Isfahan to the gulf. It was an option worth exploring more, but he didn't want to get too far ahead of himself.

"We can table this discussion for now," Foster said. "Let's head back to the hotel so I can check out of my room."

"Then where, Agha Foster?"

"Isfahan."

TWENTY-FIVE

Over the next week, Foster and Reza poured their energy into cleaning out the warehouse and setting it up as a suitable base of operations for Shinar Outfitters. They both slept on thin mattresses on the floor in the one-bedroom flat while scouring the city for reliable used Toyota Hilux trucks. Three was the bare minimum they would need to support an operation, but four would be better.

"I think I have a solution," Reza said.

In between looking at other properties and buying four-wheel-drive vehicles, the two had been discussing potential locations for a drop zone. Their biggest problem was still the insufficient distance the operators would be able to travel under canopy. They wouldn't be able to make it anywhere near the target location.

"Let's wait and see what the assault team comes up with," Foster said.

Fortunately, they weren't trying to solve the problem alone. After arriving in Isfahan, Foster had immediately reached out to Captain Cross through the dark web. The first part of his report was positive—he had found Volkov and knew where he would be—but the matter of establishing a plan for ingress and egress left much to be desired.

"What about Ahvaz?"

Foster stopped sweeping and leaned against the push broom as he appraised Reza. "We've been over this. We don't have a legitimate reason for being in Ahvaz, and that will open up a whole new set of problems."

He couldn't tell Reza that Robert had been killed because he had traveled to Isfahan when he should have stayed in the Alborz Mountains. He knew that just because he hadn't seen any kind of surveillance, it didn't mean the Iranian government hadn't been keeping tabs on his movement and activities. No matter how cordial his interaction with the director general, he could never forget that he was under constant scrutiny and only one mistake away from the same fate as his best friend.

"It's true," Reza said. "Armenian mouflon reside in the central Zagros Mountains, but that's the same distance from Ahvaz as it is from here."

The Zagros mountain range was almost one thousand miles long and stretched from southeastern Turkey, through northern Iraq, and spanned the southern parts of the Armenian highland and the entire length of the western Iranian plateau to end at the Strait of Hormuz. While Isfahan was on the eastern side and easily reached from Tehran, Ahvaz was less than forty miles from the Iraqi border on the western side.

"But we don't have permission to hunt Armenian mouflon," Foster countered. He had specifically selected the Isfahan mouflon because that's what Robert had reported Volkov hunted.

"Yet," Reza said.

Foster shook his head. They had only just received temporary permission from Director General Ghorbani for two tags for Isfahan mouflon. He knew it was an audition of sorts, and he fully expected his first customers to be members of MOIS. But if he went off script like Robert had, at best, that permission would be rescinded. At worst . . .

"Let's focus on a solution within our current capabilities," Foster said, ending the discussion.

Reza looked like he was about to argue but went back to stacking boxes in the warehouse's storage closet. Foster watched him for a few minutes as he considered the suggestion. If he could at least gain approval to do a feasibility study in the Zagros Mountains, then a second location in Ahvaz made sense. But that still didn't solve the problem of getting the team from Ahvaz to Isfahan.

And that's where Volkov would be.

Foster had returned to the mindless task of sweeping when he felt his phone vibrate in his pocket. Pulling it out, he saw an apparent spam email again notifying him that he had won a contest—his signal that there was a message waiting for him on the dark web.

He opened up his Onion browser and navigated to the website set up for clandestine communications with his command. His heart pounded in his chest as he waited to see what Captain Cross had sent him. It could be something as simple as a request for information or as complex as a warning order for a looming operation. Either way, he knew the message would dictate what he and Reza needed to focus their efforts on.

His connection to the internet was agonizingly slow, made even slower by accessing the Tor network, and Foster felt his chest tighten with anxiety as he waited for the message to load. Reza saw him standing in the middle of the warehouse floor, staring at his phone, and he stopped what he had been doing.

"Agha Foster?"

Before he could answer, the message loaded, and the blood drained from his face.

"Oh no."

"What is it?" Reza asked.

"The president authorized the mission to capture Volkov," Foster replied.

"When?"

Foster felt his throat closing and chest squeezing as he thought about all that still needed to be done. They were nowhere near ready to receive the assault team. "One week," he said, swallowing hard.

"What?"

"Intel suggests Putin has recalled Volkov to Moscow, leaving us only a narrow window."

Reza's eyes widened with surprise. "But we're not ready."

Nowhere near ready.

"We have to be," Foster said. It was the truth. Failure wasn't an option. Like it or not, in one week a team of SEALs would hurtle through the night sky toward the Islamic Republic of Iran with one goal in mind: capture the Russian arms dealer Oleg Volkov.

"But . . ."

Foster cut him off. "I know, Reza. I know we don't have anything ready yet, but we can't worry about that now. Everything we do between now and then has to be with the singular focus of preparing to get the team to the target and then out of Iran with Volkov."

Reza opened his mouth as if he was about to argue but quickly closed it. With a nod, he let Foster know he was on board. "Okay, Agha Foster. What's the plan?"

Foster motioned for Reza to follow him, and they climbed the stairs to the one-bedroom flat above the warehouse, where a map of Iran was tacked to the wall. Foster had marked off the area where the director general had given authorization for Shinar Outfitters to guide hunts in the Tangé-Sey-yed, southwest of Isfahan.

But the large-scale topographic map also showed the surrounding areas—in particular, the area west of the Zagros Mountains. He leaned in close and marked a spot on the map, then used a compass and pencil to draw concentric rings around it.

"What are you doing?" Reza asked.

"This is the drop zone," Foster replied. "The assault team will want us to provide options for vehicle-staging locations at one-mile intervals out to five miles."

Reza leaned in over Foster's shoulder and looked at the spot on the map. "Is that . . . ?"

"Yes," Foster said. "It's near Ahvaz."

Reza inhaled sharply. "I have the solution."

Foster backed away from the map and faced his companion. Reza had been pushing him to expand their base of operations into Ahvaz, but he had never given him the opportunity to explain why. Maybe it was time he stopped stonewalling the Iranian and actually allowed him to be a member of the team.

"Okay, Reza. What did you have in mind?"

"My uncle's family is from Ahvaz. He is an engineer and owns a large estate to the east on the outskirts of town. It's far enough away that a large group coming and going in the middle of the night won't be noticed."

Foster shook his head. "We can't involve your family, Reza."

"You don't understand. He's not there."

"Where is he?"

Reza snatched the compass from Foster's hands and measured out ten miles on the map's scale, then walked the sharp points across the map from the east side of Ahvaz to the Dehdez Protected Area. "Eighty miles," Reza said, not answering Foster's question. Then he measured the distance from Dehdez to the Tangé-Sey-yed. "Sixty miles." Finally, he measured the distance from there to their warehouse in Isfahan. "Fifty miles."

"I'm still not following you, Reza. What is your idea?"

He set the compass down and stepped back to study the map, nodding to himself. "This will work."

"Reza."

At last, he turned to Foster. "My uncle is a senior petroleum engineer with the National Iranian Oil Company. He helped discover the Ahvaz Field—the third largest in the world—and has been called away to help expand Iranian oil exports. His home in Ahvaz has been vacant for over a year, and we could borrow it without anyone even knowing."

At the mention of oil, Foster immediately thought back to Duncan and his cover with Shell Global. He knew the Brit probably had connections in Ahvaz, and he filed the thought away for later.

"His estate is a little over forty miles from the border with Iraq."

Foster thought about the altitude the SEALs would have to jump from to fly that far, but he knew the prevailing winds over the Persian Gulf would favor them reaching that distance.

"We can stage three vehicles there before the operation, and one of us can wait for them."

"It should probably be you," Foster said. "It's your uncle's place, and you're familiar with the area."

Reza nodded. "I agree. Because your job will be to bring Volkov to the Dehdez Protected Area."

"Reza . . ."

"You will arrange for a mouflon hunt in the Tangé-Sey-yed. During the welcome party, you will slip away and bring Volkov to the Dehdez." He stabbed a finger at the protected area. "This is where the assault team will grab him."

There were plenty of reasons why the idea wouldn't work, but Foster knew it was better than anything he had. At the very least, it was worth looking into. He nodded.

"Okay. Let's put together a plan, and I'll get it back to the team."

TWENTY-SIX

THE FRIGHTENED BOY was gone.

Foster twisted his body and placed both feet on the wall, then pushed off with the brick stretched out in front of him. Even starved for oxygen, his powerful legs propelled him another five meters before the weight carried him back to the bottom of the pool. One leg. Then the other. Slowly, he scissored his legs together and resumed his swim.

Left . . . right . . . pull . . . relax.

He had completed the task, but something compelled him to go farther. It wasn't vanity or boastful arrogance, but the discovery of an untapped reservoir of determination. One kick. Then the next. One stroke. Then another. Foster pulled and pushed his body farther along the black line, beckoning him back to the deep from where he'd come.

Sixty-five meters.

Foster tilted his head forward and sighted in on the black line that was his goal. It had never been his ambition to break the record. He hadn't dropped into the deep end intending to go more than fifty meters. But Foster Quinn was a Recon Marine.

He opened his mouth to shout in triumph as he reached the seventy-five-meter mark, but then everything changed. His lungs didn't scream at him to inhale. His muscles didn't burn from the agony of exertion. He heard nothing, saw nothing, and felt nothing. It was as if he had swum inside a bubble and dissolved into oblivion.

"Quinn!"

But then there was the voice. He knew he should recognize it, but it seemed more of a nuisance than anything else. He felt safe and warm in his bubble. Content. But the voice wouldn't leave him alone and beckoned him back into the cold.

"Quinn! Wake up!"

He felt the stinging slap of an open palm across his face, and he struggled to respond. His eyes fluttered in a tug-of-war between the comforting darkness of oblivion and the painful brilliance of life.

"Quinn!"

His eyes snapped open, and he stared not into the face hovering over him, but into the cloudless Southern California skies. Then, as if the deep blue had pierced his bubble of oblivion, each of his other senses came under assault. He felt the rough concrete of the pool deck under his back, and his skin broke out in gooseflesh as the wind swept across his soaking wet body. He felt his heart thundering in his ears and the ragged breathing of a man who was either tired or scared. Or both.

"Quinn! Can you hear me, bro?"

His eyes rolled from side to side, taking in the crowd growing around him. But the only face in focus was the one directly over him.

He coughed. "Staff Sergeant James?"

Robert James smiled. "Yeah, buddy. You with us?"

Then it all came back to him. The fifty-meter underwater swim. The weighted brick. The beckoning to push his limits beyond expectations. The pushing off the wall and returning to the deep. The triumph of breaking the record and the defeat of blacking out.

"You saved me?"

His instructor nodded. "Yeah, bro. I got you."

Foster closed his eyes and felt his body shudder with relief.

"Agha Foster?"

His heart felt light, and a happiness settled over him. His instructor had abandoned his duty of watching others swim fifty meters underwater with a ten-pound brick. To save him. To pluck his unconscious body from the deep end and revive him on the pool deck. To bring him back to life.

"Agha Foster, wake up," the voice said again.

But it wasn't Robert's.

"No," he muttered.

He didn't want to open his eyes. He didn't want to return to a world where Robert was nothing more than a memory.

No!

Suddenly, the veil of sleep was yanked away, and he remembered what he had tried to forget. He wasn't on the deck of the Camp Pendleton pool where Robert had revived him, but on his mattress in a one-bedroom flat in Isfahan. He was no longer the chiseled Marine of his youth, but an isolated operator on the eve of the most daring mission he had ever undertaken. Foster shook his head.

"Agha Foster, it's time to wake up," Reza said again.

Reluctantly, he opened his eyes, then sat up and looked into Reza's worried face. He knew he had probably been talking in his sleep again—it seemed to be happening more and more—but the dream was already fading. He could no longer see Robert's face or hear the soft timbre of his voice, and the deep pain of his absence took root in his heart once more.

"We need to get you to Tehran," Reza said.

He nodded, remembering that he had scheduled a meeting with Duncan as a last-ditch effort to come up with a reasonable egress plan for the assault team. He had less than twenty-four hours until eight SEALs jumped from the back of a cargo plane and parachuted into the Islamic Republic of Iran, and he still didn't have a plan to get them out.

"Yeah, okay," Foster said, rubbing the stubble on his face while trying to wipe away Robert's lingering memory. There would be time later to demand more than ninety minutes of sleep or answers to the plaguing questions surrounding his best friend's death. But now was not that time. "Let me get dressed."

"I'll be in the car."

Foster watched Reza's shadow retreat to the stairs from the corner of the room where he had arranged their mattresses in a neat row, then brought his wrist up to his face to examine the dim illumination of the hands on his Tudor Submariner.

Three a.m.

He groaned but didn't waste additional energy on lamenting the loss of sleep. If all went according to plan, they would return to Isfahan later that morning with the last wrinkle ironed out. Oleg Volkov had agreed to accompany him to the Tangé-Sey-yed, where they would meet their local guides for a mouflon hunt. Reza insisted he had already arranged for the guides and game warden to look the other way while Foster and Volkov slipped away to the Dehdez, but he had no such assurances that the Russian would go along with their plan.

Foster pushed himself off the mattress and staggered sleepily to the chair where he had placed his KUIU pants and long-sleeve button-down shirt. He dressed quickly and slipped on his hiking boots, then stood in silence in the darkened room while thinking about the looming mission with trepidation. There were still too many variables for him to feel comfortable with the team executing on timeline, but that decision was out of his hands.

Foster heard the Peugeot's engine turn over with a squeal as the worn timing belt groaned to life.

I know the feeling, he thought, feeling the culmination of years of abuse on his worn body as he descended the stairs and climbed into Reza's sedan.

"Are you ready?" the young Iranian asked.

Foster nodded. "Let's go."

They pulled out of the warehouse, leaving behind three Toyota Hilux Vigo pickup trucks adorned with the Shinar Outfitters logo, and headed north on the main road linking Persia's past with its present. Both men were silent as they contemplated their roles in the upcoming mission, but Foster attributed his silence to the one thing Reza didn't know.

Even though the Iranian had been fully vetted and was a vital member of their team on the ground, Foster still hadn't shared with him his suspicion that Volkov was to blame for his best friend's death. If he had other options, he might have even recused himself from the operation to prevent his personal biases from clouding his professional judgment. But he didn't. Like it or not, when he signed on the dotted line, he had become the only person responsible for the success of the mission. Just him.

Just one man.

Alone.

No, not alone, he reminded himself.

When they reached Tehran, Reza dropped Foster at the café and left to run his own errands. They had been working nonstop to put the finishing touches on the plan, but after learning Shell Global had an office in Ahvaz, Foster had returned to the café and ordered *khagineh* and waited anxiously for Duncan to show. When he did, Foster abandoned all pretense and asked the Brit point-blank if he could coordinate for a shipping container to be loaded onto a merchant ship in Bandar Imam Khomeini. Duncan had agreed to try but made no promises.

Now Foster saw his arrangement with Duncan as the one item that would either make or break the whole thing. Without the Brit's help, they were left with trying to sneak across the border into Iraq—an option that was too dangerous to even be considered.

Foster heard the faint tinkling of the door's bell as he walked into the café and took his now-familiar seat. A waiter appeared a moment later and walked to the front door to lock it, then gestured for Foster to follow him behind the curtain into the kitchen. Hesitantly, Foster got up and followed, wondering why Duncan had changed protocol.

This can't be good.

He walked into a storage room off the kitchen and waited until his eyes had adjusted to the darkness before fixing his gaze on the older man.

"Does it have to be tonight?" Duncan asked.

"I'm afraid it does."

Duncan sighed heavily and shook his head. "I'm sorry, my friend, but it's too rushed. I can't do it."

Foster felt a chill run down his spine as he took in what the British spy was saying. He'd known it was little more than a Hail Mary, but he had still hoped his one ally in Iran would be able to work miracles for him. "How much longer do you need?"

Duncan reached up and stroked his trim beard. "Another twenty-four to forty-eight hours would still not be enough, but it would be better."

"When is the next scheduled departure?"

"In four days."

Foster grunted. "That's too long."

He had tried pressing Captain Cross into delaying the operation to give him more time to put a suitable egress plan into place. But the captain had refused. And Foster was again reminded that the enemy always gets a vote.

Duncan shrugged. "Do you have someplace you can keep them secure for a few days while I keep trying?"

Foster nodded. "What else can I do?"

"Call off the whole bloody thing," Duncan suggested with a sharp laugh.

Foster might be tempted to do that very thing, if he could. Still, he was a man of faith, and even though that faith had been taxed to its limit, he believed in good triumphing over evil. He believed God would protect the eight SEALs as they descended that night from the heavens like angels of retribution. And he believed Volkov would be brought to justice.

"I can't do that," he said.

Duncan nodded. "I didn't think so, mate. I'll keep trying."

TWENTY-SEVEN

That night, stars twinkled above an Air Force Special Operations MC-130W Combat Spear as it flew north on a flight plan from Abu Dhabi to Baghdad International Airport. The plane and its crew from the Seventy-Third Special Operations Squadron had been making nightly round-trip flights for over a week, building a consistent footprint so their presence in the clear skies over the Persian Gulf wasn't unexpected or alarming.

On each previous sortie, they had been queried by air defense controllers when the strong westerly winds pushed them toward Iranian airspace. And each time, they had delayed their responses before making sluggish course corrections to return to their filed route.

This time was no different.

"Unidentified aircraft on heading three five zero at thirty-five thousand feet, you are approaching the sovereign airspace of the Islamic Republic of Iran," the bored and tired voice said for the eighth night in a row. "Please correct your course immediately."

The aircraft commander turned to look at his copilot and rolled his eyes. Major Keller "K-Money" Rholdon was the squadron's director of operations and a veteran of multiple deployments to Afghanistan, Iraq, and an assortment of other locations in the Middle East. He was at home in the skies over the Persian Gulf.

He keyed the microphone. "This is Wombat Three Three. We are an American aircraft operating in international airspace on an approved flight plan."

His copilot chuckled, then reached for the stopwatch he had started when the SEALs began their pre-breathing cycle. "That's forty-five minutes."

Keller nodded and watched the other pilot flip the switch to depressurize the cargo bay. "Think they bought it?"

He shrugged. "It's been the same thing each night. Maybe it buys us a few extra miles."

Every little bit helps, Keller thought.

Even though the Combat Spear was designed from the ground up as the ideal platform for the tactical insertion and extraction of special operations forces by weaving through enemy air defenses, the purpose of this mission was a little different. They wanted to be overt. They wanted to be seen. And they wanted the Iranians to believe they had accidentally encroached on their airspace. Again.

"Approaching the HARP," his copilot said.

Keller nodded and switched to a secondary radio to hail the Air Force U-28A Draco—a modified Pilatus PC-12 turboprop—as it orbited just across the border in Iraq. "Dragonfly, this is Wombat Three Three. Eleven minutes from release."

"Wombat, this is Dragonfly, the drop zone is clear."

"Wombat," Keller replied, then reached up and retarded the power control levers. He needed to slow the special operations Hercules to a safe airspeed before reaching the high altitude release point. They had planned the high-altitude jump for thirty-five thousand feet to allow the SEALs ten thousand feet of free fall before deploying their chutes at the highest altitude allowed and flying to the drop zone forty miles away.

"Here goes nothing."

Then he silently recited one of the few passages from the Bible he had memorized. It was an offering and prayer for their safe return.

You will not fear the terror of night, nor the arrow that flies by day, nor the pestilence that stalks in the darkness, nor the plague that destroys at midday.

In the cargo bay, Seth felt more than heard the large MC-130W transport aircraft slow, indicating that it was nearing the release point. He and the other SEALs each wore a Military Javelin container paired with an MS-360 Military Silhouette main chute—a system specifically designed for HALO and HAHO standoff operations—that gave them the ability to steer under canopy and fly to their intended point of landing.

But not without risks.

It wasn't always the smartest option for inserting a special operations team. Too many things could go wrong—unpredictable wind, extreme cold temperatures, equipment malfunctions during canopy deployment, or personnel injury upon landing. But it was necessary for a mission like this. It allowed them to insert well behind Iran's coastal defenses and put boots on the ground while the enemy focused on the transport plane that continued droning north.

Tre—the team's military free-fall jumpmaster—disconnected from one of the two six-man pre-breather portable oxygen systems, then leaned over and spoke with the Air Force crew chief. They conferred for a few seconds before Tre stood and faced the other jumpers, raised his left fist in the air—elbow even with his shoulder and forearm perpendicular to the Combat Spear's floor—and pointed to his wrist with his right index and middle fingers. Bringing his right fist back to match his left, he looked at each of his teammates in turn, then flashed ten fingers and said, "Ten minutes."

Each SEAL replied, "Ten minutes."

The rear cargo ramp lowered, and a red light illuminated, but Seth and the other SEALs remained seated. He reached back to turn on his Twin-53 portable oxygen system and verified the gas was flowing before flipping the K-valve to change sources. After a few breaths, he disconnected from the pre-breather secured to the Combat Spear's five-thousand-pound tie-downs while his leg bounced with nervous energy, and he waited for the next signal.

Tre extended his right hand, palm up, at waist level with his elbow tucked to his side. He turned his body from right to left to right before returning to center, then raised his right fist and flashed two fingers.

Two knots of wind at the drop zone.

He watched Tre walk aft to the ramp, where he leaned out and looked down into the black abyss. Tre conferred with the crew chief again—confirming their position with the flight crew—then turned to face his brother SEALs and made eye contact. He raised his right arm in an arc from his side to shoulder level.

Stand up.

They were five minutes from release.

Seth stood and went through the well-rehearsed motions of ensuring his equipment was ready while Ryan completed a check of his main and reserve rip-cord pins to ensure they were properly seated. He felt a double slap on the back of his gear.

Pin check complete.

No matter how many jumps they had made, they treated each one as if it was their first to make sure it wouldn't be their last. But they took even greater care with this jump. Even one loose fitting or missed attachment point could cause gear to detach upon exiting the plane and spin the jumper out of control.

That would be a disaster before the operation even started.

Seth conducted a pin check on Ryan before turning back to Tre. The jumpmaster extended his right arm straight out to the side— palm up—then brought his hand up to touch the edge of his helmet.

Move to the rear.

They were one minute from release.

Seth and the other SEALs made final adjustments to their goggles and exchanged hand slaps, fist bumps, and Hawaiian shakas, then shuffled slowly toward the edge of the ramp. Between the bulky clothing they wore to combat the cold and the gear they needed to complete the mission, it was a cumbersome process to reach the edge, where they stood shoulder to shoulder and waited to leap out into the darkness. The jumpmaster brought his right hand to his side, thumb extended, and raised it in an arc over his head.

Stand by.

Fifteen seconds.

The single red bulb on the bulkhead extinguished and was quickly replaced with a green light. The jumpmaster placed his arm across his chest, then pointed to the open ramp.

Go.

As the stick lead, Seth went first and dove into the pitch black. He didn't wait to see if the other SEALs followed, instead focusing on stabilizing his body in the MC-130W's slipstream. Facing away from the Combat Spear, he arched his back and extended his arms out front, head lifted, and legs bent at the knees. The premission jitters were gone. All that was left was a solitary focus on the task at hand.

Seth brought his arms back until his hands were even with his eyes and spread his legs. Turning slightly to the left, he checked his altimeter—thirty-four thousand feet—as the formation of SEALs oriented themselves east toward Iran while falling to Earth at terminal velocity—over one hundred miles per hour.

Despite the low illumination, it was easy to spot their intended drop zone to the southeast of Ahvaz—a dark patch of ground surrounded by brightly lit industrial-looking facilities. At twenty-seven thousand feet, the SEALs all turned away from the formation, put their arms back to their sides with legs extended, and tracked away from each other for a dispersed opening of their canopies.

Seth was now all alone in the darkness.

At twenty-five thousand feet, he initiated one big wave over his head, then deployed his pilot chute. As he felt the tension of his risers beginning to slow his fall, his canopy opened overhead with a *snap*. He completed a quick controllability check, then initiated a check-in with the others over the closed intranet cellular mesh network.

"Ninety-nine, check in. Angel Six."

Only the sound of rushing wind answered his call.

He felt for the single push-to-talk taped to his thumb, connecting his Peltor headset to the AN/PRC-148 MBITR in a pouch on his left. He wiggled the fittings and repeated his radio call.

"Angel Four," Ryan replied.

Seth breathed a sigh of relief as the remaining six SEALs checked in, then he flipped down a compact workstation on his chest rig, containing a compass, a Garmin GPS unit, and a smartphone loaded with ATAK—Android Team Awareness Kit. The miniature moving map immediately showed his position in relation to the others and their planned flight path. He made a subtle correction to his heading and steered toward the correct dark spot of land.

Their MS-360 canopies gave them an approximate three-to-one glide ratio and roughly twenty knots of forward speed. Adding to that an average of sixty knots of wind from the HARP to the DZ meant that the SEALs were flying under canopy with a ground speed of almost ninety miles per hour.

Seth lowered his QTNVGs—quad tube night vision goggles— before looking over his shoulder at the other SEALs stacked up behind him. They were nothing more than shadows in the night sky. Mere whispers in the wind blowing ashore.

He glanced down at his ATAK, made another minor adjustment to his chute to steer toward the prebriefed waypoint, then looked up and spotted an IR pointer circling the drop zone.

"There's Dragonfly," he said.

A series of mic *clicks* let him know his teammates also saw the U-28's mark. It comforted him to know he and the seven other SEALs wouldn't be completely alone. Even if the Draco remained across the border in Iraq, he knew it would keep its sensor trained on the patch of darkness southeast of Ahvaz as they made their approach.

The IR pointer suddenly shifted into a lazy figure-eight pattern, then steadied up on the center of the drop zone and flashed a pat-terned sequence of two short and one long.

No resistance expected. Continue.

"Setting condition alpha one," Seth said.

More mic *clicks*.

He glanced down at his ATAK again and noted their ground speed. The conditions were ideal for landing at the designated drop zone after traveling just over forty miles under canopy, but he knew the real work wouldn't begin until they were safely on the ground. Despite the dangers of the HAHO insertion, the real dangers waited beneath them in the Islamic Republic of Iran.

TWENTY-EIGHT

For easily the hundredth time that night, Foster glanced at his Tudor Submariner and mentally calculated how much longer he had before he needed to get Volkov into the Toyota Hilux and make the sixty-mile drive to the Dehdez. In his mind, he could clearly see the SEALs loading up into the back of the MC-130W Combat Spear at Al Dhafra Air Base in Abu Dhabi. He could feel the bone-chilling cold as the cargo plane depressurized and the ramp opened to the night air, thirty-five thousand feet above the Persian Gulf.

"I am honored you asked me to join you on your first hunt," a voice said, bringing Foster's focus back to the present.

He turned and looked at Volkov, who smiled as he surveyed the gathering of villagers, there to celebrate Shinar Outfitters' inaugural hunt for Isfahan mouflon. Foster studied the darkness beyond the Russian, looking for the two men who had accompanied him on the hunt. If not for them and what Foster knew he needed to do later that evening, he would have been blown away by the hospitality of the people who welcomed them into their homes—even if just for the night or three days of the hunt.

"I'm glad you accepted my invitation," Foster said, though his mind was already mulling over how he was going to broach the subject that would either make or break the entire operation.

The big Russian placed a heavy hand on Foster's shoulder and squeezed. "One day, you must allow me to return the favor and take you hunting in Russia. We have seven subspecies of snow sheep, four of brown bear, four of moose, three of Caucasian tur, wolverine, deer, and ibex. There are more big game in Russia than any other country in the northern hemisphere." He fixed Foster with a gaze and lifted his chin slightly to expose his deep Russian pride.

Foster nodded and took a sip of his tea, feeling increasingly anxious at being so close to a man he considered a murderer. "I would like that very much, Oleg."

Volkov removed his hand and slapped Foster on the back, and the two men fell into a comfortable silence. Foster knew this was the moment he had been waiting for, but he still wasn't sure if the Russian would even go along with the ruse. Or, if he did, whether he would be able to separate him from his bodyguards.

Here goes nothing, he thought.

As Volkov shifted his weight and prepared to wade back into the celebration, Foster leaned in close and spoke quickly in a hushed tone. "How would you feel about doing something a little . . ." He paused for dramatic effect but also because he knew there was no coming back from what he said next. *"Illegal?"*

The Russian froze and slowly turned to appraise Foster with narrowed eyes. They stared at each other in silence, the faint flicker of light from the celebratory fire dancing across their faces and masking their thoughts with shifting shadows. As the moment drew out from ten heartbeats to twenty, Foster worried he had made a grave mistake in believing the intelligence that said Volkov's proclivities leaned toward hunting endangered species or that the Russian would be open to such a proposition.

"What did you have in mind?"

Foster felt himself deflate with relief, but he forced a smile onto his face. "I have a connection in the Dehdez," he said, setting the bait.

Volkov's eyes twinkled in the firelight as he considered what that meant. "Armenian mouflon?"

Foster nodded.

"There are others who can take me," Volkov said. His eyes scanned over the flickering fire, darting from shadow to shadow as if searching for a trap.

Foster suspected he was actually looking for his keepers and knew the statement was intended to draw out more information without committing him to doing something that would land him in hot water with the Iranian government. Volkov was right that there were other outfitters who had been given permission to hunt in the Zagros Mountains, so Foster knew the attraction would be less about the species and more about Volkov's tendency to operate beyond the limits of what he was permitted to do.

"Tonight?" Foster asked.

Again, the Russian said nothing and only stared at Foster as if trying to decide why the American would risk something so brazen when they already had a hunt organized in the Tangé-Sey-yed. The Armenian mouflon was no greater a trophy than the Isfahan mouflon. Only the prospect of doing something without the regime's express permission set the two apart.

"Are you sure that is only tea?" Volkov said at last, gesturing to the cup in Foster's hand. "Maybe you found yourself a little of my Russian vodka?"

Foster pressed harder. "I won't have the chance again, Oleg.

The government won't give me permission to hunt in the Zagros Mountains, but my driver has arranged for a local guide to take us there tonight."

Volkov gestured to the celebration and the game warden who eyed them suspiciously from across the gathering. "What of them? Won't they notice us missing?"

He felt a tinge of excitement that the Russian was coming around to the idea, and he pressed his advantage. "The guides have been paid to look the other way."

"And the game warden?"

Foster grinned. "Also in my pocket."

Volkov threw his head back and laughed with such exuberance Foster almost thought it was forced. He smiled nervously as he waited for the Russian's fit of laughter to subside.

"You continue to surprise me, my friend," Volkov said, placing a thick arm around Foster's shoulders and pulling him in close. "But no. Let us enjoy the evening, retire early, and wake up refreshed. There will be opportunity for your *extracurricular* activities another time."

Before Foster could argue, Volkov released him and walked back toward the gathering with a smile on his face.

Well, that changes things . . .

~

AHVAZ, IRAN

Seth made several more adjustments to their flight path and guided his team of SEALs toward the spot of land on the outskirts of Ahvaz. The U-28A Draco continued to illuminate the drop zone at regular intervals, giving the operators a visual reference point on the ground to correlate with the ATAK units on their chest rigs.

The infrared pointer again shifted into a lazy figure-eight pattern before centering on the drop zone and flashing a new patterned sequence of four long and four short bursts.

Happy hunting.

"Drop zone clear," Seth said. He had been told a trusted local national would be waiting for them at the drop zone, and confirmation from the surveillance aircraft's infrared sensor helped ease his concerns.

Despite the thick layers of clothing he wore to combat the extreme cold, his fingers and toes were numb. Even as they descended into denser and warmer air, he knew it would take a while once on the ground to regain the full use of his extremities. Regardless, he wiggled his toes and clenched and unclenched his hands to keep the blood flowing as much as possible.

A little over thirty minutes after exiting the Combat Spear, they reached the holding area at two thousand feet over the isolated compound on the outskirts of Ahvaz. Seth and the formation of SEALs circled the spot on the ground where the Draco had indicated they were to land, looking for the ground markings that their local national asset was to set up for them. In addition to indicating the wind heading, the markings provided authentication in the form of an infrared beacon with a programmed sequence of lights.

Two short and one long indicates the drop zone is not compromised.

Craning his neck to look down at the ground where they were supposed to land, Seth spotted the red and green lights arranged in a line with the red light into the wind. He looked ninety degrees from the windward light source, trying to spot the authentication beacon.

But it wasn't there.

He had a choice to make. He could take the Draco's assessment at face value and continue the landing. Or he could abort and proceed to the alternate drop zone. There were additional risks with that—especially to their safety, since the alternate site hadn't been prepared for a parachute landing—but it gave them a better chance of retaining the element of surprise.

If he continued to the primary drop zone and the Draco's sensor hadn't detected a team of Quds Force operators waiting in hiding for them, they would literally be flying into a trap.

One short and two long means the drop zone is compromised.

Still nothing.

He was running out of time and altitude to decide. If they continued circling in holding, they wouldn't have enough altitude to make a turn back to the alternate location.

Come on, come on, he thought, praying for the local national to come through and set out the authentication signal. But after several more ticks of the second hand, he rolled the dice. At one thousand feet over the ground, he banked his chute to the east to fly the downwind leg to the primary drop zone.

"Making my approach," Seth said, letting the others behind him know he had made the decision. If any of them disagreed with it, they didn't voice their concerns—a series of *clicks* let him know the other SEALs understood. They were all flying on faith.

With hundreds of jumps under his belt, Seth felt the chute almost like an extension of his body, and he felt the wind shift as he turned through north at six hundred feet. Though the winds weren't as strong at their lower altitude, he still knew he had cut it close. At three hundred feet over the ground, he turned into the wind on his final leg and released his combat equipment to dangle beneath him on an eight-foot tether.

He made minor adjustments to the toggles on his risers, expertly shaping his parachute the way a bird shapes its wings to harness the wind's invisible and subtle currents and eddies. At ten feet over the ground, he brought the toggles to shoulder height and planed the canopy in the initial flare. He felt slack in the tether underneath him as his combat equipment hit, then he brought his toggles all the way down when he was three feet off the ground. Within seconds, his boots were the first to set down on Persian soil.

He vowed they would be the last to leave it.

"Angel Six at DZ Gabriel," he said in a whisper, then scrambled to gather his chute and move clear of the drop zone as the remaining SEALs touched down in silence around him. Seth brought up his suppressed AKS-74U and turned on the ZenitCo Perst-4 infrared laser as he sighted through the darkness at the compound less than one hundred yards to the north. The weapons and ammunition they used for the operation had been recovered in Afghanistan and gave the US government plausible deniability.

"Angel Six, this is Dragonfly. Single heat signature is mobile and headed your way."

Seth listened to the soft footfalls of the remaining SEALs touching down on the arid soil behind him, and he lowered himself to the ground as he traced the outline of the compound with the laser's sharp point. A second laser joined in as another SEAL brought his weapon up in preparation to engage whoever was making their way toward the drop zone from the compound.

Suddenly, a shadow appeared from a doorway on the western side of the compound. Both lasers shifted instantly and centered on the figure's torso.

"Hold fast," Seth whispered.

A light flashed in a sequenced pattern.

Two short. One long.

Seth exhaled when he recognized the authentication code he had expected. "Friendly," he whispered. "Advocate, Angel Six has made contact with Dobiel."

TWENTY-NINE

SETH REMAINED STILL AS HE WAITED for the rest of his team to collapse their chutes and come online with their weapons aimed at the compound. Through his QTNVGs, he watched each of their infrared lasers turn on and shift toward the single shadow in the doorway, then he moved his thumb to the pressure switch connected to the weapon light mounted on the Russian carbine's rail.

"Flash," he whispered, letting the others know he was about to damage their night vision. Then he pressed on the rubberized switch and shot a narrow two-hundred-lumen beam of white light at the shadow.

The target responded with two flashes of an infrared light.

"That's our guy," Seth said, rising out of the dirt and making his way across the open ground to the compound. "But keep your heads on a swivel. Remember, guys, we're all alone out here and sixty-plus klicks from the border."

"On your six, Six," Ryan replied, letting Seth know he wasn't alone as he advanced.

"Angel Five, moving left," Hunter said, leading Hayden wide to the west as they moved in on the compound.

"Angel Seven, moving right," Tre responded. He and Will would advance from the east and provide security on the team's right flank.

"Angels Eight and Nine on overwatch," Dennis said, letting the others know he and Desobry would give them sniper cover.

While the SEALs to Seth's left and right scanned their sectors of responsibility, he and Ryan kept their IR lasers trained on the shadow as it emerged from the darkened doorway and walked slowly into the field to meet them. When they were barely twenty yards away, he and Ryan stopped.

"Balak," Seth said, freezing the shadow in its place.

"Balaam."

Seth instantly relaxed at hearing the correct response to the challenge statement and lowered his rifle. *"Salaam alaykum."*

"Wa-alaykum-salaam," the shadow replied.

"You must be Dobiel," Seth said, using the code name they had assigned to their Iranian contact.

"I am Reza."

Seth advanced and shook the young Persian's hand. "You were supposed to set the authentication signal on the drop zone, Reza."

"I'm sorry. I've never done this before." His voice had a slight tremor to it.

Seth knew it was probably the most dangerous thing the young man had ever done. "It's okay. You remembered. That's all that matters." Then he pressed on the push-to-talk to transmit to the rest of the team. "It's clear. Bring it in."

As shadows emerged from the surrounding darkness, Seth felt a sense of calm for the first time that night. The nerves he had felt before leaving the MC-130W were gone. All that remained was to climb into the back of a truck and drive eighty miles through the desert and bag a Russian arms dealer. From there, they would make for the coast and egress from the Islamic Republic before the sun came up or anybody even knew they were there. Piece of cake.

"There's a problem," Reza blurted.

And, just like that, the nerves were back.

~

TANGÉ-SEY-YED, IRAN

Foster spent the rest of the evening trying to look like he was enjoying himself, despite agonizing over the operation that had gone horribly off the tracks before the assault team even set foot on Iranian soil. He had managed to sneak away and send a coded and encrypted message to Reza, letting him know he had been unsuccessful in convincing Volkov to accompany him to the Dehdez. But by the time the welcome party wound down, he was still no closer to figuring out how to get the Russian somewhere they could grab him.

"You should get some sleep, Mr. Foster," his guide said. "Morning come early."

Foster nodded and broke away from the remaining villagers, yawning but too wired to sleep. Their other guide and the game warden—both of whom Reza knew personally—had already retired and left Foster alone with his thoughts and worries. He was satisfied Reza had received the message and would keep the assault team hidden, but Volkov was a bit of a wild card, and he didn't know how to direct the team.

Will he return to Isfahan? Najaf-Aabad? Tehran?

Does he only have two bodyguards? Or more?

He slipped inside the guesthouse and found a mattress set on the floor for him in the corner of the room. It was very similar in style and construction to the home where he had stayed in Kond-Olya, but the walls felt as if they were closing in around him—squeezing him deeper into the corner and pressing him down onto the mattress. He tried the box breathing technique but still felt his heart rate and blood pressure elevated beyond what he suspected was healthy.

Come on, Foster. Think!

He closed his eyes and inhaled slowly through his nose as he pictured the assault team arriving in Ahvaz without a clear target to move on. He tried putting himself in their shoes and felt the frustration at having completed one of the most dangerous clandestine infiltrations in command history only to come to a screeching halt at the drop zone.

Failure is not an option. There is always a way.

He listened to the snoring of the men surrounding him in the room, then slipped his burner phone from his pants pocket and opened the Signal app to compose another message to Reza. It was no use trying to pretend he could salvage the original plan, and he made the decision to shift to the alternate. It brought additional risks he was loath to accept, but he didn't have much of a choice. If he wanted to complete his mission and bring Volkov to justice, it was the *only* choice.

Fortune favors the bold.

He sent the message, replaced his phone, then resumed his box breathing and said a short prayer for God's hand over the coming events. He had to salvage at least a few hours of sleep before Shinar Outfitters' first hunt in the Islamic Republic of Iran. Whether or not the operation had been botched, he still had an obligation to preserve his cover.

~

AHVAZ, IRAN

"Isfahan?" Seth stared at the young Persian in disbelief and shook his head. "No way."

"It's the *only* way," Reza said.

"It's too far," he replied, still shaking his head at the suggestion that instead of making the eighty-mile drive to the Dehdez Protected Area, they would travel more than double that distance to reach Isfahan. "Much too far."

"The Russian will not be in the Dehdez, and he is too protected in the Tangé-Sey-yed," Reza said, then repeated his assessment. "This is the only way."

Seth stood from where they had been squatting in a courtyard just inside the compound's thick walls. "Then find us another way. Because I am not about to order my men to climb into the back of a pickup truck and drive one hundred and ninety miles through the desert."

He had been on botched operations before—the failed mission to capture SANFORD in Somalia his most recent. This one was so far outside their parameters, he wasn't sure he could chance it. But he also knew a member of their task force had been living in Iran for weeks to prepare for this operation, and he knew that person wouldn't have suggested they travel to Isfahan if there was any other way.

"We have a safe house in Isfahan," Reza said, continuing his efforts to convince the team leader. "If we leave now, we can reach it well before the sun comes up."

"What about patrols?" Seth asked. As it was, he was uncomfortable remaining stationary inside the compound. He didn't like the idea of traveling almost two hundred miles without air cover or a QRF ready to come to their aid if they found themselves in a firefight.

But Reza didn't seem worried at all. "If we leave now, we won't encounter any. We are far from the border and won't pass through any checkpoints."

Seth was inherently skeptical of strangers. But he had to place his faith somewhere.

"It is safe," Reza said. "Follow me."

Seth turned to his fellow SEALs—hardened warriors who had

been through hell with him—and knew what they would say if he asked. To a man, they would agree to do whatever it took to complete their mission. But he wouldn't ask. He was their team leader, and the burden fell to him.

"Okay," he said at last.

Reza's shoulders relaxed and a broad smile appeared on his face.

THIRTY

Three days later, Foster received a single message from Reza, confirming the assault team had agreed to travel to Isfahan and delay the operation until the target was in place. He returned from the Tangé-Sey-yed with mixed emotions, relieved the mission would continue but anxious that he was no closer to having a concrete plan for their egress.

He was lost in thought as he exited the paved highway and navigated the pickup truck to the Shinar Outfitters warehouse on the outskirts of the city. The hunt had been successful, and he'd managed to guide Volkov onto a mature mouflon, but he was still focused on the logistics surrounding the operation. Even the thrill of the kill was muted by the oppressive weight of responsibility.

Leaving the Tangé-Sey-yed, Volkov returned to his residence in Isfahan, unaware that a team of Navy SEALs had also arrived in the city for their own hunt. Despite the presence of bodyguards—the number of which was still an unknown variable—Foster knew the takedown would go off without a hitch. What happened after was still the unknown he was uncomfortable with.

I need to talk to Duncan, he thought.

Foster pulled the pickup truck into the short driveway in front of the warehouse. Leaving the engine running, he jumped out and opened the garage door so he could park inside, beyond the prying eyes of his neighbors.

"So this is where you ran off to," a voice said.

Foster froze.

The garage was dark, but his eyes quickly adjusted. Without moving, Foster swiftly took stock of his surroundings and recognized the shadows moving on either side of the door's opening. Men with guns. But not pointed at him.

"Seth?"

"Pull the truck inside first."

Foster didn't bother nodding. He knew better than to act as if he had been talking with someone and nonchalantly returned to the truck. In truth, the knot of anxiety in his chest seemed to ease up as he recognized that his team had arrived. There were those who felt comforted by the presence of Navy SEALs and those who feared them.

Foster was among the former.

He pulled the truck into the warehouse and closed the door behind him. Turning around, he was surprised to see his former teammates staring back at him with a myriad of expressions on their faces—most some variation of shock.

"I thought you went back to the Corps without saying goodbye," Seth said.

Foster knew it was an admonishment of sorts—that he had been hurt when Foster disappeared from the Dam Neck compound. "Sorry. I think that was the skipper's plan."

"Doug?" Seth asked, referring to their squadron commander.

Foster shook his head. "Captain Cross."

"What squadron are you in?"

Foster glanced from Seth to the others, then gestured for them to follow him. "Let's go upstairs and have some tea."

"Tea?" Seth said with a touch of frustration. "You can't be serious, Foster. Where have you been?"

Foster stared at the SEAL officer. "What do you mean?"

"I mean, we did a HAHO infil three nights ago, and you pop up out of the blue and stroll in acting like this is normal?"

Foster had never considered how the change in the operational plan might affect them. As he looked at the long-haired and bearded SEALs encircling him, he noticed they were all on edge. Life in Isfahan had almost become normal to him after slowly embedding himself into the culture, but to the others, they were still in the middle of hostile territory.

"Let's go upstairs. We can talk there."

Seth moved out of his way, and Foster walked to the stairs at the rear of the warehouse as if he owned the place. Because he did.

Opening the door to the one-bedroom flat, Foster came face-to-face with Reza. The young Iranian smiled broadly, showing his relief that Foster had returned. "How was the hunt, Agha Foster?"

"It was good, my friend. The customer came away with a new skull mount."

"Skull mount?" Seth said behind him. "You were out hunting?"

Inhale: one . . . two . . . three . . . four.

Hold: one . . . two . . . three . . . four.

He understood Seth's confusion. While they had been hurtling toward the earth at terminal velocity, he had been enjoying the hospitality of the locals in the Tangé-Sey-yed. And while they had hidden themselves in the back of Reza's truck to sneak into Isfahan, he had been preparing to hunt mouflon with wealthy clientele.

Exhale: one . . . two . . . three . . . four.

"It's part of my cover," Foster said.

"Your cover," Seth repeated.

He nodded. "I run a hunting outfitter that just received permission from the Iranian government to hunt Isfahan mouflon."

Seth's face turned red. "And you thought preserving your cover the night of the operation was more important than getting Volkov to the Dehdez?"

Inhale: one . . . two . . .

No.

Foster might not be an assaulter with the command any longer. He might not even be a Force Recon Marine. But the blood of those who came before him still flowed in his veins. He looked from Seth to the other SEALs—all men he had been in combat with before— and saw the same questioning looks. He might not be a member of the assault force, but he was still a member of the team.

"I was hunting *with* Volkov."

"Start from the beginning," Seth said.

Recognizing that Seth and the other SEALs were uninterested in tea, Foster gestured for them to take a seat. He lowered himself onto the rug covering the tiled floor and waited until Seth joined him before beginning. "Want the short version or the long one?"

"Let's start with the short."

"When I got home from Somalia, I learned Robert James had been killed."

"I heard," the SEAL said. "He was a good one."

"He was." Foster swallowed. "After his funeral, Captain Cross called me in and told me that Robert had been killed while conducting Advanced Force Operations here in Iran."

"Looking for Volkov?"

He nodded. "He asked me to take his place, and I accepted. I've been here since the middle of September, setting up this outfitter with the goal of getting close to Volkov."

"Sounds like you succeeded," Seth said, though Foster couldn't tell if it was genuine admiration or a passive-aggressive way of reminding him he had been hunting while the operation went to hell in a handbasket. "Why the rush?"

"That was the captain's call, not mine. Apparently intel reports suggested Putin was recalling Volkov to Moscow."

"When?"

"We never learned, but Captain Cross didn't want to miss out on the opportunity."

"But he's still in country?"

Foster smiled. "He's here in Isfahan."

Seth looked up at Hunter—his assistant team leader and senior enlisted on the team. "What are we waiting for, then? Let's go over there and snatch him up and get the hell out of Dodge."

Foster understood his eagerness. If he had parachuted deep behind enemy lines and been forced to hole up for three days, he'd be just as eager to complete the mission and beat feet for the ocean. But Seth didn't know what Foster knew, and Foster wasn't looking forward to telling him.

"It's not quite that simple," he said.

The SEAL furrowed his brow as he studied his former teammate. "Explain."

"The operation was rushed . . ."

"Yeah, we know that much."

Foster took a deep breath before breaking the news. "We don't have a solid egress plan yet."

If not for the fact that the room was sweltering, Foster would have felt the chill in the air as his former teammates learned that they had completed a dangerous HAHO insertion into the Islamic Republic of Iran without any means of leaving the country.

"Did the command know?"

Foster locked eyes with Seth and saw the look of betrayal on his face. He nodded.

With a disgusted grunt, Seth pushed himself off the floor and walked away. Foster watched him pace along the back wall, then turned to look at Hunter. "I told Captain Cross to delay the operation."

Hunter nodded. "It's okay, Foster. I know you did your best."

Again, he felt like the comment was a double-edged sword, intended to both compliment and criticize his performance in preparing for the operation. Maybe he was being overly sensitive, but he couldn't help feeling like an outsider who had let the entire team down.

"I'm sorry, guys."

Hunter waved away his apology. "It is what it is. What do we do now?"

Foster looked at the other SEALs gathered around and noticed they were all waiting on him to brief them on the plan. When he made eye contact with Desobry, the dreadlocked SEAL winked at him, letting him know they were past the point of laying blame and only wanted to get on with the mission.

Like a switch had been flipped, Foster went from being contrite and reticent to confident and focused. "First, before we move on Volkov, I need to meet with my contact in Tehran and nail down our egress plan."

Seth rejoined the group. "When you said it's not solid, what does that mean exactly?"

Foster glanced at Reza, who gave him a subtle shake of his head. "It's Jell-O."

He could tell Seth was less than pleased with his answer, but he nodded, apparently willing to give Foster at least some grace. "What else?"

"While I'm in Tehran, Reza will brief you on the intel we've collected on Volkov's residence. Unfortunately, we don't have much—outdated architectural drawings, surveillance photographs of the surrounding neighborhood, and maybe a week of detailed logs of people entering and exiting the premises. His pattern of life is erratic, but I'm confident he at least beds down there each night."

"No girlfriend?" Hunter asked.

"In Iran?" Foster chuckled. "This isn't the country for late-night trysts."

Seth kept them on topic. "Guards?"

"That's the rub," Foster replied. "We haven't seen any at his residence, but he was accompanied by two armed Russians on the hunt. I'm going to say there will be at least two—probably former Spetznaz Wagner Group mercs—on site when we make our move."

Seth and Hunter exchanged glances. "Two we can handle," the SEAL officer said. "Four, five, or six? With the jump on them, we're good. Any more, and we could end up in an all-out gunfight."

"Then let's hope it's no more than six," Foster replied.

THIRTY-ONE

TEHRAN, IRAN

Later that day, Foster parked his Toyota Hilux truck at the Parsian Azadi Hotel to begin his now-familiar surveillance detection route on foot. He hadn't spotted any vehicles following him from Isfahan, even after making several brief stops and quick route changes on the way to the hotel to be sure. By the time he crossed the pedestrian bridge, he was relatively certain he wasn't being followed, but his skin still prickled with nerves as he drew nearer to the café.

The bell on the front door tinkled when Foster walked inside. Duncan sat at his usual spot, sipping tea and reading the newspaper as if he didn't have a care in the world. He looked up when he saw Foster enter but returned to the article he was reading, barely even acknowledging his presence.

Foster was about to say something when he noticed they were not alone in the café.

"Ahhh . . . Mr. Cottle!"

He felt his stomach drop with sudden fear, but he managed to force a smile on his face as Director General Ghorbani stood and made his way across the café to greet him. "Bijan, it's so good to see you."

The two men embraced in the customary greeting, then Ghorbani gestured for Foster to join him at his table. "I heard you had your first successful hunt," the director general said.

Foster couldn't help but wonder how Ghorbani had come by that information. Reza had assured him the guides and game warden had been paid for their silence, and he didn't think it likely Volkov or his men had reported back to the Department of Environment. But he nodded anyway. "Only one customer, but it was a good experience."

"And the guides? How were they?"

So it was the guides.

A waiter appeared and Foster ordered a chai tea, using the interruption as an excuse to look back in Duncan's direction. The Brit didn't appear to pay him any attention and only folded his newspaper, drained his tea, and got up from his table to leave the café.

Foster turned back to Ghorbani. "They were very skilled. And the game warden too. We were able to get our customer within three hundred yards of a mature mouflon, which made harvesting that much easier."

The director general nodded, pleased that Foster and his company understood the intricacies of their permit. If they had only wounded an animal that could not be collected, it would have necessitated the hunt ending prematurely. So it had been in their best interest to guide their customers inside a range that was within their skill set—ensuring a clean kill. "Very good."

When Foster's chai arrived, the two men sipped their tea in silence. After several uncomfortable minutes, Foster asked, "Was there something in particular you wanted to discuss?"

Ghorbani's eyes widened in surprise. "What? No, of course not."

Foster still didn't believe it was coincidence that a representative of the Iranian government just happened to be taking his tea in the café where he met with an intelligence operative of the British government. Worst of all, he had traveled from Isfahan to Tehran by car and made his way to the café on foot, and he hadn't seen a single thing to make him think he was being watched.

That meant they were either tracking him electronically or somebody he trusted had sold him out.

But who?

"What brings you to Tehran, Mr. Cottle?"

"I had some business with the bank," he said, telling the truth. "And I really enjoy the *nān-e barbari* here. If I'm going to travel all the way from Isfahan, I might as well treat myself."

Ghorbani smiled. "Well, it's fortunate I ran into you. I was planning a trip down to Isfahan and intended to drop in and see how Shinar Outfitters is faring. Now it won't be a surprise."

It was never a good sign when someone from the government wanted to make an unannounced visit—no matter what country you were in.

"It would have been a pleasant surprise," Foster replied. "But I'm thankful for the opportunity to receive you. Do you know when you might be coming?"

Ghorbani finished his tea and wiped his mouth before answering. "I'll be there in the morning."

Ghorbani left the café a few minutes later, and Foster forced himself to order the thick flatbread to keep from bolting from the café. When he and Reza had set up the warehouse in Isfahan, they had done so knowing that an unannounced visit from the government would be likely. But that was before they welcomed eight Navy SEALs who had dropped in to capture a Russian arms dealer.

He finished his meager breakfast while his stomach slowly soured with the anxiety. It fell to him to safeguard the team of elite commandos deep inside Iran, and he still had no means of getting them out. Even if he scrubbed the entire operation, it didn't absolve him of his obligation to get his former teammates out of the country. One way or another, he needed to get them to safety before Ghorbani dropped in on them.

Foster left the café and retraced his path from the Parsian Azadi, stopping at the Bank Pasargad branch closest to the hotel. His business with the bank was one hundred percent legitimate and last on his list of priorities, but it was imperative he maintain his cover— even if he suspected Ghorbani or one of his cronies was onto him. If he had elected to bypass the bank and return to Isfahan straightaway, it would have only confirmed his guilt if somebody was watching.

And it was almost certain somebody was.

When he left the branch, Foster headed for the hotel parking lot where he had left the Toyota Hilux. He was deep in thought but still observant of his surroundings, so it wasn't that surprising when a Khodro Samand pulled alongside and stopped.

"Get in," the Brit said.

Foster didn't even bother looking around. If they were under surveillance, Duncan would have never risked it. He jumped into the passenger seat and hadn't even buckled before the Silver Fox pressed on the gas and pulled away from the curb.

"What in the bloody hell is going on?"

Foster held his hands up and shook his head. "I was just as surprised as you."

The Brit drove for several minutes, expertly navigating the streets and utilizing switchbacks and cut-throughs while searching for a surveillance team. Satisfied they were in the clear—for the time being— he pulled over and turned to face Foster. "He arrived at the café only minutes before you did. You are being followed."

Foster glanced in the side-view mirror, half expecting to see a Saipa Pride sedan filled with uniformed Security Police officers turn the corner and pull in behind them.

But they were alone.

"You can see I'm not."

Duncan reached into his pocket for what looked like an electronic cigarette and held it horizontally in front of Foster, waving it across his body. "Then you are being tracked. How else would Ghorbani know you would be there?"

"Coincidence?"

The device in Duncan's hand chirped softly, but the older intelligence operative didn't seem fazed. When he had completed running it down the length of Foster's body on one side and back up on the other, he tucked it back into his pocket. "We both know it wasn't a coincidence," he said. "But you're clean."

Foster's heart still pounded in his chest. "I'm running out of time, Duncan."

The Brit nodded. "I have arranged for a shipping container to be staged at the docks in Bandar Imam Khomeini. It will be there tomorrow night and will be loaded onto the merchant vessel *Star Helena* the following morning. The ship will depart later in the day bound for Singapore anchorage."

It was exactly what Foster had asked for, but he couldn't wait another twenty-four hours.

"It needs to be tonight."

Duncan's cheeks flushed. Foster knew the Brit had taken risks to arrange for the shipping container and even greater risks by picking him up off the street to tell him. "Impossible."

"It has to be. One way or another, the operation is going down during this period of darkness, and my men will need to be on their way out of the country by morning."

"You ask for too much, mate."

"Ghorbani told me he plans on stopping by my warehouse in Isfahan tomorrow," Foster said.

Duncan still looked frustrated but appeared at least somewhat sympathetic to his plight. Like Foster, he was often at the tail end of the whip, reacting to circumstances beyond his control. In both of their countries, politicians and senior leadership often directed actions without regard for the consequences at the tactical level, and men like Foster and Duncan were left trying to navigate the dangers.

"I'll do my best," Duncan said with a resigned sigh.

"Thank you, my friend."

"Don't thank me yet," the Brit replied as he put the Samand in gear and pulled away from the curb. "Just get the bastard."

THIRTY-TWO

That night, Foster stood in the warehouse and watched his former teammates prepare for the operation. It hadn't been that long ago that he had been among their ranks, completing a gear shakedown as they kitted up to take out one bad guy or another. It didn't matter whether it was in the mountains of Afghanistan, the Somali lowlands, or the sprawling urban maze of Iran's third-largest city.

"Alright, listen up," Seth said, taking center stage as the SEALs finished conducting checks on their gear. "Ryan and I will be in truck one with Foster. Reza will drive truck two with Hunter, Hayden, Tre, and Will." He turned to look at the snipers. "Desobry, you and Dennis will be on your own in truck three. Think you can manage driving without hitting anything?"

"Just don't slow down," Des replied.

The SEAL officer took a knee as the others gathered around the city map they had used to plan their assault. "We'll leave the warehouse and proceed to release point Omaha at this intersection here." He pointed to a spot three blocks away from the house where Volkov slept. "Truck three will move to their overwatch location, here." He pointed to a building that had a commanding view of the Russian's residence.

Desobry nodded. "We'll remain at that location until the package is secure, then proceed to route Bourbon and wait for the convoy."

"Check," Seth said. He traced a finger from the release point to the target building. "Trucks one and two will proceed directly to Tucson once overwatch is set. Foster will drop us at the back entrance while Reza takes truck two to the front."

Foster looked from Seth to the other SEALs and saw the intense focus on each of their faces. He would have given anything to be in their shoes, decked out in Arc'teryx fatigues, plate carriers and quad tubes affixed to bump helmets. He would have gladly traded in his civilian attire and commercial cover for the chance to sling a carbine over his shoulder and kick in the front door with the rest of the guys.

Seth pointed at Hunter. "Once you and your men are ready to breach, give us the count. Simultaneous entrance from the front and rear. Ryan and I will clear the first floor, while you move straight to the upstairs bedroom."

"Check," Hunter said.

"Once you have Volkov in flex-cuffs, make the call and head straight for the front door. Both trucks will converge there, and we'll load up and make our way to Bourbon for the egress."

Hunter nodded.

"Foster, how we doing on that?"

He still hadn't heard from Duncan. He gave a subtle shake of his head.

Seth pursed his lips in obvious frustration. "Roger. It changes nothing. If we have to steal a boat once we get to the port, we'll do that. First things first, though, let's nab this guy and get to the coast."

The others started trading fist bumps as they psyched themselves up for the operation.

"Foster, anything to add?"

He cleared his throat. "We know there will likely be at least two armed guards at his residence. Volkov has business dealings with several unit commanders within the IRGC, but most of them are forty-five minutes away in Najaf-Aabad. I don't expect him to have reinforcements, so we should be in and out. Five minutes tops at the objective."

"Anybody else?" Seth asked. When nobody spoke up, he stood. "Alright. Let's mount up."

An hour later, Foster sat behind the wheel of the lead truck at release point Omaha, looking through the windshield at the dark street ahead of them. Seth sat next to him, waiting to hear from the team's snipers while he cradled his suppressed carbine and bounced his knee nervously.

"What's taking so long?" Ryan asked from the rear seat.

Seth's leg stopped bouncing. "Patience, bro. We just got here."

"Yeah, three days ago."

Foster glanced up into the rearview mirror and saw Ryan wink at him, letting him know the comment was just good-natured ribbing. He grinned, enjoying the feeling of being part of the team again. Beyond the other SEAL, Foster saw the second truck parked behind them, idling in the shadows with its headlights off.

"Angel Six, Angel Eight sets overwatch this time, over."

Seth slapped his hand on the dash before replying. "Copy. Trucks one and two, proceed to Tucson, over."

"Truck two," Hunter said from the truck behind them.

Foster shifted the Hilux into gear and pulled away from the curb. Though he knew it would make them stand out if they ran into local police, he left his headlights off. They would need every bit of stealth to reach the objective without alerting Volkov or his protection detail.

"Truck one is breaking off," Seth said as Foster cranked the wheel to the right and cut over to the next block. He pressed his foot hard on the gas, keeping speed so they could arrive at the residence's rear entrance in sync with Reza and the SEALs in truck two.

"Tucson is clear," Dennis said, in a voice that rumbled like thunder.

"At the objective in three . . . two . . . one."

Foster stepped hard on the brakes, careful not to lock them up. The last thing he wanted was the squeal of brakes giving them away. Before he came to a complete stop, Seth and Ryan had their doors opened and stepped from the still-moving pickup truck as it slowed to a stop.

"Angel Six, stacking up."

Foster watched the two SEALs move swiftly to the rear door and take up position on either side. Seth turned to look at him, then made an exaggerated nod to let him know he could proceed to the front entrance and wait with Reza for the egress. Foster pressed on the gas and raced away from the darkened compound, not bothering to look in his rearview mirror at the frogmen who were preparing to make entrance.

He rounded the corner as his mental clock reached zero, knowing their actions on the objective needed to be crisp and clean if they wanted to leave Isfahan without a convoy of police vehicles or Quds Force chasing them. Fortunately, he knew there was no force more professional than the group of men who had descended on the Russian's house in the middle of the night.

"Angel Five, set," Hunter said.

"Stand by to breach," Seth replied.

"Three . . . two . . . one . . . *go!*"

Foster knew the team had to surreptitiously enter the residence to avoid alerting the local authorities. As they spun into both the front and rear entrances in a choreographed movement, the only sound Foster heard was the pounding of his heart. But if he could have heard anything else, it would have been the whisper of hardened warriors brushing against the light metal doors.

Seth led the entry through the rear door and swept into the residence with his tricked-out AKS-74U raised and prepared to neutralize any threats they encountered. He felt Ryan on his heels, turning left as he turned right, their infrared lasers sweeping the room as they each scanned their sectors.

"Clear right," Seth said.

"Clear left."

On the other side of the residence, Seth heard the metallic clapping of multiple suppressed carbines firing controlled pairs as Hunter led the main force in through the front door.

"Tango down," Hayden said.

"I've got movement upstairs," Tre added.

"Go," Hunter said.

Seth heard the pattering of feet as the SEALs at the front of the house left the foyer and made for the second floor. He had studied the residence's schematics in such detail that he could clearly picture the other men and where they were in relation to him.

"Room left," Ryan said, reminding Seth that they still needed to sweep through the bottom floor and eliminate any resistance before the main force reached Volkov.

"Go," Seth replied.

Though the QTNVGs had a wider field of view than older-model night vision goggles, he still felt a sense of tunnel vision and forced himself to continue scanning his sector as Ryan swept by him into the room on their left, his rifle up and ready. Seth pivoted and covered their six as they moved. It would only take a momentary lapse in focus for the tide to turn, and he wasn't about to let that happen.

"Clear left."

Seth spun as he crossed into the room and scanned for threats. There were none. "Clear right."

"Moving."

Ryan quickly shuffled across the main room for the second room on the first floor at the rear of the house. According to the architectural drawings, there were two identical rooms at the front of the house, and from the sound of things, Hunter and his boys had run into at least one of Volkov's men there. He had to assume the same would happen to them at the rear.

Ryan stopped just shy of the door and stood against the wall on the right side. Seth mirrored him on the left.

"Ready," Ryan said.

"Go."

The two SEALs swept in and carved the room with their lasers, scanning for threats but not seeing any.

"Clear left," Ryan said.

"Clear right."

It can't be this easy.

On the street out front, Foster pulled over to the curb on the opposite side of the street, pointed east. He looked through his side window at Reza, sitting behind the steering wheel of the second truck. The young Iranian shot him a nervous look, then resumed scanning the street to the west. There was nothing for either of them to do but sit and wait for the SEALs to frog-march Volkov through the front door.

Multiple flashes drew Foster's attention again to the large concrete structure. Their carbines were fitted with suppressors to reduce the noise and minimize muzzle flash. But even so, they were hardly quiet, and lights strobed from the upstairs windows like lightning.

"Tango down," Will said.

"Moving to primary bedroom," Hunter said, letting those listening know they were about to reach the objective.

"Angel Six, Angel Eight, you've got activity one house over to the west," one of the snipers said.

Foster turned and looked over his shoulder just as the front door of the house next to Tucson opened. Two men exited with stubby AKS-74U carbines held in tense grips, and he recognized immediately that neither had accompanied Volkov to the Tangé-Sey-yed.

"We've got company," Foster said. "Two tangos."

As he watched the two Wagner Group mercs sprint up the street toward Volkov's residence, the lead man's head snapped back, and he crumpled to the ground like a marionette whose strings had been cut. The faint echo of a gunshot followed a split second later, and Foster knew Des had just scored a direct hit when it mattered most.

"One tango down," the sniper said.

The second gunman watched his partner drop to the pavement, then quickly took cover behind a cement wall. Apparently watching the air around the other merc's head turn to pink mist was enough to make him reassess his strategy.

"No shot on tango two," Des said, letting the others know there was still one more bad guy with a gun floating around outside.

"Ninety-nine, Angel Five, jackpot. I say again, jackpot. Proceeding to exfil."

Instead of feeling relief that the main assault team had taken down Volkov, Foster felt a sudden fear that they would leave through the front door and expose themselves to fire from the second mercenary. He looked over at Reza in the second truck and saw the young

Iranian looking back at him with an expression of frozen terror on his face.

"Still one tango on the street," Des said. "Overwatch moving to route Bourbon."

"Angel Six."

Foster didn't have to think about it. He never did. He just opened the door and jumped out onto the street.

THIRTY-THREE

ARMED ONLY WITH A Russian MP-443 Grach pistol that Reza had purchased for him, Foster held the gun in a loose two-handed grip and quickly crossed the street, using Reza's truck for concealment.

"Tucson is clear," Seth said. "Making our exit in thirty seconds."

Foster took two quick breaths, then stepped out from behind the truck and raced for the cement wall. So far, the second mercenary hadn't seen him . . .

The gunman peeked his head around the corner to look toward the residence's main entrance but stopped short when he saw Foster closing on him. He lifted the AK in Foster's direction, but the former Marine was quicker. He squeezed the trigger in rapid succession, not really caring if he hit his mark.

Crack! Crack! Crack! Crack!

His rounds impacted the wall, sending shards of concrete into the air and forcing the merc to wheel away from the incoming suppressive gunfire. Foster's only goal was to keep the other man's finger off the trigger long enough so that he could make it across open ground and engage the shooter from a better angle.

But he didn't have unlimited ammunition. Unlike the SEALs, who had come loaded for bear with several spare magazines of Russian ammunition for their carbines and pistols, Foster was stuck with only seventeen rounds of 9mm ammunition. He needed to keep the gunman's head down, but he couldn't afford to waste many more rounds. He needed to make each one count.

"I'm engaging the second tango," Foster said. He knew when the team exited the residence, they would notice his empty truck and wonder.

"Exiting in three . . . two . . . one."

Foster didn't have time to look over his shoulder and watch Seth dragging Volkov down the front steps to the idling trucks. His entire focus was on the corner of the wall where he expected the gunman to appear again.

What he hadn't expected was just the muzzle of the stubby carbine poking out to spray bullets indiscriminately across the street. Foster acted on instinct alone and dove to the right, sliding across the pavement and colliding with the concrete building the SEALs had just exited.

But the gunman didn't stop there. He continued firing until Foster heard the familiar *click* of the AK running out of ammo.

"Get him to the truck," Foster shouted, then pushed himself off the ground and raced for the wall.

He skidded around the corner and saw the Russian merc completing an emergency reload, slapping backward on another thirty-round magazine. He was reaching for the charging handle to chamber a round and ready the carbine again, but Foster wasn't going to give him the chance.

He lifted his pistol and sighted in on the Russian, pressing back on the trigger before his front sight post had even settled on his target.

Click.

It was the loudest sound in the gunfight, but Foster knew he still had plenty of ammunition. He fell back on the fundamental training he'd received since day one of Marine Corps boot camp in San Diego and slapped up on the bottom of the magazine to ensure it was properly seated.

Tap.

With his left hand, Foster reached across the top of the pistol and gripped the slide, yanking it back to clear the malfunction and chamber a new round.

Rack.

But the Russian was quicker. He recognized that Foster was quickly working his way through his immediate action steps to get the malfunctioning firearm back in the fight. Abandoning his attempt to aim the AKS-74U, he lunged at Foster while using the carbine like a club, bringing it down on his outstretched pistol.

Foster tried pulling the handgun in close to his body, but he was a fraction of a second too slow. The metal frame of the stock slapped down on Foster's hand like a baton, and he lost his grip on the pistol. It clattered to the ground as Foster looked up in time to see the Russian bringing the AK to his shoulder to end the engagement.

Holding his battered hand to his chest, he lowered his shoulder and launched off the concrete at the Russian, aiming for his sternum. He was injured and unarmed, but he was far from being out of the fight.

He slammed into the Russian with a grunt, and his momentum carried the two men into the wall, but they both remained upright on their feet. Foster's focus was on the short-barreled AK still in the other man's grip. He grabbed the frame of the weapon and twisted it out of the Russian's hands, but he lost control and it clattered to the ground. His opponent quickly shifted his body weight and positioned himself to gain leverage.

Systema, Foster thought.

Though it had been months since Foster had rolled with his teammates or practiced his beloved Brazilian jiu-jitsu, he instinctively recognized the Russian martial art that traced its lineage to the Cossacks. The combat method was popular among agents of the Komitet Gosudarstvennoy Bezopasnosti, or KGB, and the Spetznaz special forces, further solidifying his assessment that the man he was grappling with was a Wagner Group merc.

"Ty umresh," the man grunted, his breath reeking of tobacco.

Foster ignored the comment as he felt the man trying to manipulate his body in a flowing circular form. He knew the Russian was working up to a takedown, and Foster wasn't planning on giving him the opportunity.

Not Systema—Sambo.

He slid his right hand high up on the man's collar, digging his thumb underneath the loose fabric while using his elbow to keep the Russian from shouldering into him. With his left, he worked his hand up above his opponent's elbow and gripped the sleeve to control his dominant hand. He was moving on instinct, and his body continued with the throw he hadn't consciously been setting up for.

Foster swung his left leg up, foot turned outward, and planted it in the Russian's stomach while rolling left and pulling him over his head. The merc landed hard on his back, but Foster wasn't done moving. The *Yoko Tomoe Nage*—a traditional Judo throw—served to disorient his opponent while allowing him the opportunity to continue from a position of strength. Foster used the Russian's collar to secure a choke, sinking it in deeper and deeper as the merc fought to escape. He clawed at Foster's eyes in a panic as he struggled to breathe, but Foster hid his face and continued the squeeze.

Six to eight seconds is all it takes.

"You done playing around?" a familiar voice asked from the shadows.

He looked up and saw Hunter staring down at him through QTNVGs with his AKS-74U aimed at the scrum. Foster felt the Russian go limp as the choke finally succeeded in starving his brain of oxygenated blood. As he released his grip and stood over his opponent, he heard Hunter's gun cough twice, and the merc's head bucked from the impact.

"Let's go," Foster said.

Hunter left Foster on the ground and sprinted to the closest Toyota Hilux. It took Foster less than a second to recognize that somebody was already behind the wheel of the truck he had abandoned to go after the Russian, and he followed the assistant team leader inside.

"What was that all about?" Seth asked once he was seated.

Ryan sat behind the wheel and stomped on the gas to follow the other pickup truck to route Bourbon. Foster knew the gunfire was sure to draw attention, and they needed to be well outside the city before the neighboring residents called it in to the police.

Or before the IRGC responded to the Russian's distress call.

"Russian mercs in the house next door," Foster said.

He felt stupid they had missed that during their surveillance of the residence, but it made sense now why they hadn't seen anyone else in the house with Volkov. Foster quickly shook away his disappointment. There would be time later to pick apart all the things he had done wrong leading up to the operation. What mattered now was getting the team safely to the shipping container in Bandar Imam Khomeini.

"All units, truck one is en route to Bourbon with Angels Six, Five, Four, and Ten," Seth said.

It didn't go unnoticed that Seth had used Foster's old call sign when alerting the others to who was in the truck. It felt good being included as a member of the team again, even if he felt a lot of guilt that things hadn't gone according to plan.

But, then again, they rarely did.

Tre's voice answered in reply. "Truck two has Angels Two, Three, Seven, and Dobiel."

"Truck three is at Bourbon with Angels Eight and Nine."

That's everyone, Foster thought.

Things might not have gone as smoothly as they had wanted, but they were still leaving with all eight SEALs, one former Force Recon Marine, and a scared Iranian.

And a Russian arms dealer.

Foster turned to look at the man with a black hood pulled over his head. Seth had his hand on the back of Volkov's head, shoving it between his knees toward the floorboard. It had taken months of training and weeks being alone in the Islamic Republic, but it had been worth it. Robert's killer was in custody and would soon be onboard a Navy ship. Mission accomplished.

"We've got company," Ryan said.

THIRTY-FOUR

THERE WERE TWO MAIN ROUTES OUT of the city that led south toward the port, and both joined up in the village of Lordegan. The western route on Highway 51 would have been faster, but it was deemed too risky as it took them closer to the militant stronghold of Najaf-Aabad. Accordingly, the convoy had dubbed Highway 65 as route Bourbon. But they weren't the only ones racing in that direction.

Foster craned his neck to look through the rear window at the flashing red lights of the green and white police car chasing them. "One hundred yards," he said, letting Ryan know they had a lead, but it was shrinking.

The SEAL pressed harder on the gas pedal in response, inching their truck closer to Reza's.

Come on, Foster urged silently. *Faster!*

Seth gripped Volkov's neck, jerked him upright, and whispered menacingly into his ear. "Who did you call?"

"Nobody, you fools," the Russian said. Even after being plucked from his bed in the middle of the night, hooded, zip-tied, and tossed into the back of a truck by a group of Navy SEALs, Volkov was defiant. "You made enough noise the entire Islamic Revolutionary Guard Corps will be after you."

Seth reached behind to grip the Russian's bound hands and lifted upward, torquing his shoulders to apply pressure and a modest amount of pain. "How many in your protection detail?"

"Two," Volkov spat.

Seth wrenched harder. "Try again. We took down that many in your house. Who were the men outside?"

Ryan jerked the wheel hard over as the truck drifted around a corner.

"What . . . men?"

Foster looked from the hooded arms dealer back to the police car. "He's gaining on us."

"Truck three, what's your status?" Ryan asked.

Seth reached over with his other hand and gripped the back of Volkov's head, pushing it down into his lap as he pulled harder on his wrists. "The Russians outside your house. The ones with bullets in their heads."

"I don't . . . know what . . ."

Foster was distracted from his answer when Desobry answered Ryan. "We're in position and ready to interdict."

Foster breathed a sigh of relief and turned back to Seth's field interrogation just as the Russian denied for a third time any knowledge of the Wagner Group mercs they had engaged outside his house. "I only had two men in the house with me. I don't know who the others were."

Foster and Seth traded glances. The men were already dead, so there was no reason for the Russian to lie. But if he was telling the truth, it meant there was someone else involved they hadn't accounted for. Foster gave Seth a subtle nod, letting him know he believed Volkov. The SEAL nodded and moved on with his questions, beginning with the ones he already knew the answers to.

"What was your purpose here in Iran?"

Volkov coughed before answering. "To purchase Shahed-136 drones and arrange for their shipment."

"To where?"

The Russian shook his head, trying his best to resist.

"We already know, Oleg," Seth said, using the Russian's first name to let him know this wasn't a random abduction. The United States of America had put Oleg Volkov in its crosshairs.

"Ukraine," Volkov said, almost spitting the name like a curse.

"Okay, Oleg. Now we're getting somewhere."

The convoy had reached a straight stretch of road, and Ryan pushed his foot into the floorboard, accelerating the pickup truck to its top speed as he passed Reza and took the lead. Foster watched the other truck drift back a conservative distance, then increase speed to keep pace as they raced for the highway.

"Route Bourbon in one minute," Ryan said.

"Overwatch set," Desobry replied.

"We're running out of time, Oleg," Seth said. "Why is Putin recalling you to Moscow?"

Volkov stiffened. "How did you . . . ?"

"I told you, Oleg. We already know. I just want to hear you say it."

The Russian's reaction was telling in more ways than one. He was obviously shocked that Seth knew something that should have been a secret. But it was more than that. There was a genuine fear that Foster wouldn't have expected from someone supposedly high up within the Wagner Group.

Is there a rift here we can exploit? Did Volkov do something to earn Putin's scorn?

Volkov shook his head. "Just shoot me. If you don't, the tsar will."

Again, Foster and Seth looked at one another. There was definitely more to the situation than they knew, and Foster was certain Seth also wondered if they were unwitting pawns in a bigger political scheme. "Why will Putin shoot you?"

He shook his head harder, then his shoulders trembled with genuine fear. "Because I failed him."

"How?"

"Thirty seconds," Ryan said.

Foster looked behind them at the green and white police car that had drifted almost two hundred yards behind Reza's truck.

"I lost the contract," Volkov said.

"What contract?"

"For the drones. I lost the contract for the drones, and someone else purchased them."

"Who?"

Volkov shook his head. "I don't know."

"Oleg . . ."

Ryan's calm voice counted down. "Bourbon in three . . . two . . . one."

"I swear *I don't know*!" Volkov shouted.

Foster squinted through the darkness at the pursuing police car, just as two simultaneous rounds from the team's snipers impacted the compact sedan. Foster couldn't see it clearly from his vantage point but knew by the way the car veered off the road and crashed into the adjacent shallow ditch that one round pierced the radiator, and the other went through the windshield and hit the driver.

"Good effects," Foster said.

"You're in the clear," Desobry's voice said, assuring them they were no longer being followed.

The tension in the car abated, but Foster was still focused on what Volkov had just told them. If he hadn't purchased the suicide drones that had been used to murder innocent civilians in Ukraine, who had?

BANDAR IMAM KHOMEINI, IRAN

The sun was already up by the time they reached the port city, and the caravan of three trucks pulled off the highway into the industrial complex where Duncan had indicated he would stage the shipping container. They parked in a remote corner of the lot and turned off their engines, sitting in silence as Foster tried again to reach the British spook.

But his call went unanswered. Again.

"We can't sit here much longer, Foster."

Volkov's head jerked up and twisted toward Seth. "Foster Cottle?"

It didn't really matter if the Russian arms dealer knew Foster had been more than a simple hunting guide. Soon, Volkov would be tucked inside a shipping container and loaded onto a merchant vessel bound for Singapore. But he would never reach the island nation. After transiting the Strait of Hormuz, an American Navy destroyer would force the *Star Helena* to heave to and prepare to be boarded.

Of course, that all assumed Duncan had been able to come through for them.

"Shut up, Oleg," Seth said, forcing Volkov's head back down between his knees.

Foster's leg bounced with nervous energy as he contemplated their predicament. The industrial complex belonging to Shell Global had been vacant in the early morning hours, but it was slowly starting to fill with roughnecks and technicians. If their trucks hadn't been spotted yet, they soon would be. And none of them wanted to be around for that.

His leg stopped bouncing when his phone rang.

"Hello?"

"You blokes sure made a mess of things," Duncan said.

"There were . . . complications."

"Are you there?"

"Just waiting on you, mate," Foster replied, letting the Brit know they had handled the *complications* and were in place.

"One of my men just delivered the container," Duncan said.

"Is he . . . ?"

"An expat?" Duncan finished for him. "Yes. He will drive your third vehicle back to Isfahan once the *cargo* has been loaded."

"I owe you," Foster said.

"Oh, I know you do."

"How do we find the right container?"

"Look for the container code. Tango charlie kilo uniform four four one two eight eight."

Foster scribbled the alpha-numeric code onto a scrap of paper. It had been years since he had participated in maritime search-and-seizure operations, but he remembered learning about container codes and what they meant. The first three letters were the owner code—in this case, *TCK* indicated the container belonged to the leasing company Triton International. The fourth letter was the equipment identifier, and the next six digits were the container's serial number.

"What's the check digit?" Foster asked.

"You've done your homework," Duncan replied. "Very good. It's two."

The seventh digit on the container was boxed and known as the *check digit*—it allowed operators, terminals, depots, and other parties in the supply chain to automatically validate the container number. Together, the four letters and seven numbers were assigned to the container by the classification agency International Standards Organization through the Bureau International des Containers, known as BIC. No two container codes were alike, and it ensured the SEALs hid in the correct one.

Most importantly, it would allow the SEALs who later boarded the *Star Helena* to let them out.

"Thank you, Duncan."

"Oliver will meet you there. Godspeed."

The line went dead and Foster looked over at Seth, who was waiting for instructions. He had been given the container number, but they still didn't know where to find it in the sea of containers already staged inside the complex.

"What are we doing, Foster?"

He took a deep breath and held it for a count of four, then held up the scrap of paper as he exhaled. "We need to find this container."

Ryan chuckled from the front seat. "We might stand out here."

"Reza and I will go look for it while you guys wait here."

"We don't have all day," Seth said.

But Foster knew they did. The container wouldn't be loaded onto the *Star Helena* until the following morning, and he couldn't help wondering how hot it would get once they were locked inside. The port city routinely peaked at over one hundred degrees, even in October, and he wasn't sure Duncan had prepared for any form of life support inside. They might wish they were still sitting in the cramped Toyota pickup trucks.

"Who's this guy?" Ryan said, directing their focus to a man crossing the lot.

He was headed directly for them.

THIRTY-FIVE

FOSTER CLIMBED FROM THE BACK SEAT without hesitation, intent on interdicting the man before he got a chance to see eight SEALs armed for war occupying the trucks. He closed the door behind him and took two steps before he recognized that Reza had followed his lead and exited his truck to join him.

"You must be Foster," the man said with a clipped Cockney accent.

"Oliver?"

"Who else knows you here?"

Between the man's accent and working-class appearance, it was unlikely he was anybody other than Duncan's man in the port facility. But Foster wasn't willing to stake his life and the lives of eight SEALs on an assumption. "What's the container's check digit?"

The man cocked his head and furrowed his brow in confusion. "What?"

"The check digit," Foster repeated. "What is it?"

"Two."

The man had a one in ten chance of getting it correct, and it wouldn't have been Foster's choice for a countersign, but it was as good as they were going to get. He took a deep breath and exhaled slowly, then nodded. "Where do we go?"

"Follow me."

Less than an hour later, three Shinar Outfitters Toyota Hilux trucks left the port city after locking eight SEALs and a Russian arms dealer inside an air-conditioned shipping container. Foster again sat behind the wheel as he followed Reza north from Bandar Imam Khomeini bound for Isfahan. Oliver brought up the rear in the third truck.

Foster was exhausted, but he replayed the previous evening's events over and over in his mind. It was true that no plan ever survived first contact, but he still couldn't help feeling responsible for how unprepared they had been. He should have seen the other Wagner Group mercs well before he committed the team to taking down Volkov in his residence, but his unease went beyond a simple failure to properly reconnoiter the target location.

Volkov had no idea who they were.

He believed the arms dealer, if for no other reason than the Russian had no cause to lie. But there was something about the way they had interacted—both in Kond-Olya and the Tángé-Sey-yed—that led Foster to believe Volkov wasn't the cold-blooded murderer he had first thought him to be. Arrogant and proud? Yes. With loose morals and a skewed sense of loyalty? Most certainly. But, in his heart, Foster didn't believe Volkov was the one who had murdered Robert James.

Then who did?

That was the question he pondered on the drive, and he thought back to his discussion with Seth after arriving at the port. They had climbed out of the truck and left Volkov bound on his side in the back seat. It was obvious to Foster the entire situation unnerved the SEAL officer.

"Volkov said he lost the contract to purchase the Shahed-136 drones from the Islamic Revolutionary Guard Corps," Seth had said. "But we have clear evidence the Russians used suicide drones to attack noncombatants in Ukraine."

"It doesn't make any sense," Foster said. "Why would Putin send him here to purchase the drones if he got them from somewhere else?"

Both men turned to look at the truck where the Russian arms dealer was bound and gagged, then Seth turned back to his former teammate. "What if he didn't?"

"Send him here?"

"Get them from somewhere else."

Foster shook his head. "Are you suggesting somebody other than Russia is using them to support Putin's illegal invasion? By killing innocent civilians?"

"Maybe," Seth said. "It's the only thing that makes sense."

"How does that make sense? Doesn't it make more sense that this is all about Putin's ego? I mean, he goes from being a KGB lieutenant colonel to the president and is the personification of Russian exceptionalism."

Seth frowned in thought. "He does remind me of Philotheus."

"Pretend I didn't go to your fancy school."

"He was a monk in the fifteen hundreds. He believed in the quasi-divine status of the Russian state and called Moscow the third Rome." Seth paused. "He once said, *Two Romes have fallen, but the third stands, and no fourth can ever be.*"

Foster wasn't big on philosophy or history, but he understood the point. "Right. So, Putin is embarrassed by his military's performance against their little brother, and using the drones was a feckless decision to salve his bruised ego. I don't see your point."

"Who else had something to gain by using the drones?"

Foster rolled his eyes. "By killing civilians? Are you listening to yourself?"

Seth held up his hands to forestall Foster's frustration. "Consider for just a moment the possible existence of a third party."

"Who?"

"To get to the *who*, we need to start with the *why*. Why would someone want to use Iranian military hardware to kill noncombatants? Why would someone want to help Russia?"

"Are they really helping?"

Seth grinned. "No. They are not."

Foster thought back to the news broadcasts he had watched at home in Virginia Beach while sipping on bourbon and brooding over his new assignment in the command. He thought about the graphic images he had seen on his television in Emory of dead bodies amongst the rubble in cities like Kharkiv, Kherson, Borodyanka, Odesa, Izium, and Kyiv. Russia's indiscriminate bombing and shelling of nonmilitary targets was a thorn in their side from a public relations standpoint.

"Bad press," Foster said. At first, he had dismissed it as a casualty of war. He believed the new tsar genuinely did not care what the world thought about him. But even he had to admit the addition of suicide drones into the equation did more to hurt Russia at home and abroad than it helped Putin's war effort.

Seth nodded. "And with bad press comes sanctions. France, Germany, Italy, Lithuania, Spain, United Kingdom, and Netherlands all impounded yachts owned by Russian oligarchs. Switzerland, who had more than eleven billion in deposits from Russian citizens, followed the European Union's sanctions and was quickly criticized by the Kremlin and dubbed an 'unfriendly nation.' Fifty-three countries closed their airspace to Russian airlines and Russian-owned private jets, and lessors of commercial jets worth over ten billion moved swiftly to repossess aircraft stranded outside Russia."

"How do you know all this?"

"Don't you read?"

Foster looked around at the industrial oil facility. "I've been a bit preoccupied, preparing for this mission."

"Fair enough," Seth said. "But *somebody* benefited. The global military-industrial complex saw a boost from the international response to Russian aggression, and the United States was the front-runner."

"So *we* used Iranian suicide drones to kill innocent civilians?"

Seth shook his head. "I'm not saying that. You and I both wear the cloth of our nation. *We* would never do something like that."

"Then who?"

"Do you know how much we spent in one year providing military aid to Ukraine?"

Foster shook his head.

"Over forty-six billion dollars."

Foster thought the number was staggering, but he remained silent as he waited for the punch line.

"And do you know what our annual expenditure was during the war in Afghanistan?"

Again, Foster shook his head.

"Forty-three billion dollars. We are still recovering from the pandemic and are facing soaring inflation, but we are spending *more* to help Ukraine defend itself from Russia than we spent fighting the Taliban and taking out the perpetrators of September eleventh?"

"But we're not the only ones helping Ukraine," Foster protested, refusing to allow himself to follow the SEAL officer down his path of logic. In his heart, he knew helping the people of Ukraine was the right thing. He almost didn't care why the United States gave so much. It was for a good cause.

"The next closest nation is Great Britain, with just over five billion dollars in aid."

"So who benefited?"

"Defense contractors," Seth said. "The big five weapons firms—Lockheed Martin, Raytheon, Boeing, Northrop Grumman, and General Dynamics—all saw their shares appreciate since the Russian invasion by an average of almost thirteen percent. Collectively, their stocks outperformed the S&P 500, the NASDAQ composite, and the Dow Jones Industrial Average."

"For them, war is good for business."

"And business is good," Seth added. "But who are their customers?"

Foster saw where the SEAL was going. "The government."

Seth nodded. "Government contracts make up the bulk of their net sales, and wealthy investors and the politicians they influence stand to gain the most."

"Even from a humanitarian, geopolitical, and economic disaster like the war in Ukraine?"

"*Especially* from that. It gives politicians the leverage they need to secure public support for military aid."

Foster couldn't help hearing Seth's words from Somalia, *power and money.* He knew the SEAL was jaded when it came to politicians and senior military leaders, but there was no denying that American defense contractors—and their investors—had made *a lot* of money from the war in Ukraine.

As Foster stared at Reza's taillights, he realized he was still no closer to figuring out who might have facilitated the transfer of the drones for use in Ukraine. He was still no closer to figuring out who had actually employed them. But the one thing he was sure of was that he had accomplished the mission his command had sent him to do.

It was time to go home.

Driving with one hand, Foster fished his cell phone out of his pocket, then opened his Onion browser and navigated to the site he used for communications with Captain Cross. Glancing up at the road every few seconds, he composed a simple message that was arguably the most important part of the entire operation.

STAR HELENA. TCKU 441288 2.

After sending the message, he set his phone down in the truck's cup holder and gripped the steering wheel with both hands. His conversation with Seth had made him uneasy about his involvement in the entire operation. He had sacrificed time with Rebecca and Haili because he believed Oleg Volkov was a threat to more than just the freedom-loving people of Ukraine. He believed in the mission—believed it was the right thing to do.

But if Volkov didn't procure the drones for Russia, who did?

He was still pondering that question when he received a message back from the command.

He read it and cursed.

THIRTY-SIX

ISFAHAN, IRAN

Several hours later, the convoy arrived at the Shinar Outfitters warehouse. They parked the trucks and, after Oliver left, began a complete sweep of the property, looking for anything Seth's team of SEALs had inadvertently left behind. But Foster's mind was elsewhere. He was preoccupied with the last message he had received from Captain Cross.

Reza took a break from scouring the warehouse and leveled Foster with a worried look. "When do you have to leave?"

"Late tonight."

"But why? We got him."

That worried Foster too. The whole purpose for coming to Iran was to establish a cover and prepare for a capture-or-kill operation to take out Oleg Volkov. And, at that moment, the Russian arms dealer was safely tucked away inside a shipping container with eight Navy SEALs looking after him. But they weren't out of the country yet, and Foster wouldn't completely relax until after the Navy boarded the merchant vessel and transferred Volkov into permanent custody.

Still, his job was done. Or so he thought.

"I don't know," Foster answered. "But my orders are clear. I need to be on a Lufthansa flight tonight leaving Tehran for Frankfurt at one forty-five a.m."

Reza leaned against the wall and crossed his arms, exhibiting a confidence that had become characteristic since returning from Abu Dhabi. After his participation in the previous night's operation, he seemed even more comfortable in the role he had taken on, and he had no problem challenging Foster on their mission.

"What exactly did the message say?" Reza asked.

Foster sighed. "It said, *You are invited to the Jagd and Angeln in Leipzig, Germany. A ticket on Lufthansa flight 601 is waiting in your name at Imam Khomeini International Airport.*"

"What is *Jagd and Angeln?*"

"It's a trade show," Foster said, thinking back to Game Fair en Loir-et-Cher, where he had met Simon Gervais and been introduced to Director General Ghorbani. "A person in my position would be expected to go."

"You mean, as owner of Shinar Outfitters?"

He nodded.

"What about in your other role?"

And that's what worried Foster the most. Unless Captain Cross had some other purpose in keeping his cover active, there was no reason for Foster Cottle to travel to Germany for a trade show. But his hands were tied. There was nothing he could do other than sanitize the warehouse and pack for the unexpected trip.

"I guess I'll find out," Foster said, putting an end to the discussion.

Reza looked like he was about to question Foster further when a loud pounding on the door facing the street cut him off. Both men turned to look at the door, then at each other.

"Who . . . ?" Then it dawned on Foster. "It's Ghorbani."

Reza's eyes grew wide as he looked up the stairs toward the one-bedroom flat they hadn't yet had a chance to clean. "What? Why?"

Foster shook his head, frustrated that in the excitement leading up to the operation, he had forgotten that the director general had invited himself to pay Shinar Outfitters a visit. "I ran into him in Tehran when I went to meet Duncan." He thought *ran into* was a favorable term, when he suspected Ghorbani had purposely sought him out. "He told me he would drop by this morning to see how we were doing."

"But the upstairs . . ."

There was a second knock at the door.

"You go and give it a quick sweep while I answer the door. I'll keep him down here as long as I can."

Reza nodded, then jogged for the stairs while Foster slowly inhaled and scanned the warehouse and the still-warm trucks. They needed to be washed, but fortunately, they hadn't sustained any damage that would make them stand out from any other car or truck in Isfahan. Especially after the shoot-out at Volkov's residence and the subsequent police chase, Foster didn't need anything setting his fleet apart.

With a long exhale, he walked to the door and opened it.

"Foster! Where you been, brother?"

His mouth fell open. "Dom?"

The easygoing Louisiana native laughed, then stepped around Foster and walked into the warehouse. "Who else would it be?"

His initial shock wore off quickly, and he scanned the street before continuing with his plan of delaying their visitor on the first floor while Reza sanitized the apartment. He cleared his throat. "I actually thought you were Director General Ghorbani."

Dom turned and gave Foster a sideways glance. "Ghorbani? Why? Were you expecting him?"

"He told me he would drop by this morning."

Dom stood in the middle of the warehouse, scanning the open space and taking in the trucks' filthy appearance. "Thought you would have cleaned up a little first. Been out scouting for places to hunt?"

"Actually, I guided my first hunt," Foster said, though he suspected Dom already knew that based on the way he didn't react to the news. "What are you doing here, Dom?"

His fellow American turned to him with a hurt expression. "Well, it's good to see you too, buddy."

Foster shook his head. "I didn't mean it like that."

"Sure."

"Sorry. I just finished a hunt and have a lot to do before . . ." He trailed off, wondering if he should even mention that he was leaving. If his paranoia surrounding Dom was even remotely warranted, the last thing he wanted was to let him know where he was going.

"Before what?"

Too late.

"Before I catch my flight."

A smile cracked on Dom's face. "Wait just a second. Are you going to Jagd and Angeln too?"

Foster tried masking his disappointment as he nodded.

"Me too, brother. Beer, schnitzels, and fräuleins," Dom said with a growing smile. "And not particularly in that order!"

LEIPZIG, GERMANY

A little before eight o'clock the next morning, the Lufthansa Embraer 190 regional jet touched down at Leipzig/Halle Airport in Saxony. Foster looked through the window at the gray-hued scene of flat and unforested land of the southern North German Plain. Compared to the hot temperatures he had experienced in Ahvaz and Isfahan, Leipzig just looked cold. Overcast skies. Dense fog bordering on mist.

"Sure beats Iran," Dom said from the seat next to him, leaning over to look through the window.

Foster nodded but couldn't bring himself to encourage the American further. After convincing Dom to leave the Shinar Outfitters warehouse in Isfahan and give him time to pack, the two had reunited late that night in the boarding queue at Imam Khomeini International Airport. They had been seated separately on the Airbus A340 to Frankfurt, but Dom had worked his charm with the customer service agent during their layover and convinced her to move him so they could sit together on the shorter flight to Leipzig.

"Don't you think?" Dom asked. His words were slurred a little—a by-product of the alcohol he had consumed freely after the jet cleared Iranian airspace.

"Will be a nice change of pace," Foster agreed. But his thoughts were on figuring out how to get free long enough to meet with Captain Cross without the other American interfering.

"What are we going to do first?"

Foster looked at his companion, unsure whether he seriously thought the two would be spending all their time together. But he was exhausted and had no problem coming up with a legitimate excuse. It was the first thing on his agenda. "I'm going to take a nap."

Dom chuckled, then fell silent as the jet taxied to the terminal. Foster leaned back in his seat and let his eyes droop closed. In his mind, he could almost imagine he was sitting in the back of an MC-130W Combat Spear as it taxied to the JSOC ramp at Camp Lemonnier, Djibouti. He could feel the team of SEALs crowding him in his webbed seat while the cargo plane jostled from side to side and rocked him gently to sleep. Even the cold steel floor of the transport plane beckoned to him as if it were a Westin Heavenly Bed with a supportive pillow top mattress wrapped in three-hundred-thread-count Egyptian cotton sheets . . .

The noise was gone.

"Foster?"

He shook his head and blinked to focus. "Yeah?"

"You with us, buddy?"

He stood from the seat and stretched. "Good to go, boss."

"Boss?" Dom laughed and slapped a meaty hand on the back of Foster's neck. "You really do need a nap. Where do you think you are?"

Reality rushed in and felt like an oppressive weight pressing down on him. It had seemed so real, but as Dom's face came into focus, Foster was reminded of one overwhelming and undeniable fact.

I'm alone.

"I'm good to go," he said.

The smirk on Dom's face said otherwise. "Uh-huh. Sure you are, buddy. Let's go get checked in."

THIRTY-SEVEN

FOSTER AND DOM SHARED A TAXI from the airport to downtown Leipzig where—to Foster's dismay—both men checked into the Seaside Park Hotel. Located on the famous Nikolaistrasse in the historic city center, the hotel boasted a unique art deco style and afforded Foster easy access to multiple discreet locations. He just needed to figure out where Captain Cross wanted to meet.

Dom accepted his room key from the front desk clerk, then turned to Foster. "You're really going to nap, aren't you?"

Foster didn't have to pretend and yawned in response. "I'm a zombie, bro."

"Well, you've got my number. Let me know when you wake up, and I'll tell you where I am." He gave Foster a mischievous grin. "Just don't expect me to do all the work finding you some female companionship."

Foster shook his head as Dom walked across the lobby to the

elevators, then he turned to the front desk clerk. He completed his check-in process—asking for a room as far from Dom Theriot's as possible—and the fräulein smiled sympathetically before handing him his room key.

"I upgraded you to a junior suite, Mr. Cottle," she said in English laced with a thick Upper Saxon accent.

"Danke," Foster said, then turned to wheel his Eberlestock duffel to the elevators where Dom had disappeared only moments earlier.

He yawned again and focused on putting one foot in front of the other, forcing himself to stay alert long enough to reach his spacious forty-square-meter room. He could already envision himself collapsing onto the bed and sleeping for several hours while he waited for the command to make contact. He just hoped he didn't sleep so hard he missed his window—if he hadn't heard from Captain Cross by the end of the day, he would be forced to spend his time with Dom.

"Foster?"

It took a second for him to recognize the voice. Foster felt like he was in a dream as he turned and saw his former teammate and CIA case officer turned congressman walking across the lobby's tiled floor.

"Luke? Is that really you?"

Luke Chapman looked resplendent, decked out in a custom-tailored charcoal suit and red power tie, but he was the last person Foster expected to see. For the briefest of moments, he actually wondered if Captain Cross had sent him to Leipzig to meet with the congressman.

But the look of surprised confusion on Luke's face wasn't faked. "What are you doing here?"

"I was going to ask you the same thing."

"I'm here to attend the Jagd and Angeln expo," Luke said. "Not that Leipzig isn't a beautiful city, but I'm assuming you came for the same reason?"

Foster nodded, uncertain how to respond. If he told Luke he had come to the trade expo as the sole proprietor of Shinar Outfitters, it would lead to questions he was unwilling or unable to answer. If he claimed to have come as Foster Quinn, he risked blowing his cover. If he tried coming up with an alternate excuse for being in the hip, modern city, Luke would quickly sniff out the lie when they bumped into each other in the exhibition hall.

So Foster did none of those and quickly redirected the conversation's focus back onto Luke. "Since when have you been a hunter?"

Luke took the bait. "I'm not, but it pays to play nicely with campaign donors."

"Like who?"

"Sturm, Ruger and Company owns the largest firearm manufacturing facility in the state, accounting for over sixty-seven percent of all guns produced in North Carolina."

Foster thought he sounded like a brochure. "So they invited you here?"

Luke nodded. "They donate to my campaign, and I score points with my constituents."

Foster thought back to his conversation with Jeff Wilson at Arlington National Cemetery as they marched behind a Cadillac hearse carrying Robert James to his final resting place. The SEAL's words echoed in his ears. *Don't you mean score points with his constituents?*

He needed to disengage before the conversation turned back onto him. "So you'll be here for a few days?"

Luke nodded, but his eyes drifted down to Foster's duffel. "Looks like you just got in. Why don't you get settled, and we can meet up for drinks tonight."

They shook hands. "Sounds like a plan, brother."

"We've got a lot to catch up on, I'm sure."

Foster pressed the elevator call button and watched Luke saunter across the lobby to speak with the front desk clerk. When the doors opened with a metallic *ding*, Foster walked inside and waited for them to close before exhaling with relief. It was one thing to have to avoid Dom over the course of the weekend. Adding in an unwitting politician who could potentially blow his cover was another—even if that politician had once lived the life.

Foster rode the elevator to his floor in silence, a confused mess of utter exhaustion and nerves. He needed that nap more than ever. When the doors opened on the quiet narrow hall, he floated across the carpet to his room. He let himself in, pushed his bag aside, and collapsed face-first on the bed.

He was asleep within seconds.

When Foster woke, it was dark outside. Not that it surprised him—he had slept less than a handful of hours in the past three days. Much of the training he had endured in the military demanded he operate at a high level with even less than that. But sleep was a foregone conclusion when you were exhausted and left alone for hours in a quiet suite.

With a groan, Foster rolled onto his back and dug around in his front pocket for his cell phone. Pulling it up to his face, he saw several missed calls and text messages from Dom.

And one from a number he didn't recognize.

He rubbed his eyes and opened the text message from the unknown number, squinting at the words and trying to decipher their meaning. But they just didn't make sense. He rubbed his eyes again and reread the message.

37:33. YOU EITHER SURF OR FIGHT. 18:30Z.

Foster tossed his phone next to him on the bed and pushed himself upright. He looked around for something he could use to orient himself in his room but saw only shadows cast onto the wall from light streaming in through his window. He spun and put his feet on the floor, resting his forearms on his knees as he yawned and fought back the fatigue that had claimed him for God only knew how long.

He looked at his cell phone resting on the bed with its cryptic message, then down to the red and gold clay beads on the bracelet Haili had made for him before he left home. Foster bit the inside of his lip as he fought back thoughts of his family, remembering all the times he had paddled through the surf on his longboard to solve one problem or another. He wished he had that luxury now.

But you're not in Virginia Beach. You're in Leipzig.

Foster scooped up the cell phone and fired back a single character in reply.

?

The phone quickly returned an error saying that the message could not be delivered.

"Great," he grunted, then stood and walked over to the window. Looking down onto the street below, Foster saw what appeared to be the normal goings-on for a Friday night in Saxony. He looked to the left and saw a faint glow on the horizon, meaning that the sun had only just set, then across an expansive park at the majestic Leipzig Hauptbahnhof, or main train station, on the other side.

He turned back to the bed and picked up his phone again. There was something about the saying that stuck out to him.

You either surf or fight . . .

He had heard it before but was too tired to place it, so he focused on the numbers. They looked like times to him, but *37:33* didn't make any sense. The second number—*18:30Z*—could mean six thirty Zulu time, also known as Coordinated Universal Time or Greenwich Mean Time.

Foster glanced at the clock on his nightstand.

8:04 p.m.

He strained to remember what time zone he was in, then felt his fatigue melt away when he realized Leipzig was two hours ahead of Greenwich Mean Time.

18:04 Zulu.

If that second number really was a time, then he was running out of it. But even if he had successfully deciphered that part of the cryptic message, the rest of it still didn't make sense. There was simply no way *37:33* could refer to a time. At least not time on a clock.

His eyes shifted between the clock on his nightstand and the cell phone on his bed. "Elapsed time, maybe. But of what?"

Foster felt like he was on the cusp of unraveling another clue, but the answer remained stubbornly out of reach. He wondered what types of things were measured in elapsed time and immediately thought back to his flight from Frankfurt to Leipzig.

Fifty-five minutes. Too long.

Then his flight from Tehran to Frankfurt.

Five and a half hours, or three hundred and thirty minutes. Way too long.

He was on the right track but measuring the wrong thing. Train ride from the airport to downtown?

Fourteen minutes. Still too short.

A song was too short, an album too long. A sitcom episode was too short, but a movie was too long . . .

A movie.

"You either surf or fight," Foster said out loud, feeling the faint glimmer of light burning just a little brighter.

He looked at the clock again.

8:11 p.m.

He was running out of time. But he knew he was on the right track. There was something about that phrase and the thought of a movie that caused his heart to beat just a little bit faster.

"You either surf or fight," he said again.

With a deep breath, Foster opened his phone and searched for the phrase. When he exhaled, he saw that his search had returned several images of a man wearing a black Stetson with a black and gold braid around its base and acorns to the front. The man wore olive-drab green fatigues and a pair of aviator sunglasses, standing tall as a Huey's blades spun over his head.

"You either surf or fight," Foster repeated for a third time, almost like a mantra. "That's it."

For most men of his generation who had gone into the military, certain movies were almost required viewing. *Full Metal Jacket, Hamburger Hill, Heartbreak Ridge, Platoon.*

And *Apocalypse Now.*

Another glance at the clock.

8:17 p.m.

He buried his face in his hands in frustration, annoyed that he couldn't solve the riddle. As he listened to the sounds on the street beneath his room, his mind slowly replaced them with soaring music from an opera about Valkyries—music that had accompanied a swarm of helicopters flying into battle in the 1979 epic war film directed by Francis Ford Coppola.

"Ride of the Valkyries."

Foster knew Valkyries were figures in Norse mythology who carried half of the warriors slain in battle to Valhalla. But it wasn't the thought of a mythical afterlife that had taken root in his consciousness.

It was the opera.

Reaching for his phone again, he performed a quick internet search for the song now blaring in his mind. He clicked on the first link that appeared and slowly stood from his bed when he came to the section on its composer, Richard Wagner.

Richard Wagner was born to an ethnic German family in Leipzig . . .

His heart pounded faster, and he hurried to scan the rest of the article, stopping short when he came to a list of historical sites related to Wagner in Leipzig. He read about a plaque located on the side of a modern shopping complex commemorating his place of birth near Bruehl. In the same area, there was also a statue of the young composer standing in the shadow of a large student dormitory.

But it was the statue located in Oberer Park, in front of the Leipzig Opera House, that caught Foster's attention. It was less than a five-minute walk from his hotel.

He glanced at the clock one last time—*8:26 p.m.*—then bolted from his room.

THIRTY-EIGHT

FOSTER CROSSED GOETHESTRASSE and entered the park from Brühl. The Vienna House hotel—the one-time home of some of the world's most talented musicians—sat over his left shoulder as he reached the walking path and turned right toward the opera house. Despite feeling rushed, Foster forced himself to slow down and remember what he had learned during his countersurveillance training. He might not have had the luxury of completing a full surveillance detection route, but he could still be alert for somebody following him.

When the statue of Richard Wagner came into view, his heart skipped a beat as he realized there was nobody there waiting for him.

Am I too late?

As if in answer to his question, his phone vibrated. He slipped it out of his pocket and read the text message.

LUDWIG.

Unlike the previous message, it wasn't a complex riddle he needed to solve. But he understood its significance. He might not have had the luxury of taking a circuitous route to the statue to check for the presence of a surveillance team, but that didn't mean whoever he was meeting hadn't taken precautions. Giving Foster a second location gave a surveillance detection team the opportunity to ensure he wasn't being followed.

Foster continued walking to the statue of Richard Wagner and lifted his phone to take a picture, then opened his browser and searched for the name *Ludwig*.

Unsurprisingly, his search returned unhelpful results that ranged from a popular YouTuber and a drum manufacturer to a restaurant in Leavenworth, Washington. He added *Germany* to the search, but that yielded only slightly more useful results. Known as the Swan King or the Mad King, Ludwig II of Bavaria had been possessed by the idea of a holy kingdom by the grace of God, but he had no ties to Leipzig and seemed to be another dead end.

But when Foster added *Leipzig* to his search, he was rewarded with several promising hits. The first was Carl Ludwig, a physician and physiologist in the 1800s whose contributions resulted in the University of Leipzig naming their institute of physiology after him. But the second and most likely result was for a bookstore located eight minutes away in the Leipzig Hauptbahnhof.

Turning away from the statue, he walked north through Oberer Park on the opposite side of a small pond from where he had entered the green space. Up ahead, the sprawling train station rose like a giant above the park's barren trees, and it was easy to see why it was considered one of Europe's largest. He set his sights on the building's eastern south-facing entrance.

The evening air had a chill to it that Foster found invigorating after living in Iran's hot and arid climate for nearly a month. He tucked his hands in his pockets but was wide awake and alert for anybody following or paying him too much attention. By the time he reached the Osthalle, he was certain he had blended in with the local populace and was just another German out for an evening stroll.

Foster entered the building and passed a bank of lockers on his left before climbing the wide steps to the concourse on the upper floor. During the Second World War, the train station had been targeted by Allied bombers and the roof over the concourse had collapsed, but it had been rebuilt in a manner that blended modern convenience with old-world architecture. At the top of the stairs, Foster turned left underneath a towering stone arch and made for the bookstore.

The station's nineteen train platforms were to his right, and the concourse buzzed with activity that was normal for a European transportation hub. Foster made for the blue *Ludwig* signs and ducked into the bookstore with soaring ceilings and ornate stained-glass skylight, his eyes scanning its patrons for a familiar face.

"You're late," a voice said.

Foster didn't react but paused at the display of magazines, picking one to thumb through. "It's been a rough few days. Cut me some slack."

Captain Cross stepped out from behind a rack of books and fixed Foster with his gray eyes. "Let's take a walk."

If Foster had been expecting some measure of gratitude for his role in capturing Oleg Volkov, the senior SEAL officer aimed to disappoint. Captain Cross left the bookstore without another word, and Foster hurried to catch up. He already had enough on his plate to worry about with both Dom and Luke vying for his time in Leipzig. He didn't need any added stress.

"Did we get him?" Foster asked when he pulled even with the Navy captain.

The captain grunted in response, and Foster suspected he wanted to wait until they had reached a more secluded location before getting into details. But locations like that were hard to come by in the busy train station—even at that late hour. The older SEAL settled against a glass railing looking down on the concourse's lower level.

"The USS *Delbert D. Black* boarded the *Star Helena* this afternoon," Captain Cross said. "The naval boarding party returned to the *Black* with Oleg Volkov in custody."

"So it's over," Foster said, already feeling the siren's call of home.

"Not quite."

Foster turned to the senior officer and bit his lip hard to keep from saying something he might later regret. Even though he had suspected as much, hearing that the command intended to keep his cover active was a punch to the gut. "Excuse me?"

"Our latest intelligence suggests that Volkov wasn't the person responsible for transferring the weapons from Iran."

Foster recalled his conversation with Seth in Bandar Imam Khomeini while they waited to stuff the Russian arms dealer into a shipping container. "Yeah, after initial questioning, that was our assessment too."

"So what the hell happened?"

It felt like a slap in the face. After everything he had sacrificed for this mission, he was surprised the task force commander had flown across the Atlantic to criticize his execution of the operation. "What happened is we got the bastard you sent me to get. Even after you rushed the mission before we were ready."

The captain's face turned red, and Foster knew he had pushed back a little too hard. Though he was no longer a Marine, he still fell under a clear chain of command, and his comment bordered on insubordination.

"Take it easy, Foster. I'm not criticizing your execution . . ."

"Sounds like it."

"Seth's after-action report indicated there were additional Russian mercenaries not part of Volkov's protection detail," the captain said. "Any idea who they were? Or why they were there?"

Foster shook his head, still bothered that both he and Reza had missed the mercenaries during their surveillance of Volkov's residence. "Based on what we learned from Volkov, I think he had fallen out of favor with Putin, and the Russian president had someone else procure the drones from Iran."

Captain Cross pursed his lips. "What if it wasn't Putin?"

It was too close to what Seth had said about the war in Ukraine, but it just didn't add up. "Those guys were definitely Russian."

"But what if the Russian president wasn't the one calling the shots?"

Foster narrowed his eyes at the SEAL captain. "What aren't you telling me?"

Captain Cross turned and leaned his back against the railing, taking the opportunity to scan the concourse for prying eyes and overeager ears. "The NSA intercepted communications between an unknown person in the Washington, DC, area and Dmitri Tarasov, a Russian with loose ties to the Wagner Group through a company in Hong Kong."

"But we don't know who's communicating with him?"

The captain shook his head. "The FBI opened an investigation, but I'm sure you can imagine the pace of that given the bureaucracy surrounding anything that takes place in the capital."

The FBI's priority in DC will be ensuring they don't dig up dirt on the wrong member of the political elite.

Foster dropped his chin in frustration at the thought of the DC warmongers who loved to profit off the blood of America's warriors. "What about Robert?"

"What about him?"

Foster looked up at the SEAL captain. "Did he die for nothing?"

Captain Cross inhaled sharply. To a combat leader, the only thing worse than losing a warrior under your charge was to lose him for nothing. Foster needed Robert's death to have meaning. If Volkov wasn't responsible, then who was? Tarasov? The person the FBI was investigating?

"The drones came from Iran. There is no arguing that. Robert put us on the right track. Now it's up to you to finish it."

It sounded like another sales pitch, but Foster didn't need to be sold. He had signed on to seek justice for his best friend's death, and he wasn't going to stop until he found it.

No matter where it took him.

"What are my orders?"

THIRTY-NINE

FOSTER RETURNED TO THE Seaside Park Hotel thinking of nothing else but flying back to Iran to hunt down Dmitri Tarasov. But if what the captain had told him was true, he knew justice wouldn't be served even then. What he needed was someone he could trust inside the Beltway to batter down bureaucracy and break through the red tape preventing the Bureau from uncovering the identity of the person who had communicated with the Wagner Group leader.

Luke Chapman was the obvious choice.

Foster stopped short from walking inside as he considered how to make it work. Maybe Luke being there was an answer to his prayers. After the expo, Foster could get on a flight back to Tehran confident that the former spy was returning to Washington, armed with the information he needed to help the FBI uncover the identity of Robert's killer.

Foster scanned the street, knowing even if he didn't see a

surveillance team, the Bundesnachrichtendienst, or BND, had probably assigned one to the congressman's delegation. Foster's cover was still intact, and the last thing he wanted to do was draw attention to himself by meeting in secret. Meeting in a public place would appear far less suspicious.

Foster walked inside and turned for the bar—a space furnished in a swanky art deco style—scanning the room for the man he suspected might be there. Most business at conferences and trade shows took place in the hotel bars after hours, and the Jagd and Angeln expo was no exception. The room was packed, but Foster couldn't see Luke anywhere.

He growled in frustration and was about to leave when he spotted the congressman sitting alone at a table overlooking Nikolaistrasse and Willy-Brandt-Platz.

Foster surreptitiously scanned the room again, trying to detect surveillance on the politician, then walked up to Luke and took a seat across from him.

"Congressman."

He didn't seem surprised by Foster's sudden appearance. "Enjoying your evening?"

The bar was crowded with several patrons enjoying late evening snacks and cocktails, but Dom wasn't one of them. Still, that didn't mean Foster wasn't worried about being overheard. He spoke softly and relied on Luke's ability to read his lips. "I'm on the job."

They locked eyes for a moment while the former intelligence officer processed what Foster had just said. Of all people, Foster knew Luke would understand the importance of maintaining his cover, so the less they talked about what he was doing in Leipzig, the better.

"Here? The Jagd and Angeln?"

Foster nodded.

"With who?"

Foster narrowed his gaze, caught off guard by the blunt question.

It had been over a year since Luke had left the Central Intelligence Agency, but he still should have known better than to ask him that. Maybe his time in the House of Representatives had made him sloppy—though Foster thought Congress was the perfect place to practice the kinds of skills taught at The Farm. "Shinar Outfitters," he said, maintaining his cover even with an old friend.

"Shinar Outfitters," Luke repeated.

Foster nodded, then shifted the focus of the conversation before Luke could ask additional questions and pry into his cover. "And just what kind of *business* is the congressman from North Carolina's ninth district conducting in Germany? Spending my tax dollars?"

Any tension that remained between the two men evaporated as Luke let out a hearty laugh. "Is that what you think of me?"

Foster grinned and pressed harder. "You know it is. I've got the number to the Government Accountability Office on speed dial, and if you don't pick up our tab, I'm going to report this trip of yours as fraud, waste, and abuse."

"That sounds like extortion."

"It is," Foster replied, deadpan. "I'm glad we understand each other."

Luke's retort fell short as the waiter appeared and took their order. Foster still hadn't had a thing to eat since leaving Frankfurt earlier that morning, but he had lived in a dry country for too long to not want a taste of home. He ordered an old-fashioned and was pleased to learn the hotel carried Blanton's. Luke ordered the bourbon on the rocks.

After the waiter disappeared to prepare their drinks, Luke leaned forward and rested both arms on the table and steepled his fingers. It reminded Foster of how Captain Cross had sat in the command conference room when he told him that Robert had died. Almost as if reading his mind, Luke said, "The last time I saw you, we were burying our brother in Arlington."

He heard Jeff's voice echoing in his ear. *He's not one of us.*

"That's why I'm here," Foster whispered.

Luke's eyes grew wide, but he maintained his posture, lording over the table. "What do you mean?"

Foster tried waving away the comment, but Luke wasn't having it. "You know, just because I'm not living in the suck or going downrange, it doesn't mean I gave up the fight."

Despite what Seth thought of politicians, Foster believed him. Even in the secretive world of special operations, he had to trust somebody. And Luke had never given him any reason to think he was anything other than a true patriot. Foster had to take a leap of faith if he was going to successfully recruit the congressman to grease the wheels of bureaucracy.

Still, he remained quiet.

"Foster."

He held up his hand, gesturing for patience as the waiter returned with their drinks. Foster let the bronze liquid linger on his tongue for just a moment, savoring the smoky flavor before swallowing and enjoying the warmth spreading outward from his gut.

He took a deep breath before speaking. "I need your help."

Over the course of the next hour and another round of drinks, Foster brought Luke in on their operation to take down the Russian arms dealer. In broad strokes, he explained how the Russian private military company had been responsible for widespread death and destruction in Ukraine.

"Ukraine?"

Foster nodded.

"But you've been in Iran?"

Again, he nodded. "On behalf of Wagner, Volkov facilitated the purchase of Iranian suicide drones. Or so we thought."

Luke looked confused. "You said you got him, but now you don't think he did it?"

Foster took another sip of his cocktail before answering. "There's no question he was responsible for bad things happening to good people—if not in Ukraine, then elsewhere. But no. There is new evidence that a man by the name of Dmitri Tarasov is responsible."

The congressman sat up taller when he heard the name.

"Know him?"

Luke nodded. "Yeah, I know him. Had some dealings with him on my last overseas assignment with the Company." Foster didn't have to ask what company—it was a common sobriquet for the CIA. "Where is he now? Still in Iran?"

"No clue." And that bothered him.

"What can I do to help?"

Despite what Jeff thought about Luke or what Seth thought about all politicians, Foster appreciated his willingness to step up to the plate. Even in a swanky bar in Leipzig, Germany—far from home and far from the fight—they were still teammates, and Luke had his back.

"The FBI is investigating someone in the DC metro area who has been speaking with Tarasov. We don't have a clear understanding of the nature of their communication, but the assumption is that they are pulling the strings."

"Wagner has somebody in the States?" Luke asked.

As hard as it was to believe that was the case, Foster admitted it was likely. "Most people think of Wagner as a large entity with a single hierarchical structure. But the truth is, it is more like an umbrella over multiple smaller companies that run independent of one another with only a loose affiliation."

"And loose legitimacy," Luke added.

"Right. That's what the FBI is looking into."

Foster let the comment hang in the air, not wanting to openly ask

Luke to intervene in an official investigation but hoping he caught the hint.

"And you want me to apply a little pressure," Luke said.

"I need your help to make sure it keeps moving forward. I don't know how much longer I can be away from Rebecca and Haili." Foster let their names tumble from his mouth before he clamped it shut, disappointed that not only had he broken cover, but he had spoken his wife's and daughter's true names out loud.

Foster saw Luke's eyes drift down to the bracelet his daughter had made for him, and he quickly hid his hand underneath the table.

"You know the Bureau is good at what it does," Luke said.

"And I know their kind doesn't trust yours," Foster said, hinting at the oftentimes overt hostility between the nation's premiere law enforcement agency and its foreign intelligence service. "But I do."

Luke took a sip of his bourbon. "Okay. I can't promise anything specific. But I can promise to look into it and make sure it doesn't get swept under the rug."

They locked eyes, and Foster nodded. "Thanks, Luke. I owe you."

FORTY

Three days later, Foster arrived in the Islamic Republic of Iran just like he had done a month earlier. As he looked out on the darkened tarmac, he had a sense of déjà vu. But this time it felt a little different. Even while waiting to speak with the officer from the Immigration and Passport Police, Foster felt more confident. He was self-assured. Relaxed.

He breezed through customs and immigration and walked outside, where Reza sat waiting in a Shinar Outfitters Toyota Hilux. Seeing the truck brought Foster back to the reality of his situation, and he hefted his rolling duffel over the side and dropped it into the back of the truck.

"Welcome back, Agha Foster," Reza said as he climbed into the front passenger seat.

He wanted to say something polite like *It's good to be back*. But it wasn't. The truth was, Foster had thought he would already be back in Virginia Beach with his wife and daughter, not back in Iran surrounded by strangers and people he couldn't trust.

"Do you want to spend the night here?"

He shook his head. "Take me to the apartment."

Reza pulled away from the curb, sharing time between looking at the dark road ahead of them and the dark mood plastered on Foster's face. "Is everything okay?"

His conversation with Luke had put him at ease that somebody was watching out for him back home, but he still felt uneasy about Dom. Though the Louisiana native had remained in Germany an extra day—supposedly to flesh out some business opportunities—Foster knew his persistent presence in Iran would only complicate the mission to hunt down Dmitri Tarasov.

"Everything is fine, Reza."

"Maybe we should stay . . ."

Foster had been so absorbed in thinking about his mission that it took him a few minutes to catch on that Reza didn't want to drive to Isfahan. He studied the young Persian and saw a worried look on his face. "Why?"

Reza shot Foster a sideways glance. "No, it's okay, Agha Foster. I'll take you."

"Is there some reason I shouldn't go to Isfahan?"

Reza chewed on his lip but shook his head. "My uncle is in town for the night . . ."

Foster felt the growing knot in his upper back release. "You want to visit family. For a minute, I thought it had something to do with the mission."

"But it does," Reza replied. "He's in town for the night before traveling to Ahvaz tomorrow."

"Ahvaz . . ." Foster finally realized Reza was talking about the uncle who had unwittingly allowed a team of Navy SEALs to use his property as a drop zone.

"I want to speak with him before he goes. I don't think we left any reason for him to suspect somebody had been to his place, but the last thing I want is for him to call the authorities if he finds something strange."

Foster nodded, appreciating the initiative the young Iranian had shown. When they first began their relationship, it had been a simple business transaction. Even as it evolved into Reza assuming more and more responsibility, it still involved him only following instructions. But following the operation to capture Volkov, Reza had taken on ownership in the overall mission. They might have had different motivations, but Reza was just as committed as Foster to its success.

"That's smart," Foster said. "We can stay here for the night."

Reza squinted through the darkness at the long stretch of road ahead of them, then shook his head. "No, it's okay. You've been gone almost a week, and I'm sure you want to get settled. I'll drop you off and come back."

Foster yawned. "Are you sure?"

"Yes, Agha Foster. It's no problem."

He nodded and closed his eyes.

～

ISFAHAN, IRAN

That night, Foster spent close to an hour unpacking and getting settled back into life in Iran. He was mentally and physically exhausted, but he couldn't bring himself to flip the switch and shut down for the night until everything was in order. Structure was the one thing that gave him comfort, and it gave him something to focus on other than being so far away from his wife and daughter.

He unbuttoned his solid blue shirt, pulled it over his head, and draped it across the back of a chair in the corner of the room. Then he kicked off his leather boots and slipped off his jeans, arranging them on the chair for easy access—a habit the Marine Corps had ingrained in him. He surveyed the cramped apartment once more, then turned out the light.

As he collapsed onto the twin bed, he took a moment to recognize that his true life had increasingly intruded on his thoughts since capturing Volkov. For whatever reason, his subconscious had decided the mission was a success and could therefore think about things that would get him killed if the Iranian government discovered his true identity. He shook away the thought, then said a variation of the same prayer he had said each night since arriving in the Islamic Republic.

Lord, as the night falls and darkness surrounds me, I come before You with a humble heart, seeking Your divine protection and guidance. I ask for Your loving presence to watch over me as I sleep. Place Your mighty angels around me to shield me from harm and danger. Please give me a restful and peaceful night's sleep, free from worries and anxieties. May I awaken refreshed and rejuvenated, ready to embrace a new day with a grateful heart. In Jesus' name I pray. Amen.

Foster felt himself sinking deeper into the mattress, but he remained awake long enough to say another prayer asking for God's protection over Rebecca and Haili while he was away. When he had finished, his fatigue overwhelmed him, and he drifted off to sleep.

Then it came.

BOOM!

He knew it was a dream, but he couldn't help it. The sound resonated through the water and seemed out of place as the pool's bottom again flattened out, but Foster just tilted his head forward and sighted in on the black line that was his goal. It had never been his ambition to break the record. He hadn't dropped into the deep end intending to go more than fifty meters. It was as if he felt a direct connection to those who came before him—to James Roosevelt and Merritt Edson, to Samuel Blair Griffith and Alan Shapley.

Foster Quinn was a Recon Marine.

I shall be the example . . .

He opened his mouth to shout in triumph as he reached the seventy-five-meter mark, but . . .

BOOM! BOOM!

He squinted with confusion, and his world went dark. He bolted upright and gasped at the booming sound still echoing in his ears. It took him a moment to remember that he wasn't in the Seaside Park Hotel in Leipzig, but in his one-bedroom flat in Isfahan. Then he remembered Reza had left and returned to Tehran. He was alone.

Just one man.

BOOM!

He swung his legs out from under the thin bedsheet and set his bare feet on the dusty floor. Even in the dead of night, the ornate ceramic tile still retained a modest amount of heat from the previous day. He wiggled his toes, almost surprised to discover its smooth touch and not the pool's rough plaster.

Groaning, he leaned forward and rested his forearms on his thighs, a thin stream of light falling on the bracelet Haili had made for him.

BOOM! BOOM!

The loud banging on the front door downstairs returned his focus wholly to the present, and he rose silently from the twin mattress and crossed quickly to the window. Pulling aside the rug he had hung in front to insulate his room from the sun's brutal rays, he peered through the dirty glass onto the street below. Two red Toyota Hilux Vigo trucks were parked directly beneath his window, and a quick scan in either direction revealed similar trucks with armed men in the back at both ends of the block.

He considered going for the hunting rifle he had locked away in a case across the room. But there were too many of them, and he was just one man. Foster's heart rate dipped as he drew a long slow breath in through his nose and held it for a beat before exhaling.

The pounding on the door resumed, and Foster resigned himself to his fate and turned for the chair in the corner. He stepped into his jeans and pinched the coin pocket's left rivet to activate a distress beacon—a precaution he had thought was unnecessary, but one he was thankful for. It would be active for an hour before self-destructing and becoming nothing more than an inert fleck of metal and silicone. He pulled the partially buttoned solid blue shirt over his head, then slipped his feet into his leather boots.

The door crashed open, and Foster slowly turned for the stairs as his heart pounded in time with the beating of feet running up the worn treads. When the first man appeared, he feigned shock and held up his hands.

"Don't shoot," he said, letting a quiver of fear break through his otherwise calm baritone voice.

The first man reached the top of the stairs and swung the butt of his rifle up into Foster's chin. His head snapped back, and he saw stars ring his vision, but he had expected the strike and had already begun moving backward to soften the blow. It still hurt like the dickens, but it hadn't knocked him out cold.

A second man reached the landing and darted around the first to grab Foster's arms and wrench them behind his back. The man was strong, but his technique was flawed. Had there not been more men scrambling up the steps in reinforcement, Foster could have broken the hold and turned the tables on his assailant.

"Why are you doing this?" Foster pleaded, letting a hint of fear and confusion intermix with genuine pain. But he knew why, and the possibility of someone coming for him had been a constant fear over the last month.

They yelled at him in Farsi, but his understanding of the language was still marginal at best, and he only caught bits and pieces of what had them worked into a frenzy. Unfortunately, he caught enough to know his fears were warranted.

"You are an American spy," a third man said in surprisingly good English. He stepped forward and placed a thick hood over Foster's head.

"What? A spy?" He shook his head against the rough burlap. "N-n-no," he stammered. "I'm just a hunter!"

"No! You are a spy!"

An invisible fist slammed into Foster's stomach, and he doubled over at the blow, despite half expecting it. The punch wasn't very well placed, and he suspected the offending wrist had probably taken the worst of it. But it still took the breath out of him.

He opened his mouth under the hood, trying in vain to inhale, but the punch had seized his diaphragm. Unseen hands gripped his upper arms and the back of his belt, lifting him slightly off the ground as they carried him to the stairs leading down into the warehouse. He shook his head and continued asserting his innocence, slowly twisting and jerking his body to resist his captors' efforts to abscond with him. He knew enough about how this usually went to abandon hope of surviving through the night.

Unless Seth got the message.

"Please," he moaned. "I'm just a hunter. I'm not here to hurt you. Please, let me go."

"Just a hunter!" the man scoffed.

Foster protested, "Call Director General Ghorbani! He'll confirm I'm only a guide—"

The man struck him in the side of the head, ending the conversation as they reached the warehouse floor. He felt the cool night air wash over him as they carried him through the front door and out onto the street, where he heard only the soft puttering of a truck's idling engine through the thick burlap over his head. He knew what was about to happen.

"You're no guide . . . *Foster Quinn*," the menacing voice said in his ear. He had the presence of mind to recognize that the man had used his real name, confirming his fears that somebody had discovered who he really was. There would be no chance of talking his way out of this.

He just needed to survive. At least long enough for Seth to send help from Abu Dhabi.

A rifle struck the back of his head, and that hope disappeared along with the world around him.

FORTY-ONE

WHEN FOSTER CAME TO, his head throbbed painfully where they had struck him. He tried lifting a hand to his temple, and a brief moment of panic ensued when he realized he couldn't. They had bound his hands behind his back—the plastic zip ties' sharp edges digging into his wrists—and he felt the presence of men on either side of him, crowding him in the truck's back seat.

"Where are you taking me?" he asked.

There wasn't much he could do with that knowledge even if they told him, but it gave him some measure of calm to remain engaged in his situation. It was the first and most important lesson they had taught him in SERE school—to be an active participant in your survival and take ownership in your situation. He didn't know how long he had been unconscious, but the knot on his temple felt fresh.

Two . . . maybe three minutes?

He knew the distress beacon had a limited battery life. The

advertised duration was one hour—which, in the world of government contracting, meant it was probably closer to thirty or forty minutes. He just hoped they reached wherever they were taking him before the beacon stopped transmitting his location. It was his only lifeline to the outside world—his only hope for rescue.

"Shut up," the man to his right growled. He reeked of body odor and stale tobacco, but unlike others Foster had encountered, he hadn't tried masking it with cologne.

The truck turned and Foster tipped into the man on the opposite side, who pushed him back upright and rewarded him with a backhand to the face. It stung and made his eyes water, but Foster had been hit in the face before. He knew he would be hit in the face again before this was over, but as long as he felt pain, it meant he was alive. It meant he was still in the fight. Even in captivity, he felt tied to his mission. For God and country, for Rebecca and Haili, and for his duty to honor Robert and the cause of freedom.

I am an American fighting in the forces that guard my country and our way of life. I am prepared to give my life in their defense.

Though he was still hooded, Foster closed his eyes and recalled the words of the Code of Conduct as he focused on his breathing. In for four seconds, hold for four, out for four seconds. Repeat. His body jostled from side to side, swaying gently with the truck's motion, and a picture formed in his mind. He saw the red Toyota Hilux pickup truck with two men in the front and two in the back, one on either side of him. He saw himself bound and hooded in the middle of the back seat, sitting tall in the face of captivity.

Foster was scared. His heart thundered in his chest and his stomach knotted painfully with anxiety, but he focused on his breathing and on what he could control. It wasn't much, and he was reminded of the biblical story of Daniel in the den of lions. He clung to the lesson that Daniel's faith might have put him there, but it was also his faith that had saved him.

May your God, whom you serve continually, rescue you!

The truck came to a stop, and Foster held his breath as he waited to see if they would begin moving again. He exhaled when the doors on either side of him opened, but his relief was short-lived. The man to his left clamped a hand down on his arm and dragged him from the rear seat, letting him fall to the ground. He hit hard on his left side but made no effort to move.

"Get up," a voice said.

If I am captured, I will continue to resist by all means available.

With his wrists bound behind his back, he struggled to push himself up to his knees, but he wasn't in a hurry. The more he made his captors work for what they wanted, the better chance he had of prolonging the window of opportunity for Seth to mount a rescue. It was the one thing he had always been able to count on: They would come for him. They would not abandon him.

Just like God hadn't abandoned Daniel.

A swift kick to his ribs knocked him back to the ground and erased his fleeting thoughts of rescue.

"I said, get up."

Again, Foster pushed himself to his knees.

Again, the man kicked him back down.

He no longer wore the uniform, but he was still an American fighting man. He was still a Force Recon Marine, still a warrior beholden to the ideals of the Founding Fathers, still a husband, still a father. Foster was still a man of faith with the grit to endure even this.

I will never forget that I am an American fighting for freedom, responsible for my actions, and dedicated to the principles which made my country free.

I will trust in my God and in the United States of America.

. . . trust in my God . . .

Again, the story of Daniel came to mind as he pushed up to his knees. Daniel's unwavering faith had been rewarded by God sending

His angels to close the mouths of the lions. Foster knew he was no Daniel. He knew at times he had doubted God's hand in things and had believed he could do it on his own. He was flawed and nothing like the man God had sent His angels to save. But he still believed. He believed he was a child of God and a faithful servant. He believed he would not be abandoned to languish in captivity and suffer at the hands of the enemy.

And he believed God would send His angels to save him.

Only they would be green-eyed devils from Dam Neck, Virginia.

"Get up," the voice said again.

Foster lifted a leg in front of him and started to stand, just as a rifle struck him in the back of his head and toppled him forward onto his face. Pain erupted under his hood, and his vision flared red, then faded to black.

Foster opened his eyes as the hood was ripped from his head, but he quickly snapped them shut against the blinding light. He had seen more than enough to know he was in trouble.

"Wake up," the man said, slapping his stubbled cheek.

Foster shook his head. He was awake, but he didn't want to be. He didn't want to be naked and zip-tied to a wooden chair in the middle of a windowless empty room. He didn't want to be surrounded by men who wanted to hurt him.

"Foster," another man said.

He recognized this voice.

"Open your eyes, brother."

His eyes shot open and zeroed in on Dom Theriot. "You ain't my brother," he growled.

But the Louisiana native only smiled.

"I could have been," Dom said. "I tried extending an olive branch . . ."

"An olive branch? I knew you were garbage from the moment I met you."

Dom laughed. "You're right. I always knew there was something about you I just didn't like either."

"Like a moral compass?"

Foster knew he was only antagonizing his captors, but he didn't care. He had accepted that his suspicions about Dom were warranted, though he was frustrated he hadn't taken action sooner. Maybe if he had told Captain Cross that he feared Dom was onto him, this could have been avoided.

Dom brushed aside the jibe. "There's just one thing I'm curious about."

Foster glared into his eyes, defiant even in the face of a seemingly hopeless situation. Daniel hadn't given in to his fears when the lions began circling and prowling ever nearer. Neither would Foster give in and forsake his faith in the face of a faithless man. "What's that?"

"Who do you work for?"

Foster held his gaze and refused to look away, but the question surprised him. He had assumed Dom already knew. "You first."

Dom's eyes flicked up to a man standing behind Foster, and he nodded.

A fist slammed into Foster's right ear and toppled him—chair and all—onto his side. He grunted when he impacted the concrete floor but was inwardly pleased he had avoided answering the first question while eliciting a reaction from the other American.

"Try again," Dom said.

Two of his men grabbed Foster by the arms and lifted him off the ground to set the chair back up where it had been. Bright spotlights shone down on him, but Foster still kept his eyes focused on Dom.

"I don't think so."

Again, Dom nodded at the man standing behind Foster. And again, Foster felt the rush of air as the fist arced toward the side of his head. Only, this time, he threw his weight backward at the last moment and watched the fist sail in front of his face, carrying the man off-balance.

In a fight, Foster would have slipped the punch and counter-attacked from a different angle. But he was tied to a chair, and his momentum had committed him to continuing onto his back. The man who had thrown the punch was off-balance and slid to the right, but the chair grazed him on the way down. Foster slammed into the ground and cracked his head against the concrete floor just as he saw his would-be attacker stumble and fall to his knees, tripping over the chair's upturned legs.

Stars ringed his vision, but he allowed himself half a beat to be pleased he had thwarted his captors' efforts to break him. Even naked and tied to a chair, Foster was still in the fight.

Small victories win the day.

He looked up as Dom leaned over and stared down at him. "Foster Quinn, Force Recon Marine. From the moment I met you, I knew there was more to your bogus story."

Foster blinked his eyes to clear his vision, clinging to his cover as if it was the only thing keeping him alive. "I don't know what you're talking about."

Dom made a clucking sound and squatted low. "Of course not," he said. "But it doesn't matter. You sealed your own fate in Leipzig."

Foster's face flushed hot. He had kept Dom at arm's length while in Germany and thought he had kept his meeting with Captain Cross a secret. But his captor's admission was all the evidence he needed to know his cover was officially blown.

Still, he glared up at the other American. "By ignoring you?"

Dom laughed. "Let me guess. Your orders were to find me."

"Find *you*? You must think pretty highly of yourself, Dom."

The man above him shrugged. *"Mozhet byt."*

Foster felt his blood turn cold. "What did you just say?"

"I said maybe. Maybe I do think pretty highly of myself, but an ego is always a risk when you're in my line of work. Maybe facilitating the sale of drones from Iran to Wagner gave me a bit of an ego boost. Or maybe it was that you were looking for me and I was under your nose all along."

Foster shook his head, trying to keep his thoughts from swirling around all the clues he had missed. "Dom . . . Dmitri?"

Dmitri Tarasov grinned. "At your service, *loh*."

FORTY-TWO

FOR WHATEVER REASON, the man Foster had known as Dom Theriot kept him alive. Maybe he thought he could use Foster as an insurance policy. But for what, he wasn't sure. It just didn't make sense, and the question swirled in Foster's mind like a dervish as he slipped in and out of consciousness, and the passage of time became a blur.

His body ached from the strain of being tied to the chair in the cramped room. The walls seemed to close in on him, and the air grew stale as he lost track of how long he had been confined in the dimly lit space. The distress beacon had long ago fallen silent—its faint hope extinguished—and he struggled between the relentless feeling of captivity and the disorienting fog of his own thoughts.

How long has it been?

More than an hour but less than an eternity.

Just breathe.

He clung to that simple act of breathing, reminding himself to focus on each inhale and exhale. It was a small anchor amidst the chaos and uncertainty that consumed him as the minutes stretched into hours.

Suddenly, the door swung open and interrupted Foster's thoughts. Without warning, a deluge of ice-cold water cascaded down upon him and drenched his already soaked skin, sending shivers down his spine and causing his teeth to chatter uncontrollably. The guard responsible for the cruel act retreated swiftly and left Foster once more in the suffocating darkness.

Alone again, Foster desperately tried to make sense of the situation. He had suspected Dom Theriot wasn't just another hunter seeking the government's approval for doing business in Iran. But the revelation that he was an arms dealer—a *Russian* arms dealer—had caught him completely off guard. Dom's accent, mannerisms, and behavior had all convincingly portrayed him as an authentic American. Yet here Foster was. Soaking wet and tied to a chair in a room that was little more than a closet because Dom Theriot—*Dmitri Tarasov*, he reminded himself—had sniffed out Foster's secret while keeping his own.

Where did I go wrong?

Foster's mind churned with regret and self-doubt. He replayed the events of the last month in his head, desperately searching for the misstep that had led him there. How had he failed to see through Dom's facade?

Lost in his thoughts, Foster's brooding was abruptly interrupted by a loud *thud* that reverberated through the building's foundation. Startled, his eyes snapped open, and he strained to listen to the muffled voices shouting on the other side of the door. The words were indistinct, but the urgency in their tone was evident and punctuated by the unmistakable sound of a Kalashnikov on full automatic. The rapid-fire bursts echoed through the room and caused him to flinch as his mind raced with possibilities.

Is someone here to rescue me?

Is this a new threat?

As the symphony of chaos played out beyond his confinement, Foster could only hope that amidst the turmoil, an opportunity for escape would present itself. In the darkness, his resolve solidified, and he steeled himself for whatever lay ahead.

The staccato of gunfire continued to echo through the building, and Foster strained against the restraints holding him to the chair. The sudden eruption of violence gave him a glimmer of hope that his rescue might be at hand, though the intense exchange of gunfire and sporadic shouts painted a chaotic picture outside his confined space.

It has to be Seth, he thought.

The tension in the air thickened with each passing moment, and Foster silently prayed for his friends' safety amidst the risks and dangers he knew they were facing to reach him.

Finally, the thunderous symphony of gunfire began to subside. The silence that followed was almost deafening, broken only by the distant sounds of footsteps drawing nearer. Foster strained his ears, desperately trying to distinguish Seth's voice from the rest.

"In here," he shouted, his voice hoarse and filled with emotion.

The door burst open with a resounding crash. Foster squinted against the sudden brightness as a figure materialized before him. The sight of a masked man clad in tactical gear flooded his heart with relief and gratitude.

"Thank God," Foster whispered.

"You can thank His Majesty's Secret Service," the Brit said as he moved with precision and speed to free Foster from his restraints. "After we get you out of here."

"How . . . ?"

The British commando helped Foster to his feet. "Duncan said you were slow."

"Duncan?"

A surge of soreness and numbness overwhelmed him, and it took a moment for him to regain his balance and strength. But the commando steadied him and helped him into a set of soiled clothes before guiding him toward the exit.

"Let's talk later."

The narrow corridor outside the room bore the scars of the fierce firefight that had taken place. Bullet holes riddled the walls, bodies littered the floor, and the scent of gunpowder hung heavy in the air.

Foster studied the corpses scattered in the corridor. "He's not here," he said.

"Who?"

"Tarasov."

"We're not in the clear yet," the commando said, ushering Foster forward before keying the microphone on his tactical radio. "Tigga One, package secure. Proceeding to extract."

Foster followed closely as his heart pounded in sync with each step, adrenaline coursing through his veins. The sense of urgency fueled their movements as they navigated the mazelike building.

"Tigga?"

"The king's dog," the Brit replied, though Foster couldn't tell whether he was serious.

"His dog?"

He nodded. "A Jack Russell."

He's serious.

They inched closer to their objective, and the building's main exit came into view. But, before they could reach it, what remained of Tarasov's security team cornered them.

The commando barked out orders and signaled his team to take cover and engage the enemy. Bullets whizzed by Foster's head, and the acrid smell of gun smoke filled the air. He instinctively ducked around a corner to seek cover and watched in awe as the small team of British commandos displayed their tactical prowess and advanced on the enemy.

Foster would have given anything to have a gun in his hands.

Time seemed to stretch as the battle raged on, and Foster watched the commandos moving with precise coordination. Though Tarasov's men put up a fierce resistance, the British commandos' experience shone through, and their superior training and firepower turned the tide in their favor. One by one, the remaining guards fell, and their futile attempt to thwart the rescue mission came to a decisive end.

Silence.

The smell of death lingered as a testament to the intensity of the battle that had just taken place. The commando who had freed Foster signaled to his team, and they swiftly secured the area and ensured there were no remaining threats.

"Clear left," one of them said.

"Clear right," said another.

Foster's heart pounded with relief as Tigga One approached him with a reassuring smile. "We've got you, mate."

They might have fought under different flags, but they shared a bond forged in the crucible of battle. Foster remembered serving alongside British Special Air Service and Special Boat Service commandos in Afghanistan and Africa. He didn't know the backgrounds of the men who had rescued him, but he recognized the same skill and dedication. Together, they made their way toward the building's exit, and each step filled Foster with a renewed sense of purpose. When they stepped outside, the night air greeted them, and even the warm breeze offered a welcome respite from the confines of his captivity.

The commando lifted the balaclava up over his head, and Foster squinted at the face.

"Oliver?"

"I believe that's twice now you owe me for saving you."

Outside, the rest of Oliver's team stood ready, their gazes filled with satisfaction and determination. He took in the sight and felt a surge of gratitude wash over him, wondering if that was how Daniel had felt in the morning when King Darius came to pull him free from the lions' den.

"Thank you," Foster said.

Oliver clapped a firm hand on his shoulder. "We never leave a brother behind," he replied, his voice brimming with conviction and eyes twinkling with mischief. "Even if you throw our tea in the harbor."

"Time to move," another commando said.

"Right. Let's go."

Foster cast a final glance at the building that now stood as a symbol of his triumph over adversity and a testament to his faith. Oliver led him to a waiting Land Rover Defender and tucked him into the back seat, shutting the door on the echoes of their battle.

"What about Tarasov?"

Oliver slapped the driver on the shoulder, and the SUV raced away into the darkness. "Another day, mate."

Foster craned his neck to look over his shoulder at the building where he had been held. Had they killed Tarasov during the rescue? Or had the Russian somehow slipped through the cracks again? His mission hadn't changed just because his cover was blown—he still needed to bring to justice the man responsible for murdering Robert James.

"How did you find me?"

Oliver turned and studied him. "Your blokes in Abu Dhabi got your distress signal."

"And they called you?"

He nodded. "They knew they wouldn't reach you in time."

"What now?"

"I think you know."

Foster turned again and saw a faint glow on the horizon to their left. He didn't know where Tarasov had held him captive, but he knew they were heading south. "To the port?"

Oliver nodded again. "You're going home, mate."

FORTY-THREE

The drive to the gulf from Isfahan was almost eight hours, but the Brits delivered Foster to the sleepy coastal town before the sun had come up. There was a faint glow on the horizon, but the Defender was still shrouded in darkness as they parked behind a small house in the central part of the city. It was one of less than a thousand, and the only one owned and operated by MI6.

"What's the plan?" Foster asked as he unfolded himself from the back seat and stretched.

"Come on," Oliver said, his voice quiet and as hard as iron.

Foster followed him and the two other commandos into the house, aware that their window of darkness was rapidly fading. They would either have to hurry to finish the egress before the sun came up or hole up in the house until the next period of darkness. Foster didn't relish either option, but he didn't have a choice.

"Five minutes and we're leaving," Oliver said, pulling back several rugs to expose a three-foot square piece of wood.

"Right," said another commando.

"Oliver," Foster said, trying to get the leader's attention.

The lanky Brit removed the wood, then stepped away from the cache as the other two reached in and removed fresh magazines for their Heckler & Koch MP5SD3 submachine guns. Foster knew they needed them after the gunfight they had been in with Tarasov's men.

"We're running out of time," Oliver said. "Your blokes are already at the rally point."

Foster looked at his watch and understood. Once the sun came up, anybody caught in the open would be exposed. Whether the IRGC or MOIS were looking for them was irrelevant.

"What can I do to help?"

"Stay out of our way while we refit," Oliver said.

"Then keep up when we move," the other said.

Foster had been in their shoes before—outmanned and out-gunned, deep behind enemy lines with the odds stacked against them. The only difference was that in his past life, his race against the clock had been to escape bad-guy land and return to the comfort of a waiting Navy ship. The British commandos had risked their covers—and their lives—to rescue him from Tarasov and get him to safety. But even then, they weren't leaving. They needed to stay and act like nothing had happened.

"Got it," Foster said.

He stood back and waited until all three had stocked up on fresh ammunition. When they left the safe house, he followed hot on their heels as they raced through the dark alleys and narrow streets to reach the western edge of town. There, a wide swath of open ground was the only thing standing between them and the beach. Between Foster and his freedom.

At the corner of the block's last building, Oliver hesitated for only a second, then ducked low and sprinted into the shadows on the other side. Foster watched the other two commandos follow suit, leaving him to fend for himself. When it was his turn, he looked both ways and darted across, dropping behind a berm next to Oliver and his men.

"The beach is one hundred and fifty meters that way," Oliver said, pointing at the dark western horizon. "There is a pier three hundred meters south and a marina protected by a breakwater three hundred meters north."

"Boat traffic?"

Oliver shook his head. "Not at this hour. But soon you can expect the local fishermen to prepare for their day."

As the three men huddled underneath a palm tree, a green and white police car approached from the north. Oliver tugged on Foster's sleeve, pulling him lower to the ground as the sedan drove past. But its lights were off, and it didn't appear to be in a hurry.

Oliver watched it turn a corner and disappear into the slumbering city before continuing. "We will go with you to the edge of the clearing and provide cover until you're in the water. But then you're on your own."

Foster nodded his understanding.

"You'll have to cross through a public park with a playground spanning almost fifty meters. It's not illegal to sleep in parks in Iran, so be careful where you walk."

"I won't step on anybody," Foster said, still hoping the police had run off campers who had thought to sleep there that night.

"Once you make it through the playground, you'll have a one-meter drop to the sand from the stone seawall." Oliver looked across the vacant land at the row of streetlamps lining the beach. "It's well lit, so be quick about it."

"How far from there to the water?"

"It's close to high tide now, so maybe only twenty or thirty meters."

He felt a sense of relief to know the open water was so close, and had he been preparing to make this move at any beach in America, Foster wouldn't have even balked. But the prospect of racing the rising sun to reach the Persian Gulf and plunge into the shallow coastal waters that were the sea snake's natural habitat gave him pause. It didn't matter that the sea snake fed on bony fish, wrasses, goatfish, and dottybacks, or that it was gentle and nonaggressive. Foster hated snakes.

He swallowed. "Where are they meeting me?"

"One klick out," Oliver replied.

Aside from his irrational fear of snakes, it wasn't a daunting task as open water felt like home to Foster. Even the annual Recon Challenge in Camp Pendleton began with a one-thousand-meter open-water swim. But in the charity event, competitors swam while carrying seventy-pound rucks. He knew a good time for the distance was under twenty minutes with fins, but he figured he had less than that until the rising sun provided enough ambient light to highlight a lone swimmer making his way out into deeper water.

No time to waste.

"Thanks for coming," Foster said.

Oliver responded with a curt nod. "Ready?"

Foster rose from the depression and moved swiftly across the open ground toward the beach. He could hear Oliver and the British commandos behind and on either side of him, scanning their sectors for campers or prying eyes. But he was focused on his goal—reaching the beach and swimming out into the gulf to link up with his ticket home.

At the edge of the hinterland, Foster dropped behind a shrub and scanned the playground for movement. The swing sets and slides were illuminated by the soft orange glow of the streetlights, and he saw nothing that made him worry the park was occupied. But he knew looks could be deceiving.

Oliver sidled up next to him and lifted a flashlight to his shoulder. Pressing the rubber button on the side three times, he shot quick beams of light out across the water.

Click. Click. Click.

Foster held his breath as he waited, scanning beyond the playground for a response from his rescue party.

Flash. Flash.

"That's the signal," Oliver said. "Good luck, mate."

Foster took a deep breath, then stepped out into the park and jogged through the playground to the seawall. He knew he was no longer hidden in the shadows and that anybody who happened to look in his direction would see a man who clearly didn't belong in Imam Hassan. His heart hammered in his chest as he sidestepped a swing and ducked under a slide, keeping the spot on the water where he had seen the flashes of light fixed directly in front of him.

Flash.

He reached the seawall and launched himself over the stone into the sand beyond. Oliver's assessment of the distance he needed to cross had been exaggerated, and Foster sprinted only fifteen meters before reaching the water's edge. As if he were back in Croatan with a surfboard tucked under his arm, Foster ran into the water until a wave caught him in the chest.

Taking a deep breath, Foster dove headfirst into the surf and began swimming. His mind flashed back to the ten-thousand-meter open-water swim he had completed at the Marine combatant diver course and the hundreds of like swims he had made since. The water was his environment, and starting his swim toward the ocean's silent horizon, he felt safe.

Left . . . right . . . pull . . . relax.

It was tempting to resort to the traditional American crawl because it was one of the faster strokes, but Foster fell back on his training and began swimming the sidestroke. Like he had done countless times before to become a Recon Marine, Foster scissored his legs and used his top hand to pull him further into the water. Then he relaxed, gliding a foot or two before repeating the process.

Left . . . right . . . pull . . . relax.

Flash.

He adjusted his course slightly to the right and aimed for the last burst of light, focused on keeping his stroke smooth and strong. With each pull, he knew he was getting farther away from the man who had killed his best friend. He was getting farther away from a young man who had placed his faith in him and taken great risks to help him accomplish his mission. But he was getting closer to his wife and daughter. He was getting closer to the men he considered his brothers, who hadn't left him in his time of need.

Left . . . right . . . pull . . . relax.

"We got you," a quiet voice said.

Foster stopped swimming and lifted his head in its direction to see a fifteen-foot black rubber boat bobbing in the water less than three feet away. He could barely make out the shapes of several men straddling the gunwale to keep a low profile, but he knew who they were.

"Grab on," Seth said, reaching down and stretching his arm out toward Foster.

They clasped arms—forearm to forearm—as the coxswain started the fifty-five horsepower two-stroke engine. Seth heaved Foster into the boat just as the outboard caught with a quiet cough. He flopped into the middle of the boat, soaking wet and tired from his swim to the combat rubber raiding craft.

"Thanks for coming," Foster said between gasps of air.

The coxswain twisted the throttle on the tiller and pushed it hard over, steering the pump-jet propulsor with shrouded impeller to power the inflatable boat through a tight arc back out to sea.

"Don't thank me yet," Seth said, his voice barely audible over the wind. "You still need to climb the ladder."

Foster was exhausted from his captivity, the operation to rescue him from Tarasov, the eight-hour drive to Imam Hassan, and the one-thousand-meter swim. He wasn't looking forward to jumping back into the water and swimming through sea spray to a rope ladder dangling beneath a helicopter.

"Well, thanks anyway," he said, leaning against the hull.

The boat skipped across the water at close to fifteen knots, racing for the indistinguishable patch of water where they would rendezvous with a Navy helicopter. As a Force Recon Marine, Foster had trained for this method of extraction and knew exactly what to expect. He closed his eyes as the boat's undulating movement rocked him closer to sleep.

But a smack on his shoulder kept him from getting there. "There she is."

Foster lifted his head and looked beyond the bow at a shadow hovering over the water less than two hundred yards away. He knew they would arrive within seconds, and the SEALs would roll off the gunwales and make their way to the rope ladder the helicopter crew had kicked into the water. They would scuttle the CRRC, letting the inflatable boat and outboard motor sink to the bottom of the Persian Gulf, but it was a small price to pay.

"You ready?" Seth asked as they neared the helicopter.

Foster nodded.

FORTY-FOUR

Several hours later, Foster stood on the fantail of the Arleigh Burke–class guided missile destroyer and looked out over the placid waters of the Persian Gulf. He was safely aboard one of the most powerful warships in the world, but his experience had resulted in a nagging fear hovering just beneath the surface. He looked at the Iranian coastline through the haze and knew he would never return.

"Penny for your thoughts?"

Foster turned and saw Seth saunter up to the railing. He looked almost like every other sailor on the destroyer, dressed in a green camouflage Navy working uniform. But the subdued SEAL Trident over his left breast set him apart.

"Can't help but feel like I'm retreating." Foster's heart pounded like an exclamation mark on that thought.

"Well, you're not," the SEAL said with a nod at the shore. "You were sent there to do a job, and you did it."

He shook his head. "But we didn't get the guy who killed Robert."

Seth wrapped a hand around the back of Foster's neck and squeezed. "Was that your mission?"

He looked over at the SEAL officer. "Yeah. It was."

Seth sighed and turned to lean against the stanchions surrounding the flight deck. The MH-60R helicopter that had plucked them out of the water was back in the hangar, and they were left alone with nothing but the wind whipping across the deck as the *Delbert Black* steamed south for Qatar.

"Foster, you've got guts, brother."

"But . . ."

"I don't think you realize what you accomplished. You left DJ and came home to find out your best friend had been killed. That's enough to cripple most guys, but then you took on the burden of his death as a mantle and carried it into your next mission."

"You would have done the same."

"Maybe. But I didn't." He stabbed a finger into Foster's chest. "*You* did."

Foster shook his head again, unwilling to accept the praise. "And I failed."

Seth stood tall and set his jaw as he glowered at Foster. "Enough," he said. "You might not be on my team any longer, but you don't get to have a pity party. You left your wife and your daughter behind, entered into Iran under a nonofficial cover, built a business from scratch, and caught the guy the command sent you to find."

"The wrong guy," Foster countered.

"Still a bad guy. So what if the intel was wrong? It's not the first time we came up short because the analysts screwed up, but it still wasn't a dry hole. We got Volkov."

Foster wanted to argue with Seth, but he could tell it was pointless.

In the SEAL's mind, Foster had done the impossible, and it didn't matter that Tarasov had escaped. It didn't matter that Foster had blown his cover by meeting with Captain Cross in Germany and had almost paid the ultimate price for his mistake.

But Seth saw the look on his face, and he wasn't willing to let it go. "What's on your mind?"

"Tarasov," Foster said. "He's the one."

Seth leaned in close. "And we'll get him. You have my word, brother."

Foster knew he meant it. Even when he was held captive, he'd had complete faith that Seth would come for him, and he knew his team of SEALs were the right ones to bring the arms dealer to justice. But he was done. His cover was blown, and there was no way the command would risk letting him be a part of the team to bring Tarasov in.

"Just wish I could be with you when you do," Foster said.

Seth draped an arm around Foster's shoulders and pulled him in close. "Me too. You were one of the best."

Maybe it was how Seth had referred to him in the past tense, but it cloaked the entire operation with an air of finality. It meant that no matter how much he wanted to be, Foster would never be part of the team again. His value was in the past.

"What do I do now?"

It hadn't been that long ago when he'd had the same thought while overlooking thousands of graves at Arlington National Cemetery. He had been rudderless then, a warrior without purpose, but he felt completely adrift now. He looked up at Seth with pleading eyes.

"When we get into port, you'll get off the ship and go to the airport. You'll board your flight and fly home."

"And then what?"

Seth smiled at him. "Then you'll take care of your wife and daughter. You deserve that, and they do too. Leave the rest to us."

NORFOLK INTERNATIONAL AIRPORT
NORFOLK, VIRGINIA

So he did.

Foster hadn't told Rebecca he was coming home. Part of him was afraid of having a repeat of his last homecoming when she had ignored his messages and left him to fend for himself. But a bigger part of him wasn't ready to step back into his role as loving husband and devoted father. No matter how hard he tried, he couldn't let go of the burden he had taken on when he became Foster Cottle.

"I should probably start charging you," Jeff said, grinning from his seat behind the wheel of his Ford F-150 pickup truck. "You know I'm not an Uber driver, right?"

Foster opened the passenger door and climbed in. "Thanks for coming."

Jeff looked through the rear window over his shoulder. "No bags?"

Foster shook his head. "Left in a bit of a hurry."

The SEAL nodded knowingly. Then he put the truck into gear and pulled away from the curb, leaving a cloud of blue-hued smoke in their wake.

Like before, the two men rode in a comfortable silence. Foster tried locking away what had happened to him inside the dark recesses of his mind, but that proved more difficult than he expected. He studied every car that passed them on the freeway, expecting to see each one filled with men who had come to take him back to Iran. He ran his thumb along the angry marks cut into his wrists where the zip ties had restrained him. He felt the bracelet Haili had made for him, and his heart raced, his chest heavy.

"Now, where we going? Am I taking you home, or do you need some time?"

Jeff had asked that question before too. This time, Foster knew he couldn't put off going home. Rebecca and Haili had sacrificed so much already, and they needed him. Rebecca needed her husband. And Haili needed her father.

But he needed them just as much. His experience in Iran had shaken him and tossed his soul around like a boat lost at sea. For as much as Rebecca needed her husband, he needed his wife—the one person who could calm the storm within and settle his restlessness.

"Home," he said, choking on the word. "Take me home."

Jeff reached over and gave Foster's shoulder a squeeze, then let the rest of the drive pass in silence. By the time they pulled into the gravel parking spot in front of the cottage on Vanderbilt Avenue, Foster's nerves were shot. He felt torn between the life he had chosen to leave behind in Virginia Beach and the one he had escaped in Isfahan.

Leaving his family had been his choice. Leaving Iran had not.

"We're here," Jeff said, softly encouraging Foster to take that first step.

"Thanks for the lift, brother."

Foster climbed out and waited for Jeff to pull away before turning to look at their modest home. His eyes instinctively went to the shed in the backyard where his longboard sat in storage, beckoning him to carry it into the ocean and put off facing his fears. But he ignored the siren's call of the surf and walked through the white picket fence to the front door.

Standing on the porch, he hesitated with his hand hovering over the handle. Part of him wanted to just barge in and pick up where they had left off, but he felt like a stranger. He still hadn't shucked the identity he had worked so hard to cultivate—the life he had taken on as his own. He lifted his hand and knocked.

He heard movement inside, barely audible over the thumping of his heart, and he swallowed against his anxiety. But when the door opened, his thundering heart pounded for a different reason, and his worry melted away into his wife's brown eyes.

"Foster?"

He opened his mouth to say something but couldn't find the words. He saw the confusion and fear on her face fade into emotions he had resisted.

Relief . . . peace.

"I'm home," he said. His words came out like a whisper but carried a gravity only those who had been downrange could appreciate.

She closed the distance between them in two hurried steps and fell into his arms, burying her face in his chest. He wrapped his arms around her and felt his entire world shaking as she released months of pent-up emotion with a muffled sob. He squeezed her tighter and kissed the top of her head.

Rebecca pulled away and looked up at him with red tearstained eyes and said the words only a person waiting for their warrior's return could appreciate. "Welcome home, baby."

"Daddy!"

It took effort for Foster to look away from his wife, but the blur of motion from over her shoulder drew his attention to the nine-year-old girl who looked at him like he was a giant. Still clinging to Rebecca, he knelt and waited for Haili to fly into his arms.

"I'm home, baby girl."

Foster had loved feeling Rebecca in his arms, but there was something about Haili's hug that made his heart skip. In his wife's embrace, Foster had felt the fear she had lived with for months while she waited—the fear her husband might never return. But in his daughter's, he felt her certainty that he would, mixed with the heart-breaking longing for his presence.

"I'm home," he said again.

Haili stepped back and clutched at his hand, turning it to look at the red and gold bracelet she had affixed to his wrist. "You still have it," she said with a smile.

"Never took it off."

FORTY-FIVE

The next day, Foster woke up with Rebecca in his arms. It was the first night in nearly two months he could remember sleeping through without being awakened by nightmares or an anxious energy fueled by a combination of cortisol and adrenaline. But his body still wasn't adjusted to the time difference, so he slipped from their bed and crept toward the door.

"Where are you going?"

Her voice had a soothing lilt that froze him in place, but he quickly turned back and leaned over to kiss her soft lips. "I can't sleep, so I'm going to catch a few sets."

She reached up and held him there, letting her kiss linger before finally pushing him away. "Be back in time for breakfast."

"You don't have to . . ."

She cut him off. "In bed, Foster. I want breakfast in bed."

He grinned at her in the darkness, not sure whether she really intended for him to deliver a tray of eggs, bacon, and freshly squeezed orange juice or if she had something else in mind. "I won't be long," he said, then turned and walked out.

Foster knew intimately each loose floorboard and hinge that needed oiling, and he slipped from their cottage like a thief without making a sound, already thinking about the frigid Atlantic surf. He retrieved his longboard from the shed and made for the beach. He needed a therapy session now more than ever.

Stepping from the cracked asphalt to the cold sand of the path cutting across the dunes, Foster looked up into the starlit sky as he contemplated the coming day. He knew that by the time the sun came up, he would have already set himself on a path that would change their future. Like the last time he had been on that stretch of beach in Croatan, he needed the saltwater's clarity to prepare him for what he needed to do.

Only this time, he and Rebecca had already talked about it.

After the initial homecoming, Foster had spent the better part of the afternoon in Haili's room to make up for his absence. His fears that she resented him for leaving proved unfounded, and within minutes, they settled into their natural roles of loving father and daughter. She showed him the jewelry and art she had made, and he told her corny dad jokes that made her groan and roll her eyes. She was still his little monkey. And he was still her hero.

His alone time with Rebecca had been a little more complicated. Though there hadn't been tension like there was the last time he had come home, she could tell something was different. Something bothered him. She never flat-out asked, and he hesitated to tell her. He viewed his role as a husband to protect her and shield her from the evils of the world, wanting instead to enjoy life with his wife all the days that God had given him under the sun—all his meaningless days.

But she was a godly woman. Since the beginning, Rebecca had noticed him, regarded him, honored him, and esteemed him. She valued his opinion and admired his wisdom and character, appreciating his commitment to her, and therefore considered his needs and values. When they were alone, she encouraged him and made it clear she wanted to share in his burden So he did.

In the end, before they fell asleep wrapped up in each other's love, they agreed it would be best if he resigned his position with the command to focus on their family. They had already sacrificed so much, and she quickly intuited he needed time to resolve the trauma he had experienced.

But that didn't make it any easier for him to accept.

Standing at the water's edge, Foster stared out over the crashing waves at the approaching dawn. Though he and Rebecca had agreed on a plan for their future, he still felt guilt and shame—guilt that he had failed to bring Robert's killer to justice and shame that he had left Reza to clean up his mess.

Tossing aside his worries, Foster sprinted into the ocean and dove on top of his outstretched longboard as he crested a wave and began paddling. The water was colder than he remembered, and the wet suit did little to insulate him, but he didn't hesitate to turtle roll with each wave until he had cleared the breaking zone.

Like most mornings, Foster sat astride his surfboard and stared at the inky horizon while searching for answers. His time on the water was less about catching the perfect wave and more about finding clarity and focus. Today was no exception.

How can I fulfill my obligations to my wife and daughter if I've abandoned my brothers?

He knew it was the same conflict he had agonized over the last time he had been on the water. It was the same feeling of being forced to choose between one or the other that had tormented him while burying his best friend. How could he ever feel peace at home if he left his brothers and allowed them to go to war without him?

He ran his fingers through his wet hair and kicked his legs in an eggbeater to turn back toward shore. He hadn't caught a single wave, but he'd gotten the answers he came for. He would still go to the command and resign his position like he and Rebecca had agreed, but he knew he wouldn't be able to find peace until he found Robert's killer. One way or another, he knew.

It's not over.

Foster returned home and was happy to learn that Rebecca did not, in fact, want a tray of eggs, bacon, and freshly squeezed orange juice. They took their time reconnecting as husband and wife, then he showered, dressed, and climbed into his Defender for the short drive to the base.

He made the drive from their house in Croatan to Dam Neck as if the Land Rover was on autopilot. His thoughts were on seeing familiar faces hidden behind thick beards or under long hair, faces of men he had bled and battled with and considered brothers. He expected some discomfort since most of them probably thought he had already left the command to return to the Marine Corps and didn't know what he had been through.

Though he was no longer in Commander Belloni's squadron and had cleared out his cage long before leaving Hampton Roads for the Shinar Ranch in Texas, he parked his Defender in his usual spot. It would have felt unusual if he'd parked anywhere else. He climbed out of the SUV and turned for the headquarters building.

It was only Foster's second time there. The first time, a Navy commander had escorted him inside for what he thought was a pep talk to reenlist in the Marine Corps and stay on as an assaulter. Instead, Captain Cross had informed him his best friend had been killed while conducting Advanced Force Operations under a Special Access Program code-named SILENT HORIZONS. And he'd asked Foster to take his place.

Now, Foster was the one who needed to ask something.

"Can I help you?"

His hands hung loose and relaxed at his sides as he studied the slender woman behind the wide oak desk. Foster knew most commanding officers' secretaries held the keys to the kingdom and could either help or hurt his cause. But she didn't know him from the next guy. To her, he was just another scruffy-looking operator intent on disturbing her boss.

"Yes, ma'am," he said. "Can you tell Captain Cross that Foster Quinn is here to see him?"

If she recognized his name, she didn't let it show. She picked up the phone and punched a button before holding the handset to her ear. Foster could hear the senior SEAL's deep voice resonating on the other end, but she kept her voice barely above a whisper, and he tried to appear as if he wasn't listening in on the conversation.

When she hung up the phone, she studied Foster again as if seeing him in a new light. "Would you mind having a seat? He will be with you in just a moment."

The anteroom was furnished in spartan government chic with simple faux-leather armchairs spaced precisely twelve inches apart and set in strategic locations around the room. He sat in the one that gave him a clear line of sight to both the main entrance and the door leading to the captain's office. Rebecca liked to joke that he plotted primary and alternate escape routes from every restaurant they dined in and refused to sit with his back exposed.

But it wasn't a joke.

No sooner had Foster lowered himself into the seat than the skipper's door opened, and Captain Cross stepped out. "Foster," he said. "Come in my office."

He stood and followed the captain inside, nodding to the secretary as he passed.

"Close the door."

Foster did, then took a seat in a chair only slightly more fashionable than the ones in the waiting area.

"I didn't expect you back so soon," the SEAL officer said. "With your cover compromised, there's no rush for you to come back. Take as much time as . . ."

Foster cut him off with a quiet "I'm not coming back."

Captain Cross leaned back in his leather executive swivel chair and locked eyes with him. "Okay. Maybe you should start from the beginning."

Foster had prayed over this on the drive to the compound, and he felt at ease with his decision. "Sir, I signed on to participate in SILENT HORIZONS because I believed Volkov was a purveyor of death who needed to be taken out. But maybe even to a larger degree, I accepted this position out of a sense of duty to Robert James."

"What are you saying, Foster?"

"I'm saying, now I need to focus on my wife and daughter," he said. "I'm saying I'm out."

Captain Cross appraised him in silence, then pushed across a manila folder—like he had done the first time they met. "Before you go . . ."

"What's this?"

"We got it from Dobiel."

Foster's heart jumped, and he locked eyes with the captain. "You mean Reza."

The SEAL nodded. "Have a look."

Foster placed his hand on the folder and drew it closer, almost scared to open it and expose its secrets. But he took one long, slow breath and steeled himself for whatever was inside. After what felt like an eternity, Foster opened the folder, surprised to see a copy of what looked like a handwritten note.

"What is it?"

"Read it," Captain Cross said. "He delivered it to Seth in Abu Dhabi."

Foster looked up and furrowed his brow in confusion. "When? He wasn't scheduled for another polygraph until next month."

"He didn't come for a polygraph. He came for you."

The shame Foster felt in abandoning Reza came roaring to the surface. His fingers trembled as he picked up the note and began to read.

Agha Foster,

I was frightened when I returned to the warehouse in Isfahan and found you missing. I am ashamed to admit that I fled back to Tehran, expecting the police to knock down my door and take me away. I didn't know what to do.

So I went looking for you and thought Dom Theriot was a good place to start.

Foster swallowed and looked up at Captain Cross. "He went looking for me?"

"Keep reading."

I remembered the hunt he took you on in Kond-Olya and drove there to visit the lodge and speak with the guides. They remembered the hunt quite well and spoke highly of you, but they had a less than favorable opinion of Mister Theriot. It wasn't his first time visiting their village, and they shared stories with me of his previous hunts. Stories that didn't add up.

Again, Foster paused. It seemed Reza was drawing his own conclusions about Dom Theriot—or Dmitri Tarasov—and while he appreciated the initiative, it was a little too late. His cover was already blown, and the Russian arms dealer was in the wind. "We already know Dom Theriot wasn't who he claimed to be—"

"Just keep reading," the SEAL officer insisted.

Farhad and Ahmad took me into the lodge to show me pictures from his previous hunts. As you know, the Alborz red sheep are prized game, and the guides were eager to show me pictures of their trophies. Mister Theriot was in quite a few, but they were most eager to show me one photo in particular.

I didn't recognize the individual in the picture, but I made a copy and included it with this letter. Maybe it's nothing. Or maybe it's the one that got away.

Your friend,
Reza

Foster set the note down with trembling fingers and looked up at Captain Cross. "Where's the picture?"

"Foster . . ."

He slammed his fist down on the sturdy desk as a wave of adrenaline fueled his anger. "Where is the picture?"

The captain slowly lowered both hands to the desk and placed them flat in a gesture intended to indicate he was not a threat. "Before I show it to you . . ."

Foster felt his neck and cheeks flush hot as he strained to control his temper.

"I need you to understand we are taking this seriously. We turned the photo over to the FBI as a potential lead in their investigation to track down the individual who has been communicating with Tarasov."

Foster thought back to his meeting with Luke Chapman at the

Seaside Park Hotel in Leipzig. If he could convince Captain Cross to give him a copy of the photo, he could drive up to Washington and deliver it personally to the congressman. There was no way the Bureau would be able to sweep it under the rug if Luke took it before the House Judiciary Committee and demanded answers.

"Sir, no offense, but I've seen what happens when we allow the system to work."

The captain's hands were still flat on the desk, but he shook his head. "Foster, I don't think you understand."

"No, sir. It's *you* who doesn't understand. We can't just turn this evidence over to the FBI and expect them to do the right thing. They've been weaponized by the political elite to eliminate their opponents and every obstacle standing in the way of amassing grotesque wealth and unchecked power."

Again, Seth's words from Djibouti echoed in his mind. *That's all they want, man. Power and money.*

Captain Cross took a deep breath and exhaled loudly. "I know how—"

Foster cut him off. "You know nothing!"

The SEAL captain slammed both hands on the desk and shot up from his chair. He leaned over and glowered at Foster, challenging him to interrupt again. When he spoke, his voice was low and menacing. "You will give me the respect to let me finish, or I will have you escorted off this compound and ensure you are PNG'd. Do I make myself clear?"

Foster's entire adult life had been spent as a warrior, battling alongside some of the most talented special operators on the planet. If the command labeled him *persona non grata*, he would be cut off from even his closest friends. Seth, Hunter and Hayden, Tre and Will, Des. Doors would be shut, and calls would go unanswered.

He clamped his mouth shut and gestured for the captain to continue, inwardly seething at his impotence.

"I know how you feel about our senior-level leaders and the politicians in Washington. I know you don't trust them, and to be honest, neither do I. Before I show you this picture, you need to understand that the command has liaisons in the Justice Department to ensure this doesn't get buried. We have consulted WarCom, and their JAGs agree this is the best course of action."

Foster knew Captain Cross meant well, but he didn't think consulting with the brass at the Naval Special Warfare Command or its team of lawyers in the Judge Advocate General's Corps would keep the wrong people from squashing the investigation.

"May I?" Foster asked, not wanting to risk angering the senior SEAL further.

The captain nodded.

"I spoke with a former teammate about this investigation, and he assured me he would apply the appropriate amount of pressure through the House Judiciary Committee. If we could get him—"

"What teammate?"

Foster saw the look on the captain's face and paused before answering. "He was a case officer before he left the Agency and was elected to Congress."

"What did you do, Foster?"

The question caught him off guard, and he leaned back. "What?"

Captain Cross opened another folder on his desk and tossed the copied photograph onto the table, but Foster hesitated to break eye contact. When he did, he saw the smiling faces of Farhad and Ahmad, his two hunting guides in Kond-Olya, on either side of two American hunters. One, Foster knew was actually the Russian arms dealer Dmitri Tarasov. The other was . . .

"Congressman Luke Chapman," the captain said.

FORTY-SIX

FOSTER STARED AT THE PHOTO and tried making sense of it. There had to be some mistake.

"Luke said he had met Tarasov on his last assignment with the Agency."

Captain Cross looked at Foster with kind, apologetic eyes. "That was true. But this photo wasn't taken then."

But Foster still refused to believe it. "Maybe he went on the hunt to—"

"Foster, this photograph was taken after Congressman Chapman left the Agency."

"He had to disclose foreign travel—"

"Our liaison within the Bureau already confirmed he did not disclose traveling to Iran during his most recent background investigation."

The captain was shredding each of Foster's arguments, and anger was slowly replacing his disbelief. "When did this happen?"

"We believe he visited the Islamic Republic sometime while you were deployed to Djibouti."

If anything, that made Foster even more incensed. Not only had a former intelligence officer met with a Russian arms dealer in an openly hostile country, but he had also done so while a representative of the American people. "When he was already in office?"

"We think he traveled there after he was elected and before he was sworn in."

Foster growled. "Like that matters."

The two men fell silent and looked at each other across the desk. Foster knew the skipper was assessing how he handled the news that somebody he had trusted had engaged in illicit behavior with a person the president had personally targeted. But Foster knew it went deeper than that.

"Did he kill Robert?"

Captain Cross took a deep breath and exhaled through his nose. "We don't know that."

"Is he the one who ordered my capture?"

The senior SEAL shook his head. "We don't know that either."

"What are we doing about it?"

"The FBI—"

Foster held up a hand to stop the captain. "I know you said you've turned this over to the FBI, but we can't afford to be hands-off on this."

"We're not."

Foster fell silent and waited for the skipper to continue.

"Like I said, I didn't expect you to return so soon. But, since you're here, I might as well make my pitch now."

Foster shook his head. "I already told you I'm out."

The captain reached across the desk and lifted the photograph Reza had provided them, holding it up in front of Foster's face. "I know you spent time downrange with Luke, but so did I. He was embedded in our teams and has access to secrets that would be devastating to our operations if they fell into the wrong hands. Like you, I don't trust the establishment to take care of him for us, and I want one of our own overseeing his downfall."

Like the last time Foster sat across from the captain, he felt himself being pulled into another assignment he felt ill-suited for—another assignment he already knew he couldn't refuse. His motivation hadn't changed. There were good guys and bad guys, and Foster would always side with the good guys.

"What are you asking of me?"

"I'm asking you to stay on with SILENT HORIZONS."

"I can't go back."

Captain Cross sighed. "I'm not asking you to go back. I'm not even asking you to leave the States."

Foster furrowed his brow. "What about Posse Comitatus?"

He was referring to the federal law enacted in 1878 that limited the powers of the federal government in the use of military personnel to enforce domestic policies within the United States. Ironically, it was designed to prevent the political elite from abusing their power to punish their opponents and cow their constituents—the same abuse Foster saw being perpetrated by other federal agencies.

"Last I checked," the captain replied, "you're no longer a Marine."

"Semantics. I still report to you, sir."

The senior SEAL nodded. "I appreciate the position I'm putting you in, and I wouldn't ask it of you if I didn't think you could handle operating in the gray."

"There's no gray," Foster said. "I took an oath that makes my duty pretty black and white. *I, Foster Quinn, do solemnly swear that I will support and defend the Constitution of the United States against all enemies, foreign and domestic; that I will bear true faith and allegiance to the same.*"

"What about the rest?"

Foster knew he meant the part of the oath that said, *That I will obey the orders of the president of the United States and the orders of the officers appointed over me, according to regulations and the Uniform Code of Military Justice.*

"*So help me God,*" Foster concluded.

"That's not what I meant."

Foster grinned. "Like you said, I'm no longer a Marine."

"What are you saying?"

Foster stood and locked eyes with the captain. "I'm saying that I still live by my oath to defend the Constitution of the United States against *all* enemies, foreign *and* domestic."

"So you'll stay on?"

"Luke Chapman is an enemy of the United States, and I intend to make sure he is brought to justice."

FORTY-SEVEN

Several weeks later, Foster parked his Land Rover Defender on the street in front of the US Department of Energy, six blocks from his destination. Clouds hung low over the city, blanketing the nation's capital with a somber feeling. Foster turned up his collar against the brisk late-fall wind and thrust his hands in his coat pockets as he started walking.

For the first time in months, he felt at peace. Nightmares still woke him in the middle of the night, leaving him coated in sweat with a racing heart and a tightness in his chest he wasn't sure would ever leave. But Rebecca's comforting touch and soft words helped pull him back from the abyss. As the days passed, he was more and more thankful God had blessed him with such a loving wife.

He paused at the corner of Seventh Street with the curved

arena-like building of the Hirshhorn Museum to his north. It was midmorning the week before Thanksgiving, and the streets were bustling with the normal traffic for a city of almost seven hundred thousand people. But Foster wasn't paying them any attention.

His thoughts were almost as dark as the sky, and he looked up from the sidewalk at the sprawling Rayburn House Office Building in the distance. His task wasn't one he was looking forward to, but one that needed to be done. Ever since Captain Cross had shown him the picture Reza provided of Luke Chapman standing shoulder to shoulder with Dmitri Tarasov, Foster had known he didn't have a choice.

Four blocks later, Foster crossed the street and entered the Botanic Garden. He walked slowly, making his way to the circular fountain at the center. Though the temperature hovered near freezing, he stopped and stared at the water while he contemplated the path that had led him there. A gust of wind tousled his hair, and he looked over at the gleaming white dome of the Capitol Building.

"Foster," a voice said, drawing him back into the moment.

He took a deep breath, then turned to greet the man he once thought was his friend. "Congressman Chapman."

Luke walked around the fountain and approached Foster with a politician's smile plastered on his face. He wore a beige cashmere overcoat buttoned closed with a red scarf tucked in the collar. The American flag lapel pin caught Foster's eye and made his blood boil.

"What brings you to town?"

Foster looked over his shoulder, down the length of the mall. Though he couldn't see it, he knew they were standing less than three miles from where Robert James was buried. "I came to visit a friend."

"Well, I'm honored you made the time." Luke's smile grew. "Why don't we go into my office and get out of this cold?"

Foster locked eyes with him, then turned and took a seat on a stone bench. "I don't think so."

Luke looked up and surveyed their surroundings, almost as if he expected a team of Navy SEALs to converge on him. Despite what Foster knew he had become, Luke was still a former case officer with all the skills and training it took to survive undercover in austere environments. He had still put on a plate carrier and hefted a carbine while they tracked and hunted terrorists across the globe. Despite his pedestrian appearance, Foster knew he was a formidable opponent.

"What's going on, Foster?"

Foster removed his hands from his pockets, exposing a Smith & Wesson micro-compact Equalizer TS pistol aimed at the congressman. "You owe me some answers."

Luke's eyes grew wide as he looked down at the handgun, but he held his hands out to his sides to show Foster he wasn't a threat. "Do you need help? I'm here for you, brother . . ."

"Brother!" Foster spat. "Don't you ever call me that again. Not after what you did."

Foster saw the expression on his face harden. "What did I do exactly?"

"Tell me about Dmitri Tarasov."

Again, Luke scanned the Botanic Garden, surely looking for a surveillance team eavesdropping on their conversation, then looked Foster up and down.

"This conversation is just between you and me," Foster said.

Luke probably didn't believe him, but he still appeared to relax somewhat. Maybe he believed Foster wouldn't have been foolish enough to confront him without backup if he had admissible evidence of wrongdoing. Maybe he believed he could still control the conversation and manipulate Foster into believing his version of events.

"What do you want to know?" Luke asked, then took a step toward him.

Foster clucked and shook his head, wagging the barrel of the pistol just enough to let the congressman know it was in his best interests to remain where he was.

"I'd like to sit," Luke said, gesturing to the bench.

"Sit on the fountain," Foster replied.

Luke hesitated for a moment, then complied with the simple demand before answering Foster's question with a repeat of what he had said in Leipzig. "I told you I had dealings with Tarasov on my last Agency assignment."

Foster nodded. According to what the Bureau had uncovered during their investigation, that much was true. Before Luke left the Agency, he had been sent to Syria with an Army Special Missions Unit as they rooted out elements of the Islamic State. It was there, Bureau investigators asserted, that he met Dmitri Tarasov, an American-educated Russian with loose ties to the private military company Wagner Group.

"In Khasham," Foster said.

It was barely more than a tick, but Luke's reaction betrayed surprise that Foster knew so much. Then, like any good case officer, he rolled with it and quickly continued driving the conversation in a favorable direction. "I had developed him as an asset. When Russian and Syrian forces struck the Conoco outpost where we were working alongside Kurdish and Arab forces, I reached out to him to try to stop their attack."

Foster had read the after-action report. The outpost had been struck with a mixture of tank fire, large artillery, and mortar rounds. In response, American drones and warplanes arrived overhead and pummeled the Russian and Syrian forces for over three hours.

"It didn't work," Foster said.

Luke shook his head. "When you mess with a bull, you get the horns."

Foster didn't take the bait. "What I don't understand is why a man working for an organization that had lost so many fighters in that battle would ever go into business with you."

"Foster . . ."

Again, he clucked and shook his head. "This is the part where I ask you very pointed questions and you give me very direct and honest answers. If I don't like them, I put two rounds in your face and let DC Metro find you floating in that fountain."

Luke looked over his shoulder and shivered, as if the prospect of floating in the ice-cold water was more terrifying than two rounds of 9mm hollow points in his skull. He looked back at Foster and nodded.

"After the Battle of Khasham, when was the next time you spoke with Tarasov?"

Luke swallowed before answering. "One month."

"What was the purpose of that communication?"

"That's classified," Luke said. But Foster only needed to raise the pistol an inch before Luke reconsidered his tactic of stonewalling the former Marine. "He wanted to provide me with details of Wagner activities in Africa."

"In exchange for what?"

"Foster . . ."

Foster closed his eyes and slowly exhaled, trying to calm his heart. His rage and animus were close to overpowering him, and his finger twitched on the trigger.

Just four-point-seven-five pounds of pressure.

When he opened his eyes, he glared at Luke but didn't see the man he once had considered a brother. He didn't see a former CIA case officer or task force team member. He didn't see a congressman from North Carolina's ninth district. He saw only an enemy of the United States who had put his selfish desires ahead of the oaths he had taken and the citizens he had sworn to protect.

"Cursed is anyone who accepts a bribe to kill an innocent person," Foster said.

"What?"

"I'll never understand why you betrayed your country. But if you want to live, you'll tell me now why you betrayed me."

Luke opened his mouth to profess his innocence but quickly snapped it shut. He looked away from Foster and surveyed the Washington skyline with its museums and monuments erected to honor the beacon of freedom that was the United States. Foster didn't believe for a moment Luke regretted his decision to betray everything he held dear, but he still gave him the opportunity to reflect on his sins.

"This goes deeper than me," Luke said at last.

"What does?"

The congressman took a deep breath and looked up into the clouds as if praying for salvation from the angel of retribution who had descended upon him. "*This.* Politics is dirty, Foster. You don't get anything unless you give something."

"You're not *supposed* to get anything. You're a public servant."

Luke shook his head. "That's not the way it works. I didn't betray my country, Foster. Despite what you might think about me, I did not violate my oath."

"Don't you dare preach to me about oaths. We took the same oath to support and defend the Constitution against all enemies, foreign and domestic. When you accepted money from Tarasov—"

"I didn't."

"What?"

"I didn't accept money from Tarasov," Luke said. "You've obviously done your homework, Foster. Have you found any evidence that I have benefited financially?"

It was true. The Bureau's forensic accountants had investigated both his personal and campaign finances and found no irregularities. But that didn't absolve him from brokering whatever deal he had made with the Russian arms dealer, and there was more than enough evidence to convict him of several crimes related to not disclosing his personal relationships with foreign nationals. No matter how Luke tried to spin it, he couldn't avoid the simple fact that he had violated his oath and crossed a line.

It was black and white.

"Did you commission Tarasov to purchase suicide drones from Iran?"

Luke hesitated. "Yes."

"Why?"

Luke shook his head. "This is so much bigger than me . . ."

"Answer the question."

"War is good for business."

"For who?"

"For those who keep this country running."

Foster's blood boiled as he listened to Luke parrot the sentiments of the elite—that the ends justified the means, and the American citizen was too ignorant to understand. But there was only one thing Foster really wanted to know—one thing he knew investigators wouldn't be able to uncover.

"Did you tell Tarasov I was in Iran looking for him?"

Luke met his gaze. "Yes."

Foster had thought the admission would hurt, but it only galvanized his resolve to see his assignment through. "Did you also tell Tarasov Robert was there for the same reason?"

"What?"

Foster knew Luke had been trained in the art of lying. In its most basic form, an Agency case officer's training taught him to manipulate the truth to convince an asset to work for him. But Luke's reaction seemed genuine.

"I know you betrayed me," Foster said. "Did you also betray Robert?"

"What are you talking about? Robert was killed in a climbing accident."

His words carried such sincerity that for a moment, Foster's resolve faltered. *What if he's telling the truth? Was Robert's death really an accident?* But he shook away the doubt. In his heart, he knew the man who had betrayed him had also betrayed his best friend.

Foster lifted the pistol and pointed it at Luke's face. "Last chance."

"Foster." Luke trembled and stared into the maw of the Smith & Wesson. "I did *not* betray Robert."

Foster swallowed back his disappointment, then cleared his throat and spoke. "Take him."

Luke's body sagged as the quiet morning was broken by the sounds of roaring engines and squealing brakes. Foster tucked the pistol back into his coat pocket as more than a dozen federal agents in blue windbreakers raced into the Botanic Garden with guns drawn. They came from every direction and converged on the fountain where Congressman Luke Chapman stood with his chin to his chest and waited for them to read him his rights.

Then a gunshot rang out.

FORTY-EIGHT

It wasn't the first time Foster had seen someone die, but it was the first time he felt conflicted about it.

It wasn't that the congressman didn't deserve a sniper's bullet—Foster had secretly imagined ending his life in multiple medieval ways. He had seen himself kneeling on Luke's chest and squeezing his neck until his eyes bulged and his mouth opened and closed in vain. He had seen Luke's head, partially hidden behind the front sight post of his Smith & Wesson Equalizer, moments before pulling the trigger and bringing him to justice for his betrayal. He had seen himself holding Luke's head underwater or pushing him off a cliff. He saw knives and kettlebells, tire irons and chains.

He had been so full of hatred and rage that he knew he would do none of those things. Instead, he'd spoken with Rebecca about his fears, and they prayed for a solution together.

Do not judge, and you will not be judged. Do not condemn, and you will not be condemned. Forgive, and you will be forgiven.

But forgiveness didn't mean a pass from the justice Luke Chapman had brought onto himself.

The former spook was proud and arrogant, and there would have been no greater punishment than to have federal agents haul him away in handcuffs for the whole world to see. Foster wanted the traitor's transgressions plastered across the front page of every newspaper in the country and broadcast on every TV screen in America.

For the man who had betrayed his brother for thirty pieces of silver, spending the rest of his existence behind bars was a fitting end.

But that wasn't what had happened.

Foster turned left at the end of the path and made his way slowly down the street. He wasn't the only person visiting the cemetery, and he kept his hat pulled low to hide his face from the others. He wanted to be alone with his thoughts and try to resolve the conflict and turmoil he felt swirling inside. Nobody he encountered on the hallowed grounds could do that for him—he had come to speak with only one person. And as much as he prayed for it, Robert James would never be able to answer.

Foster turned off Eisenhower Drive and strode into Section 60, where too many of his friends were buried. It was known as the saddest acre in America, a sacred and peaceful place that was the final duty station for too many of America's young men and women. It was the final resting place for those killed in the wars in Iraq, Afghanistan, and numerous other hot spots around the globe where politicians sent them to die.

"For what?" Foster asked.

Only the wind answered, and he weaved through graves on his way to visit his best friend. His eyes couldn't help falling on the hundreds of coins scattered across almost every tombstone in Section 60. The custom of leaving coins with the deceased traced its history to the Roman Empire when coins were placed into the mouths of fallen soldiers to pay for passage and protection across the River Styx. In naval history, sailors placed coins under the masts of sailing ships to pay the "ferryman" for safe passage into the afterlife.

Foster saw countless pennies—subtle messages that someone had visited the grave—and more than a few nickels and dimes that signified the visitor had served with the interred service member in boot camp or at some point during their career. But it was all the quarters Foster saw that turned his stomach.

He started counting only the twenty-five-cent pieces as he made his way to Robert's grave but gave up when he had reached enough to buy a burger and fries at any fast-food joint in the country. When a person left a quarter on the tombstone, Foster knew it meant they had been with the service member when they died.

There were no quarters for Robert.

Foster stood in front of the tombstone, consumed with guilt that he hadn't been there for his friend at the end, and read the engraved name out loud. "Robert Michael James."

He remembered burying his best friend as if it was only yesterday. He remembered speaking with Luke Chapman before the procession led them to this small patch of grass where one of the finest Americans Foster had ever known was placed in the ground. As he looked at the coins stacked on top of his best friend's tombstone, he remembered that his inner conflict then hadn't been much different than it was now.

"What am I going to do, brother?"

Make me proud.

Foster heard the words as clearly as he had when Robert whispered them into his ear before his winging ceremony inside the First Reconnaissance Battalion paraloft in Las Flores.

"I hope I did," he said. "I took over your job at the command to finish the mission and bring Volkov to justice. And we did, brother. We got him."

Foster looked up from the tombstone as his eyes filled with tears. "But it wasn't Volkov we were after. It was Tarasov. And I don't think it's over. I discovered Luke had betrayed us to the Russian, and I wanted to make him pay for that. But somebody beat me to it. He was just the tip of the iceberg."

No matter how hard he tried, he couldn't stop himself from seeing the congressman's head snap back and disappear in a cloud of red mist. He couldn't stop himself from hearing the sickening *thwap* of the high-velocity bullet turning out the traitor's lights before he could reveal the identities of his coconspirators to the authorities. Foster blinked away his tears and looked down at the tombstone.

"I wish you were here to tell me I'm doing the right thing, but I can't trust that Rebecca and Haili will be safe until everybody involved is put in the dirt. Luke might have betrayed me, but I believed him when he said he didn't do the same to you."

In the moment of clarity he had been seeking by visiting the cemetery, Foster knew his mission was far from over. He reached into his pocket and removed a worn set of gold wings, then rubbed his thumb across the smooth surface and felt each subtle ridge of the parachute lines as he remembered his best friend in the way one warrior remembers another.

"I came to give these back to you," he whispered, reaching up to run a hand along the smooth Vermont marble while careful not to disturb the coins that had been placed there. "But I'm not sure I can do that yet."

His eyes fell to the coins stacked on Robert's tombstone, and he suddenly felt flushed. Along with the pennies, nickels, and dimes he expected, Foster saw a neat stack of two gold coins and one silver. Without touching them, he leaned over and saw that the top coin was emblazoned with a two-headed eagle with raised extended wings, set against a four-cornered heraldic shield with rounded lower corners. He leaned in closer and saw two small crowns topping the eagles' heads, with one large crown above them—all linked by a ribbon. The eagle held a scepter in its right claw and an orb in its left.

"What is this?" Foster asked, scooping up the coin to inspect it closer. The writing was in Cyrillic, but the numbers on the reverse side were easy to see. The silver coin was labeled with a *5* and the gold coins with a *10*.

His heart pounded in his chest when it dawned on him that twenty-five rubles was the equivalent of twenty-five cents, and that those three Russian coins were the same as leaving an American quarter on Robert's tombstone.

Whoever had left them there had been with Robert when he died.

Make me proud.

Foster knocked the coins off the tombstone and tucked the gold wings back into his pocket. "Not yet, brother. You can have them when the job is done."

CAMEL 33
AIR FORCE C-17

Foster Quinn stood, wedged between the bulkhead on the port side of the cargo jet and one of the two forty-one-foot boats mounted on a low velocity airdrop system platform. Each Combatant Craft Assault, or CCA, was powered by twin diesel engines that could propel the monohull at speeds of more than sixty miles per hour. He studied the complex rigging needed to carry the expensive boats from the back of the Air Force C-17 into the water five thousand feet beneath them and marveled at the effort it took to deliver two boats and twelve men to that exact spot in the Straits of Florida.

It wasn't Foster's first time conducting a military freefall operation, or even his first time jumping into water. As a former Force Recon Marine and assaulter with the Naval Special Warfare JSOC task force, Foster had trained almost exclusively in a maritime environment. But it was his first time doing it not wearing the uniform of a United States Marine.

He craned his neck to look beyond his stick, comprised of eleven other men, at the jumpmaster, who was positioned closest to the ramp. They all wore the same thing, olive drab dry suits with their fins attached to their shins with eighty-pound cotton tape and Ops-Core FAST SF high-cut helmets with goggles pulled down to shield their eyes. The jumpmaster held a fist down at his side with thumb extended, then raised it overhead in an arc.

"Stand by!"

Each man in front of Foster repeated the hand signal and shouted command as a drogue chute deployed from the rear of the cargo jet and stabilized in its turbulent jet stream. Fifteen seconds later, a twenty-eight-foot extraction parachute deployed and pulled the first CCA clear with a *clack-clack-clack* as the platform raced down the cargo jet's rollers. Ten seconds after that, the second boat followed.

With the cargo area clear and no longer feeling cramped, the jumpmaster pointed to the ramp, and the line of men moved steadily toward the rear, where they dove headfirst into the air like lemmings. When it was Foster's turn, he didn't hesitate before diving after the other jumpers in his stick—arms extended overhead and legs spread with his knees bent.

As he fell below the cargo jet's altitude, the wind hit his body and tipped him over, but he arched his back and stretched his arms long and wide to quickly correct into a stable position, then reminded himself of a parachutist's four priorities during free fall.

A parachutist pulls.

A parachutist pulls at the designated altitude.

A parachutist pulls stable at the designated altitude.

A parachutist never sacrifices altitude for stability.

At the altitude they had jumped from, he had approximately twelve seconds until he reached the designated altitude to pull his rip cord. At that point, he would be at four thousand feet over the water and close to a terminal velocity of over one hundred and twenty miles per hour. Things happened fast when jumping from a lower altitude, but like every other jumper in his stick, Foster had hundreds of jumps under his belt and followed the procedures they had drilled into him from the start.

As the other jumpers began pulling their chutes, Foster glanced at the ALFA digital visual altimeter on his left wrist and confirmed his deployment altitude. He completed his wave off signal and reached back with his right hand to grab and unseat the bottom-of-container pillow. Fully extending his arm, Foster tossed his pilot chute into the wind stream, causing the bridle to pull the curved pin from the closing loop and initiate the deployment sequence.

Foster couldn't see what was happening, but he felt the deployment bag leave the container on his back, then sweep overhead as his body swung from horizontal to vertical. Tension from his risers unstowed the suspension lines from their retainer bands, and within seconds, the lines had fully extended and pulled the main parachute from the deployment bag. The main canopy inflated with the weight of Foster's body falling to earth.

But it didn't feel quite right.

He looked up and noticed a number of lines over his main canopy.

A partial line over.

He knew there was no option to land the main canopy. Or to even attempt a controllability check.

Perform cutaway procedures immediately.

Foster arched his body, looked down, and gripped his cutaway pillow with his right hand and reserve rip cord with his left. But he froze when he saw another chute directly beneath him. For a moment, he thought to reach up for his rear risers and steer away from the other jumper but knew he was too late. He spread his arms and legs wide, hoping to bounce off the canopy and lines.

But he was falling too fast.

The impact jolted him, and he lifted his arms in front of his face, taking in his altitude subconsciously.

Three thousand feet.

He knew the emergency cutaway decision altitude was eighteen hundred feet, with a hard deck of one thousand feet to leave time for reserve chute deployment. Even with the installed Skyhook system, the reserve could deploy in two to four hundred feet, but anything less than one thousand was a gamble no jumper wanted to take.

As the canopy underneath him collapsed and engulfed him in a cocoon of silk and parachute lines, he lost all sense of direction, speed, and time. He knew the clock was working against him, but as some of the crusty recon veterans liked to say, he had the rest of his life to clear the malfunction.

Using a hand-under-hand method, Foster tried pulling himself clear of the lower canopy, knowing it was likely the jumper beneath him would cut away first and leave him stuck in the tangled mess to plummet into the water. His heart thundered in his chest, and he dug deep into his hidden reserves of energy to clear himself of the entangled lines and cut away from his malfunctioning main chute.

Just when he thought he would never see the ocean or sky again, he saw both. And he saw the terrified face of the SEAL beneath him, his right hand gripping his cutaway and reserve handles as he waited patiently for his teammate to clear himself. Foster gave him a subtle nod, then rolled into clear air and regripped his handles.

Foster arched his back vigorously while punching the cutaway pillow away from his chest, then immediately doing the same with his reserve ripcord handle. He felt the pilot chute catch air and extend the two-inch-wide high-drag bridle. The free-stowed suspension lines deployed and extracted the reserve parachute from the free bag. Foster felt an instantaneous *snap* as the canopy deployed.

He exhaled.

Looking up, Foster saw a partially inflated reserve chute and continued with his post-opening procedures—releasing the steering lines from the deployment brake setting to the full flight setting. If he had more altitude, he would have performed a controllability check—not that it would have done him any good. Instead he quickly oriented himself to the drop zone.

For as chaotic as the last several seconds had been, he appeared to be coming down almost exactly where he expected in the deep blue water where the Gulf of Mexico met the Atlantic Ocean. But because the other jumpers all had good chutes, he would beat them to the water.

He glanced at his altimeter.

Two hundred feet.

Foster wanted to turn into the wind but instead released his chest strap and focused on flaring his canopy. He lifted his eyes to the horizon, where two sleek CCAs bobbed in the water, awaiting their crew, and braced himself for the water entry. No matter how many times he had jumped into the water, it always caught him off guard as the featureless surface played tricks with his mind and made him think he was higher than he actually was. Only this time, he knew it would come even quicker.

Any second now . . .

No sooner had he completed that thought than his feet plunged into the water and the rest of him followed.

Acknowledgments

TAKING ON THE CREATIVE ENDEAVOR of writing a novel is daunting. Writing one with another person even more so. But that was not the case with this project. From the very beginning, we have been in lockstep in our goal for the series—to provide an entertaining and thrilling glimpse into the clandestine side of special operations while delivering a message of hope to our veterans. Even when Foster Quinn feels alone, he isn't. Neither are you. And neither were we.

The amount of support we received for this project is nothing short of inspiring. First and foremost, we both want to thank God for this opportunity. His hand has been apparent from the start, especially in **Karen Watson**, who had the vision to minister to male readers through fiction. She has been a stalwart champion for this series, and we are eternally grateful. Likewise, the editorial and art staff at Tyndale worked tirelessly to ensure this book was worthy of its mission. Specifically, we would like to thank **Sarah Rische, Stephanie Broene**, and **Ron Kaufmann**.

Though this is a work of fiction, we are both intimately familiar with Foster's emotions and challenges. Because of that, it is important to note that none of this would have been possible without the support of our families, who bore the brunt of uncertainty during multiple combat deployments. We would like to especially thank **Kathy** and **Sarah,** who embodied the role of military spouse and know what it means to carry the load and keep a family together. And our kids, **Hunter, Hayden, Haili,** and **Summer Robichaux,** and **Tre, William,** and **Rebecca Stewart,** who sacrificed time with their dads so we could serve our country and defend our freedoms. Each is a patriot in their own right.

In delivering a realistic look behind the scenes of the never-ending battle between good and evil, we leaned heavily on the shared experiences and expertise of several special operations, intelligence, and combat veterans. Where we got it right, we owe thanks to **Seaspray, Dennis Price, Ian Hunter, Will Taylor, Hunter Robichaux,** and **Del Roll.** Where we fell short, the blame is ours alone.

When writing this story, we wanted to make clear the distinction between the people of Iran and the regime that continues to oppress them. **Alexander Sharif** graciously offered his hunting and cultural expertise to give the story a depth that would not otherwise have been possible. He was an invaluable asset during the writing of this book, but, more importantly, he became a close friend. *Sepās-gozāram.*

Lastly, our agents, **John Howard** and **John Talbot,** deserve the credit for making this all possible. Neither of us would be where we are without their support.

Still serving.

Chad Robichaux
& Jack Stewart

About the Authors

CHAD ROBICHAUX is a former Force Recon Marine and DoD contractor who served on eight deployments to Afghanistan as part of a Joint Special Operations Command (JSOC) task force. After overcoming his personal battles with PTSD, Chad founded Mighty Oaks, a leading nonprofit serving the military and first-responder communities.

As a highly sought-after public speaker, Chad is regularly featured on a wide range of national media. He is considered a subject-matter expert on PTSD, veterans care, and national security, having advised presidential administrations, Congress, the VA, and the DoD.

Chad is the cofounder of two nonprofits focused on the rescue of Americans and vulnerable people groups trapped or captured in conflict zones around the world. In 2021, he led the largest civilian evacuation in American history, rescuing over seventeen thousand people who were trapped during the Afghanistan withdrawal, including his longtime interpreter and friend, Aziz. The story is chronicled in his bestselling book *Saving Aziz*, which is set for cinematic adaptation. His latest book, *A Mission Without Borders*, was a *USA Today* bestseller, highlighting ten rescue and humanitarian aid missions Chad has led to Ukraine since 2022.

Chad holds an MBA from the New York Institute of Technology, is a board-certified pastoral counselor with the American Association of Christian Counselors, and is completing a graduate nonprofit management program at Harvard University. He is a lifelong martial artist, professional World MMA champion, and fourth-degree Brazilian jiu-jitsu black belt. Chad is a devoted Christian. He and his wife, Kathy, have two daughters, two sons, and five grandchildren. Through his resilience, passion, and heart to serve others, Chad remains an inspiring figure worldwide as the host of *The Resilient Show*. Visit him online at chadrobichaux.com.

A native of Seattle, Washington, JACK STEWART graduated from the US Naval Academy and served twenty-three years as an FA-18C Hornet fighter pilot before retiring with the rank of commander. During his time in uniform, he flew combat missions from three different aircraft carriers over Iraq and Afghanistan and became recognized as an expert in close air support. He is a graduate of the US Navy Fighter Weapons School (TOPGUN) and former adversary instructor pilot.

Hand-selected to integrate naval strike aircraft into the Afghanistan war effort, Jack deployed on the ground as a member of an Air Force Tactical Air Control Party attached to the Army's 4th Brigade Combat Team, 82nd Airborne. He leveraged that experience on his final two deployments, as part of a Joint Special Operations Command (JSOC) task force, conducting counterterrorism missions in East Africa, North Africa, and the Arabian Peninsula.

Jack holds a bachelor of science in English from the US Naval Academy and a master of science in global leadership from the University of San Diego. A former law enforcement officer, he is now a captain with a major US airline and has appeared on international cable news as a military and commercial aviation expert.

Jack is the author of four novels in the acclaimed Battle Born series. He lives in Dallas, Texas, with his wife, Sarah, their daughter, and two sons. Visit him online at jackstewartbooks.com.

CONNECT WITH CHAD ONLINE AT

chadrobichaux.com

OR FOLLOW HIM ON

CONNECT WITH JACK ONLINE AT

jackstewartbooks.com

OR FOLLOW HIM ON

jackstewartbooks

jackstewartbooks

JackStewartBook

Jack_Stewart

jack-stewart

THE RESILIENT SHOW

Hosted by Chad Robichaux

In a world filled with confusion, self-doubt, and emotional turbulence, it's time to reclaim our strength and adaptability. It's time to be RESILIENT!

The Resilient Show is committed to bringing on the most insightful guests to educate and inform our audience through engaging discussions, expert interviews, and actionable strategies. Our goal is to help individuals build resilience beyond the challenges of everyday life, not only to improve their own lives but also to positively impact their communities.

LEARN MORE

TheResilientShow.com

MIGHTY OAKS
★★★★

Mighty Oaks is committed to serving military and first responder communities who have endured hardship around the globe through intensive peer-based discipleship programs, outpost meetings, speaking, and resiliency events. We have programs for men, women, and married couples at multiple locations nationwide and globally. Those who attend our programs are fully sponsored, to include meals, lodging and travel, ensuring their sole focus is on recovery and empowering them to identify their purpose as they move forward.

⊛ **RESILIENCY**
⊛ **RECOVERY**

INTERNATIONAL ⊛
ADVOCACY ⊛

Inspired by Isaiah 61, Mighty Oaks seeks to restore the brokenhearted through Christ, to build leaders of leaders to rise up from the ashes; they will be called Mighty Oaks of Righteousness.

MIGHTYOAKSPROGRAMS.ORG

APPLY HERE

SCAN TO DONATE

CP2033